CRIMSON BLADE
THE CHRONICLES OF LUCINDA CRANE

Mike Adamson

**Crimson Blade
The Chronicles of Lucinda Crane
by Mike Adamson**

All rights reserved. No part of this book may be reproduced or transmitted in any form or by any means, electronic or mechanical, including photocopying or recording or by any information storage and retrieval systems, without expressed written consent of the author and/or artists.

Crimson Blade is a work of fiction. Names, characters, places, and incidents are products of the author's imagination. Any resemblance to actual events or persons, living or dead, is entirely coincidental.

Story copyright owned by Mike Adamson
Cover illustration "Crimson Blade" by Jen Downes
Cover design by Marcia A. Borell

First Printing November 2024

Hiraeth Publishing
P.O. Box 1248
Tularosa, NM 88352
e-mail: hiraethsubs@yahoo.com

Visit www.hiraethsffh.com for online science fiction, fantasy, horror, scifaiku, and more. Stop by our online bookstore for novels, magazines, anthologies, and collections. **Support the small, independent press... and your First Amendment rights.**

This volume is for my sister, Jen, and my brother in law, Dave, without whom none of it would have been possible. For their patience, support and belief in me as a writer, they have my immeasurable gratitude.

CONTENTS

5   Foreword

9   Crimson Blade

35   Red Sun Rising

50   Ouroboros

107   Stalking Nemesis

128   Hellbane

165   Dance of the Trees

176   The Knives of November

207   The Last Revenant

224   Vampire House

Foreword

Everyone knows vampires, right? They have fangs, drink blood, sleep in coffins, turn into bats, are indestructible to bullets but crumble to dust if touched by sunlight. They loathe garlic, crosses, and silver, and are susceptible to the odd stake hammered through the heart. They are ancient, powerful, hierarchical, usually male, and utter chick-magnets.

Bram Stoker has a lot to answer for. That said, Dracula is the most-depicted literary figure on celluloid, just ahead of Sherlock Holmes, according to Timothy Miller in his 2022 essay *What Is Pastiche in Literature and Why Is Sherlock Holmes Perfect for It?**, though Monster Complex.com and Ultimate Pop Culture Wiki actually reverse that order. So, the undying appeal of the inhuman is clear (pun intended). That Stoker codified vampires for the public's imagination does not mean he did more than embellish legends, though. "Count Dracula"—Vlad III, "The Impaler" of Wallachia—was a real historical figure, recorded not for occult powers but as a warlord and sadist of exceptional brutality. But a corpus of legend tends to attach to such figures, and in Eastern Europe, the vampire, like the werewolf, is embedded in the folk canon, transmitting to the rest of the world down the centuries.

The existence of diseases whose symptoms resemble vampirism—porphyria and even rabies—helps to explain aspects of the folklore but also opens the door to something else—a scientific explanation for the existence of conditions otherwise seeming inhuman. Mutation is a variation from a genetic baseline condition, so a variety of states, both obvious and hidden, may result. "A genetic disease spread by physical contact" is an obvious definition for vampirism.

Vampires have not merely been popular, they were a mania and fixation during the twentieth century, and in the third decade of the twenty-first, the erotic appeal of vampire sexuality, merging as it does with the Goth movement, is a basic stock-in-trade. So much so that a great many publishers out there in the short-fiction market expressly discourage the topic of vampires, along with werewolves, zombies, mummies—essentially the whole classic repertoire of the Universal Pictures monster movies of the Thirties and Fifties. That's bad luck if you happen to love vampires!

But they do have a point. Vampires as a subgenre of horror have been done to death (yes, pun intended), especially in the post-*Twilight* era of supernatural teen romance—seriously, who saw *that* genre coming before it did?! Today's vampire writer is obliged, nay, commanded, to find a new twist—to say something fresh about the old blood suckers.

Between 2006 and 2012, I attended five conferences at the English Department of the University of Sunderland in the UK, in my capacity as an archaeologist contributing to historical, folkloric, gender, and other studies as seen through the archaeological lens. Sadly, the seminar series ended in 2013. Around that time, the department launched Spectral Visions Press to showcase newly-written Gothic fiction, and I was more than happy to show them something: "Crimson Blade," the first story in this collection. It was published the following year in their inaugural volume, *Spectral Visions The Collection*, and was one of the batch of placements that convinced me to make a serious effort to find a foothold in the short-fiction market.

My twist? My new take to breathe fresh life into the undead? Taking a scientific standpoint, I posited that vampirism is not a single genetic condition but a *family* of conditions giving rise to more than one phenotype, or outward expression. The traditional vampire—lover of the dark, drinker of blood nigh exclusively, killer, predator upon humans, plus the suite of attendant superpowers like shape shifting or defying gravity—is certainly there, and I call them *Darklings*. But there is another stream of existence, which, of course, are the *Lightlings*. These vampires have a different form of the condition that allows them to blend in with humans to a far greater degree.

They have reflections, they eat food, the sun is not lethal to them. Blood remains a constant, as do immortality, pronounced psychic capacities, and the ability to heal almost any wound.

Thus armed with a scenario, I made my heroine a changeling five centuries old, which, *Highlander*-like, allows me to hark back to that half-millennium and all it contains: people, events, memories—a rich milieu indeed for storytelling. Another formulaic device is that the stories are all set in England, each finding a new and historically interesting part of the country to explore and showcase. A land with recorded history going back to Roman times and a folklore as rich as anywhere on Earth provides an inexhaustible smorgasbord of material.

Lucinda Crane is my heroine: a vampire who walks among mortals, uses the Goth community as a shield, and has dedicated her life to defending mortals *from* vampires —indeed, from all manner of occult jeopardy. As a changeling, she remembers mortality, and her loyalty has never wavered. She was lucky enough to be changed by a Lightling who introduced her to the joys of perfect health and immortality, and she has come to appreciate the flow of time as mortals never can. Over the centuries, she learnt the ways of the warrior, and while a sword is her permanent companion, she also knows her guns and martial arts.

All stories presently completed appear in this volume. Some have been published before. Besides the *Spectral Visions* outing for "Crimson Blade," "Red Sun Rising" was picked up by Bards and Sages/Society of Misfit Stories for ebook publication, plus a spot in their second print anthology; and "Stalking Nemesis" appeared in the Hiraeth digest *Bloodbond* in May 2018. Hiraeth also optioned a couple of other stories, which led more or less directly to the proposal for the anthology you now hold. When it became clear that a collected edition was in the works, I was inspired to write the final, major story that draws together the threads and characters of the existing group, provides a satisfying climax, and leaves the door open to future adventures.

A note on timing. These stories were written over many years, and no explicit time line was needed on a tale by tale basis. However, when drawn together, a more precise chronology is desirable, and here the stories are grouped between late 2016 and early 2019. They flow better as a tighter narrative, and conclude before the coming of the pandemic, which was of course not mentioned in any piece. So:

Crimson Blade (November, 2016), Red Sun Rising (December, 2016), Ouroboros (summer, 2017), Stalking Nemesis (autumn, 2017), Hellbane (summer, 2018), Dance of the Trees (autumn, 2018), The Knives of November (November, 2018), The Last Revenant (December, 2018) and Vampire House (January, 2019).

Will there be more? I see no reason why *The Chronicles of Lucinda Crane* should not continue. I have more adventures to write, new areas to explore, and look forward to weaving new conflicts for my swordswoman, the vampire who battles vampires to save *us*.

*   https://www.writersdigest.com/write-better-fiction/what-is-pastiche-in-literature-and-why-is-sherlock-holmes-perfect-for-it

Mike Adamson
Adelaide, South Australia, April, 2024

Crimson Blade

A long leather coat and red hair drew barely a glance in twenty-first-century Whitby, but the lithe, almost statuesque woman who wore the style warranted more than a few. She was nearly six feet tall, and eyes lost in pools of darkness carried more than a hint of the things from which ordinary folk shied. To call her beautiful was an understatement, but it was an angular beauty that seemed the merest veneer concealing things best left unspoken—an animal *something* that simmered under the tightest possible control, lest it escape and create an uncivilised scene in the lap and midst of civility.

Darkness was her place. Late afternoon plunged the Old Town into blue shadow under a mantle of black clouds flying on the wind over the Esk Valley, through which the westering sun struggled at times in bursts of angry yellow. A cold wind off the North Sea tugged her flaming hair and bit at her neck. She stood on the short breakwater below Tate Hill Street, alone now, as the chill drove late-season day trippers indoors. The town was emptying for the day, and soon few people would be abroad but for the Goths and others devoted to the dark and occult side of this town between the moors and the sea.

The salt wind brushed her face with the tang of distant lands, but she closed her eyes and let the flush of sunlight paint her eyelids deep red. She heard the tide lap in the harbour, exposing the mudflats at the ebb, and rich green sea growths and black weed clothed the docks. The evening flight of herring gulls made a sweet chorus all around her, and she listened to the throb of a fishing boat putting in.

All so normal, so perfectly sane and ordinary. Yet, to one who had the skill to see beyond the mundane, nothing could ever *be* ordinary. She sensed the shimmer, not far away, of an instability portal, like a heat haze, a melding of this place and some other. Across the harbour, something stirred—a grumble as sleep faded and the entities of darkness began to sense their time was near. The ghosts at the lighthouse, the Blackdog, the Coach of the Dead, the hob, and all the old spirits that had stalked this town for hundreds of years—all were as real as the first time mortal eyes beheld them. Even the black panther would be abroad tonight; his apparition had begun to wander the east side of town by night since the turn of the new century.

But all this was grist for the occult mill. The woman was after bigger game.

With a hard smile, she turned up her collar and strode off the breakwater as the sun seemed to give up the unequal struggle and settled over the high moors, relinquishing the town to the arms of night. When she stepped through the narrow sidings onto Church Street, she found some shops closing while others still showed the sad neon flickers of a season gone by. The summer was well over, but business clung to life with the tenacity of a leech. The amusement arcades across the harbour would throb and flicker with empty foyers and windswept streets—the bizarre and unsettling air of gaiety without an audience.

Pubs did their evening trade, and the Goths were raging in their strongholds of blackness, blood, and torment, their fury against life flung in the face of orthodoxy. Some were superficial, attracted by the mere trappings of the subculture; others were deep indeed, nursing profound philosophies of society, identity, and the passage of time. And, here and there, walking among them, were *other* things...

He was here. Javirand the Face-Changer.

Oh, my foe of old, tonight will be the night, she thought as the strike of her footfalls echoed thinly in the blue evening. She walked down the centre of the old bricked road between overhanging buildings—sensing, *feeling* the world around her and reaching out for his signature. As day gave way to dusk, he would stir; soon he would wake and hunger.

She stepped aside as a car went by and a few late shoppers hurried from doorway to doorway, and flexed her neck and shoulders, working them subtly. She felt the weight of the curved sword that rode her back under the coat, the bulk of the twin plastic and carbon fibre automatics in the small of her back, and sundry other items of gear. It was not much with which to face a horror that had stalked humanity for a thousand years, but she was confident. *And experienced.*

The hour was still early, but the day had ended before 5 p.m. as she stepped into the narrow, cosy front bar at The White Horse and Griffin, further along towards Bridge Street. She ordered mulled wine and sat alone to watch the street with inscrutable eyes. Drinkers paused for a moment, cast a glance at her striking profile, but looked away before her green irises could turn towards them. Dark folk were ten a penny in this town, but this one had an aura that warned them to beware—there was nothing sham here.

In an hour, evening thickened; drinkers came and went, and streetlights glimmered on the river beyond the swing bridge. Still, no one would approach her, and she felt the antipathy of their stares. *If you did but know*, she thought, smiling faintly as she toyed with the last warm red velvet in her glass. *If you knew, you would crawl into your beds and shake with fear until the sun returned. And thank me with all your hearts.*

Suddenly, she felt the vampire wake. Like shattering icicles, a thrill of otherworldly recognition shot through her mind at Javirand's first intake of breath. No matter what face he wore in this place and time, she would know his psychic spoor. He was close, less than a kilometre away; she had tracked him here when she first felt him stirring from his long slumber, and now she would finish it.

The last warm, spiced wine passed her red lips, and her black-gloved fingers turned the glass over on the table. She rose in a swirl of leather, stepped out, and jerked a zip up to her throat against the chill. Eyes followed her as she turned towards Bridge Street. From a deep pocket, she drew a soft, folded hat, which she opened out and flexed into shape—a broad brim against the nighttime cold.

The bridge was closed; the odd car went by. She saw diners in the fish restaurants and warm glimmers from the bar in The Dolphin. Following Church Street south, she felt for her prey and at last stood in the glow of streetlights by the small boat berths, sniffing the night air. A ceilidh band played softly in a tavern along the way; she saw huge brown gulls that had settled to sleep on posts and bollards. So peaceful, so normal—but there would be blood this night, and maybe soon.

"Where are you?" she whispered, turning slowly on the spot, eyes closed. "Where are you hiding, old friend?"

A drawn-out baying answered from somewhere high above, and she smiled, thin as a razor. Only she had heard that ethereal sound. The blackdog they called *the Barguest Hound* objected to more company on his crowded turf and called from the east cliff with a warning. She crossed the street, found the ancient stone steps of Caedmon's Trod, and traced her way up between the tall houses, past where the old ship chandlers' shops and the ropeworks had stood in centuries gone by. She followed the walk towards the halls above and the sacred headland.

How like him to hide near holy ground, she thought as she rose above the town and soon looked down on its roofs. *He masks his psychic scent with the resonance of prayer...but where could he be?*

She looked back at the town lights shimmering on the languid river and felt the sea wind's bite. This was Javirand's kind of night, and some late reveller on these ancient streets would pay a terrible price. It was also *her* kind of night, and she smiled like a death's head as she felt the wind tug at the hem of her coat and play in her hair. The town was quiet below, its lights a sad reminder of campfires in the dark, that crucible of humanity where language, story, and legend had been born long ages ago. Mortals still huddled around the flames to hide from overarching nature, and the woman nodded with a maternal understanding of their needs.

The Barguest Hound bayed once more, and she

looked up to see the first silver of moonrise over the North Sea, a waning disc just past full that lit the cloudscapes in ethereal glimmers and stroked the salt-melted stone of the old Abbey's naked bones. Yes! Javirand was awake and hungry. She hurried on along the beaten trail, through early winter's rank grass, towards the long stone walls backing the Abbey house complex's old coach houses. He was close, she felt, walking on towards the gleam of St Mary's Church, which loomed against the angry evening sky. She found herself at last on Church Lane. The footpath became Abbey Lane, winding south around the skeletal remains of the abbey itself.

There was no service tonight. The graveyard was deserted and the wind played among the leaning stones like an insane piper. So many psychic resonances dwelt in this place. Their interplay was almost more than her higher senses could stand, and she knew it set her at a disadvantage. *Of course he chose this spot—he is nothing if not experienced*, she thought. But with every moment, the chances of her discovering his lair before he went out into the night to slake his demon thirst grew slimmer, and she scowled. The best she might do was intercept him at his carnage or trail him back from there.

She stood still in the blustering wind, closed her eyes, stretched out, and found only a confused melee of spoors. The Blackdog was often here, and the Coach of the Dead had circled this graveyard times without number. All left their traces, and this headland was a maze of glowing filaments leading to and from eternity. All she could do was keep watch, sure that she would know when Javirand moved.

Vaulting a dry-stone wall, she settled in the lee of a corroded, ancient gravestone, drew her coat close, collar up, and brought out the twin automatics. With precise motions, she screwed in the silencers, checked the actions, and loaded and safetied each weapon. They slid into deep pockets that formed hidden holsters before she brought out the sword and laid it across her knees, one gloved hand light on the braided hilt.

And waited...

Deep in her listening trance, the hours went by while she felt the vampire's caution, his arrogance, his anger. He was hungry now, but Javirand was aware of her just as surely as she was of him, and he knew he would not pillage unchallenged this night.

Come on, you thing of hate, she mused, *come on—try your luck.*

Twenty minutes before the pubs closed, he moved. She knew the instant he emerged from this place's background noise like a dark battering ram. A hundred metres away, Javirand cleared the coachyard wall, and at once she was up. Vaulting the cemetery wall, she ran in a crouch, sword drawn. She knew better than to *look* for him; he was too swift, too dark. He crossed the fallow land on the cliff's shoulder, raced across the open grass, and passed Caedmon's Trod. With the vampire's inhuman ease, he took flight in a springing bound to the rooftops behind the Blackhorse Yard, bounded from one to another, and dropped in a plummet into the hotel's yard.

Breath catching in her throat, the avenger repeated the feat, boots striking the red roofing tiles in precisely the same places. She felt the rush of wind as she dropped into a smashing impact in the yard, and flagstones cracked as if under a hammer. Javirand had already gone, but now she could track him. The sword slid back under her coat, and she was out of the yard onto Church Street before curious mortals could throw open doors.

His tall, powerful figure stalked towards Bridge Street, and she went in pursuit, hands in pockets on the grips of both pistols. Closing the gap as Javirand turned right, she broke into a run in the shadows. When she turned the corner, he was already halfway across the bridge, moving with a powerful, economical tread. Anyone watching from the Dolphin's door as closing time approached saw only a Goth stalking the streets of his beloved night, all cloak and pale face—and let him be. Javirand's world was his own, and his willing anonymity granted him all the licence and mandate he needed to take what he required.

Not if I have any say.

She settled to trail him at a discreet fifty metres. He looked back just once as he turned right on St Anne's Staith, and she caught the flash of a dark smile from a hard face beneath wind-blown hair. Whatever form he wore this time, Javirand could never deceive her. Her palms itched to draw the pistols and send him into the harbour in a hail of shot, but more definite—and indeed satisfying—methods were needed to rid the world of his sort.

He strolled along the harbour front, past closed-up rock candy stores and Goth boutiques, restaurants, and curio shops, before hooking left at the Marine Café. Losing sight of him, she broke into a run, certain he would be opening the gap, and when she turned the corner, he was nowhere to be seen. His spoor had moved on up the West Cliff, and she took the route by the Seaman's Mission Café, up through crumbling stone steps, across a car park, and onto Cliff Street. Nothing.

He was some distance west, his scent fading. Summoning her strength, she breathed deeply, then ran, cat-footed, along Cliff Street. She turned at a private driveway, bolted through gardens behind the tall houses, and cleared a wall in a graceful leap that put her on the open commons off Silver Street. From there, she became a blur of motion, leaping the opposite fence and taking the side street beside West Cliff Congregational Church. She came to rest in the middle of Belle Vue Terrace, panting softly.

The feel of Javirand's presence was almost a violation, as if his pallid hands were stroking her body. She turned in a half-crouch, looking one way and another until her psychic perception drew her eyes *upward*, up the church's old stonework to the lead-tile roof and spire. She saw nothing, but he was up there, and she slipped stealthily into the shadows of a side street. The clock at the bottom of Belle Vue was grazing midnight.

"Time, gentlemen, please," was the publican's cry since time immemorial, when the clock's hands struck twelve and she heard drinkers leaving the Granby in ones and twos, just around the corner. Her overwhelming impression was that even now Javirand was marking a victim. Inside her pockets, she eased both pistols into her palms. She thumbed off the safeties and stepped into the streetlights' blue wash, every nerve on fire.

A couple of Goths left the pub and nodded a courteous greeting to what they believed was one of their own, and in that moment of distraction, she lost her lock on her quarry. In a terrible rush of what might have been dark wings, a cloud of grey *nothingness* dropped from the church spire and enveloped a young tourist who had stepped out as the pub door closed. The girl had no time even to cry out before the ball of darkness swept her up and sucked her into the air.

Pistols presented, the avenger fought to find a line of fire, but in the blink of an eye the quarry was gone. She broke into a headlong run, back the way she had come, tracking Javirand by the scarlet balefire of his malevolence. Up and over the church, he went—but he could not maintain this energy output for long. He needed to strike, drink, and recover strength.

The empty lot. She ran with the pistols drawn, skated around behind the church, and cleared the fence in one bound, but the sight that greeted her stopped her short. She was far too late. The body lay in ruins, a scarlet mess where the throat should have been, clutched almost lovingly in the arms of the *thing* Javirand had become.

It was white as a worm, humanoid, but something other than human. Vicious claws tipped the massive limbs, and eyes blazed like red witchfire; blood dripped from immense fangs, and in the dim wash of streetlights, the beast leered, unafraid.

"Lucinda Crane, my old enemy," came the words, growled deep in the huge throat. "When will you lose your pity for these mortals and live up to your potential?"

For a long, terrible moment, she met his eyes over open sights from a crouch six metres away, before Javirand laughed and vanished in a swirl of grey vapour through which her rounds passed harmlessly.

She closed her eyes in the anguish of defeat, and knew she had to move. The last thing she needed was being connected with the worst murder in Whitby's history. But when she reopened her eyes, she saw something she had never expected.

A blue aura hung over the body, pulsing softly, and shapes moved in the wash of radiance. Insect-like, resembling locusts the size of dogs, the creatures worked methodically, digging like sexton beetles—opening not a grave but a portal between realities. One of the hobs glanced at her, seemed to fix her with an otherworldly stare, then redoubled its efforts. The mutilated corpse settled through the torn earth until it vanished from sight. The hobs brushed the grasses all around with raking fingers and swept the soil back together, as it had been before. Chitinous jaws chittering in triumph, they faded with the blue light.

The police would never solve this disappearance—one of the hundreds, thousands, of cases reported but never closed. Lucida Crane shuddered, pocketed the guns, and turned to vault the fence once more. Making her way quickly from the scene, heading south, she followed Silver Street down to Flowergate, took a left, and strode past the closed-up shops to the harbour frontage by the bridge.

Her heart was steadier now, and the weapons' weight was more comforting. Looking up across the river to the East Cliff, she smiled coldly.

"You made a mistake," she whispered. "Now you've fed, and your spoor is bright as the sun. You can't hide." Treading confidently, she crossed the road and took the bridge, her resolve as hard as granite. Javirand could keep moving for most of the night, but his breed had an Achilles's heel: in daylight, they needed a secret sanctuary.

Unlike her own kind.

The wind blustered, driving the clouds before it, and the moon's silver face touched the town from time to time. Lights were going out all over now, windows darkening as the streets at last became devoid of life, but for the odd cat that darted from shadow to shadow—and the unseen passage of things less mortal.

Would Javirand allow her to find his lair unopposed?

Certainly not. He must be secure before he closed his eyes, for if Lucinda found him asleep, she could take his head and stake his heart before he could react. No...he would come for her long before dawn.

Their hatred was an old one. How many times had they fought? Gloved fingers counted them off. His native India in 1865; Afghanistan, 1880, and Vienna, 1886; London in 1888, back-to-back feedings—nicely obscured by the unrelated Ripper case. Lisbon, 1912; Istanbul, 1915. Then a long sleep for them both before a horrifying pursuit through the misery and blood of the Eastern Front, where the Germans had fallen back after the Battle of Kursk. Wherever there was blood to spare, Javirand would be there—wearing a new face each time, thirsting beyond all control, and disdaining the mortals upon whom he fed.

He was trapped in Berlin at the time of the airlift, but had not starved—not when the citizens were his prey. She had not even scratched him that time. New York, 1957; Hong Kong, 1964, on the front doorstep of the world's newest and most brutal war, soaking up the flood of lost souls seeking refuge. She almost had him there, but his gorging was so vast that he slept in some lost tomb for decades and emerged into a world changed by technology. For the last twenty years, they had played cat-and-mouse —hunting by computer, calling in favours. The place changed, the tools evolved, but the game never did: kill or be killed. Her resolve had never wavered.

Indeed, as the decades went by, Lucinda learnt more about the Darkling condition as she became less guided by ancient habits and superstitions and more compelled by a gathering understanding. Javirand slept away the ages between killing bouts while she chose diversion, and with each lull in their war, she became more and more certain of her allegiance to mortals.

Lucinda Crane's own vampire nature was very different. She walked in the light, ate and drank things other than blood, but though her powers were far less developed than Javirand's shapeshifting and teleporting, they remained superhuman. Infinite life was both a gift and a curse, as ever—but it would be less of a curse when she had made her world a safer one by ridding it of an old and unwelcome competitor.

She stood in the deserted shadows of Church Street while the wind played under the eaves. All the life had faded from the town; it seemed she had stepped back centuries to a time when nothing more than brick and wood protected the frail human form from a world so vast and savage that survival itself was doubtful. Living from age to age gave her a higher perspective, and in modern society, she saw a desperate scramble for identity. In the Goth movement into which she blended, Lucinda perceived a quaint and often—it seemed to her—shallow expression of this quality. But mortal lives were so fleeting and temporary that she could forgive the Goths almost any quest for meaning.

She breathed the ocean's eternal salt tang, flexed her mind, and stretched out. She found the quarry's psychic signature without difficulty. Javirand was up somewhere high, watching, waiting. She was content to let him come to her. After so thorough a gorging, he would not feed again tonight—possibly not for weeks. She must only pick the ground on which they would do battle, and this was her prerogative: he was the one who must retreat to some lair before the sun rose. If he lapsed into deep slumber, she had all the time in the world to find him, dig him out, and finish him, so he must try to destroy her first while his strengths were at their greatest.

The sun had been down for seven hours, and at this time of year was seven hours away. They had plenty of time to play. Slowly and purposefully, Lucinda made her way along the street and turned onto the 199 steps that wound up around the cliff to the church. As soon as she moved, he would know she was coming, and he would snarl his pleasure. As far as she was concerned, Javirand was welcome to come out and fight at any moment.

She climbed one step at a time, smiling as she remembered the folklore that swore these steps could never be counted to the same number twice. The wind mounted around her, and she turned up her collar, tugged her hat down more firmly, enduring the gale with the stoicism and endurance of her kind. She took her time, paused to sit quietly on the public benches, and let her eyes wander over the quiet rooftops, the glimmers on the river, all the while feeling the presences of the unseen. Somewhere in these streets, the panther was prowling tonight—a slinking black beast with balefire eyes. The ghosts were abroad in their endless quest to break through the barrier between the worlds, and the Hound wandered in the intermittent moonlight.

My kind of town, Lucinda thought with the bleak humour of one whose province was eternity. As she finished the steps to the clifftop, she saw the ruined abbey's illuminated columns against the dark sky and remembered so many other sites—Rievaulx, Selkirk, Haughmond—each with its gothic appeal. Each was striking, and each a sad yet triumphant reminder of human travail, and of the spirit that hung on in the teeth of Nature's relentless reclamation of all that mortal ingenuity might accomplish. What better arena for this eternal conflict?

With a measured stride, she walked up Church Lane, past the graveyard, towards the old abbey walls, and experienced an overwhelming sensation of being watched. He was up there on the rotted stone columns, eyes following her every movement as she strode on by the gatehouse and into the sea wind's full bite. She heard the roar and tumble of breakers below the cliffs while the wind sang in the columns. The moon's face lit their pitted stonework as the clouds parted...this was as good as any place.

She strode onto the open lawn between the cemetery and the Coastguard radio station, further along Abbey Lane, and eased the sword free as she turned east. She stood like a black statue, senses closed to everything but the need to perceive Javirand. She could do this all night, if need be; her endurance and concentration were unmatched by any mere mortal.

Come to me, she urged, projecting the thought. *Come to me and taste my steel; let us do battle as we have for a century and a half. I will end your reign of terror, as I have vowed.*

Now that she was centred, grounded, the wind and the dark had lost their power. The dim wash of light from the lane was all she needed; her pupils were wide. The sword vibrated thinly as the wind hummed across its razor-honed edge, and she adjusted its angle to vary the tone until the blade sang with a life of its own, its song thrown out in defiance of the dark power above.

Perhaps Javirand enjoyed the sound of the singing blade, for it bridged the ages, harking back to times when the sword was master. An age they both remembered well. They recalled the world before the coming of engines and electronics—a time when firearms were crude, and the measure of a warrior was somewhat different. She imagined him sitting up there, somewhere on the towers, eyes closed, head moving softly as the ethereal tone transported him back.

In the simple sharing she admitted, with a sense of faint revulsion, they had more in common with each other than either had with mortals. *Why do you love them?* Javirand had demanded long ago. It was 1915 in Istanbul, and they fought sword-to-sword on the Grand Bazaar's rooftops while the Great War worsened around them. *Why do you love them so? What makes them more worthy of your allegiance than your own kind?*

Her only answer had been *compassion*. Hers for the mortals who were trapped in a single lifetime, and the humans' for each other, and the good of which they were capable. He had snorted in derision and mentioned the war; she had shrugged and laid him open from sternum to groin. The fight was bold and bloody—he sliced her to the bone, but they disengaged when Turkish police swarmed the rooftop. She healed with the same speed as did Javirand; in a day, even the scars were gone.

As she waited, she meditated on his term, 'your own kind.' In the hundred years since he had spat those words at her, she had often thought of them. There were more vampires in this world than anyone knew. Lineages and allegiances, houses and cliques, tribes and clans, all interwoven through thousands of years of secretly recorded history—history that lived best in the memories of those who had seen it unfold and yet endured.

Two great lines had emerged. Those whose mutation —for it could only be mutation—imprisoned them eternally in darkness, raging in cold fury against the world, outcast and proud in the terror they inspired. And those whose mutation was different, those 'changelings' who found themselves far less susceptible to the effects of full-frequency light, with digestion that did not reject normal food. *Yes,* Lucinda Crane drank blood. She metabolised whole blood as part of the vampire's life process. But over the years, she had cultivated a taste for O-negative over ice in a martini glass. It was less primal than the hunt, and the likes of Javirand considered it a weakness, but Lucinda's preference made it far easier to blend into the mortal world from which both vampire forms originally came—and she had a much deeper understanding of mortality, even an affection for it.

Thus, her allegiances, and she was not the only one of her kind who fought on behalf of mortals. Humankind was a beast capable of scaling sublime heights—or wallowing in unspeakable depths. Neither of the two extremes mattered to the universe. But vampirekind dwelt not among the stars, but on a single living world, and sometimes sides must be taken. She had chosen hers long ago.

Javirand came at her like a whirlwind, a flurry of formless vapour that solidified into the worm-white killing apparition, dropping out of the dark as he cleared the abbey walls in his descent from the crumbling towers. Speed was his greatest asset. He hit the ground in a crouch, sprang like a massive cat, and his claws whistled over her head as she went to one knee. Her sword wove a tapestry of moonlight. Now, the song of air over the honed edge was a demonic wail as she moved like lightning, and the blade became a blur.

No one in the sleeping town would believe that this drama was playing out; none would trust any glimpses caught on the CCTV covering the abbey gatehouse. The shadows hid a conflict as old as the world. In his combat morph, Javirand was a seven-foot killing machine able to defy gravity and teleport at will, but these gifts made him both arrogant and predictable. Lucinda had minimal ability in the former skill, and none in the latter. As always, she put her faith in speed, agility, and the ability to defeat strength with intelligence. The sword created a zone of exclusion around her that the Darkling strove to defeat—trying to get through with his grasping reach and distract her long enough to take out her throat, then finish her at his leisure.

At last, he flipped away a few metres and morphed back to his human guise, panting shallowly as he rested after the enormous effort. The face Javirand now wore was stern, broad, but not unattractive in a dark and forbidding way. His black clothing left his face no more than a pale, disembodied image in the gloom. "Come along, Lucinda," he said pleasantly in a rich baritone that still reflected his native Indian accent. "Much as I enjoy our infrequent wrestling matches, we both know it can only end one way. I have always been the stronger, and one day your luck will run out."

She took the almost contemptuous offer of rest stoically. The upraised katana was a bright steel crescent between them. "What could we possibly have to talk about? Since we first fought in Jaipur, there has been no quarter, nor will there ever be."

"A shame. If I could but mingle our mutations, who knows what you would become? Your powers would triple."

"My powers are fine as they are," she whispered.

"You are weak!" he snarled, folding his arms on his chest. "Weak in body, mind and spirit! Compassion—" the word dripped scorn "—is your failing. Only in ruthlessness is there strength, and only in strength is there survival. Our kind, yours and mine, will still walk proudly upon this Earth the day the sun swells above us, but theirs—" He waved a hand abstractly at the town below. "They will be dust, blown on the winds of hell and rightly forgotten for the vermin they are."

"'Vermin' from which we are descended!"

"*Evolved!* We are the next step—they are obsolete. They are to us as the monkey is to them!" After a long moment, Javirand gestured dismissively. "Enough. Lucinda, has it never occurred to you that I would rather turn you than kill you?" He smiled faintly, let the words hang on the night wind, and studied his fingertips. "Over the years, I might have killed you a hundred times, but what a waste it would have been. Elevated to the ranks of my kind, what a force you would become. Tell me you do not wish to feel *real* power." The last was said almost seductively.

Her voice was a gravelling purr, her eyes like black coals. "We are worlds apart. The greatest rush of power I shall ever feel will be the satisfaction when your head leaves your shoulders."

He shook that head sadly. "Not this time, then. The more strength I waste, the sooner I must drain another of your despicable mortals. So, enough." He shrugged, threw his arms wide, and vanished in a swirl of grey vapours.

For long seconds, Lucinda stood panting, watching the darkness over the sword. She reached out psychically, stretched for his signature, but he was nowhere nearby. Javirand was some distance away now, under cover, hidden. He need never expose himself when he could merely walk through walls to leave and return. Solid stone lay between them, and the status was quo.

She returned the blade to its scabbard under her coat with slow, practised actions as her mind raced to process his words. Had he really been playing with her all these years? Or was he bluffing because this time he really had his back to the wall?

The night was undisturbed; their battle had gone unnoticed—in fact, it had been only a few minutes in length. She jogged to the cemetery, leapt the dry-stone wall and crouched in the lee of a grave to marshal her thoughts. Should she walk away this time? Leave Javirand's playing field open, let more unsolved murders stain this town, then track him down for an eleventh time somewhere, somewhen, else?

I am weary of this game, she thought. *I want it over. Now.*

Gathering her thoughts, spirit, and strength around her, she found a thread of her vampire nature envying him the hot, fresh blood on which he had supped so deeply. For all her compassion, Lucinda was what she was: a predator who could never wholly cease to be what nature had made her. But she put hunger aside for now and wrapped her coat close against the chill air. She had the strength to finish this business before finding her own nourishment in a far less traumatic way.

The church's clocktower showed 2 a.m., and the passage of time surprised her. Her wide pupils perceived the world in greys and greens, silver and the deepest blues —not darkness but a rich palette. She had studied Whitby and its occult traditions in depth before embarking on this mission, and she knew this headland's history intimately.

It had been home to the first wooden abbey in the seventh century and to the abbess St Hilda until her death in 680. Hilda hosted the Synod of Whitby in 664, which fixed the dating of Easter, and legend swore that her ghost still walks, sometimes seen in luminous majesty between the towers. Vikings razed the original abbey in 851, but a Norman knight rebuilt it in stone in the eleventh century, and it met its end in 1540, in the great dissolution under Henry VIII.

The Church of St Mary is more recent. Its earliest structures date from 1110, though most of what exists in the present day is eighteenth century, especially the interior. The famous cemetery, with its salt-corroded stones, hosted many a seaman's remains, and the town's seafaring tradition had it that the Coach of the Dead welcomed newly-buried sailors by circling the grave three times and collecting the departed's soul for a proper seaman's repose among his own kind. The last burial here took place the very year she first fought her nemesis, and part of the cliff edge had recently broken away in heavy rains, spilling ancient bones into Henrietta Street below.

That was the Sunday-school version of the headland's history. Lucinda knew many other tales and sat brooding on them as the clock's hands wound away the minutes. She remembered a story—a tale of the time when Captain Browne Bushell had held court at Bagdale Hall, across the river, where stories claim that his ghost still prowls the manor. He was something of a scallywag, and during the Civil War, fought first for one side, then the other.

The mid-seventeenth century was a brutal time of immolation, pitch-capping, racking, and gouging. Contemporary records reported that a party of Parliamentarians spent several weeks on this headland—they created an escape tunnel after a section of the old abbey grounds collapsed serendipitously, revealing chambers that were part of the foundations under the eleventh-century structure. The men dug a tunnel into those chambers for use as a hiding place from royalist forces, and would retreat there at a moment's notice. According to the story, the entrance was through a grave in St Mary's cemetery—consecrated but empty.

What would be more cynical than for Javirand to secrete his physical remains in a chamber beneath an abbey's deconsecrated soil?

The inscriptions on the oldest gravestones were no longer legible. Salt wind had corroded the stone, turning smooth-worked tablets into rippled layers of chemical-stained rock, leaning and falling in disarray. Among the vertical tablets were many other designs, including 'pillar and altar' tombs; some were very old. She knew the oldest surviving tombs' approximate location, and if those chambers in the abbey foundations were vital to the Parliamentarians—and to Javirand—it would surely be close to the abbey. It was unlikely the entrance was in any grave on the side destroyed by landslides in the intervening centuries.

In fact, she was almost on top of the site, right where she crouched. From a deep pocket, she took a thermal scope, switched it on and held it to one eye to sweep the gravestones around her. Equal heat values returned a mosaic across the cold grass, stone after stone, and she walked slowly along the ranks of graves, scanning the oldest, most weathered. At last, she paused beside an early modern period altar tomb, weathered so severely that it almost seemed to be a natural boulder. And there, she registered a slight difference in the stone's temperature, as if an airspace behind it conducted heat at a different rate from the dense earth of others.

Putting away the scope, she let her night vision gradually correct itself before examining the grave with a brushing touch of gloved fingers. She put an ear to the smooth, cold slab and rapped hard, listening to the echo's quality...yes, it was hollow beneath. This, in itself, meant nothing; many tomb graves were sepulchral chambers containing a freestanding coffin. She would not know until she had done what was necessary.

The task would have been impossible for a human, no matter what one saw in movies. The cover stone weighed at least three hundred kilos, and only the vampire's inhuman strength could move it unaided, without tools. The slab shifted grudgingly and emitted a draft of stale air. She noted how carefully it had been fitted to its supports; it was meant to deflect water from reaching the interior. When she put a penlight into the tomb, and flicked on the beam, she saw minimal water damage. The chamber was empty, around a metre deep, lined with smoothly-cut stone; at one end, steps disappeared down into total blackness.

Now she steeled her courage. She was about to enter the real night. This was the monster's world, and though vampire resilience would bring her through any ordinary trial, fighting the beast in this narrow space had both advantages and drawbacks. She dropped into the hole and used her shoulders to ease the stone back into place, then crouched to use the thermal sight once more.

The steps led downward for perhaps three metres. They were curiously unworn, as if they had never known human tread. Her footfalls were a thin echo as she stepped down into a tunnel whose roof was so low that she stooped. It ran straight into the blackness. Now she brought out a single pistol to cover the darkness ahead and moved slowly into an icy stillness that seemed to have evaded all passage of time.

Slowly, slowly...there was no rush. There was only cold stone behind her; all the threat in her world lay ahead. The thermal sight showed her a uniform gradient of heat from floor to ceiling, where the soil temperature varied with depth, and she fought to make out anything useful. She could use the torch or even a flare, but with her wide-open pupils, it would be like staring into the sun. It would destroy her night vision, and even vampire eyes took minutes to reset. A mortal's would take hours—but even minutes were more than Javirand needed.

The implicit threat to turn her knotted her belly with fear. She had no idea what the result would be of mixing the two vampire strains, and she did not want to be the test subject to find out. She just wanted to find him and finish the job—it would take just one surgical stroke of the blade to immobilise him, and immortality would become his living hell.

The tunnel stretched on ahead, a silent vault. He was somewhere out there, in the abbey's old cellars. At this distance, his psychic spoor was bright, and its modulation told her he was probably already asleep. The penalty he paid for his powers was exhaustion, and in his complacency, he might not have deigned to research mere human industries in this place. He could be oblivious of the existence of this tunnel.

Give him time to settle into deep slumber, she thought, easing down to kneel on the flagstones. She set down the pistol, found the torch, felt for the switch, and lit only a single LED. Eyes shielded from the glare, she peered down the arched stone way in the sudden blue-white brilliance. As far as a wooden partition perhaps fifty metres ahead, the tunnel was clear. She crept on slowly, with strict noise discipline.

At the partition, she killed the LED and flicked on the thermal scope to scan the joints between vertical planks that were hoary with age. A definite temperature increase showed in the chamber beyond, and she played the scope along each division between the boards, looking for anything she recognised beyond.

Nothing. She listened for a long while, but no sound reached her inhuman ears. After a time, she turned the single LED on the partition. It seemed less a door than simply a barricade fitted into the tunnel's mouth—probably a last line of defence, should this hideaway be found. Lucinda would have expected it to be barred, assuming Javirand was aware of the tunnel and this chamber. The abbey had many underground chambers—folklore told of a young nun walled up alive in one of them for adultery.

After careful inspection, she slid a knife out of a boot sheath and probed through the gaps between the ancient boards. Sliding the blade up and down, she encountered no horizontal bars and smiled wolfishly. She had a chance. She set her shoulder against the wood, took a deep breath, and focused before exerting vampire strength. Timbers creaked under the first new force applied to them in 360 years. Going slowly and carefully, she changed her position and the angle of thrust. The mass of oak gradually began to move, grating against the stone around it. Dust trickled down the walls as, with one boot against the wall for leverage, she kept up the pressure. If the timber shifted suddenly and crashed down, she would lose the element of surprise, so she must catch it before that could happen.

Switching from pushing to pulling, in a split second and in near total darkness, would have been beyond most mortals—but not a vampire. When the moment came, Lucinda rebalanced in the blink of an eye, snaked a hand around the massive panel's edge, and stabilised it as it swayed.

At once, the psychic impact doubled. Javirand's essence had imbued this lost lair for some time now, and she concentrated to block out the foul feeling. Now, she could ease aside the barricade and step through. The LED illuminated a stone-flagged chamber in which were stacked boxes and barrels—gunpowder and flints, pistol balls, long-ago decayed packages of food. Muskets leaned against a wall.

The centuries fell away as she imagined the last

hands to have worked in this storeroom, so long ago. On the chamber's other side was a heavy, iron-bound timber door of mediaeval design, arched at the top. On cat-light feet, she stepped through the dust of ages, extinguished the LED, held the thermal sight to the dry-rotted gap around the great planks—

And froze.

Heat bloomed in the eyepiece, and she saw part of a humanoid form, stretched out on a pedestal made from crates and tarpaulin—the few things Javirand had teleported into this place to accommodate his meagre needs. He may have chosen to live in luxury elsewhere, but he prided himself on Spartan virtue when hunting. He sank into his otherworldly trance without need of comforts. Lucinda watched his breath plume in the chill air, a long, slow exhalation. His metabolism had already slowed.

She examined every rotten gap in search of the right perspective, observing Javirand where he lay, just three metres away. He had never been so much at her mercy; she had never located his sleeping place before. The monster was vulnerable, and, in this enclosed space, Lucinda suddenly became the beast, the hunter.

The massive old door was rotten; its timbers were at least five centuries old. She knew she could break them by force, but it was a question of time. He could wake far faster than she could break. The barrel hinges must be rusted into place, and would squeal like banshees if they swung at all. If this was all about speed, she had only so many options.

Stepping back, she soundlessly placed the light on a shelf in the storeroom and drew the automatics. The magazine slipped out of one, and she replaced it with another; its rounds were colour-coded red: explosive shot. One standard round remained in the chamber above the explosive rounds, with the weapon primed to cycle from the open-bolt position. The second pistol slid into her belt. Drawing the sword, she began to breathe deeply, cycling her oxygen level before extinguishing the LED.

Now, Lucinda went to one knee at the door and

brought the silencer to the crack between the boards, with the thermal scope balanced over the sight.

The *squit* of the silenced round was painfully loud in this deathly silence, and the burst of heat obscured everything, but from the tumbling body's sound, she knew she was on target. The shot had passed cleanly through the brainpan. That in itself would not kill a vampire, but it would certainly slow Javirand down for long enough. Flicking the LED on full, she stepped back and thumbed the pistol selector to full auto.

With a braying snarl and flickers of muzzle flame, the entire magazine ripped free as she tracked an arc. The pattern of detonations filled the air with flying splinters and bits of flame, and when she hurled her weight at the door, the timbers burst inward in a collapsing chaos. She dove through, dropped the first pistol, snatched the second, and hurled herself over Javirand's sleeping pallet.

The body was not on the floor.

In the torch beam's harsh contrast, Lucinda looked up in time to see him morph into his hunter form. The gaping wound in the side of his head closed as she watched, and his snarl thundered in the confines. Muscles swelled to herculean proportions as his rage magnified, and when she raised the second pistol, he laughed in her face.

"You are less than pathetic," he growled. "How many times will you try the same thing and expect a different outcome? Why are you incapable of learning?" He nodded, flexing his hands. "And now I shall turn you."

She looked over the open sights, calm and clear, and almost regretful as she savoured the moment. "Oh, I can learn," she said softly, and triggered a single round.

The rosette of blood over his heart should have meant nothing, but at once the towering creature staggered back against the wall, pawing at its breast. An expression of dawning horror contorted its terrible features. "What...?" Javirand whispered. "What have you done?"

Lucinda pumped two more rounds into his chest before she dropped the weapon and hefted the sword.

Dancing in closer than she had ever dared, she thrust with all her might. The razor-honed blade passed through the enormous, pallid body, nailing it to an ancient timber before she whirled and snatched up the pistol.

His eyes were desperate. Pain racked him now; wisps of smoke rose from the gaping chest wounds. "What have you *done*?!" Javirand roared. Immense hands seized the blade and worked at it, but his strength was failing fast. In moments, he was unable to sustain his form and returned to human guise, an almost pitiable spectacle of a man impaled and dying in an ironic tribute to old Vlad himself, whose hideous, fifteenth-century exploits inspired Bram Stoker to write his classic novel in this very town.

Javirand's flesh began to smoulder, and Lucinda came in even closer. "These are wooden hollow-point bullets. They shatter on impact; I had them lathed from the wood of a sanctified cross, and each carries a silver dart inside. It makes no difference if *I* believe in such antiquated things, but if *you* do...ahhh." She winked one dark eye. "That was a twenty-first century staking. Enjoy eternity dead."

His eyes widened with the knowledge of his impending death, his total and ultimate failure. One hand pawed at the air before him. One last, desperate defiance spat at the fates from slack and drooling lips. "My brothers will avenge me!"

Snapping up the pistol, she emptied the rest of the magazine into him. As he burst into flames, she wrenched the sword out of timber and chest. Javirand folded to his knees, and Lucinda stepped back for the massive stroke that took his head off cleanly.

In the balefire of the reaction, as conflicting energies consumed the vampire flesh, she stepped clear. One hand rose to shield her eyes, and her nose wrinkled at the offensive odour. It was over in moments. The entire body, head included, shrivelled in a wreath of gold-green flame that heated the chamber, then faded away. A pile of white ash collapsed on itself.

Silence. The torch's LED glare was the only energy left here. Javirand's spoor had at last vanished from the world. She sank heavily onto the sleeping platform, panting, shoulders heaving as the reality of victory finally hit home.

They had warred for 151 years. Lucinda felt suddenly lonely—what would her world be without Javirand? But a moment later, a smile crept through. It would be peaceful. Cleaner. And he was far from the only Darkling. She would not discount his warning of revenge, but the affairs of vampirekind took many years to unfold. By the time Javirand's siblings and comrades knew anything about this sad tableau under the ancient headland's sod, she would have found newer pastures.

The world was once again worth living in. Lucinda cleaned the blade with slow deliberation before sheathing it with a decisive thrust into the scabbard at her back and retrieving the pistols. The way out was clear. Moving the grave slab slowly aside with a feat of inhuman strength, she emerged into the night wind's cold sting ten minutes later. She squared up the slab and gazed at the abbey—feeling the ages flowing about her, hearing the plethora of ghosts and spirits, entities and beasts that boiled through the dimensions in this focal place—and she smiled faintly.

This was a new century, a time of fresh beginnings and new directions. Vampirekind had survived for thousands of years and would accompany mortals into the future, but their place remained in the shadows. She squared her shoulders, looked up at the clouds flying before the westering moon, and vaulted the wall to make her way down the 199 steps. The slow strike of boots on stone would caress the sleeping residents' subconscious minds, but this was a town that never really, fully, slept.

She would watch the sun rise over the North Sea in a silver-pink wash while the herring gulls took flight. When the first pubs opened their doors she would take a breakfast of mortal food and enjoy it. But, sitting on the breakwater below Tate Hill Street among sleeping seabirds, Lucinda Crane could not help hearing the siren song of her own world.

Battle left her hungering—*really* hungering. Not for mere food but for the sustenance of her kind, the strange ambrosia that would forever force her to walk apart from the humans she respected.

She needed blood. Warm, fresh human blood.

When the day had begun, and she would disturb no one, she would take out the mobile and punch an often-called number. The difference between the Darkling vampires and those who walked in the light was that the Lighting's 'victims' were perfectly willing, and thus, not victims at all.

Red Sun Rising

In the centuries of her life, Lucinda Crane had learnt one thing before all others: more evil slept than ever walked abroad.

The timeless ones had come to sense when others of their ilk opened their eyes. A tremor rushed through the soul; a whisper, somewhere on a deep and etheric level, reminded the walker in eternity that he or she was never alone. For some, it was the eternal confirmation that darkness has its soldiers, while for others, it meant simply that new prey had stepped out onto the playing field.

But not every evil was of vampirekind. Indeed, vampires were a single—if divided—species among a plethora, a universe of entities in which mortals no longer believed.

Lucinda was tall, hard, and beautiful. Hair the colour of old blood counterpointed her pale complexion. The long leather coat completed a Goth image that was common enough in twenty-first-century Britain to draw no more than a raised eyebrow as she walked the evening streets. She was a loner who chose company only fleetingly, always moving on—eternally the outsider, the curiosity, and humans were glad she did not linger. She was content; her business could be bloody. The few people who knew her were all the sanctuary she needed.

She had followed a scent—a spoor in the world's ether; a psychic sigil that told her a malevolent *something* had crossed over onto the mortal plane. The trail led her down from the Yorkshire dales, across the Midlands and the Pennines, and on to the village of Shifnal in Shropshire, on the railway between Shrewsbury and Wolverhampton. Her black Jaguar XKR had purred along country roads as she followed her unearthly senses. In the first days of winter, she found evil's nesting place at last. The snows that bit early in this new, broken climate made November a chill, white wasteland of hard streets and bare trees.

Shifnal is a small town where she could walk from edge to edge in fifteen minutes without hurrying. But it is a *nice* town, embodying country England in so many ways, from ancient timber and stucco buildings to reminders of the nineteenth century. Its businesses serve the farms all around, and the railway line passes through the centre of town on an elevated embankment.

The station straddled Bradford Street overhead. The Victorian edifice of brick and riveted iron had seen better days, but its permanence defied the harsh season. The bitter winds that swept down from the Welsh mountains when the Atlantic threw gales at the British Isles rimed the iron with ice. Evening came in early; streetlights and shops glowed cheerily through the twilight blues. Christmas decorations were already up, and Lucinda could smile at the endless cycle of commercialism that masqueraded on one hand as religion and on the other as a distorted half-memory of ancient, forgotten, suppressed lore.

No matter—Christmas was what the world made of the old festival, and the institution was a good one. She had read *A Christmas Carol* in its first edition, and more than once had heard Charles Dickens perform his inimitable renditions on stage. So long ago.

Memories flooded in as she stood outside a newsagent, eyeing a widescreen above the counter, which quietly played what she recognised as the classic 1984 production. Thirty-plus years was an aeon for mortals; several cast members were no longer in this world. To her, it was the merest blink of an eye, a single episode punctuating her 150-year war with the vampire Javirand the Face-Changer, which was so recently resolved in a chamber beneath Whitby Abbey.

Shaking herself free of the memories, she stretched out with the vampire's senses. She shut out the sounds of passersby, traffic on the main road, the rumble of a train going through the station, and concentrated. The entity was here—not corporeal but *anchored*. It had chosen its host, its link to the physical world, the one it would consume, suck dry like a spider with a fly, before moving on. Her object was to sever that link—draw the entity like pus from a wound, and hurl it so firmly into the cracks between the dimensions that it would be a thousand years before it oozed back into this world.

She had no difficulty spotting the host.

The girl was perhaps sixteen years old. It was less her Goth appearance than the black aura surrounding her that informed Lucinda she carried a curse. Touched by evil—although unconscious of it and its nature—the girl was already damaged. Pale-faced and thin, she had the look of a cancer sufferer, an impression that was doubled in intensity by her voodoo makeup. Her eyes were lost in pools of blackness beneath a hood that underlined her separation from the daylight world.

She sat with a few other teenagers at café tables outside the takeaway chicken, pizza, and kebab house on Bradford Street, the main thoroughfare heading north through town. She picked at the food, trying to laugh with kids who had been her friends, but Lucinda's trained eye saw how those friends perceived the *strangeness* surrounding her. They were backing away, bit by bit. Soon, the entity would have isolated its victim from all possible sources of help; then the consumption would begin in earnest.

Lucinda sat on a bench a little way along the street, under the trees outside the now-closed confectioner's shop, and watched lights glimmer on a slushy residue of snow in the gutters. As yet, the snow did not lie long, but its thawing made the night no warmer. Her breath was a regular pluming in the glare as cars went by. She heard the teens chattering and grating music from a mobile—but the girl had noticed her.

Something the kid could not possibly understand, let alone name, drew her to Lucinda like a magnet. When her friends at last headed for home, or to the local pubs, the girl remained, sitting like the queen of the damned in her hood and cloak while white flakes began to fall.

The psychic aura was strong. Lucinda knew to the moment when to turn her head slowly and make direct eye contact. The shock was almost physical. She watched the teen flinch, then gather herself, rise, and approach with timid steps—the pathetic mental gymnastics of a victim trying with every remaining shred of willpower *not* to be prey.

At last, she stood a few paces away in the bitter evening. Lucinda had to admit that this one was the epitome of the troubled teen at war with the world. She did not expect to make much of her vocabulary. To one whose ear had been trained long ago, the new century constantly grew more difficult to understand.

The girl's West Midlands accent overlaid the lingual drift with curious patterns. "Who...?" she began. Fear of the unknown was obviously tempered by the thrill of the same—a dangerous trait that the entity fostered. The more trouble it could get the host into, the richer it would feed on the ensuing anguish.

"Lucinda," she replied, a deep burr in her throat like a lioness's growl. Had the girl known that a razor-honed sword rode in a scabbard under the long coat, she would have been especially fascinated. Morbid glee in the violent and unnatural could not have been written more clearly on her.

"I haven't seen you around here before."

"You're a local?"

"Yeah, I was born here. Miserable dump. I've had enough. I'm off to Birmingham in the morning, first train."

"And what is it that makes Birmingham better?" The question was too philosophical, phrased in a far too Victorian way.

The girl blinked, and a scornful smile flickered on her lips before she smothered it. "It's a proper town, for a start —there's things *happening*. This place dies at sunset."

"You know nothing of death," Lucinda whispered, her gaze boring into the girl with such intensity that the kid stepped back half a pace. The vampire shrugged, dismissing the thought with a faint smile. "And you are?"

"Annie. Anna. Anna Darkholme."

"Your stage name, no doubt." A carefully modulated, almost-silent chuckle edged Lucinda's words.

The tone made the teen flare up. "Who d'you think you are? You're wearing the black—you know how it's done."

"Who I am is none of your business," Lucinda returned with a faint smile calculated to infuriate the entity that dwelt somewhere behind the girl's eyes, anonymously absorbing her experiences. "And the difference between us is that only *one* of us is living out a fantasy."

Anna's hand flashed in the streetlights, a leather-mittened blow aimed at Lucinda's teeth, but Lucinda's own hand moved faster than the eye could see. She snatched the fist and trapped it in an iron grip. Anna squirmed for a few moments as anger pulsed, and then the knowledge she was out of her depth quelled the fury.

"Let's just be friends," the vampire said, staring up at Anna with snowflakes shockingly white against her red hair. After a few moments, she released the girl's hand and brushed away the snow as if its stabbing cold meant nothing. She took a hat from a pocket and unfolded it into a soft, broad-brimmed style. She drew it on and thrust her hands into the deep pockets. "Nasty night, Anna," she added, staring levelly across the street at the Barclay's Bank near the station overpass's massive footing.

"It doesn't seem to bother you." The girl's voice hinted at fascination as she cautiously edged onto the bench at Lucinda's side.

"I've felt colder." Lucinda stared at her for a long, disconcerting moment. "You must have somewhere warmer you could be."

"I like the cold. It's like the dark. It tells me I'm alive." The words came from somewhere deep down.

In them, Lucinda heard the entity's silent coaxing. Now, she must be cautious. Was the thing sensing her yet? Sooner or later it would realise it was in contact with another immortal, and it would defend itself. That would make her job a lot harder. She must pluck it like a ripe plum, but only when the time was right, so as not to sacrifice the host in the process.

"So, what's your grand strategy?" Lucinda's question

caught Anna off-balance. "For your war against the whole human race."

"I dunno what you're talking about."

"Of course you do. Anybody who wears the black knows this world is one vast lie and chooses another reality. What are you going to do about it?"

Anna shrugged, wrapping the cloak closer. "Travel. See as much of it as I can; try to meet other people who know the truth."

"Truth?" Lucinda smiled, her lips like a knife-slash, eyes hard. "A word to beware of, Anna Darkholme, for we all have truths, and they are not necessarily constant between people. You and me, for instance."

"I bet we have more in common with each other than either of us has with *them*." A leather mitten gestured at passersby on the other side of the street.

"In ways, perhaps." Lucinda fell silent, watching snow fall in the haze around the streetlights. She heard clearly as Anna began to shiver, no matter how she tried to hide it. Establishing a psychic link, she sensitised herself to the girl's aura so that she would always recognise it and could follow it. Until she had freed this child's soul from the entity that clung to it like a leech, she would never be far away. "Of course, a day might come when you wake one morning and shake yourself, ask yourself what you're doing, and realise there is less to be at war about than you thought."

"I doubt it!" The reply was scathing.

"There are better causes to fight for than feeling badly done to." Lucinda turned a hard face to Anna, and saw both a flash of anger and the sudden tempering of the kid's memory—that violence achieved nothing with her.

"What would you know?" The outburst betrayed frustration. "You must be at least forty—what do you know about anything?"

The roar of laughter from Lucinda's throat was as good as a slap in the girl's face. It piled scorn upon youth's limited perspective and told Anna that she was indeed a child.

And in that instant, some part of Anna acknowledged

her own limitations. "I can only do my best," she mumbled. "And I won't live by their code."

"Codes, is it?" Lucinda echoed, recovering her composure. "Now you're getting somewhere. Codes are good. Codes tell us who we are, and what we must do to be true to ourselves."

They said nothing for a few difficult moments. A passing car splashed them with too-bright light before Anna prompted, with seeking words, "And what's your code?"

Dark eyes met in a silence that seemed judgemental before Lucinda spoke softly. "Make a difference for good in any way necessary or possible." She raised a finger. "That is the soul of bushido. Look it up; there is wisdom in this."

The pallid teenager gave a shiver that had nothing to do with the weather. "You're *out there* somewhere. I thought I'd met the weirdest of the lot online, but they've got nothing on you."

"Glad to hear I can still surprise." Lucinda looked up into the drifting snow, which had now begun to lie. "Go home, Anna. You're hypothermic." She breathed a plume of breath that mocked her own words, and did not look back at the girl.

After a minute, she heard footsteps as Anna rose and hurried away, more troubled than ever by the strange encounter. The aura faded, but Lucinda had a firm trace on it now. She was fairly sure the entity had not yet recognised her as a hunter, and tomorrow morning would be the perfect time to strike. If Anna were leaving town, the entity must go with her, which meant extricating itself entirely from the rocks and timbers around it, gathering itself up into one complete—vulnerable—package, and tagging along. That was when it would find itself... diverted.

When Anna had disappeared up Bradford Street, Lucinda rose and wrapped her coat closer. She strode under the bridge, through to the opening of Church Street, which forked off to the right. Soon, she was turning into the yard belonging to Henri's of Shifnal and strolling on into the cheerful restaurant and bar.

She took a stool and slipped her credit card across the counter to the young barman as she folded the hat and shook snow from her hair. "Tab, please," she said with a smile, knocking on the bar's electric stockpot. "Mulled wine, and keep it coming."

Freezing nights and mortification of the flesh were for troubled mortals. She may be a walker in eternity, but Lucinda knew what comfort was for. She had booked into this well-known hotel as soon as she zeroed in on her quarry. The Jaguar stood in a nearby lane.

The barman was a chatty fellow who, since she arrived, had been trying his luck with what he saw as simply a statuesque redhead with a flair for the dramatic. She was happy to flirt while the wine flowed, though she would retire upstairs alone to hone the sword and rest in the meditative sleep she had learnt.

The first train to Birmingham went through at 8.36 a.m., and she would be on the platform to relieve Anna Darkholme of the demon on her back.

* * *

Anna had less appreciation for comfort than a vampire, which was irony in itself, Lucinda thought. She lay in a semi-dream and *felt* the world around her with the immortal's psychic gifts, keeping loose tabs on the quarry in the dark hours. Snow fell for much of the night; she knew the late sunrise would be a grey affair—England had made an early start on the hard months as climate change began to bite.

But not long after 5 a.m., she sensed that the entity was in turmoil. Anna was awake, perhaps driven by the relentless gnawing of the hidden soul parasite, and already in a blazing row with family—screaming, threats, slamming doors, and tears. The girl was now wholeheartedly throwing herself into escape.

As six o'clock went by, Lucinda rose and prepared. She dressed warmly, pulling on leathers over her thermals. By lamplight, she took up the sword to meditate and perform a slow kata, flowing through the forms effortlessly until, satisfied, she resheathed the blade and slid it into the deep carrier inside her coat.

At last, she settled her hat, pulled on gloves, and pocketed her room key. Putting on the coat was like applying warpaint; it committed her to battle. She stood silently, listening to Anna's distress with her most acute senses. The girl was packing, throwing things into a carryall, and cramming herself into as many clothes as she could for warmth.

Dawn was nowhere near, and only the kitchen staff were working downstairs as Lucinda left the hotel by the courtyard. Streetlights glimmered on a white carpet under the dark sky; the crunch of her boots was the only sound as she walked slowly up Church Street towards the intersection where the station bridge crossed over.

No traffic; not so much as a barking dog. The world was still as a tomb, and her breath made crystal fog in the air. Anyone looking out would have dismissed her as a fringe crazy, as surely as the teenager who came wandering down Bradford Street, dragging a valise, face hidden in her hood. But even from a hundred metres, Lucinda sensed that Anna was crying. She let the girl cross under, turn the corner, and enter the long, inclined tunnel of Victorian brickwork leading up to the platforms. She glanced at her watch. 7 a.m.

Now or never.

She stood quietly for a few minutes, hands folded, meditating on what she must do. The entity had disengaged from its surroundings now, which compelled it to go with its victim. Such creatures were adept at this. It rode like a parasite on the child's back, parcelled up into a ball of hate, malice, and otherworldly hunger, and attached to her heart by a tentacle—a sucker of energy. It was at its most vulnerable right now, and Lucinda knew she was running a supreme risk.

To detach it from Anna, she must take it into herself. If it proved too powerful, the entity would gain access to the vampire's bottomless strengths, regenerative abilities, and immortality. It would have reached the ultimate feeding ground, after which dislodging might not be possible at all.

This was the ethical price. Lucinda was willing to pay

it; she was certain that she understood this *thing* and could do what was necessary. As she had told Anna, making a difference, at any cost, was her code. Her sword, once the property of a samurai of revered honour and skill, was centuries old and a lost national treasure of Japan. If she ever parted with it, it would return to its origins.

At last, she looked up into the still-dark sky and exhaled a plume of breath in the streetlights. The crunch of boots remained the only sound in the wicked predawn as she strode to the station access, and up to the platform. Stepping out into the lights' glare, she found Anna sitting with her case, huddled in the familiar hooded robe, looking more miserable and afraid than ever.

"Early to be out," Lucinda said softly. "The train won't be here for an hour and a half."

"What do you want?" The reply was barbed. "Just leave me alone."

"I want to help, my dear. I know you don't want to be helped, but right now I see someone who does not have long to live. You'll end your days with a needle in your arm, a backyard abortion, or a knife in your ribs. The method is irrelevant, but no matter what, it won't be a natural end. It will be painful, lonely, and utterly futile because, at the end of the day, it will all be for nothing."

Anna could find no response.

Lucinda heard her crying quietly, face lost in shadow. "Rock and a hard place," she whispered. "Nowhere to go—can't stay here."

"How do you know?" Anna mumbled.

"I've seen it too many times not to know all the signs. And there's more." Lucinda paced slowly along the platform and set her back against a light standard, where the hat cast her face into utter darkness. "There's a goading anger, isn't there? A fury that comes up inside. You don't know where it comes from, but when it takes hold, you don't know who's a friend or not. You just need to lash out. It feels good when you do."

"You've been there." Sudden realisation, spoken in a small voice.

"The flash of pleasure is your morsel of reward for being a bad girl. It doesn't last; you have to be bad to get more."

"You're thinking of drugs," Anna observed with a chuckle.

"No. I'm thinking of possession."

Anna looked up. Her eyes bored into Lucinda's, and in that split second, a psychic flash lit the railway platform like day. The entity had realised it was in danger.

As the thing took over completely, Lucinda watched Anna's presence fade. In that instant, she threw her entire force of will at it, like a shaft of pulsing energy that washed around the entity and wrapped it in flabby coils of psychic force, against which it could rage ineffectually, like a man trying to punch his way out of a fairground paper bag.

It screamed on the etheric levels as it felt itself ensnared, and with grim determination, Lucinda began to reel it in. Anna was unconscious, slumped in her seat, panting shallowly as battle raged around her—just as well, for she was helpless while the creature clung on tenaciously with the limb of itself rooted in her heart.

Lucinda was glad she had a chill, lonely spot in which to do this; it was better this way—extracting a demon *early* was far preferable to doing it later, and having space to do the job was vital. The station's CCTV recorded only two Goth women talking quietly, one seated, one leaning on a lamppost, arms folded. No simple camera could capture what was truly happening.

Teeth gritted, the vampire poured her inhuman strength into the effort, breathing hard as she wrestled the demon. She stretched the anchoring pseudopod near the breaking point, but it must *not* break. Severing it would leave a kernel of evil in the host, and in time the entity would regenerate. She parcelled the thing up in an impenetrable sphere of lambent energy, cradled in her left hand. With the right, she exerted ever-increasing force to open the grip of the demon's repulsive fist—she *saw* it clearly, clutching the child's heart from behind.

That heart had begun to flutter dangerously. This

was traumatic for the host, too. Lucinda must end it quickly. With a deep breath through flared nostrils, she doubled the force and overpowered the grip, tearing it open. The tentacle retracted like overstrained elastic, flying into the mass within the energy globe. As her abused body was relieved of the load, Anna relaxed spontaneously.

Lucinda visualised the greenish-blue sphere of energy in both hands. Within it, she could halfway make out a writhing, distorted shape—snatches of face or limbs manifesting from moment to moment and dissolving once more into swirling chaos. With a faint smile, she toured her own aura, cleansed herself, and poured all negative energies into the microcosm in her hands. Now came the difficult part. If her concentration broke even for an instant, the entity would exfiltrate from the field and attack her. She must take it somewhere safe, and dispose of it.

The station CCTV recorded only that the tall Goth, who had leaned on the lamppost, slowly left the platform and disappeared down the ramp. It was not for security personnel to know that she took with her a vile, writhing focus of hate.

Concentrate, Lucinda whispered silently into her own mind. Nothing must slip; nothing must knock her off balance, and she could not permit distractions. She retraced her steps, aware that the first lights were already on in many buildings—she would soon have company. One step after another, she perceived the scene around her as an overlay atop the visualisation of the sphere in her hands.

She was soon back on Church Street and reached into a pocket to key the Jaguar. Locks released, lights flashed, and she glanced quickly around before removing the sword and propping it on the seat at her side. She slid in, closed up, and coaxed a cold start from the big engine. The entity raged in its cage of psychic energy—it knew it had been taken from the host by some power stronger than itself, and its fury was terrible.

At last, the V8 began to purr, the demisters cleared

the windows, and the wipers shifted snow. Lucinda pulled out onto Church Street, drove under the railway bridge, turned right into Aston Street, and followed it a few hundred metres to the village's edge, where it became Stanton Road and ran away east towards Tong and Bishop's Wood.

This would do nicely. She negotiated the hedgerow and tree-lined, dry-stone wall as farm country opened out, flat and deserted, clothed in white. Half a kilometre from the village, the Jaguar pulled over by a stand of trees, not far from Stanton Hill Wood. She switched off the engine and sat quietly, gathering her strength. She could not maintain the projection of the sphere for long. She must end this *now*, once and for all. Extraction was only a temporary solution.

When she took the sword and stepped out, the sky had lightened. At this time of year, dawn was around 7.40 a.m., and when the sun struggled through, the countryside would be a study in rustic harshness. Taking the mental projection with her, she cleared the wall and found herself in open country, among bare fields and skeletal trees. Clouds in the east flushed up in greys and yellows, at times flurrying away to let the new daylight through.

Striding slowly towards a bare copse by a frozen pond, she knew the time could not be better. As the Darkling vampire would be retreating to its lair to avoid the sun, her kind blossomed in daylight, and she welcomed the energy the sun would bring.

No traffic went by; no lights showed yet in the scatter of farmhouses and halls. She had her moment. Drawing the sword, she focused, concentrated on the sphere of energy and gently placed it on the ground a few paces before her. Carefully, she released the energy, filtered it of all taint from its contact with the demon, and gradually reduced the shield to the minimum force necessary to contain the ravening entity.

As the field faded, the thing sensed that it was about to be released. It crouched, ready for battle, wild as a starving wolf—but the knowledge that it had been humbled and must not underestimate its opponent tempered its fury.

With a final exertion, Lucinda withdrew the field and let it slip away. The energy snapped back into a lambent protective shield that formed around herself, leaving the entity abruptly naked in the world. Without host or anchor, it was obliged to *manifest.*

What came grudgingly into being was horror incarnate, a creature never intended to exist in physical form. It was a misshapen and distorted travesty of life—a gnarled and terrible apparition, all slavering jaws, rending teeth, and eyes that blazed from outside the spaces humans knew, set in a contorted package of mighty limbs upon a shrunken trunk. The terrible form began to fade into hazy nothingness as the entity fought for a foothold in three-dimensional space. Its eyes lit on the vampire, and it snarled its rage through blood-flecked fangs.

The sword extended to it; the honed tip centred unerringly on its dark brow. Lucinda spoke in the ancient tongue of vampires, handed down from time immemorial. The very words struck the entity like a blow. *"I name thee...Incubus. And in the naming, I strike thee down!"*

Naming was an ancient art for stealing the power from anything that would do harm. With its identity revealed, the creature convulsed. Terror appeared in the crazed eyes as it realised that its advantage was spent. Lucinda danced forward, and the blade passed through it, pinning it to the frozen ground. Its limbs thrashed wildly, and a terrible cry bubbled in its throat.

A stink like the grave washed over her, but she closed her nose to the corruption, watching as, bit by bit, the beast began to shrivel away, contracting around the sword like a deflating balloon. All its hate became a futile fluttering, a profane outpouring of impotent rage. It shrank, collapsed into a wrinkled vessel of skin and organs that twitched, refusing to die. At last, it crumbled into a pile of black dust among the frost. With a swirl of chill breeze, it was gone, no more than a stain that the rain would wash away.

Panting lightly, Lucinda let herself relax. It was done.

She could detect no vestige of the entity now, and as she waited—sword poised, eyes closed, alert for any returning vibration—she felt a sudden flush of warmth against her eyelids. The sun was struggling over Stanton Hill Wood, a red fireball in the icy mist above glimmering snow and hoarfrost. The wood's shadows contracted before her.

A new day, and a cleaner one. She wiped the blade in the snow and quickly made her way back to the wall. She went over it with a hand on the apex, and moments later was in the car with the sword resheathed and secreted in clips under the back seat.

She rested for some time before starting the engine and heading back into Shifnal. Passing the station, she looked up at the elevated platforms and smiled cynically. "You're welcome, kid. Have a better life." She did not know what would become of Anna Darkholme, but the child was free of the curse of possession, and whatever course she chose would be of her own volition, unclouded by the darkness her own troubled nature had invited in.

The hunt always made her hungry, and Lucinda was in time for breakfast. She would have enjoyed fresh, hot human blood—and would soon need to visit one of her patrons—but for now, bacon, eggs, and sausage would do, followed by a long, hot shower and some deep sleep.

In the lane, she locked the car, produced her room key, and traded sleepy nods with the dining room staff as she went in. Where she had been was none of their business. It was not for them to know that, although they would deem her unnatural, she was one of the few who kept the world just safe *enough* for mortals—so that humans could go on refusing to believe in anything occult.

Ouroboros

Shepley Hall had dominated the north side of Marshland Fen since the great drainage of the 1600s opened up an area that had been the lakes to farming. In the twenty-first century, the Cromwellian manor remained impressive, nestled in its copse of trees in the arms of Shepley Farm, just west of the River Ouse.

This was a land of waters, with canals, drains and rivers that were ranged in an endless battle with the elements to win back land from the sea. Fully half of England's richest farmland lay here in the Fen District, south of The Wash, a region so steeped in history that, for those who had lived through much of it, returning could sometimes be difficult.

Lucinda stirred in the predawn darkness. The night was still in its middle hours, but high summer at England's latitudes meant early starts. She heard the tick of a grandfather clock along the upstairs hall and the subtle breathing of a body at her side in a luxurious old bed, and she felt as calm and fulfilled as her wild nature would ever permit. She knew many patrons around the country—humans who understood the vampire nature and did not despise her. Though she travelled far on lonely roads, from time to time she came home to one or other of them. For a while, she could imagine that she was as human as any mortal.

When she arrived, there would always be a fresh-drawn pint of warm human blood for her—the gift of one who adored her. She was profoundly grateful for the kindness, which went a long way towards repaying her battles on behalf of an unknowing humankind. Whenever she needed sustenance, it was there for her, and more besides. A few days in the summer scenery of reaped fields, while warmth lingered before the year's inevitable turn back to greys and whites, were balm to a warrior soul. Just for a while, Lucinda could set aside the sword and guns.

But something troubled her rest this morning. Her eyes opened as *something* thrilled unmistakably on her nerves' etheric levels; her body was a sounding board for vibrations to which mortals were usually oblivious. She stiffened as an ancient rhyme ran through her mind: *By the pricking of my thumbs, something wicked this way comes.* Shakespeare had appreciated much that passed unseen in this mortal world—and a deep sense of dread washed through the vampire.

She lifted the cover aside and rose, naked in the summer night's comparative warmth. At the bay window, she looked out over the star-silvered countryside, where the distance drew her eyes. Heavy with foreboding, her soul reached out; *something* was out there. *Something* that did not belong in this time or place. Eyes closed, she concentrated on the sensation while it lasted—a vibration in her nerves, as if of falling; a sense of catching a half-remembered tune or a voice from far away. She had the strongest feeling that the disquiet's source was passing some distance to the east. Despite the warmth, she shivered, for this was unlike anything she had encountered before. If an indestructible immortal could feel fear, Lucinda was afraid.

The view across the fenlands from the upstairs window could not have been more peaceful—or more misleading. She returned to bed and relaxed, though she could not sleep. The feeling faded, but it left a troubling realisation that this too-brief stay in the gentle farmland was already over. Places to go, things to do—her unending way; time and space would reveal her course soon enough.

As the new daylight cast a golden haze over the fields and summer's birds chorused in the dawn, her companion stirred and folded her into his arms. The warmth was welcome. This simple human fulfilment was a rarity in vampirekind's lonely journey, and Lucinda acknowledged the gulf separating her from the mortals who provided her life's nourishment. She had 'turned' *none*. Each patron gave their blood willingly in order to touch, even fleetingly, the immortal kind and share a brief intimacy.

Would she turn any of them? Lucinda did not know. She was one of those vampires who walked close enough to the light to make luring any mortal away from it, even by chance, the gravest sin.

John Hales had asked her to make him a changeling. He was a strong farming man of middle years, descended from a local squire, and a long-time landowner, though he had no family in the area. He was widowed now, with a son at university down in Cambridge. The young man was glad that his father had found someone who stopped by occasionally. John had dabbled in the occult for interest's sake and met Lucinda through a Goth gathering long ago, and he finally came to accept her as the real-life incarnation of his fascination.

From that moment, he had been hers for the asking. At a fraction of Lucinda's true age, John wanted more than her undeniable charms. For many years, he had provided her with the blood that was vital to her nourishment, and he made no secret of the fact that he desired immortality and the regenerative powers of her kind. Lucinda had promised to consider it.

Part of her felt that she should reward his years of loyalty by passing on the condition that made *Homo vampirensis* such an enduring subspecies. Science was rapidly catching up. The twenty-first century would see many of the qualities of vampirekind engineered into the human organism—but not perfectly, and not yet.

"What is it?" John asked softly by her shoulder. "You're tense as steel."

"I...felt something earlier. There are more strange powers in this world than you would believe, even now. And there's no mistaking it—something *is* out there."

"Something?"

"I have no idea what, but I felt it."

"And that makes it Lucy Crane's job?"

She turned, drew him over on top of her with one powerful arm, and kissed him firmly. "You know it does."

"I wish I could do more to help."

"You do, John, you do." She could have said more, but he had heard it more than once.

"But I have just one life to lose, and it would haunt you all your days if I lost it fighting a battle fate brought to *your* doorstep." He nodded with resigned acceptance. "I hope one day you'll give me the ability to make the fight more equal."

"I *have* thought about it. It's more than the strength and long life, John; there's the knowledge that goes with it. For all your learning, you're still a beginner."

"Then grant me the time to catch up with everything I don't know." He kissed her neck, then looked into her troubled eyes. "If a day comes when I misuse the gift, you can always take it back."

"There's only one way to do that, and it would break my heart." After a moment, she rolled him off and sat up. "But it's not a choice to be making today. Today, there's a new problem to solve."

"A new beast for this knight to ride in quest of?" John asked quietly, looking up at her. "Well, the least I can do is organise some breakfast."

* * *

The high summer day was an hour old when Lucinda coaxed life into John's bike—an old Yamaha XJ 1200 in midnight black—and sent it down the lane from Shepley Farm to the road that ran ruler-straight across the reaped fields. She gunned the bike into the east. Hedgerows blurred past, and the machine's bass snarl punctuated the morning, sending birds up from the fields in chattering flocks.

Country lanes flew by as she angled north, following the psychic spoor she had felt in the night. Whatever had caused it was long gone, but like any occult disturbance in the mortal world, it left traces. Her senses guided her unerringly to water, and when she pulled in beside the bridge at the village of Wiggenhall St German, which spanned the River Ouse's grey-brown roll, she knew with grim certainty—*this* was the place.

She rolled across the bridge spanning the flow's fifty-metre width and, on the east bank, turned around in the car park belonging to the Crown and Anchor. Shutting off the bike, she kicked down the stand and walked back in the long morning light to stare at the languid waters.

Almost as many holidaymakers flocked to the fens as to Britain's coasts, and the commercial summer season was barely half over—boarding houses and hotels were doing the year's briskest business. Lucinda's nightmare was that one of her paranormal foes would awaken in such a time and place. She had often been lucky. Winter's grip had tightened on the land when evil raised its head; she could deal with it in the dark, icy months' solitude. But this was something else.

The village was still silent. No traffic passed through; no human saw the figure in riding leathers, helmet in one hand, blood-red mane tugged by the early breeze. It would be a beautiful day; people would enjoy the summer haze while cider presses turned and birds reaped their harvest of insects and shellfish. The fens' abundant birds had months left as yet before they became restless, awaiting the moment when the swirling, shrieking flocks would rise and begin the migration to Africa. The time when they streamed away from the north was usually Lucinda's cue to be vigilant. Now came *this* disturbance, on a warm morning in the peaceful season.

Every hunt began with a clue, and she was waiting for it. She hoped it would not be traumatic for some mortal out there.

She had learnt to cast her net wide and let the universe whisper to her. When she pulled the helmet back on and swung a leg over the bike, she let her vampire senses lead her north. Heading out of Wiggenhall St German, she passed through the village of Saddle Bow. She was in King's Lynn in a few minutes, while the town began to stir as the day warmed. The A148 took her through the heart of town, and she worked through the country roads on the other side to find her way to the last road.

It ran, straight as an arrow, beside the Ouse, where the river threw itself through its estuary to The Wash. The road petered out a kilometre from the sea, and she stopped the trembling bike to look out across the river's broad, greenish-brown flow.

Yes. Whatever had disturbed her came this way.

The bright morning mocked her fears, and she frowned under the lifted visor that protected her delicate skin from sunlight. Lucinda knew her own abilities and never doubted them, but whatever she was dealing with here carried no recognisable signature. She had battled many an entity from the World Unseen—the Darkling vampires, incubi and succubi—and her knowledge of them was adequate to the task. Shapeshifters, werebeasts, and simple restless spirits, all these, she understood. But *this*, she acknowledged with a sharp fascination, was beyond her experience. Even for one so old and well-travelled, the world still had surprises.

She slapped down the visor and sent the bike back east. Eyeing the GPS, she threaded through the rural roads towards Snettisham, home of the great Anglo-Saxon treasure hoard that identified this as an old, old land. Fifteen minutes took her to the north coast of Norfolk, through Tichwell, past Brancaster, and the old Roman site of Branodunum, before she passed the Scolt Head Island National Nature Reserve.

Now her head was clear, no hint of a shadow at the edges of her mind. This alone was significant. Just short of Brancaster Staithe, she pulled in again, and gazed across the wild dune grass country towards the sea's swirling inlets. No, there was no psychic taint here—at least, nothing impacting on her at this point. The focus was definitely back in the fens.

Grim-faced, Lucinda turned the bike around again and retraced her way. But the fenlands cover two thousand square kilometres—among those endless waterways, not even the vampire's nose for trouble could dowse out the quarry.

* * *

When it came, the first clue would have been easy to miss: simply a news item on the large screen in the Crown and Anchor's dining room. Lucinda had rejoined John during the day, but he had left her alone as she pondered the problem, walked in his fields, and stared at the fenlands' waterways as if she might wrest the facts from them through sheer force of will. Eventually, he talked her around, and they went out in the early evening for a quiet meal and a couple of drinks, something Lucinda found irresistibly quaint. She traded leathers and jeans for something more feminine—a rare indulgence—and let John drive them up to Wiggenhall St German in his old Range Rover.

The pub was its usual cosy self; the food was excellent, and they passed the time with small talk. John knew she was monitoring the river, which seemed to be the heart of the problem, and he let her do what she must. He was simply delighted to be out with her, seen as a gentleman farmer having an evening with a wonderful partner. Lucinda rarely had the chance to indulge him, and she enjoyed doing it.

The big screen showed the local channel, and as the news went to air, the ticker along the picture's foot provided the first hint. *Holidaymaker missing at Stowbridge.* The village lay further down the river, four or five miles south. *Police searching nearby waterways.*

Stiffening, Lucinda stared at the screen for long moments, then sipped her wine thoughtfully and at last whispered under the general murmur of conversation, "This disappearance won't be the last."

John knew better than to ask how she could tell. He had known the ageless vampire long enough to put nothing beyond her. "Do you have any thoughts?"

"Not as yet. It feels old—but everything is, really; old as the Earth, old as the stars." She was only musing, and he did not conceal his awe for the gulfs of space and time into which Lucinda peered in these moments. She pondered for a while, swirling the wine in her glass. "There's someone I need to see."

"I know," John sighed. "You'll be heading off." He smiled faintly and chinked his glass against hers. "I hope you'll drop by again when this is done."

* * *

An hour into the night, the Jaguar purred off the road in the woodland east of Northwold, some twenty kilometres from Marshland Fen.

Lucinda had called ahead to ask a favour. All she would tell John was that she was looking up 'an old friend,' which he took to mean *old*. After their quiet evening, she had changed back into jeans and jacket and packed a few things into the car. The sword slid into the compartment under the back seat, and the automatics into the hidden carrier beneath the passenger's seat. Then she kissed John farewell, and honestly could not say when she would be back. Matters had a way of developing of their own accord.

The Elizabethan house nestled back into the trees off a forested road. As its owner preferred, it did not even appear on maps. An ancient stone wall fronted the road; no lights showed, but the tall iron gates purred open in invitation. The Jaguar passed into the woods' silent gloom, as if it had never existed. Lucinda pulled on, around a dry ornamental fountain, and killed the supercharged V8 at a portico where carriage lanterns cast mellow tones over brickwork and timbers that had endured since Drake.

She stepped out, keyed the lock with a blip from the lights, and her eyes strayed to the stars in the summer sky, which was not quite dark beyond the woodland's true black. Her gaze snapped down when the door opened on soundless hinges to reveal a silhouette against the hall lights.

"Greetings, young Crane." Smooth words as Lucinda stepped up to the door and accepted a hug of welcome. "It has been far too long."

Timelessness was a true vampire trait. Caroline van Alt looked as young as Lucinda, but those who knew could tell from her manner, eyes and voice that the soul within was *ancient*. She seemed delicate by comparison with Lucinda—Caroline was no warrior—but this was an illusion. Vampire strength was rarely displayed, and only when the stakes were grave.

Blonde hair fell in tresses, framing a face that seemed to look out of a Rembrandt painting, though Lucinda knew Caroline had taken the name of 'van Alt' only in the seventeenth century. She constructed a Dutch heritage to blend in with the arrival of drainage engineers from the Low Countries, who pioneered the conversion of this land from lake to field. Her true age was much greater.

They hugged for a moment before Caroline closed the door, and Lucinda went ahead into a house she remembered well. The stones and timbers had not changed, and she reminded herself of how many centuries were encompassed by these halls. Blackened beams supported a whitewashed plaster ceiling, and ancient furniture lined the walls of study and lounge.

Caroline led her through to the back garden, where comfortable chairs flanked a lawn table. Insects and frogs called in a reed-lined pond at the foot of the lawns, and the stars shone majestically in the sky's bowl, framed all around by the oaks that preserved Caroline's anonymity.

They sat, and her fine hands opened an aged bottle. "Dom Perignon, '62," she observed. "Can you tell me the significance, Lucy?"

"'62?" She frowned. "I don't recall that being a particularly banner vintage."

"It was not. '61, yes, but not '62." Caroline eased the cork out. It flew into the darkness, and, by the light of a lamp on the table, she poured frothing gold into tall flutes. "It was the last time you came to see me. I bought this in the '80s and have wondered how old it would be before there was a reason to drink it." She passed over a glass, and crystal chinked in the evening air. "Now I will buy a bottle of the current vintage when it appears and put it away. We shall see how long that one gathers dust."

"Fifty-four years." For some time, Lucinda enjoyed the champagne silently, appreciating its antiquity. "I'm sorry, Caroline, truly."

She waved a dismissive hand in the starlight. "What is half a century here and there when we have forever? And you have been busy, if the stories are even halfway true." Caroline gestured at the tall house that lofted behind them. "Little changes here, other than for the better. We have the privacy to talk. I gave my valet some time away; he has taken the dogs." She paused, savoured the moment, and then set down her glass. "I feel your disquiet; it is like a flare in my eyes. Tell me, what brings you to see your elder in the world of the turned?"

In quiet words, Lucinda told the story—feelings in the night, a sense of malice in the waters. The older vampire listened patiently, eyes half closed and fingers steepled before her as she placed these things into the context of the ages. At last, Lucinda took a deep breath and continued with a little less certainty. "I remember something—a story I heard long, long ago. You turned me in 1541, and it must have been a century after that. Around the time you took your Dutch identity to blend in with the dyke-builders."

Caroline smiled cynically. "It was well to leave behind the last vestiges of Henriette of Anjou, who had endured too long. No one save myself even remembers Gwenifre the Saxon. Each had been her own dynasty, as far as mortals were concerned." She sipped, then smiled, realising she had strayed into reverie. "I am sorry. You were saying?"

"A story went around at that time—it became part of the folklore, and in those days, any unusual occurrence *had* to be due to the working of a curse! But I remember a spate of disappearances."

"Yes." Caroline breathed the word slowly. "Bargemen, hunters among the islands and meres, boatmen around the villages. Always, it was on the water. All through the months of high summer, in..." She concentrated. "1636."

"A barbarous time," Lucinda said softly. "The Thirty Years War savaged Europe, and the Burning Times were well alight." The tone of her voice brought Caroline's hand to her arm.

"I have not forgotten, my young friend."

Lucinda squeezed the hand for a moment. "I escaped; that's all that matters."

"Indeed. Now, you see a similarity to that summer, 380 years ago?"

"A disquieting one. It's just gut instinct—as so much is, when intuition is all we have to go on. I felt *something*." She hunted for words to express ideas for which everyday English is not designed, and fell back on the quaint, formal speech of centuries gone by. "Something of great and terrible antiquity has woken from a slumber on timescales mortals may only dream of, and it is compelled to act—with a blind compliance, perhaps, or the feeding of a dumb beast, though no beast was ever as dumb as legend pretends. Someone went missing today, and I fear there will be others."

Caroline smiled fondly at the words' familiar, old-world form. "There could be a mundane explanation. Accidents *do* happen."

"Yes. But so soon after what I sensed? That would be asking a lot of random chance. I cannot prevent a tragedy if I don't understand it."

"This is not part of the common folklore," Caroline said in a studious tone, cradling her glass and sipping from time to time. "The fens are as rich in legendry as any other part of these islands, but the one that comes down to us most strongly is Black Shuck—the old blackdog—a common enough apparition in this land. They say he is a manifestation of Odin's death wolves. He appeared in the Viking psyche in the ninth century, and he remains very much at home here. Old Blacky is real enough, and *not* the villain he's painted." She sighed, looking up at the stars. "No, this is very different. Old, you say? Then let us *feel* for it. Something so ancient leaves a bevel in the smooth curve of time, and we can find it."

Setting aside the glasses, they both concentrated—drew strength from the world around them, channelled energy in a bright cascade, and opened their charged psychic senses. It was not that they were *seeing* beyond their own closed eyelids—rather, they became acutely sensitive to whatever dimpled the world's meniscus. It might have been the boost of being paired with another powerful walker in eternity, but Lucinda once again picked up the spoor, out in the night.

"It's still here," she whispered.

"Far away, but awake...hungry. Questing. And angry. So very angry."

"Why is it angry?" Lucinda wondered in a voice as faint as the wind in the trees. "How has it been grieved?"

"Shh," Caroline countered, throwing her own

considerable power into the effort to locate the creature. "Too far away...back west."

"Heart of the fens..."

They could not maintain such effort for long. Opening their eyes, both panted quietly, and took a while to recover equilibrium. At last, Caroline turned in her seat. "You were right about its antiquity. There is a cold eternity about this beast that affrights even the likes of us. It does not belong in the modern age. Today's world must baffle its senses with vibrations, heat, light, and noise."

"You think perhaps it's simply afraid of a world it no longer recognises?"

"Maybe. But there's more. There is malevolence. It would be wrong to assign this entity the status of an innocent pawn of nature." Caroline shuddered involuntarily. "I felt *intent* and a sentience capable of hate."

"A hate of old," Lucinda mused. "Not of this world, but bound to it." She breathed deeply and sat forward, hands tightly folded. "Caroline, I have never shrunk from a foe, no matter how powerful. But this is unlike anything I know. Can you even guess what we're dealing with?"

"I need time to think," Caroline returned in a troubled tone. "You know I have kept very much to myself; that's how I've lasted so long. I have my patrons, as do you, but unlike you, I never courted conflict. You've fought a running battle for a century and a half, but that's your choice."

"Longer," Lucinda said with a chuckle. "That was just how long I hunted Javirand. There were others. Like you, I came to love and pity mortals—and since Lightlings can walk among them, why not? I would not turn my back on them now, especially since they are entirely unqualified to confront this foe."

Caroline gave a silvery laugh. "Babes in the woods. They will be looking for a murderer, an abductor, an accident—anything but reality. Thus, they will never find it." She rose and paced in the mild air. "It is a terrible thought that something even more wicked than usual shares the world with us. Just as we can feel it, perhaps *it* can feel *us*. Have you considered this?"

"I confess—no. The thought that, far from having to hunt it, it might come seeking us is terrifying."

"Bear it in mind, as shall I." Caroline shook her head and raised a hand, asking for peace, solitude. She walked away down the garden, a pale figure in the starlight.

Lucinda sipped the Dom and pondered her role. John might be right; maybe some things were not necessarily her job—or not hers alone. Perhaps it would take more swords than hers to deal with this. Knowing where to draw the line took skill and intuition, but this horror threatened all of vampirekind—and also the witches, the werefolk, and all manner of the Unseen—not just in this land but perhaps throughout the world. She might be justified in bringing them all together in a way that had never happened in the living memory and records of the oldest of the old.

She watched Caroline down by the pond, where she walked—pausing, pacing, thinking. She had always trusted this timeless woman, who had been a pivotal part of her life since before Henry VIII drew his last breath. And even then, Caroline had been as old as this land.

At last, she returned and collected the bottle, saying softly, "I have remembered something. Come into my study."

The office opened off the hall, where lights bathed the most sophisticated computer array Lucinda had ever seen. The system came off standby; screens lit, and Caroline sat down to concentrate. Long, slim fingers danced across the touchscreen interface as she called up the digitised image of an ancient document.

"This is my diary," she murmured. "You may remember it. The original is in an airtight vault, or it would fall apart with age. Paper is less resilient than flesh. I kept this diary for many years—a secret volume. Many would have deemed it a Book of Shadows, so I hid it all through the Civil War." She scrolled through the document, eyes racing along lines of handwriting that were, to Lucinda, utterly undecipherable. Caroline had recorded the dates not in years, but as degrees of right ascension.

After a while, she shook her head in frustration. "It is not here. I was sure I had referred to it."

"What?"

"Well, it seems to me that this *has* happened before, but earlier than the time you spoke of. I am remembering something much older."

"It's woken *before?*"

"Maybe." She snapped her fingers as a thought occurred. "The Chronicles of Saint Bjorn."

"Who?" Lucinda was out of her depth.

"By the eleventh century, the Vikings were largely Christianised. They had several saints among their settlers in this country. These days, those saints are largely overlooked, but they *were* there. In the days when these lands were islands among the marshes, Bjorn was a wandering monk who wrote a history of his times."

"It still exists?"

"It does. I know of a single copy—in the collection attributed to the scriptorium of Crowland Abbey. The current custodians will let me consult it." She smiled at Lucinda's expression. "Not many scholars are fluent in the written and spoken dialects of the Middle Ages. One of my chief sources of income is translating ancient documents."

She took a mobile from its cradle, paced as she selected a number, and made a personal call to someone obviously of importance in the collection's management. She returned to the desk to note down a password she had received. Replacing the phone, she sat down once more to log onto the abbey's archives and sort through menus.

Prompted, she entered the password. "The internet is a wonderful invention. There was a time when we would have spent two days on horses just to get there and ask permission. Now we merely call it up, like magic." She crackled keys, struck *enter,* and the digitised document appeared on the monitor—a dark vellum manuscript covered with Latin characters. "This will take a while, sweetie. Would you make us some coffee? And there is fruitcake in the fridge."

Entering the spacious kitchen that had been installed in the ancient home, Lucinda had to smile. Every modern convenience was to hand, yet she remembered Caroline long ago presenting to her a gentleman who had been invited to dinner along with several of his retinue. A person of some regard in London, it seemed—highly regarded for his popular works. His name was Shakespeare, and he entertained the dinner party with dazzling wit. The scene took place in the year before the Spanish Armada set sail. Technology defined the passage of time, but Shakespeare's rhetoric still rang in Lucinda's ears and was no less valuable.

She set up the automatic espresso machine with Caroline's favourite blend and opened the tallest, broadest refrigerator she had ever seen to find a sumptuous cake, but the knife with which she sliced it was centuries old. Van Alt Hall was the most delicious melding of the ages—a perfect expression of vampirekind's brand of timelessness.

The house was built by one of the 'gentlemen adventurers' of the time—the investors who put up the money for the voyages of exploration that, little by little, filled in the world map. When he had gone the way of all mortals, Caroline once again established herself as her own dynasty. She was reclusive enough for years to pass while people forgot about her. Each time a daughter or granddaughter appeared with some new story, locals would marvel at the family likeness, which was so pronounced. The strategy worked surprisingly well.

Lucinda returned with steaming coffee and Victorian china, gold-rimmed and beautiful with gothic charm. She took a seat and remained silent as Caroline worked, spectacles perched on her pert nose as she scanned the text.

The enlarged image filled the screen. "This is probably Bjorn's own handwriting," she mused. "He used the Latin contractional conventions, so in its own way, this is as dense as *Magna Carta*. It is always an eerie thrill for me to look back on the writings of, say, the 1300s and pick my way through a lost age. Geoff Chaucer is always a hoot, but one does not have to be his contemporary to know *that.*" She sipped coffee as she traced along lines of text with one fingertip, her mind flying through the translation.

The sense of peace and security eventually lulled Lucinda, and her eyes closed. She sat back in a sumptuous armchair between tall mahogany bookcases crammed with nineteenth-century volumes, and after she had set aside her cup, she fell into a light doze, still aware of the tick of a mantel clock and the breeze in the trees. She could not have said how long she slept, but she stirred at Caroline's light touch on her arm.

"I found it," Caroline said gravely.

Lucinda knuckled her eyes and hung over her shoulder as she zeroed in on a specific passage.

"I am paraphrasing into English, you understand. Latin does not translate as directly as many people like to think. Anyway, in the 1200s, when much of this region was still thickly forested, landowners attempted to drain several marshes. A thousand years earlier, the Romans had tried, but they mostly stayed out of the fens—they made too secure a refuge for outlaws and rebels. Later, Hereward the Wake fought the Normans from these parts. By the Middle Ages, people were starting to think in terms of modifying the landscape. Local landowners attempted to cut drains to channel the water away into the rivers, opening up rich farmland. It was during those attempts that people began to disappear."

Their eyes met for a long moment, and their thoughts raced before Caroline returned to the screen. "Bjorn records that in what had been the Spalda people's tribal territories—the Bedford North Level, near present-day Spalding—a 'great commotion' arose in the summer of 1242. Barges carrying the trees felled to open up the country lost men to what he called a 'water serpent.' Men-at-arms from as far afield as Nottinghamshire arrived to guard the shipments, but the beast was very cunning. It would strike from behind, snatch even armed soldiers from the decks, and disappear into the lakes with them. No one was ever seen again. At one time a local lord—fearing that the beast was in his lakes—ordered a fortune in oil set ablaze on the water in the hopes of destroying the monster. But despite his best efforts, nothing was ever seen of it."

"An isolated incident, or...?"

"The 'water serpent' was feared—local priests exorcised it more than once, and they rounded up a few witches for summoning it." Caroline made a disgusted face and passed over the point with grace. "But it struck a number of times, in a number of places. It never left without making its mark in the people's memory." She traced on through the chronicle. "*Blood and death and misery attended its arising,*" he says, "*and though stout blade and heart be raised in defiance, all human guile and will availed men naught. To the grace of God did they commend their souls and lives, and in due time did the beast return to the deep places from whence it came.*"

"Drainage," Lucinda observed softly. "They interfered with the fens in the 1200s and the beast put in an appearance. They tried hard in the 1630s, and again after the Civil War. Another round from the beast." She licked her lips and produced a tight smile. "I suppose the question is, has there been any significant variation in fen levels recently?"

"The final drainage was complete by the 1820s," Caroline mused, sitting back to polish her spectacles. "These days, it is all automated; hundreds of pumping stations regulate water flow throughout the region on an ongoing basis. If there has been any variation, it could only be minor."

"The impact of technology in the 1200s could not have been great—but it was enough to draw the beast's attention."

"It is worth checking." Caroline moused through odd menus and found her way to the University of Cambridge. She entered through a science department, logging in as a scholar, using a name Lucinda did not recognise, then passed on to the websites of the local Internal Drainage Boards responsible for maintaining water levels in these sensitive areas. Graphs came up, followed by tables of recent activities. She pored over them for a while. "Hmm.

Going by these figures—and compensating for anticipated rains—recent pumping has been about five percent above average for this time of year. It is an El Niño year, after all."

"I wonder...if this thing, whatever it is, responds violently to attempts to reduce the water levels in the lands around The Wash, perhaps it senses the pumping."

"It could be even easier to explain. The sediment and nutrient load that reaches the sea via the rivers is heaviest at times of peak flow. If this 'water serpent' is some kind of marine creature, it could be sensitive to relative turbidity."

With a few crackling keys, Caroline pulled up a remote data package. Satellite images showed sea conditions in The Wash, where the rivers exhausted long, dense plumes that fanned out into the North Sea. A comparison of the data over time indicated that they were somewhat heavier than average.

"So, why did it go quiet while the main work was underway?" Lucinda stood with both thumbs hooked into her belt loops, staring hard at the screen. "We're building an interesting theory, but our monster disappeared around the time drainage got serious. The windmill-powered pumps in the late 1600s and 1700s went a long way towards establishing this region as dry land. Then came the steam engines, diesels, and electric units that finished the job, but no monsters rose from the deep to attack during the industry of the age."

"A good point. The folklore probably made people edgy—remember, each attempt to drain the fens met with vigorous opposition from the locals, whose homes were under threat and whose lifestyles were becoming redundant. Hunters in the marshes, poachers, fishermen, and outcasts of all kinds flourished in isolation among those wild islands and waterways. Not wanting to be displaced by crop farmers, they fought progress as best they could. Perhaps some remembered whispers from the past—that *something* out there had as little liking for the idea as they did themselves."

"More than likely. But what kept the beast down?"

Folding her arms, Caroline shook her head slowly.

"There are no indications at this point. It is just a theory, after all."

"But a good one. I'd bet that if records existed, we'd find *something* haunting the Romans when they attempted a clearance. They called Britain a land of magic and monsters at the best of times."

Caroline saved data and pushed her chair back silently. "Well, my friend, what do we have? A long-lived entity of some sort that inhabits this part of the world; it is angry and it is savage; it responds to what it perceives as interference in the natural balance of its world, and it reacts by killing. It has been here for at *least* eight hundred years, probably a lot longer. And it is back."

"That's about the size of it."

"Any ideas?" Caroline asked with grim humour.

"A few. Offer it bait, see if it shows. If it does, I'll be ready—not to kill it, but to learn more about it."

"But, ultimately?"

"Killing it is the final option." Lucinda shrugged. "If there's a way to compel it to return to some long sleep that it uses to span the ages, so much the better. Remember, this could be a genuinely antique creature from far back in the geologic past, a living fossil. If so, killing it is the last thing I want to do. And yet there seems to be more to it."

"The malevolence."

"Yes. If evil truly dwells in this thing, then there are no options."

With a nod of her honey-blonde head, Caroline stood. "Good luck—I shall help however I can, but at the end of the day, *you* are the warrior."

* * *

The elder vampire was right. Warriors tended to walk alone, especially in these latter days. The idea that St Bjorn's 'water serpent' was out there somewhere sent a crawling sensation down the spine—worse yet was the suspicion that whatever sentience it possessed might sense *them* as certainly as they sensed it. The beast surely stood apart from the world's common creatures—a horror that could crawl out of the nearest river in the night and come for them as they slept. The notion chilled Lucinda, yet it barely seemed credible in the twenty-first century.

It was the stuff of nightmare, but the more she and Caroline considered it, the more they recognised the fears that had haunted the human collective consciousness since time immemorial. The Viking Ragnarok, expressed as Jormundgandr; the world-girdling Midgaard Serpent, marking the boundaries of a flat cosmos; the legendary Lambton Worm in England's northeast; the sea serpents of even earlier times—even Bram Stoker appealed to the archetype of human horror in his novel, *Lair of the White Worm*.

Sleep did not come easily to Lucinda as she lay in a guestroom upstairs. Bare to the air, for a time she stood at a latticed window, stared at the forest and the stars, and let her psychic senses wander, searching for the beast. She needed a plan, and it formed gradually as she pondered. If the creature did not belong in this world, destroying it might be beyond her ability. But returning it to whatever realm it called home remained an option—if she could find the door via which it travelled between the worlds.

First things first: she must understand the foe, which meant gathering information. She could sink into an ever-deeper state of trance and force her mind to confront it on the ethereal level—but this also held dangers. The physical level was all brute force and materialism, but in some ways much safer. She had not been joking when she suggested setting bait, but she was not about to offer herself up as a sacrificial goat. In this technological age, other possibilities were worth exploring first.

Her senses ranged far afield, but now she caught not the faintest trace of the beast, and she composed herself to rest. Still, the twin automatics and sword lay on the coverlet at her side—for all the use they might be against such an enemy.

* * *

A British summer could be a tough place to be a Goth, and at times Lucinda let the act go. The costume allowed her to blend into a fairly omnipresent subculture, but in the absence of other Goths, the disguise became redundant. Jeans, boots, long sleeves, and the broad-brimmed hat to keep the sun from wreaking too much damage too quickly were all she needed to walk out in the noonday heat. The night's ominous presence remained oppressive, and she was grateful to be among humans.

Not long after first light, she had made a call. She tried not to exploit the generosity of her patrons, but this situation called for extraordinary measures, and by luck, she reached an associate professor from the marine biology department of University College, London—one of her most trusted associates.

Lucinda had not tasted Warren Fuller's lifeblood in a year. He was more than happy to hear her voice—less pleased to know she needed the tools of *his* trade rather than her own. But he came through for her with the same selflessness each patron did, and they met in the early afternoon.

The Bell Hotel in Thetford was an old favourite of Lucinda's, like the George and Pilgrim in Glastonbury, for the simple reason these places were even older than herself. Approaching the Bell's overhanging, fifteenth-century façade was like coming home; the old bar's stone and carved beams brought a strange sense of comfort, as did Caroline's house. Lucinda knew she must return to her own home one day soon. She had travelled the British Isles seemingly without pause for much too long.

The hotel was busy with the holiday trade, but she had managed to book a table for two in the courtyard garden. Warren—a tough, square-cut man in early middle age, weathered from the pursuit of his profession at sea—had come up from London, and Lucinda met him partway, making the ten-mile drive down to Thetford. Lunch simply provided an excuse for the rendezvous, but it was a pleasant one. They cradled sparkling red while they waited for the food—beef and ale pie for one, open seafood pastry for the other.

The brisk holiday season business would convince anyone the world was its same old self, but the morning news reported another disappearance, this time a fisherman on the banks of the Broads, around sunrise. Lucinda recognised the ancient pattern. If the beast gained strength with each life it consumed, it might soon be unstoppable.

She and Warren whiled away an hour over lunch, ordered Kentish Bramley apple pie and coffee, and chatted about this and that, though Lucinda knew he must be desperate to ask what she wanted with a fish aggregation device, an infrared digital video camera, and a radio tagging/biopsy rifle.

They had met through their patronage of an occult bookshop ten years before; he fell for her blazing red hair and haunted face, and he had the plasticity to understand, accepting what she revealed about the vampire world's reality. Fascinated on personal and professional levels, Warren would do anything for her, with the same willingness as John Hayles.

Finished lunch, they ambled out to the cars and drove a little way west into Thetford's woods, the great forest's last remnants in these parts. The cars pulled off the road at a service trail, and, hidden from the main road, Warren unloaded the gear she had asked for and briefed her on each piece.

He went over the use of the radio tracking locator, and watched her load and unload the tagging rifle. "What are you after? A pike?" he asked, only half joking.

"I'm not sure," she returned truthfully. "If I can get a sample, I would be very interested in your analysis."

"It can be arranged," he said affably. "It might take a few days. Will you be around? I couldn't interest you in a room at the Bell for the night? Or anywhere else?"

Lucinda chuckled and embraced him in a bear hug for a moment. "Sorry—things to do. But if you can stick around, I'll be in touch, and you can grab the gear back. Hopefully, I'll have something for you to put under a microscope." She tapped the dry-ice-filled, insulated sample case.

"Well, take care in these parts. The news says people are going missing—they still haven't found them. They're thinking of dragging the Broads."

"It's a worry," she agreed, letting nothing slip through her composure. If she were even halfway lucky, she would shed light on this very problem.

* * *

A map of the Fen District lay spread on Caroline's dining table. Using pins, the women had marked the locations where disappearances were reported. A third had happened during the afternoon—this one further west, in the North Level near Crowland. "It moves far and fast," Caroline observed. "Even the local authorities cannot help but see a pattern soon."

"So widespread? They'll be slow to connect them; there's nothing but coincidence to account for three cases fifteen miles apart. This time, it's in the Nene's drainage basin, not the Ouse. There's little chance of any creature the police could imagine making the journey in such a short time—except an abductor." Lucinda raised an eyebrow. "Mind you, if a severed leg comes to light, they'll be looking for one thing, and one thing only."

"An anadromous shark," Caroline agreed thoughtfully. "The bull shark transitions between salt and fresh water at will, is global in distribution, and is especially aggressive. It is theoretically possible."

"Also, incorrect." Lucinda gestured at the steel cases that stood on the end of the table. "Whether this thing will come to the fish aggregator is a long shot, but worth trying. If it puts in an appearance..." She slapped the longer case. "I'll do what I can."

"Where will you set your trap?"

"We can trance for it again. If we can gather a rough impression, I'll aim for that region. Ideally, I want a bridge to give me a vantage point over the water."

"It moves quickly; in the time it takes you to get there, it may have travelled a good distance."

"I can only try."

Caroline shook her head slowly. "I do not like this one bit, Lucinda, my dear. You have dealt with your fair share of evil over the centuries, but this...this is *big*. It has *teeth*. You cannot appeal to it, you cannot reason with it, and you cannot threaten it."

With a sigh, Lucinda nodded in agreement. Opening one of the cases, she brought out two small boxes. She flipped the card lids and, with a wry smile, showed Caroline the ammunition's wicked points. "I keep these in stock for the tougher sorts of physical manifestations." She hefted one box. "High explosive incendiary." Then the other. "Armour-piercing incendiary. I'll load the magazines with alternating types because I have no idea what the target will be. It might have hide that a 9mm round couldn't possibly penetrate; it might be armoured like a crocodile—who knows?" She set down the rounds. "I've ordered some heavier ordnance, but it won't be here until tomorrow." She slumped into a chair. "You're right. I've never been a big-game hunter before, and I have no desire to be. But this situation is ours to deal with, and no one out there, *no one*, is capable of tackling this thing on its own terms."

"You know best," Caroline said softly. "It will be dark around nine. I assume you will be using darkness to cover your movements?"

"I'm obliged to, although this beast has struck three times in daylight." Lucinda glanced at her wrist. "I'd better get some rest. It could be a long night."

* * *

Those words haunted her an hour after dark as she waited by the bridge on a canal prosaically called the North Level Main Drain, about five kilometres south of Sutton Bridge and ten from the sea. The nearest houses were a couple of hundred metres each way from the bridge spanning the dark flow. The flat, reaped fields were eerily empty, silent but for the night breeze under the sickle-slash of a westering moon. Tydd St Giles Golf Club was a wide expanse of trees on the canal's west side. Where Sandy Lane crossed the waters, Lucinda sat in the car, off the road, and under a large tree opposite the east end of the bridge.

The fish aggregation device was an acoustic pinger, a controversial gadget that concentrated fish for commercial trawlers, earning it a bad reputation. Warren's scientific model was small enough to be deployed unobtrusively from the bridge. The hydrophone dangled half a metre under the dark canal's surface, broadcasting the kind of sounds known to attract fish. Lucinda was simply playing a hunch, not that the beast itself would be attracted by these sounds, but that when it was in these waterways, it would feed primarily on freshwater fish. Concentrate the prey, and the predator should come to *their* sounds.

Both automatics were silenced, and she wore them in a double rig under her jacket. She would not fire unless she had no option, since the detonation of these shells would attract attention. Most of all, she needed to do this without losing her anonymity. The tagging rifle lay on the back seat, loaded and primed with a low-power charge. When the time came, all she needed to do was connect the recovery line. The dart carried two barbs: one locked in a radio tracer—the GPS signal would register on the hand tracker—and the other was a simple tool that would take a biopsy sample and slip out cleanly. If the beast appeared, given the luck of the gods, the job would be complete in one silent minute.

This was the plan, but Lucinda's mouth dried as she waited, trying to *feel* for the creature with her inhuman senses. She would so much rather have been tackling her own kind. Darkling vampires walked in territory she understood. Here, she was armed with popguns, waiting for something the size of a dinosaur and hoping it would allow her to jab it.

You must be crazy, she thought for the umpteenth time. Vampires were tough but not actually indestructible, and the crawling cold at the edges of her mind told her this creature kept one foot—if it *had* feet—in eternity. This was the reason for the tag; she must build a model of its movements. She did not expect it to run back to its gateway, but at some point it would. So long as the radio tracer registered on the GPS tracker, she was amassing a database of its movements.

The system had a thirty-kilometre range, provided the tag had access to clear air for transmission. Given that no part of this drainage system was over four metres deep, the tether that anchored it to the creature's body would be more than long enough. She could track it by road as it moved through the low-lying lands, but she was most interested in where it had come *from*.

The FAD had been pulsing for less than thirty minutes when she saw glimmers in the river under the bridge. Milling fish, drawn to the emitter, stirred the freshwater plankton to fitful green flashes. *So far, so good,* she thought, and narrowed her concentration to a tentative feeling for the beast.

It had been in the Nene drainage basin two hours before—she and Caroline felt it distinctly as they dowsed for it over the map. It was disturbing, Lucinda admitted, to look out across the silent, lightless countryside and know something terrible was out there, not very far away, stirring in this world like Sauron in Mordor...an evil in the rivers and lakes, passing through these channels' turbidity without humans ever knowing it was there. Her uneasiness evoked thoughts of lake monsters the world over—and how very real things were dismissed as myths and legends because they dwelt outside this age's accepted *normal*.

Eyes closed, she stretched out. Her thoughts wandered across the reaped farmland behind her, turned a wide circle in the cold silver moonlight, and traversed the drain, which ran ruler-straight across the countryside. *Where are you?*

I am near.

The thought cannoned into Lucinda. She recoiled, becoming aware in one terrible instant—this had just become personal.

That was two-way communication, and it denoted a sentience of great power. An unmistakable cold accompanied it, whispering of other places and times. She shuddered involuntarily. The beast was feeling *for her*. It was no remnant creature from Earth's distant past—or, if it were, sentience had taken undreamed-of pathways to bridge the mundane world and the Unseen.

Judging the right moment was difficult, but at last Lucinda could wait no longer. She slid out, took the tagging rifle and cold case, and crossed the road in a skirmish crouch. The camera stood on its tripod on the bank above the green slope at the water's edge. It covered the area where she had deployed the FAD by the near-side support columns. She dropped to one knee to connect the biopsy dart's recovery line and laid the neat coil on the bridge's railing; it must pay out smoothly or ruin the shot. The case sat at her feet, with the latch disengaged but the lid down. As she thumbed a remote, the IR video began to record.

She shouldered the rifle and, in her own way, prayed that no human would pass by in the crucial minutes ahead. *Come on, come on!* Her nerves stretched taut as she stared into the dim water. The nearest streetlights were some distance off, serving the houses backing onto the waterway. With the anonymity of darkness, she watched the glimmers as milling fish schooled around the suspended device.

A sigh of waters was building behind her, but she did not dare take her eyes off the channel below to look back. In seconds, the green flashes multiplied into a sulphurous cloud, in which she made out fish darting in confusion and panic.

Suddenly, a massive shape moved among them— jaws snapped shut on the shoals, and water crashed up the embankment in a burst of spray. Lucinda held her breath, kept her finger outside the trigger guard, and waited for the shape to turn, uncoil, and present some part of itself for a clean shot.

She did *not* expect the beast to look at her.

In a roll of spray, the water parted. A head such as she had never dreamed of rose before her; three metres of neck lofted it up close to her level. At first, she made out only eel-like characteristics before she realised the skin was scaled like a reptile, despite the gill slits pulsing in that neck. Two huge eyes, arranged for binocular vision, stared from a hideous face above a gash-like mouth that streamed water and stank like death itself. Would the creature recognise the source of the psychic contact? How could it fail to?

For long moments, Lucinda held its gaze while the head swayed almost gracefully. She half-expected to hear its thoughts hammer into her mind, but as it turned away from her she squeezed the trigger, and the rifle's muffled cough sent dart and tag on their way.

The range was short, the impact high. The line to the biopsy dart streaked cleanly away. The barbed tag connected on the upper surface of the neck, where the jaws could not reach back to dislodge it, but a second later, the beast shuddered with shock and affront. The neck collapsed in a curving pillar of flesh as the head dove under—the dart jerked out neatly.

The tag's LED flasher activated. Lucinda spotted it in the dark water as she slung the rifle and hauled in the line. Was the encounter done? The channel roiled as the creature thrashed, trying to shake loose the tag. The water level was no more than two metres, barely enough to contain the long, sinuous body, which seemed to fill the drain. Its bulk collided with the bridge's pylon, and the structure shuddered.

With a convulsive spurt of energy, the beast ran, heading north. The LED flash receded along the watercourse with breathtaking speed. Heart in her mouth, she hauled in the line, and slipped on rubber gloves before disengaging the dart. When it had dropped into the insulated case, she flew through retrieving the equipment. She would check the digital recording later. Video and FAD units landed on the Jaguar's back seat. Lucinda hauled out the rifle case, dropped the weapon into it, and slid it away before the driver's seat rocked back into place.

The GPS tracker snicked into its holder on the dash and displayed a blip moving against a large-scale local map. The beast was already a kilometre away. The V8 fired, and the Jaguar crossed the bridge quickly onto Hannath Road. Lucinda overtook the signal as she passed through the village of Tydd Gote, and she pressed on hard until she drew abreast of the pumping station that regulated the drain's flow into the River Nene, half a kilometre ahead.

The station effectively barred the way. If the beast

were heading for the sea, how would it deal with the obstruction? In the moonlight, she clearly saw the disturbance in the water—a broad wake surging towards the pumping station that stood foursquare across the channel. The tag light's flicker might have been a firefly in the shadows. The creature hesitated, investigated the underwater structures, then reappeared, and Lucinda watched the head rise up like a sea serpent of old.

Then the beast committed to its course. It moved up onto the bank, extruding its length into a serpentine S-curve that crushed bushes and fences as it passed *around* the station. Its size was astonishing, and the darkness made the length hard to estimate. Holding her breath as she watched, Lucinda would have guessed twelve metres or more, and long, ribbon-like fins made it appear even more eel-like.

Intruder alarms went off in the pumping station; lights flicked on automatically, but the creature's sheer size made it swift. It swept aside a fence and undulated across the road that bridged the river behind the station before plunging in a smooth dive back into the shallowing waterway beyond.

By some miracle, the tag's tether had not torn loose. Now, the monster had unobstructed water all the way to the sea, and Lucinda headed away before the disturbance attracted attention. Security CCTV at the pumping station must have recorded the creature—nothing was surer. But such evidence would be 'lost,' as always happened when anything beyond human comprehension put in an appearance.

The GPS tracked the beast as, with the speed of an arrow, it headed for the junction where channel met river. Crossing under the twin road and footbridges, just short of the junction, it seemed to gain speed with depth. Lucinda nailed the speed limit north to Sutton Bridge and threaded through the corner of town, past the Cross Keys Bridge's wide metal span. She sped north on West Bank Road, while the GPS reported the creature surging up the river, right through town, towards the open sea.

Holding to the speed limit, she passed the twin

lighthouses, where the road angles away from the river at the western tower. Now, she threaded through the last roads that wove among the final, cultivated fields to the salt marshes' landward edges, and there, she pulled in at a lonely turnaround.

Grabbing binoculars from the glovebox, she stepped out into the night breeze and focused hard on the Nene's outfall, half a kilometre away across treacherous shallows. She waited one minute, two, before spotting the tag's cold, distant spark. "Got you," she breathed, watching the glimmer move out to sea. Lowering the glasses, she breathed the cool, salty air and rested against the car.

That had been a strange adventure for her collection—and it was not over yet. When her spinning thoughts calmed, she checked the GPS. The trace was wandering about three kilometres northeast—already a tenth of the system range. She must keep the contact inside its envelope, but fortunately, The Wash is not a large place.

The Jaguar purred south back to Sutton Bridge and recrossed the river on the A-17. In minutes, Lucinda passed through King's Lynn before rejoining the north road, towards Snettisham. Fifteen minutes later, she pulled in at the access gate to the beach on the Heacham foreshore, near the caravan park where South Beach Road dead-ends.

There, she turned off the engine. A few lights showed at the windows of nearby holiday chalets, but the night was quiet. The GPS placed the tracer a few kilometres offshore, idling at walking pace. It was reassuring to know its location, but with the physical aspect attended to, Lucinda must confront the abstract.

This dragon possessed enough sentience to recognise her psychic presence, but Lucinda sensed nothing she would describe as empathy. For all its unique nature, the creature's malice placed it with the Darkling vampires, incubi, and assorted denizens of the shadows she had battled for so long. Part of her regretted seeking its destruction, but she was not about to watch it consume another innocent life.

She checked the gear in the back seat, assured herself of the cold case's seals, and stood by the car's warm hood, looking out to sea as she called Warren. The sparks of towns and villages glittered in the darkness on the far side of The Wash.

She watched the glow of Boston on the horizon as she waited for him to pick up. "Hi, Warren, sorry to bother you near midnight. Hope I didn't catch you in the middle of anybody." At his grunt of humour, she went on. "I have a sample in the case. You know your gear better than I do—will it be okay till morning?"

"That case is your full-pro lab gear—liquid nitrogen, the works," he assured her. "A sample should be stable for days."

"Right. We'll have first light in about five and a half hours. I'm in Heacham. At this point, the target isn't making any moves. If it heads out to sea, I guess I'll abandon the watch, but until then, I'll keep tracking it. I want a full record of its movements."

"Heading straight out—open sea?" Warren's tone was guardedly excited. "Did you catch a glimpse? Care to speculate?

"You mean, what *is* it?" Lucinda chuckled and glanced at the metal case on the back seat. "You tell me, Warren—you tell me."

He spoke for a while about being lonely in a hotel bed, and she indulged in some pillow talk while she watched the GPS. Lifting the binoculars to scan for the tag out in the dark bay, she saw nothing now. Part of her would not put it past this creature to come right for her in a fit of spite, but its retreat to the sea also suggested caution. She made appreciative noises as Warren chattered on, but at last she brought him back on topic.

"Okay, set your alarm for five—give me a call. If we're still in range, you could shoot up and collect the gear. You'd be back in Thetford for breakfast, then home at your lab preparing slides by nine."

Minutes later, she pocketed the phone, slid back into the Jaguar, and turned up the heater. It would be a long night, and she was grateful for the thermos and packed meal Caroline had persuaded her to bring. She *could* spend a freezing night exposed to the elements; her vampire constitution would shrug it off, but small comforts were welcome.

An hour crawled by while she drank coffee and monitored the GPS. The beast was making circles in the bay; its pattern almost suggested that it was sleeping. She had seen dolphins cruise the same way, with one brain hemisphere asleep at a time. At this point, she perceived no activity from the creature, but she was more than cautious of that 'psychic brushing' occurring again without warning. If it happened at the beast's discretion, she might find herself at a distinct disadvantage. The less it knew about her, the better—she did not want a presence of such power and malice haunting her dreams.

Remembering how the serpent undulated across the land like a colossal snake, a sudden image sprang into her mind. *I wonder how vindictive it is.* If it should gain access to her memories through a coupling of minds, it could attack and manipulate her—the fastest way to turn the tables on its only threat among the two-legged species. Water courses crisscrossed the fens, not merely the main ones. Drains and ditches ran within a few hundred metres of Shepley Farm—

Ten times its own body length? Twenty? If the creature had the ability to exist long enough out of water, it would have little difficulty crossing that much dry land, and no ordinary house would resist the weight and strength it could bring to bear. The very possibility of the beast finding a way to attack her through her mind was too great to ignore. She could not afford to allow John to become her Achilles's heel.

She punched his mobile and waited as it rang. He might be asleep, but he kept the phone at the bedside when he knew she was in the area. The call forwarded to his answering service, and she thumbed off the phone and summoned patience to wait. Sure enough, thirty seconds later, John was on the line, sounding a bit groggy but glad to hear her voice.

"John, I want you to do something for me. I can't

explain why just yet, but I'd be very grateful if you would jump on the first train in the morning. Go down to London for a couple of days...I know it sounds odd, but you know there's *something* happening."

"You know I'll do as you ask," he yawned. "No chance of the odd detail, I suppose?"

"I'll tell you all about it when it's over and done, I promise. But for now, can you go? The crops are in, so there's nothing to be done around the farm."

He assented readily enough, and they spoke softly for some time—Lucinda admitted to herself that of all the humans she knew, she did indeed have a softer spot for this one than most. *Don't let your fondness for humans take over*, Caroline had said once, long ago. *They die, and the only remedy is to take away their mortality.*

Maybe it would be the best thing to do, Lucinda reflected. But she was not yet ready to make the choice. Turning the mobile off, she closed her eyes for a while, and listened to the roll of the sea. The sigh of each wave onto the sand was almost mesmeric. She relaxed into the seat's comfortable padding, opening an eye from time to time to check the GPS. The tracker was still out there, seven or eight kilometres away. The battery would last at least three days. Its extensible five-metre tether kept the float at the surface and transmitting, save for moments when the beast dived deeper, which seemed infrequent.

She could afford to relax, and settled for the night—jacket zipped, hat pulled down for warmth, doors locked. The automatics were still under her coat; she did not feel secure enough to set them aside. Driving gloves on, she turned up her collar. Even in summer, England could be a chilly place, and the breeze off the North Sea was historically unkind.

Knowing she might have to relocate at some point, she meant to rest, not sleep. A knock on the window from a heavy police hand might have unwanted side effects. Still, as she watched the GPS, her eyes grew heavy. Before she knew it, her chin fell forward and her eyes closed.

Perhaps she was overconfident, but in all her centuries, she had never so misjudged a situation. Maybe it was easier to be focused when the enemy was personalised, in human form and near at hand. This time, she found herself drifting into fleeting vulnerability, and the shock was profound the instant the beast took advantage of it.

Lucid dreaming is a skill as old as shamans the world over. Balanced on the point between waking and sleeping, the conscious mind can access the dream cortex, yet maintain a detached perspective on the images generated in the dream state. In this highly suggestive condition, the conscious and unconscious minds communicate through visual metaphor. It is also the level at which gifted people are most psychically active—and at their most *open*.

It began as a dream and, perceiving it as a dream, Lucinda did not resist. She was in deep before she suspected the truth, and by then it was too late. She felt warmth on her skin, and a flood of deep, goldy-saffron light filled her closed eyes. When she opened them, she found herself on a shore she had never known.

The sea lapped low and calm, and dense thickets of rich, green vegetation streamed across wave-smoothed rocks. The sun seemed big, intense, and the landscape was strangely silent. She stood on coarse sand, looking down into a limpid tidepool with the human urge to dive in and hang in the cool, weightless world. She did not question where she was or why she was there; as a mute observer, she simply basked in the strangeness for a long while. But when a shape moved in the deep, clear pool, she caught her breath and stepped back.

The creature moved through the water in a smooth, graceful glide. Its scaly snout broke the surface with a near-soundless roll of wavelets. The enormous head, with its unnerving binocular stare, lofted above her on the massively muscled neck. Scales shone in the warm light; gills pulsed gently. Gradually realising that this was both a dream and *more* than a dream—one in which she maintained a measure of control—Lucinda was not afraid.

She looked up at the beast, outlined against the warm sky, and *thought* a wordless prompt. She had not really expected a response, but a voice reverberated inside her head, toneless but with great gravity.

Why do you hunt me? The question was direct, fully formed. The unblinking eyes demanded a reply.

She was taken aback for an instant.

You, alone among the millions who swarm upon the land, can hear me. How?

In her surprise, Lucinda struggled to remain in the narrow band of brain cycles at which she was capable of this connection. Above or below by even two cycles per second, the connection would break. "I hunt you because you are killing," she explained as directly as she could. She raised one hand towards the creature in the dream. "*Why* do you kill?"

The two-legs remake the world; they are parasites that have changed these waterways, which are my hunting grounds of old. Each time I revisit this realm, they have done more, changed more, and taken away more.

"It is their world now," she said softly.

Theirs?! They are nothing—they are vermin!

"They have been successful. In the long ages while you and your kind were absent, the two-legs have made this world their own, and there is nothing you can do about it."

Nothing?! The long neck swayed, and the jaws snapped in thin air.

"Nothing! Listen well, spirit of the waters." Lucinda spoke from the heart, oddly moved by their encounter and unafraid of the giant. "The mortals are limited and many are duller than a lake at midnight. As a race they have prospered, but their world is *closed.* They do not welcome anything they are not familiar with—especially not what they fear. You are a water dragon of old and they no longer believe in you. You could not *make* them believe, not even if you paraded before them in broad daylight. They will kill you, cut you up to see how you work and put your skin and bones on display before they admit that you were *once* real."

She felt the dragon's fury but did not flinch. The huge body thrashed the water, and the jaws snapped over and over, gaping to reveal stupendous fangs.

"Rage all you will—mortals do not care. To them, you are a myth. If you make yourself more than that, you will become a problem to be *dealt with*." She spared the dragon nothing; she knew this was a dream and could easily snap out of it. "But it does not have to be this way."

How else shall it be?

"The age of dragons is long gone. Return to the Otherworld. Sleep away the aeons, and perhaps a day will come when the mortals are more accepting—or less powerful. It is not beyond possibility that they will destroy themselves. But here and now, the power is theirs, and this is a battle you cannot win. Fifty dragons could defeat them. They are individually weak but collectively strong."

The water beast calmed somewhat. The massive head came down towards her, floated level with her face, and the huge eyes stared into her heart.

The coldness of the Otherworld clings about you. You walk the way of forever, just as do we Elder Ones.

"If you feel this, then heed my counsel. I would not harm you by choice. Give me that choice, and I will do all I can to help you. But you cannot hunt in these shallow waters. Human souls were never meant to feed yours."

The two-legs once called me a god and made sacrifice at their altars, the giant whispered, a regretful lilt in Lucinda's mind.

"Dragons are remembered well, but few humans understand them anymore. Even fewer believe you ever really existed. When this land was marshes and the two-legs were just scattered tribes, it was easy for them to accept your kind. They saw divinity in the beasts of forest and hill—why not of the waters? Perhaps the Vikings called you Jormundgandr, the Icelanders, the Skrímsli. But times change. Those like you, whose lives span aeons, sometimes do not appreciate how quickly change comes."

The great head twitched. The beast seemed to sniff around her aura—not that it was capable of inhaling physically. It was silent for some time as it inspected her, and Lucinda felt a sudden apprehension.

Long have you lived, yes, but only for the merest few

beats of a dragon's heart. You had not long been alive, when last I saw this world. You are a hatchling! By what audacity do you lecture an Elder One?!

"I do not lecture. I state facts. I ask that you do not make me your enemy."

Mayhap we always were, for your sympathies lie with your own kind.

"And they always will. Do not expect me to stand idly by while you exact a pointless vengeance upon mortals who are innocent of the crimes you perceive."

And what will you do about it? The question was blunt.

Its challenge could be met in no other way. "I will stop you. I can do it. *Don't make me.*" The jaws gaped with a hiss and a cascade of water, but Lucinda was unimpressed. "This is the age of the machine. All your strength and size cannot prevail. Your physical form can be destroyed. Could you remanifest? I doubt it. Take yourself back through your doorway; let us hear no more of the serpent of the waters, and in a thousand years we shall see how the world fares." She smiled with very real compassion. "I will still be here—and I, at least, will welcome you."

For the moment, the serpent seemed calm. Though its face was expressionless, she felt a reaction from its great heart. *Yes,* it said. *I believe you would. But you ask a lot of dragon nature if you demand that I put away my pride, forget my anger and become a spectator to the doings of mortals.*

"I appeal to that nature to recall its own grandeur. Dragons are more than the monsters that legend has painted them. Nobility is not found in pure strength but in other qualities—understanding, wisdom, forbearance. There is nothing admirable about brute force. If you choose that way, it is a path the mortals understand all too well. They have slaughtered each other in endless multitudes for so long that slaughter is second nature." Candour communicated to the dragon at a level deeper than words, and with a twist of anguish, she bade it, "See my thoughts..."

Inviting the giant to see as she saw, she summoned memories—a torrent of wicked imagery, not just of humans' cruelty but of their destruction. She conjured images of cities blazing, vast tonnages of explosives raining from the sky to create devastation on a massive scale. She visualised depth charges flinging water a hundred metres high, flame throwers belching death, chemical weapons striking down all in their path...finally, nuclear detonations that wiped cities clean.

When she was done, she hoped the dragon understood enough for the message to be clear. The vast head hung before her as if it were weary. The beast did not speak, but she perceived the turmoil of its soul and they shared enough empathy for her to stretch out very gently and stroke the snout with her bare hand. The serpent accepted her touch, acknowledging that, in perceiving and understanding something of each other, they were alone in this world. And companionship was valuable.

At last, its voice rumbled in her mind. *I must consider this. These mortals have come far, and their brutality is astounding. If they treat all life with equal contempt and have developed the means to shatter worlds...* The words trailed off, and the head withdrew from her hand. It rose against the sky and hung there for long moments before the voice returned. *I thank you for your compassion, small one. But you must understand that I struggle with many conflicting imperatives, and my own survival might not be first amongst them.* The serpent backed away towards the glittering sea, and its neck slipped into the waves little by little. *I must think...I must think...* It slid beneath the water and vanished. *I must think...*

* * *

Lucinda's eyes opened with a start, and her heart beat like a triphammer. The event was the most intense psychic coupling she had experienced in a long time, and she did not underestimate the beast's power. It was probably for the best that they had been able to meet in neutral space. With a glance at her watch, she realised she had been entranced for over half an hour.

Her eyes went to the GPS, and a thrill of horror shot through her. The beacon lay just a few hundred metres away in the blackness. She had been on the threshold of sleep while the dragon—wide awake—cruised directly to her. On a whim, it could have left the water and crushed the car with a blow of its huge head. She might have known nothing about it, except to wake up in hospital and baffle her doctors as to how such injuries could heal.

But the serpent was at least amenable to reason. She had shown it what the human animal was capable of, and she hoped it made the connection—that, despite her immortality, she was enough of a human animal herself to understand them. Unless the dragon could dematerialise at will, it was vulnerable, which must give it a great deal to ponder.

Lucinda was too adrenalin charged to sleep now, even if sleep had been wise. Drinking more coffee, she scanned the dark with the binoculars, and glimpsed the beacon light's flicker at times. *Go back where you came from*, she thought earnestly. *I don't want to be the one who kills the last of all dragons.*

It was going to be a long night, and she found herself thinking as deeply as the serpent. Could she do it? If this were the Norse *Vurm*—the sea dragon that haunted legend, the very embodiment of the ancient—she found the very idea of killing it repugnant. Yet she had meant what she said. Her loyalties lay with the human race. The thought of innocent people vanishing into those terrible jaws filled her with at least as much loathing. What was she to do?

She checked the time again and squinted at the tracker. Yes, a long night.

Dawn found her standing on the seafront, staring out into the fading darkness as the first holidaymakers stirred. The tracker had moved offshore in the gathering light when Lucinda made her way to a public bathroom to let the coffee be on its way. A drop remained in the thermos, and she drank it for the warmth it had left. The sun had struggled above the Norfolk countryside when the phone rang.

First, Warren confirming that he was on his way up

from Thetford to retrieve the gear. To avoid attention from the locals, she arranged to meet him on a road outside town. His trip was a fifty-kilometre drive on twisting roads, so he would be a while. Soon after, John phoned to tell her he would be on the morning train.

As she warmed the Jaguar to leave Heacham, she found Caroline calling. "I'll head up to meet you," the elder vampire said. A strange note in her voice told Lucinda she had something important to say but did not trust an open line. "If we could meet around seven...?"

"There's plenty of quiet country around here."

"Excellent. I'll bring breakfast."

Things had a way of moving, and Lucinda set aside the night's discomforts as she headed up out of the village. In the pale green summer countryside, she found a roadside pull-in, enjoyed the sun's warmth against the backdrop of The Wash, and smiled at the irony: holidaymakers in Heacham would soon be on the beach, oblivious to the fact that a twelve-metre carnivorous serpent swam in the bay.

The GPS was still tracking it; if it moved inshore, approaching the beaches, Lucinda would assume the night's heartfelt discussion to have been ineffective. As long as the marker patrolled the vast inlet, no one was at risk; she could only hope that there would be no more bloodshed on *anyone's* behalf.

At about 5.50 a.m., Warren's university SUV appeared up the road, guided by her phone calls. They exchanged sleepy greetings and a warm hug. "Okay, what do you have for me?" The scientist raised an eyebrow.

"A tissue biopsy," she told him as she rocked the driver's seat forward and lifted the cases out of the back. She placed the cold case in his hands first. "Do whatever it is you do, and let me know what you find, okay?"

"Sure. But—I mean, you actually *saw* it. What was it? Shark? Turtle? Seal?"

"Might have been an eel," she said mysteriously.

"So, likely a fish." He eyed her strangely. "You're not going to give me any details, are you?"

"Not at this point, Warren." She shook her head with

a small smile. The sun struck sparks from her shades and the morning breeze tugged her hair.

He spread his hands with a huge shrug and transferred the case to the SUV before returning to pick up the rifle carrier. "What about the camera?"

"I'll hang onto it for the moment; I might need it again."

"Which means the recording caught something and you want to download it first."

"Something like that. Same with the GPS—it's still doing its job."

"Okay." He sighed. "I wish you'd let me in on the secret, though."

"Call it 'vampire business,' Warren. Need to know. The biopsy is hard evidence that *might* be augmented at a later date. That's the bottom line."

"There's no point in me giving you the speech about one's duty to science? About advancing the cause of human knowledge?"

"Not really. I'm aware of all that, but I have to balance it against other considerations."

Warren scowled for a moment at the long arc of blue sea over the slopes. "You certainly don't make it easy. Well, I suppose I'd better get going. I confess, I'm more than fascinated to put a slide under the microscope, no matter what."

They hugged again, shared a kiss, and then he was back on the road. In a way, she felt shabby for taking advantage of his goodwill—but reminded herself that she had to be practical. Warren had the facilities and the know-how, and no matter how long she lived, Lucinda would never gather every skill these situations might demand.

She listened to the birds of high summer and watched swallows darting and dipping over the fields after insects. One or two vehicles went by, and, resting thankfully in a comfortable doze, she waited for Caroline. When the phone rang, she passed on her location.

Ten minutes later, Caroline's Daimler purred up the country lane and pulled in behind the Jaguar. The ancient vampire had dressed in jeans and jacket, shades and boots—the casual comfort of the long-term well-to-do. She had been gentry for a very long time. She had secured her place in the world centuries ago through marriage and cleverness, and in the last fifty years, through personal merit and strength of character. All this showed in Caroline's self-confidence. Lucinda recognised that even someone as old as herself was still evolving.

A picnic basket appeared, and they shared sandwiches and coffee on the Jaguar's hood, enjoying the morning air. Lucinda drew on her broad hat against the brightness and described the nocturnal melding with the beast. She spared Caroline nothing, finishing with an outline of her difficult position.

"At this point, it—he—has made no further move. The thing I need is to see that GPS tracker moving away from this area altogether. Otherwise, my offer of peace blows away. I'll have to deal with him." She wore a bitter expression. "I don't want this task, but who else is going to do it?" She glanced at the time. "There's a man I have to meet later; he's bringing the hardware, but I pray to all the gods that I won't need to use it." She drank, staring at the horizon for a long while, then looked sidelong at her friend. "Now, what was it *you* needed to tell me?"

Caroline smiled thinly. "Well...last night, I did a little psychic eavesdropping. I could tell you were in a deeply meditative state—it was fairly obvious, and I was watching in case you needed a hand. But while the beast's attention was on you, I sensed something else." She took out a driving map of the Norfolk coast, folded it, and indicated a point sixteen kilometres north, on the wild shore beyond Holme and Thorham. "Another dimple in our so-called curve of space-time. That point is special; it is the absolute hotspot in the energy ranges this creature is using."

Their eyes met. "The doorway?" Lucinda wondered. "I rode by that area two days ago and sensed nothing."

"Maybe you were not properly centred to feel it."

"Perhaps." Lucinda bowed to Caroline's experience. "The exact location where he opens the gate between this world and the other must be highly energetic, even when the gate is closed, so..."

"This is my thinking. If you can find this gate..."

"It might be no more than a place in the wilds—and just by being there, I'll attract the serpent's attention. It may or may not be possible to interfere with the gate itself. And I definitely do *not* want to find myself on the other side of it."

"In a realm of dragons? Certainly not."

"But just knowing where it is might be the sort of leverage we need to get the serpent to simply go back. Let the world forget about him again."

"I hope so. I have no more wish than you do to see this visitor harmed."

"I think we have an answer as to why he was absent throughout most of the major drainage works. He withdrew to his own world and slept away the centuries, probably hoping humans would return to their ancient apathy and pettiness. He reckoned without the march of technology. He might have no understanding *of* technology—what it means to build and to invent."

"It is possible. And this makes him truly a stranger in a strange land."

Lucinda stared at the map and thumped the marked spot. "The gate won't be easy to find, but I must. It's on the coast, so unless the dragon heads south into the fens again, the GPS will maintain contact at this distance." She checked the time. "It's still early. I won't move until I've seen the man with the firepower."

"I have never been comfortable with that side of things. Especially in this day and age." Caroline sighed. "What can I say? The warrior was never in me."

"Ask yourself this. If the beast should come for you tonight, how would you rather face it? With wits alone—or wits plus a bloody big gun, in case intellectualism didn't work?"

They listened to the wind in the grass and the birds over the hedgerows, and at last Caroline stirred. "If it came to that, I would be glad to have you there. I have no wish to kill this creature—and even less to be prey. And I felt a definite malevolence. No matter how much we understand its anger at human actions, we cannot stand aside."

They hugged briefly, an acknowledgement of the misgivings they shared.

"It's decided, then," Lucinda said softly.

* * *

The man with the hardware was a character she had dealt with several times when the need arose. She saw Kruger infrequently, but when she wanted firepower, it usually originated with this grim-faced, taciturn weapons dealer. He had supplied her 9mm H&K Specials, along with the silencers and 'super-stopper' ammunition. This time, Kruger delivered a weapon that had gained popularity in the US since 2001 and just might do the job. In fact, Lucinda was staking her life on it.

They met on a byroad on Massingham Heath, beyond the woods at Grimston, twenty kilometres from Heacham. The transaction was swift. Kruger had known her so long —he asked no questions, and she paid via direct deposit between foreign accounts. He barely said a word as he passed over a long case and a satchel containing magazines and ammunition.

The weapon was a .50 calibre Beowulf assault rifle— basically, a re-chambered AR-15 platform that fired a 12.7mm round at medium velocity for massive knockdown at short range. She had ordered the 400-grain cartridges, for maximum destructive energy. Those cartridges drove hollow points that would go through quarter-inch steel plate at thirty metres.

She felt sick inside as she accepted the hardware and covered the case in the back seat with innocuous gear and travelling rugs. Kruger departed in one direction, and she took the road in the other. This was the most destructive weapon she had ever used, and she was aware of the massive recoil forces. The Beowulf was designed for hunting big game, and would probably penetrate the serpent's scales with ease. The hollow points should inflict lethal damage.

I don't want to do this, she thought, lips compressed

into a hard, bitter line. It was not the same as dispatching the true malevolence of evil—destroying parasitic soul-eaters and other supra-natural organisms that lay outside mortal perception. The dragon was none of those things.

Heading back to the north coast of Norfolk, she monitored the tracker and saw that the beacon was still out in The Wash. The creature appeared to be lingering to consider all she had shown him about human ways.

This was fine with Lucinda; it bought her time.

Caroline had returned home; she could do nothing to help, and Lucinda was as pleased to have her as far out of harm's way as John. With a certain sense of irony, she stopped at a fishing shop to buy waders and a tide table. There was no way to know what she would need when the time came, and she was more worried about the firepower she was carrying. She did *not* need an encounter with the law.

But nonchalance was a skill. Confident that the serpent was many kilometres away around the long headland, she pulled off the road in Thornham, where she took a seat in the Lifeboat Inn, and ordered lunch. She kept the GPS tracker in her pocket and, from time to time, glanced at the bright display. Could the dragon feel her close to its portal? Maybe not yet.

The summer afternoon was bright and mild, the wind off the North Sea clement enough, but Lucinda was painfully aware of marking time. Careful to give no hint that she was anything but a traveller breaking her journey, she idled over seafood and wine, coffee and dessert. Noticing several locals appraising her over raised glasses, she kept to herself. Another time, she might engage in a little verbal fencing for its entertainment value, but on this of all days, she could not afford the distraction. Glancing at the GPS, she seemed to be merely checking phone messages—these days, no one noticed.

She let the wine dwindle in her system for an extra hour and enjoyed the ancient brick and timber building's ambience over a last coffee. But she must get moving; she had some deep psychic work to do. As the lunchtime trade wound down, she left the inn and explored the access points to the vegetated dunes and tidal inlets that dominated the long stretch of coastline.

Parking at the most northerly access point she could reach, she swept the area with binoculars. This was a birdwatcher's paradise, and though it was wild, there would be plenty of people around—fishermen, beachcombers, hikers. She might not have the chance to uncover the Beowulf until after dark, by which time she would be in danger of becoming lost in the marshes, with only the vampire's sixth sense to guide her.

She headed north again, to the turnaround at the end of Staith Lane, which ran beside a tidal creek where many craft, mostly pleasure boats, moored at private jetties. There, she sat for a while, stretched out with her senses, and felt cautiously for that 'dimple in the curve of space-time' Caroline had sensed. She tried to the limit of her abilities, with no reward. The open sky, where clouds drifted over the waters, remained mute, as did the countless tidal creeks that laced the long stretch of dune grasses beyond.

At last, Lucinda turned back and took the main road east to the bird sanctuary at Titchwell. On minor roads, she threaded through the forest in search of a rough track that took her all the way to the last dune overlooking the North Sea. A couple of SUVs stood at the end, and from the crest of the path leading down to the beach, she saw a scatter of bright colours on the sand—sun-lovers taking advantage of this open shoreline.

The North Sea was as blue as she had ever seen; the afternoon warmth was idyllic, so unlike this sea's usual cold greyness. It was difficult to believe that a creature so alien to this world could pass by unnoticed, but it did so with ease—wary of humans, despite its contempt for them.

Now, Lucinda felt *coldness,* the moment she closed her eyes to concentrate on the sun on her skin and listen to the sigh of waves falling on the shore. It told her plainly that she was in touch with the ripple in time and space where the dragon came and went. The portal had to be very nearby. Her senses turned eastward, across the roughly vegetated dunes. Coarse grasses and sea buckthorn rustled in the salt breeze; she heard insects and the crackling hum of dragonflies.

Taking binoculars and camera, she stepped off the track into the waist-high grasses and walked cautiously. This was a nature preserve, and she must be careful where she put her feet. If she came this way after dark, there would be far less finesse—but she could not imagine doing what she must in full daylight.

She was close now. The impressions impinging on her consciousness were becoming too insistent for comfort, and she felt sure the dragon must sense her presence. To reassure herself, she checked the GPS, but the marker had not shifted from its patrols in The Wash. She strode on, and soon came to a tidal creek, an inlet that curled through a channel in the sands.

At high tide, the sea would fill this creek and lap among the tough, salt-resistant vegetation—and there, in the stony, muddy backwater, she found it. Nothing was visible; it was merely a wild place on a wild coast, but all at once she seemed to stand on the verge of a precipice with a vertiginous drop at her feet. She swayed for an instant before catching her balance. The gate was *here*. Merely walking by would raise gooseflesh on a mortal's neck, but to a vampire the veil was nearly stripped away. She could almost see through the yawning abyss to the world beyond.

Marshalling her senses, Lucinda pulled out a compass and took a rough return bearing on the car, which was a glimmer of polished black among the bushes. Glancing around the lonely reach, with its mud and sand, shellfish and birdlife, she marked the spot: a sad line of weathered timber posts marched across the dunes, remnants of some earlier works on the coast. With a sigh, she made her way back, grateful to retreat from the dreadful, invisible pit.

Had the dragon sensed what she was doing? The GPS showed no change, and she murmured in relief. If she needed to, she could deliberately call out to it; with the lensing effect of the energies by the gate, calling would be all too easy.

Back at the car, she studied the tide table, checked sunset and moonset times, and thought through her options. She must bring the beast here, and convince it to leave. The alternative was to use the Beowulf, which was the repugnant option—not to mention that the dragon's death would leave the twelve-metre carcass of an unknown species on the Norfolk dunes, along with evidence of its violent end. The moment the discovery was made, conservationists would rightly castigate the 'hunter'. If the creature's digestion were slow enough, its victims would still be in the gut. The gruesome facts would come out in the autopsy after the British Museum had finished with it.

At this time of year, daylight lasted until about 8.50 p.m., and darkness was imperative. The tide would fall from its peak about an hour before sunset, while the crescent moon lowered in the west. She called Caroline, let her know she had found the gate, and settled herself to wait.

Each hunt had its own flavour, but Lucinda was more certain than ever that this was no hunt. During the afternoon, she walked the beach with binoculars, camera, phone, and GPS, enjoying a long stroll on the hard-packed sand above the rising water, where the sea wind blew and birds flocked in droves. Hat tugged down against the salt breeze, she appeared to be just a holidaymaker; no one spared her more than a curious glance as she photographed the shoreline, sat on the dunes, and scanned the seascape.

She was at ground zero for an incredibly rare event and could not afford to go far. At no time during her own span on this Earth had she even heard of a dragon returning. Resting in the car, she finished the last of the food and drank from a water bottle. The tracker had moved north a short way, as if the beast were no longer interested in humans, and this heartened Lucinda.

With the windows rolled down to let the breeze blow through the Jaguar, she whiled away the time with the radio. She dozed, and came awake with a start as the coastal station's talkback show reported something that had the announcer almost laughing. The media was abuzz; it seemed yachtsmen sailing off Skegness, on the west side of The Wash, had sighted a sea serpent. The massive creature reportedly raised its head as it came alongside and viewed the sailors with apparent friendliness. The sailor in question—clearly calling on a mobile from out on the water—claimed to have actually touched the animal, and he declared it docile and inoffensive. He had plenty of photographs to make his point, and a few seconds of video.

Lucinda heaved a sigh and rubbed her face. Perhaps the dragon was rethinking his role, or perhaps the sailors had simply been very lucky. Scientists would pull apart the story and images and doubtlessly publicly dismiss them as pure fabrication. But behind the scenes this visual data would be correlated with the CCTV recording from the pumping station on the North Level Drain. Warren would surely put two and two together, and guess that she had asked him to biopsy an unknown species.

The GPS tag hovered off the Lincolnshire coast, meandering lazily as if the dragon were hunting, but no longer for warm-blooded prey. Lucinda felt confident enough to relax. The range was now high, but contact remained good. Taking a fix on her starting position, she drove back along the beach access track to the main road, then east to Brancaster.

There, she casually locked up the carload of illicit arms outside the Ship Hotel, ordered a Norfolk ale, and spent an hour or three in the sunny bar of the whitewashed old pub. Time could be an enemy, but she had one ultimate advantage over mortals: her ability to wait. A day spent in observation was hardly wasted; she was going nowhere while the dragon bided his time. The mere fact that he had not taken a human life in twenty-four hours gave her reason to hope their meeting of minds had borne fruit.

As the afternoon wore on, the sea serpent story appeared on the news on the pub's big screen, and she indulged in a smile, recognising the beast in the yachtsmen's blurry phone pictures. 'Experts' debunked the sighting as a clever digital fake, latest in an endless series of claims that were never backed up with tangible proof. She chuckled quietly. That proof was already in Warren Fuller's lab, and she confessed a curiosity to see what the human mind would make of this challenge to its 'reality.'

Enjoying another ale, she watched the beacon, which was moving out to sea. If it stayed on that heading, she would soon lose contact. To keep in touch, she must head for the bend on the coast north of Hunstanton; she needed the beast to *come* to her.

The hotel began serving dinner at six, and she passed the evening with an excellent meal, still monitoring the beacon while contact started to become intermittent. She could no longer wait for the dragon. She must call it.

Low, golden sunlight filled the sky as she headed west—shades on, squinting into the evening glare. In ten minutes, she had threaded through the narrow roads to Holme and was on the final track to the beach north of the Hunstanton Golf Course. The contact had firmed once more when she stepped out into a breeze that rushed above the now-high tide. She closed her eyes against the warm glare.

"Hear me," she mouthed silently, throwing her strength into the projection as she visualised the dragon cruising out in the blue, off towards Lincolnshire, and tried with all her ability to touch its mind. Making the beast aware of her was one of the hardest things she had ever done—Lucinda possessed no skill comparable to Caroline's—but at last the link clicked into place. The beast heard her.

Now, she had its interest, and felt its flash of annoyance at being approached by a land creature, but she did not try to explain in words. She projected an image of the creek where the gateway yawned open. This would serve as the message.

The response she registered most clearly was consternation. The doorway's discovery could mean much to the dragon—or perhaps nothing at all—but the secret to *how* it moved between worlds was surely the deepest it possessed. Throughout its long existence, it could never have imagined land dwellers ever finding the dimensional gateway, much less understanding it for what it was.

Now, the dragon must confront this threat, and the contact changed course, closing the distance with astonishing speed. Whether it was coming for Lucinda or for the gate made no difference—she must be there.

* * *

The long summer evening was done. A soft night had fallen when the Jaguar purred to the beach track's end. The sea was dark; the coast breathed with tumbling waves as the tide began to turn, and a quarter moon settled in the west. The cooling wind had sent holidaymakers back to their hotels and camp grounds; sweeping the shore with binoculars, Lucinda saw no spark of light.

The beast was close. She felt it easily here, where it could come up the tidal creek, unseen, and into the dunes. The moment came, and she pocketed phone, tracker, and automatics, grabbed the IR video unit, and slung the Beowulf over one shoulder. The lights flashed as the car locked. She watched the luminous compass carefully, making her way through the cover of tall scrub—just a hundred and fifty metres, though it seemed much further than it had in daylight.

The vampire pupils expanded like a cat's as she picked her way without difficulty through the bushes and grasses to the line of the creek. Quickly, she set up the camera to cover the waterway. There was no chance of exhausting its memory; this would not be a lengthy encounter.

But in minutes, she began to feel a chill creeping into her bones—not just the vertiginous sensation of the nearby gateway, but a real, profound cold. It made no sense; no wind blew out of the north, yet the chill gradually intensified. She zipped the jacket to the neck, thrust hands into pockets and watched the stars. A halo was developing around the crescent moon. Her breath appeared in the air as mist crawled over the dunes.

Meteorologists would attribute the fog to an upwelling of cold, deep water coming into contact with the warm surface air. But Lucinda was sure no part of the North Sea was deep enough for an upwelling to make the kind of impact one saw on tropical coasts near deep oceans. She sensed *strangeness* at work. Perhaps the gate had yawned open to admit its lost traveller, consuming the environment's ambient energy as it did.

Tension built little by little until the chill also invaded her mind. Certain that she was on the event's cusp, she unslung the Beowulf, chambered the first massive round, and wrapped the sling under her left hand on the foregrip.

What do you here? The thought hammered into her brain with enough force to make her gasp. *The place between the worlds is not for you—and in the realm that lies beyond, you would not long endure!*

Lucinda closed her eyes to the mist drifting through the silver-mauve night and willed her consciousness to fall towards the level on which she could make full contact. Her lips moved soundlessly, but she spoke more in her mind than aloud. "I will share this secret with no one. But you made a grave mistake today."

And that is?

"You exposed yourself to the mortals' view. They made images of you and sent them to others. Few humans believe them, but those who do are aware of you—and in this world, you will know no peace. You *cannot* fight them. You cannot avoid them forever. You can only go."

Go? I am not at your command!

"I appeal to your reason. To mortals, you are a beast —a large, dangerous animal that must be controlled. And if not controlled, then killed. Only in anonymity did you have safety, and you forfeited your anonymity today."

I come and go; they see me not. I may taunt them with momentary appearances, but I shall avoid them.

"Not forever. I found you easily, and there are many more like me. Some walk in the night, and would come to you with offers of power and sacrifice in exchange for your strength, wooing you with stories of the strange new world they would build. They are the kind that *I* hunt, and I hunt them very well. They would lure you to your ruin."

The cold creek waters rippled as an immense body coursed in from the sea with a serpentine curve, and the dragon's head rose against the stars to look down at her. Exhaling a frosty breath, Lucinda made a grave bow in acknowledgement of the beast's might.

I believe I can judge the worth of those who seek me out, the great voice rumbled in her mind. *I judge you, at least, and in you I feel no malice. Healthy caution, yes. And...regret. What is it you regret?*

"I regret the possibility that you will refuse to see the sense of what I say."

And thus, cause you to act. The beast seemed to sigh. *Now I see why you called me to the gate.*

"Just so," Lucinda said softly.

This, then, is our final moment. And how shall you compel me if I do not care to leave this realm?

Lips compressed, she raised the Beowulf and took aim on one of the rotten timber posts. She visualised the enormous recoil and the booming report; in her mind's eye, the post flew apart in splinters. She did not stroke the trigger, but let the image serve its purpose. Her eyes rose to the dragon's, half-seen in the mauve gloom.

You believe this tiny noise-maker will damage me?! The tone was grand, but currents of uncertainty stitched through its voice.

"You already know it will, and it can do so many times." She infused all the sincerity she possessed into the words. "Don't make me. Please, *don't make me*. Just leave. Go while you can. Let the mortals forget again. Live. When another aeon has gone by, perhaps they will be ready to believe in such beings as yourself—and, more importantly, to respect you."

Anger boiled up in the dragon's heart, but there was also an overriding clarity in its thoughts. She clung to this while her muscles twitched, poised to drag the heavy rifle around on target. If she committed to the action, she would be compelled to fire because the dragon would lunge. It would be one life or the other.

Even now, Lucinda was unsure if the weapon would really do the job, and even more afraid that the job could not be done cleanly. She might inflict a terrible death. Being psychically coupled with an entity as it suffered would add dimensions to the horror. Everything pivoted on the next few heartbeats.

Flashes seemed to break around them—the will of dragon and vampire at war for the upper hand. As the energy peaked, Lucinda was a split second away from swinging the weapon, but the battle of wills quickly began to abate.

The beast sighed soundlessly. *Mayhap you are right. And I would not visit such anguish upon one who has compassion for those of old.* The massive head drooped on the towering neck and fins flexed and rippled. *This does not mean that I have discovered compassion or respect for mortals. It would seem, their ant-like industry notwithstanding, that they neither grow nor accumulate wisdom, no matter how much time elapses. But I have naught to lose by doing as you suggest. The mortals win another age in which to play in their world before a judgement of dragons inevitably shall come.* A strange flicker of humour glowed behind the words. *You have,* after all, the beast allowed, *educated me as to the true nature and capabilities of these humans. Next time, we Elder Ones shall be less casual in our dealings with them.*

The words could mean much or little. Lucinda would ponder them for many years, but at least she now had that time.

Stand away, small one, lest you fall into the space between the planes and see stars streaking about you...

She backed away, heart racing, not knowing what to expect. Before her eyes, crackling blue-white energy appeared to envelope the serpent, but the flare was in her psychic senses rather than a real manifestation of light. The energies built, and the dragon seemed to be haloed in cold fire, a regal beast, noble, terrible, overwhelming.

Instinctively, she flung up a hand to shield her vision, but she did not perceive the flood in the normal way. Sunlight broke over her, an icy fury shot through by vast discharges of lightning. At the vortex's centre, the serpent slowly submerged backward into the creek's waters, gliding slowly and purposefully away. As the energies began to abate, Lucinda dared lean forward to see more clearly. For an instant, she perceived abyssal depths—a chaos of energetic discharges—and the serpent's outline, now like luminous glass that refracted the light all around it as it receded into a rainbow cosmos.

Farewell, small one, the fading voice rumbled in her mind. *I shall hold you to your word.*

She raised a hand to the departing giant; no words would come.

In a thousand years, came the whisper as the portal began to collapse. It folded in on itself, taking with it the ice-cold of space. *In a thousand years...*

The gate closed with a rush, a thunderclap of rebalancing forces. Thrown from her feet, Lucinda sprawled, panting in the long grass. She clawed at her spasming eyes and began to relax. The probability was that nothing she had perceived had been visible to humans—no tornado of energy had actually stormed over the Norfolk dunes.

And she had not needed to fire a shot. She sat up, taking a deep breath of air that had already grown warmer as the mist faded. Rubbing her frozen hands, she fumbled for a penlight. Shading the beam with one palm, she hunted for the rifle, flicked on the safety, and searched out the GPS and phone.

Soon, she had recovered enough of her senses to haul herself to her feet. Only residual feelings flickered around the gateway now, and she recognised the 'otherworldliness' that always surrounds haunted places. Satisfied, she recovered the camera. Its contents would be archived—but *not* by science.

With a wistful feeling, Lucinda gazed across the starlit creek to the rush of the sea in the summer night and told herself resolutely—the dragon had *gone.*

*   *   *

The age-old clock ticked heavily in the quiet parlour at Van Alt Hall. Clad in a crimson silk gown, her freshly-washed hair glistening, Lucinda sat tiredly in a vast armchair. She cradled a tall glass of wine; the bottle standing on the occasional table between her and her elder was half empty. Midnight had come and gone—the small hours were the time for deep introspection. A hot shower, clean clothes, and wine helped.

Caroline relaxed in a pale, yellow gown that matched her hair, toying with the wine, which was as red as Lucinda's own hair. "You have managed a great thing, my friend," she said quietly. "I never imagined anyone could talk a dragon around."

"First, I appealed to its nobility; then I threatened it." Lucinda shrugged. "They're highly intelligent creatures with minds of enormous clarity and power. When I showed the truth of what human destructiveness has become, it chose discretion over valour. But one of its final remarks has me baffled. An inevitable judgement of dragons."

"Bluff? Or do they really mean to return?"

Lucinda drank again. "In a thousand years, apparently, we'll know."

"Time seems to have no meaning for them," Caroline mused. "They see out the ages as we do, but they can also step *sideways* in time. A mind capable of forcing open a rift between spaces—between parallel worlds—must be able to channel energy on a grand scale. And we should not underestimate it." She summoned a thoughtful smile. "The worm in the wormhole?"

"Well, the main thing is that the *disappearances* will stop. I'm glad I didn't have to do anything drastic. I'd far rather not be at war with dragonkind."

"Which is called choosing your enemies judiciously." Caroline closed her eyes and, for some moments, seemed to have fallen asleep. Then she murmured, "The great serpent that lies outside of our reality and always returns...the snake that eats its own tail. Cycles without end."

"Maybe our distant ancestors were not imagining things when they constructed their cosmology." Lucinda nodded tiredly. "Perhaps they knew more about this world than humans in our modern times like to admit."

They were silent for a while before Caroline drained her glass. She set it on the table as she rose, bent, and kissed Lucinda. "I am going to get some sleep. I think you could do with some too."

"I'll be up in a while." Lucinda watched her old friend step out of the mellow lamplight. She sighed and stretched, trying to find some balance amid so many overlapping memories. If she closed her eyes, she could still see into the abyss, and she was deeply fascinated. What science could learn, if only humans set aside their preconceptions! Warren would soon be in touch with numerous questions to which she had no answers—though she might share the GPS data and infrared video.

The recordings were safely backed up on Caroline's computers. She would return the equipment with the memory dumped. This was on a strictly 'need to know' basis, and regarding the biopsy, Warren was working for her. Still, Lucinda was perturbed; there would certainly be consequences. But perhaps, she decided, she had always intended to open that door. Hard evidence eventually changes paradigms—humans must grow up one day.

She smiled tiredly. Even immortal vampires grew and matured, gathering wisdom as decades became centuries. Today, she had glimpsed something she had previously only *felt*. She thought back on the chill psychic wind that blew from spaces beyond any world she knew...and contented herself with familiar comforts. She was, she admitted, far more a creature of this Earth than many others whose paths she crossed, and she perceived something comforting in the thought.

Finished the wine, she turned off the lamps and padded silently upstairs.

Stalking Nemesis

Cambridgeshire held dire memories for Lucinda. Bad old memories, which she had long ago put to sleep.

One could not live nearly five hundred years without amassing experiences one would rather avoid, and the countryside at England's heart had not always been peaceful. She had seen turmoil come and go, and had embraced her place in eternity. But though she had been *vampire* since 1545, she had never renounced her allegiance to the mortals among whom she was born.

She sat in the Wheelhouse Bar in the Five Miles From Anywhere pub, beside the River Cam in the hamlet of Upware, and attracted little attention on a grim winter's afternoon: a tall Goth at a corner booth, where grey daylight spilled through high windows. She sat with mulled wine and a tablet before her, presenting the dark visage of social rebellion so common in this new century. Hair like old blood spilled across the shoulders of the long, black-leather coat; the hat lay on the table beside her, and few drinkers passing through on this bleak day cared to meet her dark-eyeshadowed, green-eyed glare. She looked dangerous. Looks were not deceiving, though few humans would have credited her true strength and agility.

Memory flowed in a cascade across the ages. She recalled the original pub on this site, which burned down in 1955. In the early nineteenth century she knew it as The Lord Nelson, and as The Black Swan in the eighteenth. Her memories stretched back, clear as bells, long before those years. She recalled Upware as a collection of thatched cottages serving the river traffic between Cambridge and Ely in darker, rawer days that ran even further back, into times from which even her memory recoiled. Shortly before the English Civil War, she had posed as the respectable wife of a merchant who was always mysteriously absent. Life could be precarious, but so long as Lucinda never tarried among humans who did not know the truth, she was safe enough. In the age of secular reason, no one believed in vampires anymore.

Along the river, the trees were bare, and the reaped fields were barren. Hard morning frosts turned the world to crystal, and rare, clear days made the frost sparkle in the low sun of these northerly latitudes. Soon the snow would lie, but she hoped to be heading home before then. She rarely reminisced about Cambridgeshire, and only dire business would bring her back, especially at this time of year.

The tablet was her link with the world. She ignored the pub's two big screens, with their endless sport, and concentrated on her own newsfeed and datastream. The murders had taken place within spitting distance—in Aldreth, eight kilometres west, and Isleham, ten to the east. Murder, *per se,* did not interest Lucinda. Mortals had always made merry with each other's lives, which was a perpetual puzzle to an immortal. It seemed to her that having only one life to live should make it precious, enshrine it as the most valuable commodity mortals possessed. But history had demonstrated otherwise, and she had dedicated many years to fighting for fragile humans, wherever and whenever she could.

Two qualities made *these* murders special. First, they were just two days apart. Second, though the victims were unaware of it, they were all related—historically, if not by blood.

Farmer George Calthrop's SUV rolled into a ditch after apparently swerving to avoid something in the road, a few kilometres from his fields outside Isleham—so said the tyre marks. There was not a mark on him; his neck broke upon impact. The police were treating it as death by misadventure, though several questions remained unanswered: what could Calthrop possibly have swerved so suddenly to avoid, in broad daylight?

The other death was less ambiguous, more gruesome. Local shopkeeper David Hornington had been taking a dawn walk through the meadowland outside Aldreth when he fell into an illegal jaw trap. The event could be classified as an accident, but the police were satisfied that

Hornington had been *pushed* before the trap closed on his torso—meaning the assailant must have known the trap's location. Hornington died of blood loss, and police had found his mobile phone some distance away, clearly taken from him to prevent him from calling for help.

In recent years, the Cambridgeshire Hunt had run afoul of the Hunting Ban, but it was common knowledge that illicit hunting still went on. Controversy surrounded their methods. Jaw traps were not unknown, but since David Hornington had no known connections to either side of the Hunting Ban debate, the police were following other lines of inquiry. At this point, the detectives perceived no parallel between the cases—

But Lucinda suspected that she knew at least *one*. To be certain, she pulled up a chart and enlarged it until it filled the tablet's screen. She traced the genealogical records of both families backward, generation by generation, until they converged in the seventeenth century—in a village called Meresford.

Which no longer existed.

She had watched Meresford burn in the snows of 1712, claiming many lives. Other hamlets and parishes gave refuge to the wretched survivors.

Eyes closed, she let the memories come—just for a moment—and snapped back to the present with a sharp intake of breath. She covered her unease with a deep draught of mulled wine. The rich, spicy red soothed her, helped her face her gut instinct. The police were hunting a murderer according to modern profiling techniques, but she knew a killer who had a far superior claim on both Calthrop and Hornington.

If she was right, it was Lucinda's responsibility to end this—because it was not the first time murder had visited this place.

Against her will, the memories returned, and alcohol did not banish them.

* * *

Meresford was a sheep town, one of many that each year provided wool for the prestigious royal chartered markets. Her business took her there as a buyer for her merchant husband—who, of course, did not exist. She traded goods to secure her livelihood and social standing, and to provide for the few trusted souls who knew her for what she was. She never took life for granted, perhaps because she watched it end so easily for mortals. She possessed the resilience of vampirekind, but was under no delusion of indestructibility. Fear was a constant companion.

The Burning Times were a plague of insanity, consuming Europe. Tens of thousands of victims had already died, from Scotland to Finland and all places between. Simply being a woman was dangerous. One could be accused of witchcraft as easily as looking the wrong way at the wrong man, or riding through a town the day before a farmer discovered blight in his fields. Lucinda had learnt to keep a low profile. From time to time, she would take a lover, and she presented the best as her partner for a decade or two before she must move on and resume her life elsewhere under a new identity—daughter or cousin.

Her worst sin, she freely admitted, was turning another mortal as she herself had been turned.

Jane Covette was lissom and wonderful, and she suffered the vampire's curse in a moment of passion. Her blood had been sweet beyond words, but that moment in 1625 remained branded in Lucinda's memory as the most perfect example of good intentions paving the road to hell. Conferring the gift of eternity was far from a selfless act. The consequences still reverberated down the corridors of time.

Vampire resilience smacked of witchcraft. When Jane survived a violent assault and yet by the next day carried no visible injuries, Lucinda could do nothing to prevent the trial. The fact that Jane's assailant confessed to abusing the travelling companion of a respected merchant's lady did not alter the accusation. The woman was *abnormal*, not of this Earth.

While Lucinda fretted in her lodgings, surrounded by her retainers, the parish council sent for a witchfinder from Bury St Edmunds. According to the law Jane should have been hanged, but wicked coincidence added fuel to the witchfinder's fire. As the interrogation and trial unfolded, wolves tore apart the town's flock; a grain store burned; and other misfortunes compounded the fear and loathing.

The witchfinder extracted a dubious confession through sleep deprivation and 'pricking' for the devil's invisible marks—and Jane easily survived a long immersion that would have drowned any human. The sentence was ancient and evil. As a punishment for heresy, burning would not be abolished until 1676, and as a penalty for witchcraft, it had always been rare in England.

Nevertheless, Meresford's terrified villagers built a pyre in the town square, and the local constable could not dissuade them. Given her vampire nature, Jane would have survived a hanging. The same nature meant that fire was equally powerless to kill her.

But her sanity was forfeit. Lucinda would never forget the terrible choice: use her vampire strength to save Jane —and betray herself in an unforgiving world...or betray Jane Covette.

In 1639, Lucinda Crane was not the warrior she would much later become. The twentieth-century Lucinda would have taught Meresford's people a new definition of fury, but four centuries earlier, she turned her face away from the horror, covered her ears, and prayed for life to end swiftly. The witchfinder administered a drug to make Jane compliant on her way to the stake—chains notwithstanding—but the villagers' jeering was as vile as the stoning.

Lucinda would forever remember that day, January 21st, 1639, as the worst of her life.

* * *

Other patrons avoided the tall Goth, and she cried bitter tears as the past resurfaced in a flood of emotion. The memories would endure as long as she lived. The Five Miles From Anywhere pub stood only a few kilometres from where it all happened, and the River Cam itself was part of the story. She dried her cheeks with a napkin and looked out at blowing grey clouds, skeletal trees, and the dark roll of the Cam. The river flowed past the marina and pub. On such days, when life's cruelty clicked sharply into focus, she wondered what immortality was *for*.

It was time to close this circle.

The police could search for mortal miscreants, but Lucinda knew Jane Covette was the murderer. Since the defining moment of her 'death,' Jane had sworn vengeance on the people of Meresford—*and upon their children and their children's children, unto the Nth generation.* She had been true to her word, but even after three hundred and seventy-eight years, she had not yet extinguished every bloodline present on that day—despite visiting on them the flames of her own demise in 1712.

Some vampires needed rest and chose to sleep away long decades, walking through time in leaps and tumbles. In each waking cycle, Jane returned to her grim quest. Working with genealogists and parish records, she would assume a new identity before researching the Meresford folk—who was the seed of whom? Each century recorded outbreaks of murder as, inexorably, she continued to snuff out one after another. During the Civil War, death in the countryside was easily ascribed to the rival factions, but as time progressed Jane became adept at arranging accidents.

At last, Lucinda repacked the tablet, slid it into a deep pocket, and drew on the broad hat. Walking into the dreary afternoon, she looked up at the glowering sky. *I made her,* she thought with profound bitterness, *then I failed her, as I have failed every human Jane has killed in this pointless revenge. Well, no more.*

The Jaguar stood in the car park behind the pub. She slid in, fired up the V8, and let it warm through while she washed her face in the mirror. She locked her feelings down firmly—she had a job to do, like so many others before. This one differed only in that it was personal. Jane would try to kill again—but this time, Lucinda would be in her way.

According to her own genealogical survey, the descendants of Meresford's people had scattered. However, geneticists found that people in Britain tended not to wander far from their ancestral lands; genetic lineages always seemed to cluster around ancient tribal domains. Lucinda had not been surprised to discover that many people claiming ancestry in the lost village still lived within a radius of fifty kilometres. Some were on the far side of the world—immigrants in the US, Canada, Australia—and in time, Jane's wrath would descend on them all. But for now, she remained focused on the heartlands, which made her predictable.

Bringing out the tablet, Lucinda pulled up a map marked with the last known locations of more than a hundred distant descendants of Meresford's folk. By now, they were all over the region, from Cambridge to King's Lynn, from Peterborough to Norwich. Any of them could be next. She had chosen Upware as a starting point merely because it was central to the two coordinates already on the 'kill map.' Using ancient skills, she could dowse the map to find Jane—but there was a more direct way. Vampires could always *feel* when they were close to each other—in fact, she was counting on it.

The long, low Jaguar purred out of the car park. Putting the hamlet behind her, she headed ten kilometres east to Fordham, where she pulled in on Collins Hill Road, opposite St Peter's Church. She looked out across bare fields at the dark line of woods towards Chippenham. The church was as old as the ages. She loved these ancient places, even if popular myth maintained that she would burst into flames if she set foot on hallowed ground. Salisbury Cathedral had not elicited such a reaction, nor had York Minster or St Paul's, so Lucinda was confident that she was in no jeopardy.

Ears closed to the winter afternoon's passersby, she cast her psychic senses far and wide, hurling her sensitivity into the southeast. She vaguely felt the mass of humanity as far away as Bury St Edmunds, but the returning glimmer of her own kind was nowhere to be found. She relaxed for a while, drank from a water bottle, and stretched her shoulders. Nothing in this quadrant—she could cross it off and move on.

She drove north, this time to Isleham, passed

through the town, and pulled over on Prickwillow Road amid barren fields. The place's name sent shivers up her spine, evoking memories of bad old days. Now, she sat quietly and extended her feelings to sweep the bare land. She *felt* crows in the skeletal trees; farms grown quiet as the grave in the low season; infrequent traffic on the long road that snaked across the checkerboard landscape; even the 'glow' of people in the Lark River marina estate across the way—but again, no hint of vampirekind.

Patiently, relying on the vampire's senses to guide her, she quartered the region. At no time had her senses failed her in all the centuries since Caroline van Alt taught her to use these skills, in the early years after turning her. She had absolute faith in them, as surely as in the twin 9mm automatics under the passenger's seat and the sword in its compartment under the back seat.

In ten minutes, she parked again on Ely Road—east of the town of Ely and close to the east-west railway line—and repeated the procedure. She took her time to sift through the signatures of such a large community. More than likely, she would sense vampirekind here; they were not as rare as this world liked to believe.

Hunting for one specific vampire, Lucinda must be careful, but she would know Jane Covette from a thousand others. This was always the way. The affinity with one's changelings lingered, almost as strong as the connection back to the vampire who had bestowed the gift. And the curse.

Half an hour later, she cruised on into the town, past the Norman cathedral and, close by, the house in which Oliver Cromwell had lived. She spent a wistful moment, savouring the psychic 'flavour' of things that were even older than herself. The stonework of the Middle Ages resonated with time's echoes, an almost hypnotic melody that only one who walked in eternity could hear. When this hunting was over, Lucinda decided, she must return and bathe in these frequencies, luxuriate in sensing the very flow of the ages.

Promising herself a boarding house, a bath, and a meal—perhaps even a glass of fresh blood—she headed west on the Witchford Road, purred back out into the bleak countryside, and a couple of minutes later took a right turn to the village of Witcham. She had to smile. These villages were so Christian and filled with churches, but place names spoke clearly of another time: Witchford, Witcham, and Wicken all lay within a dozen kilometres.

This was stud farm country. The thought of fresh, coursing horse blood distracted her. No horse had ever missed its contribution to her well-being, and while vampirekind found it less potent than human blood, equine blood was more than welcome. Horses were also immune to the curse. It could be transmitted *only* between humans, which, to Lucinda's mind, provided ample proof that humans and vampires had far more in common than most Elderlings chose to believe.

North of the town, she stopped again in the grey light as the westering sun grew low, and the fields' silence enveloped her. *Where are you?* She sent her senses venturing out over muddy tracts, scrubby hedgerows, stubbly fields, scattered farms—

And abruptly, Jane was there.

At the first brushing recognition, Lucinda pulled back from the contact, disengaged skilfully, and watched from afar. North...farther north...like a candle in the wind, the psychic spark danced on the edges of perception, and she held it as lightly as a butterfly. Sensing the location precisely—six or seven kilometres north-by-east—she opened her eyes to check the chart. Yes, a descendant of the Meresford folk lived beyond the village of Pymoor, very close to the spot where she sensed Jane.

Now, she had a choice. Show her face to her fellow changeling in an overt threat or rely on mortal authority—the law—and hope Jane complied. She stared at the data, musing over it for a while. The target was almost certainly Mrs Lesley Morris, who had lived for years at a farm north of the little rural village. Her ancestry ran back to Meresford's witch burners, via the distaff line. Lesley Morris was an only child and as yet childless herself—an entire bloodline could be terminated with one kill. The contact was too perfect to be wrong.

Grim-faced, Lucinda took a selection of mobile phones from the glovebox, chose one, and turned it on. These phones were on clean accounts, with no obvious connection to any of her holdings or interests. She used them briefly for calls that inescapable AI surveillance might build into patterns of information, and quickly discarded them.

With a cloth over her lips, she called the Cambridgeshire Police and delivered an anonymous tipoff. Implying a connection to the deaths in Aldreth and Isleham, she named the new target, and spelt out the likelihood that an attempt would be made in the near future.

She refused to be drawn farther. *There*, she thought as she headed back into Witcham. *Let's see what the uniform boys can do.*

* * *

Judging how *long* to give them was more art than science. She had no way to monitor their response. It was a question of intuition: *this* long for information to be passed, *this* long for the detectives to evaluate it, *so* long for orders to be cut, *so* long to assemble a tactical response team to back up the principal squad drawn from the local uniform branch plus County CID. George Calthrop's death had been an arranged accident in daylight, and David Hornington's was a first-light-of-dawn entrapment. But the same intuition told Lucinda that Lesley Morris's death would be simple violence by night.

She gave the police ninety minutes to put a team around the Morris farmhouse on the long, flat country north of Pymoor. The sun had disappeared into the purple overcast; dusk fell before 3 p.m., with full dark before four o'clock. Taking the long way around, to get behind the area of operations, Lucinda headed through Chettisham and Littleport to reach the north side. On B-roads, she made her way among lifeless fields and copses, reaching a point on the far side of a wide field that was now rutted by winter runoff and full of standing water.

With thirty minutes spare, she was in place to observe. Shrouded in darkness, she left the car, zipped her coat, and uncased the infrared binoculars. Effortlessly, she swung up into the branches of an oak in the hedgerow that concealed the car, put her back to the trunk, and stared at the farm, which lay a generous thousand metres away.

Windows gleamed yellowly through the thickening twilight, fluorescing in the thermal glasses as she panned across the house and yards, but she was more interested in what waited out in the darkness. Picking up glimmers of engine heat, she counting five assorted vehicles spread out, all within two hundred metres of the house. She estimated two officers to each car, and the tactical squad must be close. Bodyguards were probably already inside the house.

The police should be using nightscopes, but the Jaguar was hidden from view; they would not be looking so far out. She did not expect them to make an arrest. She *did* expect Jane to see the police long before they saw her—after which everything depended on how bloody-minded Jane felt tonight.

If she resolved to retreat and return another time, only Lucinda could stop her. Or, knowing how quickly police tired of unproductive tipoffs, she might choose another target. If she were determined to press this attempt, the result would be a 'contact situation.' The police would know the tip was good. They would also witness vampire fury in action. Someone could easily die—and it would not be Jane Covett.

You!

The psychic communication came like a slap in the face. Lucinda blinked, heart racing. Jane *knew*—it would be difficult for her not to—and Lucinda smiled, hard and bitter. The endgame was now only a matter of time and place, but first, anger must run its course.

The IR glasses picked up a flicker of heat as *something* moved in a blur across a distant field. Police motion sensors triggered simultaneously; other night vision systems zeroed in, and the response team quickly spread out in a fan around the house.

Tension crackled as Lucinda sensed the trap being

sprung. She *felt* Jane's consternation and furious frustration as, for the first time, she found armed men between her and a target. Jane specialised in the clean kill —slipping in and out, unseen—but this had the potential to be messy. A lucky stream of rapid fire might not kill her, but she would recover in a high-security cell, at the very least—or wake up in a morgue, where a whole new chapter of life would unfold.

Even for vampirekind, discretion was sometimes the better part of valour. The thermal source faded, and the officers lost contact. Lucinda watched them deploy in a skirmish line; five minutes later, a police helicopter joined the hunt, sweeping its blinding floodlight across the fields, south and west, towards Pymoor.

The search rapidly widened, but her senses had already told her that Jane was moving away—and furiously angry. Lucinda had *made* this personal in a way that had never been before. She dropped down from the tree and slid back into the car, but the police had to disperse before she dared start the engine. She brooded, driving gloves tapping impatiently on the wheel.

She *must* lay to rest the memories that tormented her...

* * *

When the pyre died down, the townspeople lost interest. With pikes and billhooks, they dragged out the sad, gnarled, charred shape, which lay shrunken and contorted among the cooling ashes. The constable, the parish council's representative, and the officiating priest knew the execution would officially be frowned on, but they made the most of the iniquity by refusing even a sinner's grave. They wanted the evidence swiftly disposed of. They ordered the remains rolled in waxed cloth and placed in a wagon, which set out after dark with just a driver and his mate.

Dressed in a dark cloak and the forbidden breeches of men, Lucinda stalked them. Sick at heart, she slipped out of her lodgings unnoticed, with instructions for one of her retainers to follow the wagon on horseback. Vampire senses turned the dark into gleaming silver-blue, reflecting the snow that lay crisply in the January night. She loped silently through the countryside; the wagoners saw nothing while their fretful horse clopped along a rutted road.

They drove for hours, winding between copses and hedgerows, lakes and creeks, always skirting the peasantry's hovels as silently as they might. At last, they found their way to the River Cam, which gleamed palely with a long sheet of smooth, fresh ice. By starlight, they dragged out the gruesome load, bound it with chains, and hurled it onto the ice. The surface shattered, and the mass disappeared from sight, though never from memory.

Anguished, Lucinda waited while the men turned back, hurrying to be home before the cold overcame them. In the silent winter night, she poured out her grief for the agony wrought by ignorance and injustice. Summoning all her formidable strength, she opened her psychic senses, and when she flung off the cloak and plunged through the frozen surface, a ghostlike illumination from the broken ice lightened the river's inky blackness just enough for her to see.

The cold struck like branding irons, but she found Jane a fathom down. The chained package had wedged itself among weeds that trailed in the current like spectres' feathery hands. With inhuman strength, she grabbed up the shrivelled corpse, kicked towards the surface, and put her head into starlight that at first seemed bright.

Striking out for the bank, she followed her own smashed path through the rime of ice and dragged out the prize. John of Harrow had been Lucinda's retainer for many years; she trusted him with her life. He had made good time and waited in the deep shadows under the trees to watch the wagon go by before hurrying to his beloved mistress.

He knew her abilities but was still appalled to find her soaked in such conditions. The river would have killed any human. Only iron will kept the shaking at bay as Lucinda wrung the icy water from her clothes before swirling on the cloak. She hefted the body over one shoulder and pushed herself hard to keep out the cold.

The outline of a building rose far across the sodden meadows. She saw it clearly and called John towards it—a sheep shed, disused, draughty, but it would do. He swiftly set a fire with flint and steel, dry straw, and the rotting remains of a broken barrow. With brute strength, he dismantled parts of the shed to build the flames, and when they were crackling, he gave his own cloak to his lady and stepped out into the snow and starlight.

Lucinda had no memory of getting out of the wet clothes and huddling beside the fire in John's riding cape, but she remembered marvelling that this power—fire—that destroyed living flesh was also precious to it. A mortal might have died of exposure; the vampire was simply numb with cold for a while. Her attention dwelt on the terrible package at her feet.

Jane was not dead. As long as her physical body remained appreciably intact, it would regenerate, though not quickly. Such damage would take days to restore. Lucinda must do two things. Find a safe place for the process to occur, and make the gift of her own blood to begin it. She could not afford to trigger regeneration before they had sanctuary, and through the hard, cold hours, she brooded by the fire while her clothes steamed.

Ready to move at last, she and John concealed the body in its sad wrappings, under broken timber and rank straw, and shared his horse. They slipped back into Meresford before the late winter daybreak, and the lady and her entourage made a formal departure that morning.

She knew from the people's surly glances that she had not been welcome, and she would never return by choice. Her coach, riders, and baggage wagon plodded out on the Ely road, but when they were well out of sight, Lucinda and John took three horses and rode hard for the shed near the Cam.

They lashed the body over the third horse until they caught up with the baggage cart. Safety lay a day's journey ahead, with the body secreted in the vehicle. She had chosen the ruin of an old chapter house belonging to Ely Cathedral Priory, which had been abandoned for a hundred years, since the dissolution.

The day was grey, with a harsh wind whipping across the fens. As twilight thickened and snow began to fall, they spotted the ruin. It stood on an islet amongst waterways and sodden meadows. Hundreds of years ago, it had been the monkish brothers' isolated outpost, but after Henry VIII's brutality, it soon fell into decay. Stonework had crumbled, roofs had collapsed, but some rooms remained habitable.

John built a fire before bringing in the body, but Lucinda sent her people away. "This is not for mortal eyes," she insisted. She herself was terrified of what she would see. With privacy, in the dancing firelight of an ancient hearth, she steeled her courage, cut the sailcloth bindings, and unwrapped the dreadful parcel.

That this charcoal-black, shrivelled, and contorted mummy should be the physical remains of one she held dear was a horror she could never have imagined. Yet part of her knew that if she had put a foot wrong, it might be herself lying there—or both of them.

The body was pathetic, almost unrecognisable as a human, let alone a particular individual. Lucinda wept as she examined it in the firelight, but enough remained, and the only hope she possessed was to enable the nature of vampirekind. She drew her dagger and, with a deft slash, opened the veins in her left wrist.

She held her hand above the corpse's stretched-back lips, so the blood ran freely between the blackened stumps of teeth, and let it flow until the wound began to close. It was more than enough. She licked her wrist, and the tang of her own blood resonated in the vampire senses. When the gash had healed, she sank down beside the hearth to watch.

Gradually, the corpse's contorted position began to relax. Little by little, the shrunken tissue that clothed the bones so tightly seemed to fill out—a process so slow that she perceived no change until she had snatched a brief, disturbed sleep and looked back. The tissues' blackened crusting began to flake away and slough off like dead scales from a snake.

By the second morning, fresh, pink tissue appeared

beneath. Each day, Lucinda fed the corpse blood at dawn and dusk, and the magic's pace quickened. The regeneration grew swifter as hours went by, while the wind worried the repaired thatch. Her people hunted in the fens and kept guard, and days blurred together. She walked in the snow, brooded, pondered her place in the world, and returned from time to time to tend to her companion.

Lucinda swept away the body's cast-off debris and let the fire consume it. By the third day, Jane lay in a bed of straw and cloaks. The marks of the flame paled away by the hour; tawny hair regrew from a fresh scalp; lips had reformed; eyes had returned to the open sockets. Ruined teeth were shed and new ivory swiftly reappeared from the gums.

When Lucinda fed her one last time, she sensed a quickening of the breath and knew Jane would soon wake. But *who* would waken? The woman she had known for so long—or some creature the fire had made of her?

* * *

Long roads between frost-locked fields made the night stark. Lucinda knew Jane would come for her at once. No more stalking. Given the option of choosing the ground, she led her into the winter's dark, further north. She felt the shadowy presence out there; she needed only to wait.

The fens were properly drained in a process beginning around 1650. Before then, chains of shallow lakes and innumerable waterways formed much of this landscape, and points of elevation that had always stood tall and dry were today's subtle hills. Lucinda knew the way blindfolded to one such islet; in summer, seas of grain would surround it rather than rippling water, and on its low, bluff brow stood the ruins of an ancient structure—perhaps mediaeval, perhaps much older. It was *ancient*, which made it *right*.

She parked as close as possible, buckled on the pistol belt, and slid both automatics into holsters in the small of her back. Taking the sword from its hiding place, she thrust the scabbard through the belt, samurai-fashion. Through the brittle, shattery, frosted grass, she made her way to the brow of the hillock, where generations of farmers had removed all trace of stonework on the surface. The foundations remained, and they were enough.

By 10 p.m., she stood in a chill wind, watching clouds scud before the moon and ignoring the cold as she waited like a sentinel outlined against the blue-grey-greens of night. The quarry was so near; their minds were almost touching when she laid a gloved hand on the sword's hilt and breathed a plume in the moonlight.

"Hello, Jane," she said quietly.

"I wondered when we'd cross paths again." A hiss from the dark.

Turning to find Jane Covette a scant dozen paces away, she blanched faintly. The face was the same—the hair a pale spill in the gloom, the outline of dark, close-fitting clothes—but a sick aura hung around her old protégé. Jane felt like a coiled spring, pent with furious energy. The sardonic twist of her lips was enough to make Lucinda ill; it was the perversion of the woman who still lived in her memories.

"I tried to stop you in 1712," she said, the words as sibilant as a drawing blade.

"Ah, the year the village burned. I always thought that was one of my more fitting achievements—such a delightful irony. It spread the survivors far and wide, though, which made my job much more difficult. You were right; I should have spared the village itself."

"Four hundred years, and you still cannot let it go."

"Four hundred years, and you're still asking why." Jane stabbed a finger at her. "You, above all, should know why!"

"The mortals who violated you went to dust long ago. Punishing their descendants is sheer spite and madness."

"It is an oath! A solemn vow!"

"Punishing the innocent today for an act of fear four *centuries* ago cannot be just."

"*You* did not burn!" Anguish filled her voice. "You were not even there! In my last moments—to see your face..." The hardness returned. "It is not yours to decide." The words were like a razor. "If it was justice you sought, you should have left me where they flung me instead of reviving me to a whole body with a soul driven by *one* thought. If you speak of justice, what of my turning? You wanted me to stay eternally young and free of disease, but I have spent all save the first fourteen years of my immortality as a harpy intent on revenge. How do you cope with all this on your conscience?"

"With difficulty!" They circled very, very slowly, judging spacing and footing. Vampire pupils opened wide, like cats' eyes; the night was a luminous blue gloom. They could have read by the starlight. "This is why it ends now. I missed you in the past, but this time you woke in the age of computers. Tracking you by your victims was not hard —and I will never *not* be between you and them."

"Then we had best have this done," came the casual reply, an instant before Jane erupted into motion.

She came for Lucinda in a blur, a ball of fury, all scrabbling limbs and claws, as primal as any wild beast. A savage cry escaped from some deep place where nothing human dwelt. But Lucinda reacted with lightning speed and the elegance of composure—a pivot on her left foot; pitch and lash out with her right in a perfectly-timed side kick that took Jane in the middle and flung her back five paces into a groaning heap in the frost.

For long moments, Jane coughed and cradled her middle before she rolled over and glared up. Lucinda poised like the crane that was her namesake, standing with her right leg still upraised. She lowered it with smooth grace. The sword had not budged in its sheath; her hand rested on the hilt.

"You are a murderer," she said quietly, "driven only by passion. *I* am a warrior, and my head dictates my actions, not my heart. You cannot win."

"I do not recognise the word 'cannot.'"

Again, Jane exploded in a whirl of force, pivoted in the air, and came at her in a rush of animalistic fury—no science whatsoever, only raw force. This was the predator's elemental hatred, once guile had been spent, and only the need to kill remained. It was enough to overwhelm any ordinary human and match many a warrior, but Lucinda sidestepped. She turned and gave ground. With inhuman ability, she avoided Jane and predicted the line of attack, so that the scything blows failed to land. Still, her sword had not left the sheath.

When they parted—Jane panting, face twisted with frustrated rage—Lucinda adjusted her hat against the night wind and breathed steam at the swift-setting moon, which had blurred among the low clouds. "There is another life, Jane."

Uncomprehending eyes blinked at her. "What, you would have me back and all will be as it was?"

"Time cannot be undone. What happened to you cannot be changed. The only power you have is to change how you deal with it."

Jane's laughter was scathing. "New Age tripe."

It was Lucinda's turn to explode, with a venom that startled Jane. *"You think you're the only woman who ever burned?* They burned tens of thousands in Europe—for more than witchcraft! Yes, it was terrible, but you have done far more than they ever did to you. You had the providence-given gift, the ability to survive, and what have you done with that gift? All this passion, and *this* is the best cause you can find to fight for?" Lucinda spat into the frost. "Grow up, you snivelling child!"

Jane was nonplussed. "Are you ever going to draw that blade?"

Lucinda glanced down at the katana's gleaming pommel and guard. "If I do, you will die. Even now, I would rather not end your days."

"Please. End them." Flat words, devoid of hope or any emotion but rage.

When Jane came at her a third time, it was with the gleam of twin daggers. The katana whispered free and moved like a blur of quicksilver; the air sang on the razor-honed edge. Steel chimed on steel, thin and small in the winter air—a sound these fens had not heard in centuries. Lucinda admitted to herself that Jane might leave her with no option.

Fury would not be denied. The daggers kept coming—feinting, weaving their web. Lucinda felt their hot kiss on her forearms and cheek as she continued to pull her blows. The wounds were immaterial, but when she and Jane froze for a long pause, and their eyes locked, warrior training insisted that she was being a fool. Did the unwillingness to kill show in her face? Did Jane see it as her weakness?

With a snarl of undiminished fury, Jane came one last time, faster than even Lucinda's eye could see. But this time Lucinda followed through in an extended crouch—and the katana's point stood a foot out of Jane's back.

Shock locked Jane in place. The daggers tumbled from hands that had grown nerveless. Her eyes went to her old, old friend with an expression of surprise, as if she had believed she held the advantage through sheer ruthlessness.

Lucinda pulled out the sword and delivered a terrible, slashing blow across the midriff that sent Jane down. A flood of blood from her abdomen robbed her of consciousness, and with stony resolve, Lucinda wiped her blade on Jane's coat, resheathed it, and turned back to the car. Everything she needed lay in the boot.

* * *

Soft snowfall before dawn came as a gift, covering the new grave in a coat of fresh white. Lucinda had dug it two days earlier and stashed a metal coffin nearby. No rotting timber for Jane Covette; no worms would feast upon her. She lay in the long, cold sleep of vampirekind, an endless hibernation ensured by anoxia. Lucinda had waited until the wounds closed, then laid the body in the casket and sealed it tight using a small blowtorch and molten solder. She lowered it into the earth beneath an oak tree in this bare, harsh land. With inhuman strength, she shovelled in the frost-hardened sod, tamped it down, and packed away the gear. The world would soon be stirring, and she must be moving.

She stood in the snow, looked up into the silent drift of flakes and let the tears come one final time. She had failed Jane in every possible way—perhaps even now. Her inability to end a life of torment only perpetuated the failure. But the moment she discovered the answer, she would exhume Jane with the means to mend her broken mind. Until that day, she would search for the remedy.

Alone in the freezing dark, she let the anguish spend itself and, at last, slid back into the Jaguar. She started the big engine, and let it warm through. Hands resting on the softly-trembling wheel, she looked back once at the tree marking the spot. She had done the only thing that *could* be done to end a meaningless rampage.

Lucinda badly needed blood now, and John Hales was not far away, just ten kilometres north at Shepley Hall, on the reaped fields of Marshland Fen. She must presume upon him. He would never refuse, just as John of Harrow had never hesitated to drain a vein into a goblet when she needed it. These were the humans she valued and loved, and their dedication was the reason she must remain true to her creed.

She dropped the car into gear and purred away into the falling snow.

Hellbane

The air was still and mild, one of those rare moments in summer when the Earth seems to stretch and relax, take a breath, and release it. Lucinda Crane had never seen the Irish Sea so calm, and she knew it could not last; the first morning breeze would ruffle the surface and destroy its mirrorlike perfection as a new day dawned over the high fells of Cumbria.

But the beauty of dawn was not on her mind as she parked on Scotch Street, along from the green beauty of Trinity Gardens. She walked with cat-footed quiet through the still-dark morning towards the yard of an old house whose gables had overlooked Roper Street since the 1600s.

As British sea towns went, Port Whitehaven was young. Its origins were well post-mediaeval, but it still reeked of time—all the centuries since it had been one of the most important gateways for the arrival of tobacco from the New World and the export of coal. Time was native to all things. She could *feel* the antiquity in the stone, brick, and timber. But more than age, there were things that passed unnoticed in the light of day and yet clung tenaciously to a strange and hungering life.

A tall timber door in a plastered wall was deliberately left unlocked. She winced at the squeal of hinges as she stepped through and went down ancient stone steps to a narrow yard. A key slid into a bright new deadlock, and in moments, she was inside. The air was flat, cool; she knew no one would be at home. Lucinda had asked to be alone, and her patrons never defied her wishes.

The cellar had been a kitchen once, long ago, but now only the hum of a fisherman's catch freezer disturbed the whitewashed room's peace. On a plain, old-fashioned table beside it stood all she needed—not one but two sterile bottles of fresh blood, and beside them, a rose in a glass vase and an envelope, hand-addressed.

The rich red quickened the vampire's pulse. She panted softly as she broke the seal and tilted the first bottle. She was a fastidious feeder and never wasted a drop. Her canines extended automatically with the thrill of the smell, the taste, and the rejuvenation coursing through her tissues, but all too soon, the bottle was empty. With a sigh, she sank into a seat and luxuriated in the impact of plasma, iron, and trace elements.

Savouring the satisfaction, she smiled, laughed quietly with a shake of her blood-dark mane. She was just lucky her mutation was along the Lightling path. She tolerated sunlight almost as well as mortals did, and traditional food remained a source of pleasure—which made passing among humans so much easier than for the Darklings. They must haunt the shadows and the night, sleeping from one bloodletting to another.

Luck had set Lucinda on this path, but conviction made her the enemy of all that stalked in darkness. She would soon be five hundred years old, and in those centuries, she had learnt almost all there was to know about how the world—the universe—worked. She had come to the west coast, between Wales and Scotland, because *something* had begun to stir in the blackness outside the visible world.

She sat for a long while, staring into space while dawn brightened, and guarding the feelings that swirled at the corners of her mind. The immortal's wide psychic field touched all shores, sensed all truths. Often, she felt that such abilities were a curse. Not choosing to count herself among those vampires who took the ages as their privilege and their physical resilience as a licence to debauch, she found herself compelled to *act*. And those actions had a way of being final, lethal—the kind that devoured Elderlings as surely as fragile humanity.

At last, she shook herself and reached for the envelope. Taking the rose from the water, she inhaled its perfume while she read the bold hand. Ian Craddock was a tour boat operator. Port Whitehaven had switched largely to tourism and leisure, and the summer season was his busy time.

As requested, she read, *all the nourishment you need for whatever adventure fate brings you. I managed two— one is a few days old but nicely chilled. I won't pretend to not be sorry that you won't be saying hello on this visit, but I respect your needs, and I know what you do to protect me. So, I'll just say I miss you and hope you'll stop by when you can.* He signed with a flourish of the pen, so unlike writers in the modern age.

Lucinda set aside the letter. She had many patrons scattered across the country, and called on them all for nourishment. None ever missed a pint of blood, and as it was given willingly, she never *turned* another human being. Never again, since Jane Covette. She returned the letter to its envelope and took her time enjoying the second bottle. The best feeding in a long while left her charged and invigorated; the pulsing sense of power spreading through her veins and muscles was the very strength she would need this time.

Finished, she held the bottles under taps in the chill-enamel sink to wash them thoroughly. The envelope slid into her inside pocket, in the leather jacket that counterpointed her dark jeans and T-shirt. She took a deep breath, held it, and let it sigh away before she walked out. With the house locked up, she headed purposefully through the fragile morning light towards her first confrontation.

Vampires always knew when others of their kind were around, and her senses had been prickling the warning all night.

* * *

Carnelios was older than Lucinda by almost a century. Turned by a vampire who died in the 1700s—fallen in a clannish battle with a Darkling—he had always chosen to absent himself from the squabbles of House and tribe. He favoured the ways of the scholar and the patron of the arts, much as did Carolyn van Alt, who had turned Lucinda in the last days of Henry VIII.

"We are not all warriors." His deep, calm burr had an odd accent—English, perhaps, but overlaid with the strains of many lands through which he had ventured in his time.

Morning shadows lay thickly in a backstreet in the old town. Sunlight crept down the stonework, far above, as Lucinda hooked her thumbs into her belt loops and squinted at the older vampire, who sat on the worn stone of a backdoor step set into the ancient brick walls. He wore his hair long and braided, his jaw bearded, and though Carnelios might not have studied the arts of combat, he obviously valued his fitness. He was still long and lean, with well-defined muscle in arms displayed by a cutoff denim vest worn over jeans and cowboy boots.

"Not every vampire needs to be," she replied smoothly, while her inhuman hearing listened for the intruders' footfalls. "It might be centuries since you studied the blade, but if you have the speed and strength, what more do you need?"

"For what lies before us? Perhaps much." He looked up at her out of clear hazel eyes and rose smoothly to his feet. "You felt it." It was a statement, not a question.

"Why else would I be here?"

"So true. Lucinda Crane, the avenging angel. You keep carving notches on your sword hilt, don't you? The Darkling Javirand." He smiled and pressed one finger to his lips. "We know you *did* him—but his kin will never hear it from us. Then that incubus, out Shropshire way... that odd business in the Fen District...those murders in Cambridge—"

"That's all my business," she said bluntly, cutting him off.

He raised both hands with a soothing expression. "By all means. But you must understand that although you fly under the mortals' radar, it's not dificult for your own kind to perceive patterns of vengeance."

"So, it's no mystery that I'd be here. What brings you?"

"Dreams." He breathed the word with difficulty, looked away, and glanced up at the pale blue sky between the buildings. He shook himself and seemed uncomfortable. "We're friends, are we not?"

"For several human lifetimes, at least."

"Then there is trust between us. We can't talk here. I have a room."

A B&B came expensive in a holiday town by the sea in summer. Lucinda wrinkled her nose at the 'boarding house smell' of age-old carpet and paint as Carnelios led the way up creaking stairs from the keyed foyer to his third-floor room. When the door had closed and the deadlock snicked sharply, he gestured at the one chair and took the end of the bed for himself. Their eyes met, and, far from the brightness of street and harbour, something dark seemed to enfold them.

"I have dreamed my death, Lucinda."

When an immortal contemplated such a notion, it must never be taken lightly. She sat forward, elbows on knees. "Beware the self-fulfilling prophecy."

"I know, I know...but this is something I've never sensed before. It's *old*." He whispered the word as if that one concept encompassed all possible dimensions. "Not all of us are blessed—cursed—to sense each manifestation that breaks free of the netherworlds and comes crawling into this one. This time, it falls to you and me, perhaps together, to face it."

"Why must you face it at all?"

For a long moment, the young face with the old eyes stared into some space Lucinda could not perceive, then Carnelios shrugged. "It is *my* death." He lay back, pillowing his head on his big arms. "I would hate to leave this world, which has brought me such pleasure over the centuries, but if I must, then let me go awake and aware, fighting to my last breath."

"If it comes to such an impasse, I'll not be far away," she murmured. "But, from this moment onward we go into this with the intention of avoiding it—if we can."

"Done," he said softly, and caught her eye. "What do you sense?"

Now she let out the breath she had been holding, shuddered involuntarily, and studied her palms' sword calluses. "Darkness. Hunger. And...fire. Always those three, in no particular order."

"As do I. I don't believe the entity is aware of our

interest. I have the strongest impression that it's older than vampirekind—much older—and it has contempt for everything but itself."

"I've never encountered anything like it." She thumped back in the chair and hooked one knee over the other. "I'm not even sure what to call it. A demon? Perhaps. This creature hungers like a Darkling; it comes from some remote plain or level of the World Unseen, and fire is a theme recurring over and over."

Nodding silently, Carnelios reached for the tablet on the bedside table. In moments, it displayed a newsfeed, which he turned towards her.

She read swiftly. "A haystack fire; two people dead, up in the farms to the east."

"Next tab."

She tapped, and her eyebrows quirked. "House fire; three dead in the village of Braithwaite."

"Next."

Tap. "Highway collision; a tanker rolled and burned—three dead."

"One more."

"Bonfires on the hills—no one knows who lights them." She passed back the tablet. "Interesting. Pattern?"

He lifted a driving map from his case, spread it out between them, and let her draw her own conclusions. "They're all in a ring to the east, between the farms and the high moors."

She rubbed her chin. "Yes. If this *thing* is anything even vaguely like those I've encountered before, it'll need an anchor in this reality. A place to inhabit, or, more likely—"

"A person."

"The kind of person who matches the self-interested nature of such an entity." Lucinda tapped her lips with a fingertip as she thought. "We must step carefully. This thing mustn't realise we're aware of it until it's too late." Her eyes met Carnelios's in a hard stare. "You know what I mean."

His expression remained unchanged. "I dreamed my death," he said simply. "Not yours. But to lay this spirit, destiny might demand a sacrifice."

She smiled faintly. "I've never been sure I believe in such things. We choose our course—and make what luck we can."

"I hope you're right," he whispered.

* * *

Clad in their summer bracken and heather, the high fells of Cumbria rose up against the Atlantic skies. The cries of hunting hawks broke the moorlands' silence—the occasional red kite, the bleat of sheep, and the distant murmur of cars on roads that wound like lonely inscriptions across a green and russet page. The Romans had built here. A day's horseback ride south of the crumbling Wall of Hadrian, an old fort had once stood at the north end of Lake Windermere, just a dozen kilometres away, and the region boasted stone circles as old as Stonehenge. Lucinda loved antiquity for its own sake. Standing in a building that was older than herself gave her a perspective on the world and her place in it.

But the entity that had come oozing through the pores between dimensions was something else again; something so old that it subverted ordinary notions of time. It was contemptuous of millennia the way vampires scorned mere centuries, and such ancient spirits were often imbued with arrogance—and cruelty. Just as Darklings played with mortals as a cat toys with its prey, this entity might play with whole worlds, if it were given the chance.

The Jaguar stood at a pull-in on a track that wound up the lonely hills above the village of Buttermere, and Lucinda walked in the wind-stirred quietness. Broad hat pulled down against the sun, driving gloves protecting her hands, she let herself *feel* the living world. This way, she had often located other vampires—and more mysterious forms of life—and here, she sensed the currents of the World Unseen.

Not every 'dweller in the dark' craved the shadows. She could afford to be amused by the mortal fixation with night—the gothic fantasy that had shaped humans' perceptions of the Elderlings in recent times. More evil walked in broad daylight than mortals might ever understand. Lucinda sometimes despaired of her efforts ever rebalancing a world that was so filled with savagery and hunger.

From a safe distance, she felt the crackle of energy from a lifeform that was utterly alien to the season's calm. Thigh-deep in green bracken on the windy hillside, she turned slowly, hunting for the direction of her enemy—her prey.

Satisfied, she drove on, back down to Buttermere, then southeast on the B5289. Passing lakes and forests, she continued around to the north and up the long shore of Derwentwater to Keswick. Every few kilometres, she would stop for a while and cast her vampire senses into the world. At the last stop, she texted Carnelios, who had skirted the country roads to the north, to flex his psychic muscles the same way.

Time to talk.

* * *

The oaken beams in the George Hotel on St John Street, Keswick, told of the ages: it was three and a half centuries since this oldest coaching inn in the region was built. When Lucinda walked in, Carnelios already had two tall pints of Jennings's ale set up on a table by a window and was working with his tablet. She sank into the seat opposite, sipped the local brew, and tried to shut out the holiday season's airy pleasantness. As strange as it had been to hunt a dark traveller in the Fen District the previous summer—this was surreal.

"I think I have our man," Carnelios mused, passing her the tablet.

Her brows rose as she studied the material in the open tabs; her cynical smile told him she agreed. One developed a nose for trouble. The subtle changes wrought by wickedness when it occupied an unwilling mortal were like a fingerprint. The coldness of mouth and eyes; the creases of skin, worked into the living flesh by expressions of demonic fury. Lust, sick enjoyment, the worst of all emotions distilled into a concentrated form—all these hid behind the thinnest veneer of civility.

His name was Jacob Martel, and he was a new-styled country squire. A few years ago, he arrived from London—*novo riche,* to be sure—and bought the old hall on the wild hills above Braithwaite, not far west of Keswick. The hall was a grouse lodge in the days of industry and privilege, but in the twentieth century it fell into disrepair. Now, it enjoyed a new lease of life as a remote moorland retreat for people of 'eclectic tastes.' Martel ran salons for artists and writers, frequent social gatherings for the 'in' set. The pattern was familiar enough for Lucinda to smell what, in human terms, might be called *grooming.* Or simple corruption.

But this was corruption of a darker sort. She had no doubt they would find evidence. Carnelios scavenged the internet for missing persons missing persons within a twenty-kilometre radius, and the search term appeared in several news features. In the last year, two women had been reported missing without trace on the high moors. A third was last seen at a party at Braithwaite Hall. Correlating this data with society page entries and social media posts told them Martel was a lothario of the first order. Making the connection to darker intentions was not difficult.

"So," Carnelios mused as they digested the implications, speaking softly under the lunch trade's general buzz, "what's his game? The playboy with the wicked habits is just a front. What's the *purpose* behind it?"

"Typically, it's simple mayhem," Lucinda replied just as quietly, "in the vastest quantity the possessing entity can manage."

"This isn't normal, though." The words were barely a whisper, and the two glanced around. Perhaps they should not be speaking of such things in public, yet at this moment, daylight might be the best defence.

"Truly, I don't know," Lucinda sighed. "As I've said, it's beyond my experience. I just know evil when I smell it."

"Then—voice of caution—perhaps we'd better know our enemy better before making any moves."

"Observation: evil typically grows over time. The longer we wait, the stronger it becomes."

Carnelios folded his hands. His shoulders gave a twitch that could have been a shrug. "We both know the powers out there—and you better than me. The *things* that find their way through the angles between the three dimensions we know so well, and the scope of their mischief with mortals. That knowledge has won battles for you as often as your skill and willpower."

"Point taken." Lucinda drained her glass and, with studied deliberation, set it on its coaster. "My impression is that this Martel character was always walking the dark side, always the 'bad boy.' He opened the door willingly, if not consciously."

"The vessel was prepared, and when the time was right, the passenger merely took up occupancy."

"Precisely. Those early disappearances might have nothing to do with him, but the third and the fires...? I don't *think* the possession has developed its full power yet, and it's far from having run its course. My gut tells me this is one possession the host cannot survive."

"I don't think survival was ever on the cards," Carnelios whispered.

But Lucinda was sure that he referred to his own. "For Martel, certainly not." She scowled. "For the likes of him, I wouldn't even try. I've seen every sort in my lifetime, same as you have. There are some I'd bust a gut for, and some I would *not*."

"Then we must learn what dwells behind the mask," he murmured, staring at the depraved face in the newspaper photo.

*   *   *

Learning came from unexpected quarters. Lucinda's phone vibrated in her pocket, and the message made her hackles rise.

West Strand, Whitehaven, by the museum. 10 p.m. Bring the boy. Things to discuss before you get us all killed.

No signature; unknown caller. But whoever it was clearly knew them, and with nothing more to go on, she and Carnelios had no choice but to follow through. She thumbed in, *We'll be there,* and stared at the device for some moments, realising uneasily that she was riding the tide of events, not controlling them, as she preferred.

She found Carnelios grinning cynically. "Welcome to my world," he whispered.

They spent an anxious day waiting, wandering the shores of Windermere and Derwentwater before heading back into Whitehaven. They left the cars in the free Quay Street South car park and eyed each other in the glow of streetlights, in the cooling breeze off the sea. At this hour, the town was settling for the night, but plenty of people were still around; the pubs would not shut for some time —this was a public place and consequently safe. Almost neutral ground.

All the same, Lucinda carried the twin automatics in the small of her back, under a long coat, and had tied her hair against the wind. Unarmed, favouring the innate reflexes and strength of the species, Carnelios zipped his jacket against the sea breeze before they walked west towards the rounded turret of the Beacon Museum on the Strand.

Uncountable hulls gleamed on the marina's dark waters, below weather-worn railings; old stone walls brooded high above the museum and café's gay blue paint. Uncomfortable, on edge, the two vampires waited in the salt air. No one was close. As the stroke of ten approached, they felt a crawling in the nerves that spelt *trouble.* Hackles rose, and they traded glances as familiar etheric scents warned them of the danger of this contact— a trap? Both gradually tensed, poised to react. Eyes narrowed and fists balled.

"Be at ease; I come in truce."

The words materialised as if from the air, and they spun to find they had company: a tall, lean figure in dark, subdued clothing, long coat and gloves. His pale skin and angular, haughty features could not have spoken more eloquently.

Darkling.

"Yes." The voice was deep, unhurried, seeming ancient by comparison with the smooth features and dark hair. "I am Anathriel, and I feel safe in speaking with you —*avenging angel, thou.* My clan has never come to quarrels with you in your war with the more indiscreet of our kind. May we treat with amity?"

Lucinda shared a long glance with Carnelios. She swept her coat aside, fists on hips—in quick snatching distance of her weapons.

Anathriel chuckled. "Loaded with silver, are they?"

"One is," she grunted. "The other is hi-ex."

"Then we know where we stand," Anathriel returned easily. "I am unarmed and alone. I could have come with a retinue; you know how it is with the old, proud Houses. But this matter is much too grave for me to stand on ceremony, and I would rather catch your attention than scare you off." He turned, rested his gloved hands on the railings, and looked out across the gently riding yachts. "We are here in common purpose."

"You also have scented the evil in the air," Carnelios whispered.

"Of course, young scholar. It shines like a black lighthouse. It screams upon the winds of the mind. Even mortals can hear it, although they prefer to take their tranquilisers and assure themselves that it's all in their heads." He smiled with the dark humour of his kind. "But what do we Elderlings mean to do about it?"

"I came here to stop it," Lucinda said bluntly.

"Ah, but stop *what*?" Anathriel caught her eye with disturbing directness. "All you know is that it is ancient, hungry, and very, very powerful. I, on the other hand, am in a position to tell you what you face."

The breeze ruffled their hair, and they heard faint music from a boat somewhere on the lapping waters. At last, Lucinda took her hands away from the guns. "Very well. Far be it from me to refuse a source of information. Enlighten us."

Turning, Anathriel gestured at the Strand, which ran by the museum and old walls, towards the western of the two breakwaters bracketing the harbour. "Walk with me."

They ambled along the broad paving stones above the marina, silent for some time. With the privacy of distance from the evening's wandering mortals, Anathriel clasped his hands behind his back and spoke with a gravity beyond any lecturer.

"I have known the ways of this world much longer than either of you—as long as you both added together. A thousand years ago, I studied at the knee of a mage from the east, in the Desert Arabica." He broke off, his expression distant, as if hearing the name spoken aloud brought back long-buried memories. "The river of time has not dulled the things I learnt from him, though much wisdom has succumbed to the march of progress. Astrology has lost its credibility, for instance. Alchemy gave way to chemistry, metallurgy, and nuclear physics. But some things remain immutable, for they were better perceived in the ages before human wisdom became human conceit—the absurd notion that because so much is known, *everything* of any importance is also known."

They knew what he meant and did not comment. Only the crunch of boots on the paving stones punctuated the monologue.

"Mamoor ibn Hassan was both wise and learned, and he was feared by his countrymen because he also had tasted of immortality. In a century, I saw him age not one day. In that time, I laboured to observe the stars, record the mysteries of nature, and understand the occult lore ibn Hassan held in strict confidence. I read his lost texts—some of which he swore were the sole surviving copies. A treatise by Archimedes, not rediscovered until the late twentieth century, for instance. But among the darker works..."

Lucinda and Carnelios respected Anathriel's reverie while he collected his thoughts. With the Strand behind them, they headed towards the breakwater's base. Leaving the comfortable human world and entering the primal sphere of the sea lent a fitting atmosphere to the Darkling's tale; something in his words sent a thrill through Lucinda's nerves. Any ancient lore was valuable to her, regardless of the source.

"Berossus the Chaldean is recognised as an ancient scholar who predates Eratosthenes of Alexandria by a century, perhaps two. The bulk of his work has been lost, but fragments remain. In his library, ibn Hassan had an *obscurum liber* attributed to Berossus by other scholars. It was written in Koine Greek, and, though very fragile, it remained quite legible. I was permitted to read it." He fell silent as they wandered on.

Out on the arc of stone, fishermen cast into the harbour here and there; sparks of light from their torches showed occasionally, off towards the lighthouse tower at the end. Stars glimmered in the mild summer night though the wind off the Irish Sea was developing an edge. It skipped over the wall that protected them on the seaward side as they moved out over the harbour; quiet water surrounded them. Passing the last railings, they walked on carefully. Vampire pupils opened wide in the blue night, and the town to the east became a blaze of streetlights reflected in the marina waters.

Far from the nearest fisherman, at last Anathriel came to a halt, folding his hands. "Berossus spoke of the nature of matter; how it is composed of energies of competitive nature, and how the balance between those forces gives rise to the differing characteristics of matter. The Chinese called these qualities the *opposing furies*, seeing in them the complementary tensions that hold the world in its dynamic balance.

"To be more specific, Berossus was addressing the ancient notion of the elementals." He raised one chiselled brow at the younger vampires. "Does this give you a clue?"

Lucinda let out a slow breath. "A fire elemental?"

"And not just any salamander, I'm afraid. Most are mischievous imps who, for amusement, trip us when we're carrying valuable things. They are amenable to being moved along with firm but respectful intent. No, this one— this is the king of fire elementals. Berossus named it with an ancient term that translates well enough into the Latin as *Ignius*, igniter. That's descriptive enough. The elemental does little else. It has slept long ages but, as is wont to happen, from time to time every spirit wakes.

"Like the other Royal Entities, this one feeds upon carnage. The last century's wars gave them nourishment such as they had never known. Those with the eyes to see spoke of fire elementals walking abroad in the streets of London, Coventry, Dresden, Berlin, Tokyo...in another time, when human destructive potential rivalled that of the spirits themselves."

"What about now?" Carnelios asked softly.

"There is just the one. But Ignius remembers those orgies of feeding on the flames' energy, and I can tell you without fear of contradiction that it would burn the world if it could." He folded his arms and smiled faintly. "A whole world on fire. All life subserviated to an elemental that is rampant and unchecked." He raised one hand in invitation. "Your turn."

"We've identified the host," Lucinda began. "The kind of human whom the darkness touched while he was still in the cradle—ripe for possession, isolated, highly intelligent, well-to-do, and given to indulgence in every whim."

"His isolation also offers us a discreet approach," Carnelios added.

"Let me guess," Anathriel said with barely suppressed humour. "You were planning to cross paths with him. Tap his lusts to win an invitation to the sanctum, all the while with a rock-solid psychic shield keeping you safe. Terminate the host at the first opportunity and draw the demon from the carcass by traditional methods." He shook his head, lips pursed as if to keep a laugh at bay. "Not this time, my young friends. Ignius is too powerful. The effort of maintaining powerful shields would lay you open to discovery. Not even our kind may divide our minds so completely as to outwardly behave with normality while inwardly concentrating our entire being upon arcane effort." He sighed, appearing to reach a decision. "You cannot do this alone."

The Lightlings blinked at each other, and discovered a grim humour of their own. "You're offering to help?" Carnelios asked with the suggestion of a chuckle.

"I would not be here otherwise."

"If the Darkling clans fear the coming of Ignius," Lucinda demanded, "why don't they wage the battle themselves?"

"Why should they?" Anathriel parried. "You're the crusader, Lucinda of the Light, and you do it so well. You brought this eternal war upon yourself—and you would strike off *my* head in a heartbeat, should it suit you. The Elderling clans know this, and they are sitting back to see what you do. I merely brought the ammunition you need—and a helping hand. It is in the interests of us all to see this demon laid."

The silence that followed was long and profound, before Lucinda laughed quietly. "An alliance of divided Elderlings. There's nothing like a third player in the game to motivate compromise."

"We all know how the world works," Anathriel murmured, stretching a gloved hand towards the water below. "It is about predators and prey. Big fish eat little fish until there are none left, then nature hits the great 'reset' when winter comes." As he spoke, a greenish haze of bioluminescence began to shimmer below the breakwater. "This is the privilege of immortality. We three walk in eternity; we may look at nature from *outside.*" He nodded at the half-seen fishermen further along the breakwater. "Trapped in an ephemeral moment, they measure all events against the scale of their own lives; if they will not live to see something, it might as well not exist. But it *does,* as do we. And we alone have the perspective to understand." In the water below, the glow had intensified as fish—swirling and darting, breaking the surface in soft rushings—stirred the summer plankton to glimmering life. "So, what if we give mortal affairs the odd push now and then? Privilege is reserved for the powerful, and no one is more powerful than the individual who both knows the facts and is unafraid to use them."

The water blazed. Lucinda flinched as a small shark looped through the shoals.

Anathriel snapped his hand closed and laughed softly into the breeze. "It is thus with all mortality. But *not* with Ignius."

"How shall we do this?" Carnelios asked, both big fists on his hips. From his expression, he had grown tired of the Darkling's posturing.

"Teamwork," Anathriel said without hesitation. "It will take all three of us. We must raise a shield such as we have never before employed to cover our approach—take the host before it can transmute and deliver fire into the embrace of all-quenching water."

Lucinda snapped leather-gloved fingers. "A holy well."

"Bright girl. Catching on?"

She smiled, warming to the challenge. "In the Dark Ages, monks venerated a sacred well—a sinkhole—up on the moors. Since time immemorial, it's been associated with water spirits, and there are Neolithic standing stones close by. Legend calls it bottomless, but a deep aquifer is just as good. We need to bind Ignius securely and send it into that cold black place where it'll sleep another thousand years before fate brings it back to air and light. If we can do this—fire's *potential* will be restored."

"Can just three of us take down an elemental?" Carnelios's was the last voice of caution.

"We must each do battle in our own way," Lucinda murmured, recalling his prophetic dream. "But I doubt we'll get out of this unscathed. Follow your heart, my friend."

"I know what I must do."

"Very well." Anathriel thrust both hands deeply into his coat pockets. "We have plans to draw. But let me promise you this: if we get through in one piece, you must take dinner with me at my London club. It's a progressive one that allows females, of course; where would be the fun without them?" He smiled, perhaps at Lucinda's expense. "Don't worry, my dear; there are places in the city where you can hire something decent to wear."

*　　*　　*

The Eden District Council office building, off Corney Square in Penrith—a magnificent old red brick structure dating from centuries past—was one of the few venues in the moorlands that were upmarket enough for the likes of Jacob Martel to feel comfortable.

His arts society was quite obviously a grooming

system for potential partners and prey, which gave Lucinda a way in—also the means to test their assumptions in public. Martel Arts was hosting a week-long exhibition in the council building's function room. The man himself would make the speeches on the first night, when the artsy folk appeared. The *artists* were on display as much as the exhibits, and no invitation was necessary.

The car park between the offices and Penrith Police Station had been opened for the event, and Lucinda parked early, while the late summer sunset flushed the sky over the high fells to the west. She sat for a while in the Jaguar, watching the coming and going, and at last called Carnelios. He answered in seconds; he and Anathriel were in the Glendale Guesthouse, about fifty metres away.

She sighed softly. "Here goes. Is our friend ready?"

"As he'll ever be."

She knew the Darkling would be sitting comfortably behind drawn curtains, deep in concentration. He had taken on the task of creating her shield, and if she passed by the possessed mortal unnoticed—invisible to the fierce psychic power behind Martel's depraved mask—they would know Anathriel was equal to this task.

"Let's get this done." She felt naked with only a single automatic in her handbag, but it should slip past the modest security at a local function in a country district.

Stepping out into the cooling evening air, she wrapped a shawl loosely over a slinky scarlet dress and heels. Her red hair was loose and set in waves. Far from her usual Gothic image, she had dressed to be noticed, by one man in particular.

Making her way around to the portico with languid grace, she followed signs deep into the old building, found the display hall, and accepted champagne and a programme while she feigned interest in the exhibition. The bubbles were of the best quality, as were the canapés —which was more than could be said for the art.

At nearly five hundred years old, Lucinda had seen genius from every corner of Europe. She was born around the time when Leonardo passed away, and in her ascendancy as a vampire, she had taken most of the privileges that accompanied immortality. An appreciation for art from the sixteenth century onward was a facet of the vampire life, and she still tended to weigh everything she saw on those scales. Modern expressionism and the surrealities always seemed a poor graft on an old stem.

After half an hour, she took a seat, draped one knee over the other to rest her protesting arches, and simply watched the people. Most were wannabes—a few art college hopefuls; hungry young artists looking for connections; hangers-on and groupies—and the kind looking for a life among at least a *little* money. She intended to appear in the latter group. When Martel made his appearance, clad in Saville Rowe's finest and chatting with a nubile young assistant, her eyes narrowed. She found the charade distasteful and would rather have tackled this problem head-on, but a public test was necessary. How could she walk up to the entity in private, unless she was sure the eye that never closed had been lulled?

Her own senses were wide open. Watching from behind a protective screen, she perceived nothing untoward about the squire. Ignius, the driving force, had hidden itself deeply tonight. Martel was its willing vessel, though even now Lucinda wondered if any conscious acceptance had occurred on his part. It was possible the elemental lay entrenched at a depth that placed it beyond even the host's dreams.

As Martel wandered around the exhibition hall, chatting animatedly with one person after another, Lucinda's eyes narrowed further. She opened her senses to see with the *extra* eye, and, gradually, an impression developed of what lay just out of sight. An amorphous mass clung to the host's back like a dark cloud, a sac of something vile, with various tendrils embedded in his organs and chakras. It played Martel like a puppet, and just for a moment, she pitied him.

Then she opened her eyes properly and took in the thin and venal features below the bulbous forehead and thinning hair—the suggestion of a round-shouldered stoop that hinted at how bearing this burden was dragging down the host. Yet Jacob Martel's inclinations and persuasions made him fertile soil; it took a certain kind of mortal to provide willing accommodation to abomination, and he fit the description in spades. Lucinda had no interest in learning the things he had done to make him so attractive to an entity that, given the chance, would scorch the Earth clean of life.

When the speeches came around, she took fresh champagne and found a place to one side, but visibly forward, where she listened and applauded at the right moments. Martel's eyes returned to her over and over—red on red had that effect. To the lothario, it was like the red rag before the bull. He finished his speeches, and as the crowd mingled once more, she was unsurprised to find herself chatting one-on-one with the squire within five minutes.

He was a little shorter than Lucinda herself, over-anxious and over-ingratiating, yet his manner suggested that he was used to getting what he wanted. She played the part of the bored, well-to-do lady, assumed an accent from one of London's better areas, flashed her best smile—and found his handshake less wholesome to the touch than a snake.

Every moment, she monitored her shield for any chink through which the entity would shine like a black light, but it seemed secure. She let Martel lead the conversation to his impressive manor on the moors, the 'private showings' and soirees he held amid the beautiful countryside for his 'inner circle,' a term he whispered. She pretended fascination, and they exchanged cards. Her own was one of the dozen bogus identities she used from time to time.

Martel spent too long with her, ignoring the others until the message was quite clear. She was eagerly invited to his country home, where he promised some rare delights in the form of culinary pleasures, art treasures, and the more *eclectic* diversions for which the affluent were often notorious. She smiled, nodded, and slipped his card into her bag, giving Martel every reason to believe she would be calling. It was no deception—but the reality would be somewhat different from what the flesh-puppet imagined.

*   *   *

"Well done, boys," Lucinda said softly over a tall lemon and lime bitters in the Robin Hood's bar on King Street, a few hundred metres away, where Carnelios and Anathriel had joined her. The Darkling looked suave and elegant in a dark suit; in a nondescript jacket and slacks that did not go well with his braids and beard, Carnelios was simply impatient with society.

"My pleasure," Anathriel murmured. "Ignius is more or less dormant at the moment. Martel genuinely believes himself to be in control of his own destiny, yet he knows something special gives him an edge—some strange means to get away with anything. It is more than the aristocracy's inbred presumption, the conceit of their boarding schools, or the savagery of their pastimes." Realising that he had just described his own kind, the Darkling rolled his eyes. "Martel's conceit goes right to the core. He *knows* he is invulnerable, and he means to satisfy every appetite. My dear Lucinda, were you mortal, your days would be sorely numbered."

"While it's Martel's own that are in short supply." She studied the hand that had shaken his. Arriving back at the hotel, she had spent several minutes in the bathroom, washing it. Under the hum of conversation and the thud of background music, she leaned across the table to the others and whispered, "The shield works. If you can protect me from his nose for trouble, just long enough for me to get close, get him alone, we can do this." Then she frowned. "But the host is forfeit—I see no way to winkle out Ignius."

Something in the way she spoke drew Anathriel's attention, and he raised a cautioning finger. "Be very sure, Mistress Crane. Is your heart dark enough to dispose of the host? If not, leave the job to one whose heart has the full measure of this task."

"I take no pleasure in it, but I understand what must

be done."

Anathriel would not let the question rest, and Carnelios's eyes darted from one to the other as he hunched over the table. They whispered below the beat of music; the Darkling had a point. "No hesitation?" Anathriel insisted. "After you have fought on behalf of the mortals for so long, you can *compartmentalise* the task?"

"I'd be less than a professional if I couldn't." Her eyes hardened, brooking no further questions, though a ghost of regret acknowledged the grim responsibility that came with it. "Only in absolute surprise do we stand a chance. So, yes—no hesitation. In fact, we must bind the entity even more firmly to the host if we're going to control it long enough for us to put it where it can do no more harm."

"Then, that will be our job," Carnelios added, moving on from the issue that persisted uncomfortably. "Anathriel provides you with the anonymity to get close to the prey while I deal with his house staff. Get them out of the firing line. You take down the host—then we bind the possession to the carcass...the *old* way."

"You remember?" Anathriel lifted one chiselled brow. "The centuries of your scholarship have not been wasted."

"I *did* it once, Master Darkling," Carnelios returned with an easy smile. "I was not always the retiring dilettante. I might have forsaken the ways of battle, but I never actually disposed of the blades, if you follow me." He took a long pull at his pint. "To keep restless spirits from wandering, vampires of old had a special method with which to seal the ethereal being to the mortal remains. It is still considered the most binding of all curses, for it endures down the ages."

"*Vincula mortuorum,*" Lucinda breathed. "The chains of the dead."

"*Maledictus eris in pertuum,*" Anathriel added in a similar volume. "Cursed in perpetuity." He nodded, smiling thinly. "The chains that once bound a powerful vampire in the grave still carry the magic that first imbued them. The vampire they bound is long-since dust and likely reincarnated as another who walks among us—but the binding charm remains effective."

"High magic from ages past. It's rarely been performed," Lucinda murmured. "Few remember such incantations. It's sacrosanct. It also means desecrating the graves of our own kind."

Now Anathriel snorted a laugh. "We Darklings are strong on tradition and the grimness of our laws, but we never flinch from hurling bones around if the need arises. Well, it has." He thought for a long moment before frowning at the others. "The untouched bones of the great, deposed *Dominius*." The name sent a thrill of unease through them all, though the tyrant had died in the Middle Ages. "The sleeping place of the Lord of Old, cursed be his name."

Carnelios sighed over his ale. "He was indeed bound with the *vincula mortuorum*. Weighted with chains that were enchanted by the most powerful of his kind, sealed into a sarcophagus, and laid to rest in a satanic crypt."

"Little wonder the perverted rites performed there got the church torched during the Civil War," Lucinda observed. "Not to mention the mass burning of black coveners at the hands of Roundheads. The ruin is just west of Harrogate, as I recall."

"A mediaeval church overlooking the lake that became Fewston Reservoir," Anathriel affirmed, drawing the details from his long memory. He raised the finger again. "Be aware that several of those who brought down Dominius still live, deep in seclusion. We might make enemies with his desecration."

"They could prepare a fresh binding for us," Carnelios added darkly.

But Anathriel shook his head. "The binding enchantments take months to forge. By winter, Ignius may be too powerful for us to stand any chance."

"Then I suppose it's the Elderlings' problem," Lucinda said, draining her glass. "If they don't want to fight this battle, fair enough—but they lose any right of objection over our methods." She glanced at the clock above the bar. "I can be there and back by first light."

"*We,*" Carnelios corrected. "You'll need a second pair of hands. And I've been there before."

"Which leaves me to while away the dark hours in research." Anathriel finished his drink. "Go like the wind."

* * *

Penrith to Harrogate, Lucinda calculated, should be around 140 kilometres—England is not a large country. She changed into jeans, boots and jacket at the boarding house, tied back her hair, and stowed the automatics under the Jaguar's left-side seat. While she filled up at a servo, Carnelios found a late-night DIY shop and bought a pick, two short-handled shovels, work gloves, a propane torch and its gas bottle, and a plastic storage tub.

With the equipment loaded, they threaded onto the M6 before 11 p.m. and headed south at the national limit. Lucinda had picked up road food, and as the motorway blurred by, they snacked on chocolate and biscuits. By turns, the M6 gave way to the A65 and A59, and half an hour after midnight, she pulled over on the shoulder of the Skipton road. On the left, late summer's reaped fields stretched away under the dark moon's clear starlight. To the right, south of the road, the region's last substantial forested area led down to Fewston Reservoir. At this hour, other vehicles were infrequent, leaving the road deserted. In the stillness, they took their bearings with both map and GPS.

Carnelios tapped the screen. "There...about 200 metres."

He pointed into the black wall of trees, and she turned off the road onto a narrow access track that looped around to farms further east. A little way in, she pulled into a forestry accessway and killed the engine. Silence enveloped the car; they let themselves soak in the sense of place and time. A Roman road ran directly through this region. One did not need the vampire's time-sensitivity to feel the centuries' depth—to almost *hear* the tramp of marching legions.

Dark summer bracken carpeted the open woodland; tall stands walled the forest off from the highway. They stepped out into mild night air where treetops rustled softly in the breeze. To monitor their progress, Lucinda set her phone to GPS, with the screen on minimum brightness. Their pupils were cat-wide, turning the night into a soft blue twilight as they made their way among the trees, through crackling leaves and twigs.

Across the hillslope above the waters, they *felt* it. Any black ritual site would have shone like a beacon to vampire senses, but the enchanted burial place of a Darkling lord shimmered so brightly in their perceptual range that they had no need to search. They walked directly to the few tumbled blocks, all that remained of the razed church. The Civil War was a period Lucinda would rather forget—it conjured too many foul memories—but here, at least, the soldiery had put an end to something dire.

Shifting in their vision, the forest floor swam in the etheric ranges. Carnelios turned this way and that, paced, and turned again to find his bearings. "Here," he said at last. "The signature is strongest right *here*. The crypt ran beneath the old nave, and from what I recall, we should be right above it. A stair opened off the tower foundation's right side. When they destroyed the place, the way down would have filled in with rubble and soil."

"We have some work ahead of us," Lucinda said mildly. "Do some dowsing; pick your spot. I'll get the gear."

In minutes, she was back with the tub filled with hardware, and they were soon working hard. Carnelios swung the pick into the rich, yielding soil, while Lucinda bent her back with the vampire's inhuman strength to shovel out earth at a prodigious rate until they struck stone. Carnelios dowsed once more, pacing the foundation's outline as he struggled to match it to his memory. At last, he extended their cutting a little way southeast, and they began to encounter broken stone on one side of the smooth, buried slabs.

"This should be it. Follow it down."

He dropped into the cutting, heaved up the blocks, thrust them aside, and helped shovel out the backfill. Slowly, the long-buried steps emerged. After an hour's digging, they took a break under the stars, drank water, and caught their breath.

"Do you feel it?" Lucinda whispered.

"Of course. The place spits at us. Too many spirits still swirl around it."

"They died badly, and no wonder they're angry. But most probably postdate our man by centuries."

"Our man," Carnelios echoed. "Dominius was many things, but I'd never call him a *man*." He sighed. "After eight hundred years, expect only dust. The enchantment did its work—he's gone."

"In a sealed coffin?"

She would say no more, and on that ominous note, they set to work once again, exposing the stairway step by step as they excavated soil and crumbled stone. Archaeologists would have sound reason to call this vandalism, but every important historical event here took place *yesterday* as vampires measured time. There was no mystery to uncover.

In the night's middle hours, they found themselves before a rotten door. The iron bindings had rusted away to orange and brown smears; massive vertical timbers had splintered and bowed inward under the weight of earth, and demolishing what remained took only moments. Carnelios tore the door apart and flung away the decaying boards, while Lucinda tripped the powerful LED torch. Its beam angled into a crypt that had not been seen since 1644.

The feeling washing over them was indescribable, physically driving them back for a moment. A thousand voices seemed to scream out of the shadows—incoherent babbling, madness and despair, agony and hate—all bound up in one amorphous cry. But it was more than this. They had scratched the veneer of other ages, and when they stepped into the crypt, where the floor was sodden with mouldering soil and water seepage, an unearthly cold struck to the bone.

Caskets had once stood on the stone shelves, but little remained, just warped timbers and piles of dust with, here and there, the ghostly glimmer of a bone shard. The atmosphere had been disturbed now; those shards might disintegrate by morning. But at the crypt's end stood a raised stone plinth, on which rested an unusual casket.

Its stone was worked in curious designs; its lid had been carved with the likeness of an ancient warrior. The design was common enough among the era's nobility, but this casket deliberately mocked the great and wicked Dominius. The vampires who tore down his rule had buried him as a Christian knight, which undid all memory of him as a grand master of vampirekind while at the same time ensuring that his resting place would remain undisturbed.

Under the edges of the sarcophagus's lid, the LED beam picked out a bright line where melted lead sealed the gap. Lucinda sparked the propane torch, held the sharp blue flame to the solder, and watched it flow like water while the burner hissed, a snake in the dank silence. Carnelios slid the pick into the gap to force it apart, and she worked along one long edge.

In ten minutes, he could lever up the lid, and with inhuman strength, he moved it aside. She killed the flame, and their eyes met. After a long moment, she turned the LED light down into the sarcophagus, and they held their breath.

Dominius. He lay in state on the dusty remnants of rich fabrics, arms folded on his chest, and he gave the impression of a man merely sleeping. His perfect preservation almost stopped their hearts—for a split second, the dread that the binding enchantment had failed fired arrows through Lucinda. Dark hair swept back from his strong brow, above an impressive nose. Whiskers common to his time framed a mouth shaped by untold cruel frowns. He was clad in silk and leather, yet a chain of surpassing workmanship bound his limbs.

The *vincula mortuorum* itself. They dared not breathe. Then, before their eyes, Dominius began to change, to fade —the stasis that had gripped his physical form had broken. Abruptly, in utter silence, the body collapsed into a deep pile of dust. Flesh, bones, fabric—all were gone in seconds. The chain's weight bore down through the body as physical matter itself lost the interconnections that had held it together.

Lucinda let out an uncharacteristic sound of

revulsion. She stepped back, put a hand to her mouth, and fought her spinning thoughts. She had never imagined she would be privileged to *see* the lost tyrant of mediaeval vampirekind—the legendary figure who had been many times more powerful than herself. His face would be etched in her memory forever, like a demonic King Arthur entombed in a far less noble vale than Avalon.

But it was *done*. Carnelios was equally unnerved, and for some time, they clung together until she shook herself hard. "Right," she said, gruff and businesslike. "Let's get that chain out."

He reached in gingerly, found a loop, lifted it out of the dust that had been a body, and brushed it clean. "Might as well leave his lordship here," he murmured, fighting for humour as Dominius's mortal remains cascaded out of the links.

He gradually paid out the chain, laying it in the tub, which Lucinda held ready. The metal shone with an untarnished silvery hue, as if its iron were alloyed with arcane elements. Lucinda whistled softly. "If I didn't know better, I'd say this was chrome steel."

"I wouldn't put anything past the great vampire metallurgists," Carnelios decided. "A steel that won't rust? Why not?"

As the chain's final loops dropped into the box, they regarded each other anxiously. "Let's get out of here," Lucinda suggested.

They scrambled to repack the gear. They might be vampires, but they had rarely been so relieved as when they emerged into the blue starlight and put the bleak tomb behind them.

* * *

An hour short of daybreak, they were back at Penrith, and Lucinda pulled over outside the town to rest. Arriving too early would attract attention. She used the time to send an anonymous email to the archaeology department at the University of York, advising them of an open mediaeval crypt in the woods west of Harrogate. She smiled at Carnelios's raised eyebrow. "Believe it or not, I don't enjoy messing with relics. I've done it, but I'd rather leave them be. Let the specialists record what's here before it's all gone. What they'll make of the open coffin is anyone's guess."

"Whatever they imagine, it won't be the truth. I can hardly believe what we just did, myself."

"Few will. Despoil the tomb of Dominius? Presumptuous!" She grinned for a second, then sobered. "Ignius is the problem now."

Sunrise was around 6.30 a.m., and they arrived at the boarding house before the guests stirred. They were upstairs in moments without meeting anyone. Anathriel had taken refuge behind tightly drawn curtains and looked ready to sleep as they conferred quietly.

"You got it?" He wore a tight smile. "Then, we are well positioned, my friends. Through some internet magic, I have managed to learn all we need to know. Jacob Martel has just two resident staff—a housekeeper and groundsman—and he is known to give them leave when expecting certain kinds of company."

"Then..." Lucinda smiled. "One phone call, and we can get them out of the way."

"That simplifies matters," Carnelios mused.

"I'll use a clean phone and discard it," she added. "Nothing traceable. There's going to be a helluva mess on the high moors, and I'd rather not attract legal attention. What about the holy well? Do we have a location?"

"About half a mile from the house," Anathriel told them. "Just a pool of black water among the heather, leading down a long, cold way into the belly of the hills."

"Perfect. Let water and earth quell Ignius's fury." Lucinda looked from one to the other. "We're on for tonight, yes?"

Each nodded in grim silence.

"Let's get cleaned up, and get some sleep." She turned towards her room. "We've got dire business ahead."

* * *

Braithwaite Hall looked late Elizabethan and wore its centuries like a shroud. It squatted on the high moors, alone against the sky. Lucinda could picture it in winter, when Atlantic gales brought black thunderheads and snow. Now it was silent, with just a few lights showing. The hulking outline of the gables and tall chimneys cut a silhouette against the evening stars.

The call had been simple enough. She used the upper-crust London voice, took Martel up on his offer of rare treats and experiences, and made a date for 8 p.m. The staff laid on dinner for two, and at half past seven, they departed with the sun. Lucinda watched the two cars negotiate the gravel track from the house to the B road, which snaked across the moors and down towards Braithwaite village.

She let another half hour go by, every moment sensing the other vampires out in the dark: Carnelios to the north, Anathriel to the south, flanking the hall. A few hundred metres away, they were watching, crouching in the heather, armed and ready to move. She breathed deeply, steadily, and calmed herself with mantras while she checked both automatics and reloads one last time. During the afternoon, she had patiently honed the sword with long, smooth strokes of a whetstone along the blade's gentle curve, until the edge was like a razor.

She could almost *feel* as the Darkling, relieved of daylight, shed his gloves, mask, broad hat, and UV shades —the desperate measures his kind needed to survive even brief exposure to sunlight, which would burn, blister and blind. Anathriel was ready, and she did not underestimate his contribution. She had fought his kind often enough to respect their strength. The moment they passed through Keswick—Anathriel in the back of Carnelios's SUV with blackout cloths at the windows—the Darkling retreated into deep concentration to blanket the area with the same shield that had defeated Ignius before. It only needed to hold until they sprang the trap.

At the stroke of eight, Lucinda breathed a long, deep sigh and jacked rounds into both pistols. They were set to fire from the open-bolt position for fast reloading, and silenced. She slid them into the holsters in the small of her back and twisted the key. The V8 throbbed to life, and she turned onto the track, crested a shallow rise, and saw the house. Now it should go like clockwork.

Except that plans rarely did, and her pulse quickened in anticipation.

Carriage lanterns burned with old-world charm under the stone portico, where she parked below the broad steps. She headed quickly up and tugged an antiquated iron bell-pull. The moment had come. Reaching behind her back, she felt the cool, nonslip grips in both palms and thumbed off the safeties. Footsteps in the hall—the sound of an ancient handle turning, before light flooded out over her.

Jacob Martel had been expecting the glamorous lady he met at the exhibition, and over two seconds his expression shifted from lustful and ingratiating eagerness through consternation to apprehension as he saw the bound hair, black T-shirt and jeans, the katana's grip extending above the right shoulder, and Lucinda's direct, unsmiling stare.

Anathriel's words came back to her. *Is your heart dark enough?* Now was not the time to debate the question. Looking into the host's eyes, she asked herself if she were a warrior, an executioner, or just a murderer. Judgement was irrelevant, and she had wasted the two seconds of his reaction time debating her own resolve.

"Remember me?" she asked, one eyebrow rising as she surveyed his expensive dinner jacket and slicked hair. Then she exploded into action.

The automatics levelled on his chest, and she triggered, point blank, as fast as they would cycle. Martel staggered backward; his arms flailed as bloody rosettes opened across his torso. At the sound, Carnelios and Anathriel would break cover and run with all their strength. Carnelios carried the *vinculum*.

The host hit the long hall's polished wood floor. Life flew out of the wide, stunned eyes and Lucinda darted forward. She dropped the guns, drew the sword with a steel rasp, and stepped aside. In one massive blow, the katana struck off the head.

Yet as it left the shoulders, its eyes flashed open, black as night. A terrible scream—not of pain, but of fury —began, perpetuated without lungs while the body twitched and pawed the air. The writhing limbs pummelled the floor. Lucinda was dimly aware when Carnelios and Anathriel pounded into the hall behind her.

She snatched up both automatics and slammed home the reloads. "Ignius is awake," she snarled.

Horrified, they watched the squirming corpse. Surreally, it flipped over and began to crawl towards its head. Had Lucinda's hesitation given the elemental time to manifest—had it begun to shapeshift? Had her sentiment doomed them?

In the instant's revulsion, they had not noticed that the face was no longer Martel's. It had undergone a transformation—the shapeshifting common to occult ambush hunters. Its features thickened; jaws pushed forward; teeth became predatory; hair receded as the skull took on an almost reptilian aspect. Splitting apart the fabric, the body swelled out of the confines of its clothes to match the head's metamorphosis. Hook-like paws scrabbled after the decapitated skull. The narrow hall offered no space to manoeuvre, and Lucinda and Carnelios risked the terrible claws to get between body and head.

"Distract it," Anathriel snapped as, with the studied motions of centuries, he removed his jacket and shirt, kicked off his shoes, and threw aside his belt.

Carnelios assumed a fighter's crouch with ornately engraved battleaxes in both his fists, arcane weapons from long ago. Stepping ahead of him, Lucinda emptied both automatics into the swelling abomination's back.

The head was now snarling; the face had transformed far beyond any human state while the rounds slammed the body into the floor, and the moment the fusillade finished, the malformed hands stretched out again—and this time found the head.

"Get back!" Carnelios gasped as the thing swelled once more.

The corpse rose into a crouch, head in its hands, and before their eyes, it set the severed skull onto the raw and bloody neck. Horrified, they watched a sulphurous flame run around the wound, sealing and cauterising. In moments, the manifestation was complete. Towering above them, two and a half metres tall, it spread gorilla-like arms tipped with black talons.

"Step aside," Anathriel commanded quietly from behind them.

Lucinda and Carnelios flattened against the walls while, stripped of the expensive clothes, Anathriel stood in an open pose, his features composed, his eyes closed to slits. Then his own transformation began. Fangs erupted; eyes blazed as he became the quintessential Darkling—driven by hunger and passion, the fury of his kind. Hands morphed into predatory hooks, and a cry from the grave broke from foam-flecked lips as he distorted, shapeshifting in seconds into the battle-morph of his species.

In a blur, he took the abomination in the midriff with a rugby tackle that drove it the length of the hall, into the timber panels. The two became a ball of frenzied violence. Immense blows thudded home; the very walls shook. In an explosion of splintering timber, a partition gave way, and the combatants plunged into a parlour beyond, sending furniture spinning and crashing.

The energy output was so incredible that not even a Darkling could maintain this intensity for long. When Anathriel was compelled to pause, Lucinda and Carnelios took his place in a flurry of blades. Striking high and low, they inscribed red lines across the beast as Ignius flailed and bellowed, seemingly untiring despite the grievous wounds it had suffered.

The thought flickered in Lucinda's mind—was it unkillable? It was an unnatural organism, so why should it obey any rules at all? Perhaps they had stumbled to the brink of Armageddon; if Ignius succeeded, darkness would fall. Flame and shadow would rule—*all* life would end, even the ancient vampires who had declined to intervene when they might have made a difference.

Lucinda felt a grim satisfaction, the simple conceit that the Lightling kind had been the first to step up and protect the existence of all. Anathriel crouched, panting, while his wounds closed one by one. When he resumed the attack, his fury doubled. The entity sprang at him, and they met in midair with a thunderous crash that brought paintings down from the walls and toppled high shelves. They rampaged through an archway into an old-fashioned kitchen where dinner had been ready to serve; tables upturned, and scalding showers hit the walls.

How do we win? Lucinda fretted. She had never before gone into a battle without knowing her foe's fatal weakness to the last degree. Could this be her own end? Vampires were immortal but, as she had demonstrated more than once, they were far from indestructible.

But this possession had not reached its full potential, and Ignius was not yet able to bring its world-spanning power to bear. Little by little, and with unremitting effort, the vampirekind wore it down. The rain of blows wore away its regenerative capacity, exhausted its faculty to maintain and repair its unnatural flesh.

As the three realised that they had it on the defensive, Lucinda gestured back into the hallway. Carnelios ran for the *vinculum* while she and Anathriel held the beast in the kitchen's shredded ruins, wading in smashed crockery and tumbled pans as they struck and parried. The monstrosity was now visibly smaller, its reactions slower, and they confined it against the timbers of the kitchen door. Though its desperate flailing and reptilian screeches sprang from an undimmed hatred, it was now very weak.

Ignius shapeshifted uncontrollably back into the host. Jacob Martel was dead, and at once the entity became dormant—helpless.

Leaning on her sword, Lucinda panted as she peered at the Darkling's exhausted ruin. Anathriel stooped with exhaustion, but the red lines that crisscrossed his pallid, massively muscled body were slowly closing. A web of similar streaks decorated Lucinda's forearms, and a gash trickled at her temple, but none of this mattered to a vampire. Such wounds were ephemeral.

As Carnelios returned, Anathriel gave up the struggle and morphed back into human form. "Quickly," he gasped, "we have but moments before it regathers its strength!"

From a shelf, Lucinda snatched a massive, ancient tablecloth. They dragged Martel's body onto it, rolled him tightly, and, with reverent hands, passed the *vinculum* around his limbs. The links tightened, and they bound them hard. Anathriel murmured an incantation from long ages past, and the three looked down at the pathetic, bundled corpse.

"It's done," Carnelios whispered. "The curse of Dominius is transferred."

"Almost," Lucinda whispered.

She turned the deadlock to open the back door, and Carnelios hefted the corpse over one shoulder. The three strode out onto the moor, where Anathriel led a silent, sombre procession across the rough bracken and heather country. In the starlight, they could see as well as by day, and they found the the sinkhole without difficulty.

Lucinda and Carnelios waded out, hip-deep, on the rapidly-shelving bottom before pushing the cursed bundle into the mirror-black pool. Air gushed out of the cloth, and the chain's weight dragged the body under. Lucinda submerged to watch in the dim starlight as the enraged elemental, sealed inextricably to a ruined human body, sank into the cold, black depths of its antithetical element.

Forever.

She hoped.

* * *

Like a battery, the house stored the black charge of the entity that had inhabited it. The Elizabethan manor felt *bad*. They could imagine the scenes enacted here as Ignius fed on Martel's depravity, and the only defence was to distance themselves, keep the shields up high and hard. They would not stay long.

Lucinda collected her spent magazines and cartridge cases and counted every round, leaving nothing for police forensics to find. The hallway was a mess of blood and shattered timbers, which they avoided. They took only enough time to clean the grime of battle from themselves and, just short of midnight, they gathered in an upstairs parlour.

The Darkling was back in his suit and looked

unflustered; the others wore robes while their clothes spun dry in the laundry facility downstairs. "This is... bizarre," Anathriel remarked, pouring glasses of brandy from a crystal decanter.

They chinked rims and drank the fiery spirit, but their eyes were hollow, haunted by all they had seen. "The elemental is laid to rest," Carnelios said gruffly. "That was the purpose, and balance is restored—there will *be* a tomorrow."

Lucinda struggled to find words. Something felt *off* and strange about the whole affair, and at last she simply smiled and sipped the spirit. "We know how this has to end," she whispered.

"Of course," the Darkling said with a shrug. "I am loath to destroy what little remains of the past, but...what is tainted must be cleansed."

"And our own tracks covered," she added. They fell silent, absorbed by what they had done, and at length, Lucinda raised her glass to Anathriel. "Thank you. I've rarely dealt in amity with those who walk the night, but I readily acknowledge that we couldn't have done this without you."

He bowed his head and smiled graciously, but his words carried a sharp edge of humour. "I am delighted to hear it, Mistress Crane. We have battled for a common purpose, but this does not change what we are. I must feed soon, and I hope that, in deference for services rendered, I may do so unhindered."

Making a generous gesture with her glass, she summoned a smile. "One understands which battles are winnable—and which are not."

An hour later, they packed their gear, walked out, and Lucinda pulled the Jaguar well away from the house before she and Carnelios returned to the kitchen. Very deliberately, they had spilt a lake of spirits and cooking oil throughout the ground floor, and now she struck a match on the rough stone by the door and lit a rolled newspaper.

The society pages flared brightly; an edge of flame charred its way across a photograph of a devilishly smiling Jacob Martel before she breathed a sigh and tossed the brand into the kitchen. The flammable mess caught alight, and a wavefront of fire raced through the house, sparking timber, paper, curtains and books. In thirty seconds, it became an inferno.

Carnelios clasped her shoulder and promised to be in touch before jogging away to the SUV, but Lucinda lingered, staring into the burning house. Fire had begun this terrible business, and fire marked its end.

The heat beat at her, and she glanced after the SUV as it disappeared on the trail to the B road. Alone with the flames and the night, she felt suddenly as if she dwelt at the bottom of an interminable well, trapped on every side by invisible walls that defined reality, time, space, and her place within them.

Perhaps this was what Ignius felt now, confined by magic strong enough to hold back one of the pillars of the Earth—enchantment before which even immortals felt insignificant.

Just for a moment, she indulged in a genuine sense of fear. Terror of the vast and obscure reaches of the reality in which all her kind were destined to walk throughout their long days.

Then, as the house blazed up, she turned away to the car and did not look back.

Dance of the Trees

Life was good when Lucinda took her ease by the Irish Sea. The top-floor room in a comfortable boarding house in Barmouth offered a pleasant panorama from the sea to the mountains at her back, over the Mawddach's vast estuary, which cut a swathe inland. She ate well, walked on late summer's mild shores, and let the trials she had recently weathered fade into life's background.

And still, she could not shake the memories of Ignius, its trickster game, and the cost of its defeat. In centuries, few battles had taken so much out of her. She felt the need to let the crusade rest, if only for a while, and perhaps live closer to the mortals' world. Ian Craddock, up in Port Whitehaven in Cumbria, had provided the blood to replenish her strength, and she spent several weeks with him before moving on.

A Lightling would always be a misfit, and in the constant travelling, Lucinda found a sense of security.

She had not visited Wales in too long. The ample wealth an immortal amassed bought the best accommodation, and she dined, drank, and wandered the wild estuary as September went by. Holiday trade had slackened. By October, the beaches were largely empty, and the first cold Atlantic winds reminded her that winter was just around the corner. For the moment, all seemed well.

She disappeared into the sameness of human life around her, just a face in a crowd—albeit one with hair like dark flame and the persona that held people at arm's length. She valued privacy and had no room in her life for anyone beyond the circle of patrons she had cultivated over the years—and a few of her fellow Elderlings.

Mellow days lingered, blurring together in peace and comfort, and one glorious sunset after another flushed the west. Lucinda felt a peace she had rarely enjoyed, and though she had learnt enough cynicism to know that good things cannot last, she also believed she was due a reward. She accepted the good times gladly.

The blow hit doubly hard when she opened her eyes in the small hours of a calm night and, with a thrill of existential dread, realised she was not alone in her own skin, heart, or mind.

An echo, like a reflection of consciousness, followed her thoughts a fraction of a second out-of-phase. She felt *watched*. A cold sweat broke on her brow, and she felt utterly alone, except for the glimmer of a presence where none should have been. With a sick feeling in the pit of her stomach, she understood instinctively what had happened.

Even those who walk in eternity make mistakes.

Berating herself was pointless. She knew when darkness gained the upper hand, and in nearly five hundred years, she had never been so afraid.

She had believed Ignius was contained for a millennium of slumber in the embrace of its antithetical element. But close contact risks contamination. Ignius was the consummate spirit of possession, one of those occult entities that inhabit living flesh for their own gain.

The catharsis of victory had blinded her to the tiny sliver of the entity that persisted in hiding, unnoticed in the brilliance of her own aural field. Assured of triumph, she had dropped her guard, and, scrupulously careful to pass unseen, the mote of evil had taken hold.

In the room's silence, she marshalled her mind, controlled her heart, and reminded herself that she was a vampire in the full bloom of her strength. She had forged a career in opposing *things* from the world's darker places, and she felt out the entity with the merest brushing of psychic contact, dancing around the edges of its presence. It was still embryonic, not yet properly aware, but it inhabited her parasitically, and, very gradually, had begun to consume her vitality.

It had implanted an etheric tentacle in the back of her heart and was now feeding on her coursing life energy, which fuelled swift regeneration. Ignius had been growing since the moment it took hold. By the time it grew large enough for her to notice it—this waking in sudden dread—it was, Lucinda realised, too deeply entrenched for her to extract it by sheer force of will.

Withdrawing from the *thing*, she compartmentalised her own mind to pretend that she was oblivious to it. When it became fully cognisant, its assault on her waking mind might become more than she could resist. She had time to think, but at first, what to do was beyond her. Days went by; a week became two in the coast's now hollow peace and beauty while she struggled with her few choices.

She might have sought the help of other vampires, but in the grip of this possession, she could not trust herself. Her sword might kill friend as easily as foe—it was all she could do to maintain a wall around her soul and remain clear-headed with independent will.

But as time passed, she would also starve. Carrying such a malevolent passenger, she dared not approach the patrons who willingly gave the blood all vampires needed. Eventually, she could only revert to taking the blood of horses in the night.

But far older and more eldritch things than vampires persist in the land's wild places, and after days spent alone in an agony of helplessness, she remembered where she might turn. A single hope burned like a beacon. She concealed it from the entity as she made her way doggedly through autumn, while the sun dwindled and Britain once again became the Dark Island.

In the shortening days, Lucinda girded her spirit, packed the weapons, dressed in denim and leather, and booked out of the hotel. She turned the Jaguar east and drove steadily, with absolute focus. She must reach the goal uninterrupted. If the parasite in her aura ever took control, she might be lost beyond redemption, and a lifetime devoted to the service of her fellow creatures would become the mockery of defeat.

A kilometre above Ladybower Reservoir in Derbyshire's Peak District, Win Hill was a wild hillock of heather and bracken under the wide sky. A mixed forest clung to the slopes, as it had since the Romans carved roads through these parts, and among those woods lay something very special—a place Lucinda had not visited in over a hundred years.

The road followed the lake's south shore. She skirted the western end of Ladybower Dam, parked on the turnoff to a forestry trail off Carr Lane, and stood in the high country's crisp, clear air, trying to recognise the low autumn sun for the gift it was.

With the car well out of sight under the trees, she looked across the Derwent's valley to the holiday lodge high on the opposite bluffs. She valued this calm. The summer season had ended by now; business was slow, so the odds of her being spotted were correspondingly slight. She must take the risk.

Settling the sword across her back, she vaulted a locked gate and headed up the trail into the woods, navigating from memory and veering from the track after a few minutes to push carefully through the understory of bracken, which had turned red with the season.

She listened to the birdsong, smelt the earth's rich aromas, tried in every way to be a creature of nature—and keep her mind off the objective. If her passenger realised the danger it was in, it would make a powerful bid for control, and Lucinda was unsure if she could resist.

Breathe, she thought distractedly. *Be a free thing of the world...you have the strength.* Above all, she must not address Ignius directly. It knew vaguely that she was aware of it, but its level of cognition was still low. Engaging it would provide it a bridge into her mind, and that would be the end. *Put one foot in front of the other.*

Her goal lay just half a kilometre into the woods, and she reached it with a sensation of compressed time. Had it really been a hundred years? So very long, but to a vampire, time was nothing, and the living world endured unchanged. Birdsong grew quiet as she entered a thinner patch of trees; the low autumn sun shafted through the boughs, where a dappled glade surrounded a figure, which since time immemorial had been known as *The Dance of the Trees*.

Once, long ago, it had been a single mighty oak, until

lightning struck this giant of the woods and great storms worked on the weakness to split the trunk. The tree had collapsed to each side, yet the grievous wound did not kill it. The spirit within was alive and well; in its division, the tree spirit became the keeper of all duality—so said the shamans and druidkind of old. The tales came down to the present by word of mouth, and among the eldritch kind, the site was widely known for its deep and ancient power.

Trees rose all around, the riot of their green scattered with autumn's red and gold. Lucinda found herself hushed with profound respect. Here was something whose antiquity made her five centuries pale. She paused before the oaks' majesty, dropped to one knee, and breathed the forest floor scent for moments of deep introspection.

She appreciated how these survivors had been named. The twin trunks were curved, contorted as if in the midst of violent action, and yet frozen in time. From each, a single bough extended—gnarled, dripping with the rich moss that clothed the trunks and connected them—as if the dancers joined hands in an intimate caress that would endure forever.

Treading silently, she advanced and knelt once more. One bare hand on the earth before them, she concentrated. *Thou who art all moiety*, she thought, deep down where the heart spoke, *hear one who is in binary divided.*

The conscious thought would slowly register with the entity. As she waited for its reactions, she sensed a flutter of alarm from the ethereal *thing* she carried—the rising tide of anger and panic. What she did not expect was the cool shaft of energy that washed over her, lambent as light filtered through green ice, a calming presence that shushed the embryonic demon's chattering fury and filled her mind with profound comfort.

We, who are eternal, hear you, child of the centuries. The whisper of two voices in concert, one male, one female, spoke deep in her mind. She could have wept, for she heard the trees and felt their compassion. *In duality do you exist, where oneness should prevail. You bring an unwelcome guest to this glade, but we know whereof you seek. There is a path you must follow, and we shall set you upon it. We bind you to this action—return not to this place of peace unless you are divested of your burden. Take with you our understanding that balance must be restored—the light to the light and the dark to the dark. Seek the spirit of the waters in the depths of Glen Deep, and may all that watches over your kind stand by you in your struggle.*

A breeze stirred the treetops, and a shaft of sunlight marked the path. Barely daring to breathe, Lucinda rose from her pose of reverence, bowed before the mighty forest spirits, and made her way into the light.

* * *

She walked now as if in a dream. The cool energy stayed with her, seeming to guide her while it held Ignius in thrall, enforcing its passivity. The greater powers never took sides; they only maintained the balance, which reminded Lucinda of how much closer she was to mortals than to any other lifeform—eternity notwithstanding. She had chosen this path long ago, and she *had* made a difference for humans in a world teeming with preternatural beings. She regretted nothing, though her road would end here if she were unequal to the task. In the grand scheme, she accepted this. A few people would miss her; she wished she could have done more for them, but in the hour to come, she had space only for herself and her own universe.

The trail descended through the land's folds, probably towards the lake, which lay so close to the north. But soon she sensed an ethereal quality, as if this were no longer the woodland of an autumn day in the Peaks but part of another time, another reality. The forest colours seemed touched by a luminosity beyond anything mortal vision perceives; the lushness of bough, rock, cloud, and fern bore an ineffable quality, caressed by some ancient magical hand. The trees rose against the sky in serried ranks, giants ready to do battle. The mortal world faded until Lucinda might have been the last human being in existence. The thought made her smile: *human* was the last label most people would apply to her.

Birdsong drifted far above as she followed the trail down mossy rocks into deep shadow, smelt the rich humus, and heard the trickle of falling waters. A grotto opened out, a narrow chasm into which plunged tiny waterfalls feeding a dark stream in a black pebble bed. With some effort, she clambered down by slippery ways until she stood on a shore of shale and broken stone at the water's edge. She looked through the dim green twilight towards the gaping cavern that swallowed the stream and where the echoing spaces invited her—*compelled* her—to go. There, she would find destiny.

Without question or hesitation, she stepped forward, hearing the pebbles clatter and crunch under her feet as she passed under a rock arch into a cavern of surprising dimensions. Her eyes adjusted; she saw the stream tumbling down slick stone into the earth and followed it, down and down, until daylight became a corona overhead, and her cat-wide eyes made out a broad, calm pool in the depths. Black as night, the water drew her on with inexplicable power.

All thought was suppressed now. Her heart raced with a thread of fear; her hand went automatically to the katana's hilt at her shoulder as she stared around the grotto in the gloom and heard the sibilant echoes of falling water.

Something crouched in that darkness—feral, predatory, watching. She felt nothing malevolent about this entity, as if it did not pass judgement. The *thing* in her aura was keenly aware of it and fluttered around, afraid and snarling in ineffectual threat. The fragment of Ignius had been far too strong for her to extract by herself, but she was no longer alone.

The water shifted and swirled; the surface puckered, rippling into languid, oily black rolls. Then the pool's midpoint rose up against gravity and against all sense of normalcy. The water's up-doming gleamed like polished obsidian, and its surface undulations took on vaguely anthropomorphic characteristics—repellent, frightening.

But Lucinda had passed beyond such reactions. She smiled, icy and hard, as she recognised a water elemental as old as this land and as powerful as eternity. Ignius was a fire elemental; they were diametric opposites. The tree spirits had known precisely what to do.

Stepping closer on the shingle that fringed the pool, she extended one hand. She needed no words; in this meeting of ancient opposites, she was merely a vessel. The act of faith came as she relinquished control, something she had never done before.

Now, she lived or died according to chance, and she endured the horror as the fire spirit surged out, crushing her into a tiny corner of her own mind as it seized control of her body and soul. It had snatched the vampire's strength; she felt her own hand draw the sword as her features distorted into something inhuman, and she crouched like a beast. She sensed Ignius's need to flee from the water elemental—but she had succeeded in bringing the fly to the spider. The ever-shifting, vaguely humanoid shape rising out of the water snarled with a rush of foam, and flung out huge surges of boiling spray. The very waters at her feet rose and wrapped her in a frigid grip, like death's hand.

Ignius roared its fury. Without her volition, the sword wove a web intended to destroy, but the razor-keen blade passed through the water, which surged back together, undamaged. The dark pool was alive—a single gelid being of immense size and strength. Its crushing weight dragged her forward, knee-deep in the shallows. She stood inside a tornado of spray, half blind and deafened, while the cave magnified the plunging cataracts into surreal thunder.

Perhaps Ignius's final remnant knew it was outmatched. It turned its hate on Lucinda, sending spikes of pain through her—fire and ice in her nerves, up and down her spine. As it crushed each chakra in a blaze of malice, she spasmed, screaming incoherently. Her consciousness withdrew into the last corner of her skull that she possessed.

She felt even those walls close in, about to squeeze her out of existence, but the water elemental produced glassy tendrils that plunged into her chakras from behind, stabilised them—and it began to extract the entity like pus from a wound. Ignius railed and shrieked, endlessly babbling its hate and insanity, but little by little, its fury weakened.

Lucinda began to feel her body and world coming back. She looked up at the water elemental as if from the bottom of a crater, but as Ignius's last fragment tore loose, her perspective shifted. She seemed to grow, and saw the entities on equal terms. The water creature was all around her, inside her, a vast, cool presence, incalculably powerful yet gentled by a deep and inherent concern.

One atom at a time, she relaxed; the pain became a terrible memory, and she listened as the fire elemental's cries became fainter. Its vitriolic fury was pathetic, infantile. Hate for hate's sake.

Swaying, all her strength expended, she shuddered in the chill as she became aware of the cave once more. When the parasite left her, she collapsed into the pool, fought to turn over, and floated on her back, panting shallowly. Above her, suspended in the air, cradled in a rainbow of swirling spray, Ignius's flame burned feebly, a corona surrounding a core as lightless as a black hole. This was the *thing* that had tormented her; for a few difficult moments, pure energy expressed itself as matter.

Deep down, she felt a strange compassion. The fragment of an ancient, terrible entity could still grow back into all it had been—but not here, not now. It must return to the darkness, and an aeon might pass before it came snarling and tearing into the world once more.

The burning darkness rose on a pillar of droplets, which she realised was the water spirit's outstretched hand. The hand reached into the sky above the grotto and, in seconds, the fragment of Ignius vanished.

The last thing Lucinda felt was a gentle wave nudging her onto the shingle before she lost consciousness.

* * *

Cold. Swimming in darkness, all she knew was a knifing cold that struck to the bone throughout her lower body. She opened her eyes in the cave's soft gloom and smelt the earth against her face. She was stiff and sore. Memories of blinding agony made her flinch, but she forced herself up on hands she could not feel and dragged herself out of the pool.

Her wide pupils easily resolved the cave—the water had returned to a calm black mirror, and the elemental was at peace. She bowed before it in profound thanks, one hand over her heart in an expression of gratitude. A mortal would have died. Only the vampire's resilience had carried her through. Her aura was cleansed; the entity had gone. She was herself—she *knew* this instinctively and felt more thankful than she could ever have put into words.

A silvery bar glimmered in the pool. When she was able, she gritted her teeth against more cold, stepped into the water, and reached under to retrieve the sword. Thanking the water spirit from the bottom of her heart, she resheathed the blade and turned to resume her journey, one shaky step at a time.

She followed the way up by the trickling falls that fed the pool and the underground streams beyond, and climbed towards the late afternoon sky. The sun was up there—seeing its gleam on treetops far above, she craved its warmth.

In the climb, she discovered a metaphor for her own life: the need to overcome the base nature that could so easily have overwhelmed her. Power, strength, and immortality created a formula for arrogance and the cruelty that went hand in hand with it. But she had taken those gifts and shaped them into a fist that struck for right. She had no other way to understand it. This brush with an occult nemesis underlined her own fragility: even vampires were vulnerable. But as she climbed back to forest, daylight and birdsong, she felt balance return, and the comfort of normality—not an epiphany but a confirmation that she stood for something.

The sun was mellow and golden in the woodland. She found a nook between tree boles, like a gift from the forces swirling around her, where ferns caught the light and the sun warmed a bare rock. Sinking down on it, she luxuriated in the fleeting comfort. The quiet bower was the opposite of every chill road she had wandered and every icy river she had crossed. Just for a moment, the world was saying *thank you.*

Her resilience had begun to rebuild. Ignius had gorged when it had the chance, but it had not taken *all* her energy. She could feel her life-force rekindling. In an hour, with confidence and purpose, she walked back the way she had come, and in the glade of the Dancers, knelt once more to give a wordless thanks to the forest's watchers.

The land sighed. Leaves rustled in a last mild breeze, and she sensed the small animals scurrying to prepare for winter. All was well; all was *right.* The woods were at peace —and, by their grace, so was Lucinda Crane.

The Knives of November

With the last flush of the holiday season six weeks in the past, the days were shortening and downpours were more frequent. Reaped fields stood fallow all over Britain, and storms swept in from the Atlantic, dumping heavy rain for days at a time. The last flocks would soon depart for France and Spain, sweep over Gibraltar, and pass on into Africa's warmth.

A melancholy time of year, Lucinda Crane reflected as she stood on the verge beside the Jaguar, looking steadily across Somerset's deserted fields. Clouds flurried on the ocean wind; standing water in the saturated land reflected their blues and greys; the sparse trees wore their autumn reds. All Hallows Eve had gone by a few days ago; a time when *real* vampires stood back and watched mortals in their revels—the bastardised, dumbed-down celebration of things of which they had no real understanding.

Sometimes Lucinda walked out in a large town to watch children scrounging for candy, the American custom that had spread across the globe; but England's real traditions were the bonfires, lanterns of carved turnips—not pumpkins—and old tales told from the heart to put shivers in the spine. Firelight and cold nights, scarecrows in tatters, tugged by the tormenting wind, darkness by late afternoon...these things defined November in England.

She could have told a few tales of her own five centuries of life, but day by day, she was still writing the story. Now, she stood in the wind to stare at farmsteads and the distant outline of roof and steeple, which were little changed by the long years. She frowned deeply. This was the village of Oldfields, halfway between Bristol and Bath, still rubbing shoulders with the countryside, though one would see both towns from the church's belltower.

The name itself echoed antiquity, and some strange shadow lay over its thatch, whitewash, stone and timber. Lucinda suspected that, for those who knew how to sense it, the shadow would persist even on a bright summer day.

Something dark dwelt in this land, this place of fallow fields, empty grain silos, and horses blanketed for winter. Something that kept a secret, treasured it, held it close and never spoke to outsiders. But modern pattern recognition software challenged the memories of the Elderlings themselves. Things inconceivable to mortals suggested themselves to the vampire mind with sibilant whispers. Trapped in the eternal present moment, mortals could not even imagine the unseen world that surrounded them.

And if Lucinda was right, there would be a murder somewhere nearby within a few days—just as there had been every thirteen years since Rome ruled this land.

* * *

The Lodge of Transcendent Glory—a seventeenth-century manor house on the Somerset Levels north of Glastonbury—had been turned over to New Age arcana. Or so the public was encouraged to believe. Lucinda knew differently, and when she pulled in at the gate and showed her face to the camera, the iron portals swung obediently apart. Passing around a lawn whose turf had been laid before the Civil War and whose oaks had seen all of English history, since King John at least, she headed up the gravel driveway towards the rambling old house and strode up the wide steps to a portico whose oiled timber doors opened before her.

Not exactly a butler, Hungerford was the estate manager—mortal, and a patron of vampirekind. Clad in dark formalwear, with his gaunt face, tall, thin physique, and balding head, the wizened old retainer let no flicker of a smile betray him as he looked her up and down. He was apparently unimpressed by the flaming locks under Lucinda's broad-brimmed hat, the long leather coat, burgundy sweater, blue jeans and boots.

After a long pause, he grunted and gestured at the wide mat before the door. "Wipe your mucky feet," he said in a broad Yorkshire accent, by way of greeting.

Lucinda laughed as she did so. "I've missed you, too, Hungerford," she said lightly with a pat on his shoulder as she stepped into the dark timber hallway. "Is Mistress Silver at home?"

"Aye," was his taciturn reply. "What's it about?"

"The library," she replied softly, tapping the polished wood floor with one toe. "The *special* library."

"You can wait in't parlour," he grunted before heading away like Lurch to locate his mistress.

The parlour was decorated in an antique style, tasteful enough for public contact. Few mortals ever penetrated deeper. Lucinda seated herself in a Georgian armchair and let the place's age wash over her, the comforting—the soothing feeling of permanence that emanated from things that rivalled herself in age. Silverware gleamed in an ornate cupboard; occasional tables vied with whatnots and other familiar objects from bygone eras. She chided herself not to let so long go by before revisiting such a sanctuary for the Lightling kind; enough vampires were born with the genes to walk in daylight—or *made* with them—to constitute an entire subspecies, after all.

The sound of heels on the hall's floorboards brought her to her feet, and she smiled a greeting. Two centuries her junior, Desdemona Silver had done very well for herself, which was to be expected since she had been turned by the already-wealthy vampire with whom she was still partnered. Silver was her trademark: flowing silver hair, silver stilettos, silver talons, and a silver Chinese silk suit.

"Lucinda Crane, what brings you to the Levels?" She spoke with a West Country accent, but centuries of contact with *money* had smoothed it. She embraced Lucinda briefly. "You're still blending with the Goth set, I see."

"It's cheap camouflage." Lucinda shrugged. "I need to consult the library."

"It's another of those crusading moments?" the lady of the house asked, mock-judgemental. "Well, whom can we assist you in terminating this time?"

"I'm not sure yet. But a mortal is going to die very soon, and I need to know whether to tip off the Somerset Constabulary...or deal with it myself."

Finely delineated brows quirked with a smile. "Well, let's not impede investigations."

Desdemona escorted Lucinda down the main hall and turned into a rear passage. In the ancient scullery, she pressed a hidden contact to release a covering panel, revealing a hand scanner, and placed her palm against it for identification.

The wall retracted to give access to a hidden elevator, and they went down, deep below cellar level, to a place so old that it made even Lucinda's flesh creep. When they emerged, lights flicked on automatically over the towering stacks of an old library. But these were no ordinary volumes; their musty antiquity was made doubly obvious by the modern terminal, which stood on an ornate desk in the only clear area.

"You know the protocols," Desdemona said softly. "Gloves at all times. Light levels remain low; temperature and humidity in here are strictly controlled. If you need anything, the intercom on the desk will find Hungerford, wherever he is." She smiled. "When you're ready, come up for some tea."

Then the mistress of this vampire House left her to her work, and Lucinda slid the tablet from her inside pocket. She folded the coat over the chair, dropped her hat on the end of the desk, and slipped on white cotton gloves from a box by the terminal before she called up the library catalogue. She remembered just enough to point the way.

Thomas Malreward. The name swam back from long ages past, and it was associated with murder. This she recalled like a bright star in darkness, and she found it a troubling match with her observations of recent criminal activity. Murder was a common enough crime, but patterns spoke volumes to investigators, and she wondered if the local force had made the connection.

She scrolled through the data she had gathered, refreshing her memory. The last disappearance in the vicinity of Oldfields was in 2005, but no corresponding vanishment was recorded in 1992. There *had* been an accidental death in the village in the November of that year. Nothing appeared in the 1979 records, but a crossmatch between parish registers revealed that a village resident passed away of apparently natural causes and was buried swiftly at precisely the correct time of year and month.

1966—a disappearance in the region. 1953 saw another disappearance, though in the age of paper records, it was less surprising that no connection had been made across such a gap. In 1940, amid the war's chaos, nobody was reported missing, but villages in the area had lost enough people in the services to easily account for one being diverted to a more nefarious end. Lucinda had no doubt that if she continued searching, using all available means—eventually, microfiche archives of country newspapers from the nineteenth century—she would find the pattern continued ever backwards through time as far as records existed.

But memories older than any mortal could imagine pointed her in other directions, and she browsed the electronic catalogue for the volumes she needed. These books were from centuries past; some were very old indeed, and stored behind glass. Many were handwritten, created by vampires, for vampire eyes only.

The name of Thomas Malreward was intimately associated with this part of the country, and so old that it 'tasted' like legend—the name persisted in at least one village name. Lucinda settled down to browse the oldest works. She puzzled over Middle English, Chaucerian, and Shakespearean prose, and, where memory failed, consulted the digital reference guides.

An hour later, becoming despondent, she stumbled over an engraving in a book dating from the 1600s. The scene depicted country children, playing in a town square on some festival day; the rhyme they chanted as they danced a circle was recorded below. Adjusting for the language, she whispered:

"*Thomas of the mal-reward,*

"Ingratitude of cruel lord,
"Bring us fruit and corn and meat,
"Against the days with naught to eat."

This was it. She had heard this rhyme in her own youth, and she frowned now as, with some difficulty, she recalled the story surrounding it.

From a twenty-first-century perspective she suspected the tale she recalled to be a mediaeval retelling of something much older. In a God-fearing parish where crops often failed—centuries *before* the witch hysteria—the story said that a villager named Thomas made a pact with the devil to deliver a human soul in exchange for bountiful crops and fertile livestock. According to tradition, nothing was ever proven, but the area never went hungry again, not even when the local lord, in a fit of piousness, had Thomas strangled. Death was his *mal reward* for serving the community, though records noted that Lucifer kept his bargain. The moral of the story being that he claimed *two* souls instead of one; thus, the wages of sin were death.

With the Christian veneer stripped away, to Lucinda the tale seemed very similar to much older stories from the pagan canon of earlier times. Ensuring a good harvest or hunting by striking bargains with deity was as old as human life. Just as the tales of King Arthur were coopted from their Welsh originals in the twelfth century and became Norman Christian fables, she guessed that this bit of doggerel recalled an event whose roots were buried more deeply—in Saxon times, perhaps even earlier.

This gave her a line of inquiry, and she probed further into the most ancient transcripts. There were undeniable parallels to the Irish Crom Cruach, the dark deity propitiated with human sacrifice in exchange for fertile land and livestock in County Cavan until—so the story went—St Patrick struck down the idol and the spirit within it. To Lucinda's knowledge, the worship of that particular entity had not crossed the Irish Sea, but something disturbingly similar was emerging. The legend of Thomas and his demise fit the pattern.

At last, she found what she needed. The volume was

one of a rare handful kept in locked cases: a treatise by a vampire sage of the Middle Ages, long ago imaged and stored digitally. An English translation from the Latin had been done, and as she scrolled through fascinating tales of lost times, she reminded herself that they had been written down in the hundred years after the Norman conquest, centuries before her own birth and turning. Here was *true* antiquity.

Among the observations of his era, the writer—one Feniculus, a Lightling born in the reign of William Rufus and writing in that of Henry II—related stories handed down from ancient times among the West Country peoples. He spoke of King Arthur, a powerful chieftain who gathered an alliance of tribes in the days before the Roman Empire ended in order to shore up the west against the tide of new peoples calling Britain home. Angles, Jutes, Saxons. Modern archaeology questioned much of this, but the essence remained. Feniculus wrote of dark times, old gods, and the north's Painted People, who raided far south of the Roman wall once the legions had gone and the *civitates* became responsible for their own defence.

Yet among such vistas of history, tales emerged of the ordinary folk and their spirit world. Feniculus had known a vampire of even earlier days—a resident of the Roman *civatatum* of Aquae Sulis, which became modern Bath, in Somerset. The Elderling remained in the town throughout the centuries when tribalism resurged. Aquae Sulis became *Bad* in the Saxon tongue, softening to *Bath* in English. In the late seventh and early eighth centuries, a curious cult arose. Folk in the region began to worship a dark, old god that went by no name but resisted the new deity from the east. The people of meadow, river and hill took holy communion on Sundays but gave their *first* fealty to a spirit whose veneration was said to grace the west with abundant grain, milk, and fruit.

The story recorded an attempt to expel the worship of the pagan spirit. An early king of Wessex found a villager reputed to have dealt with the unholy entity, trading life for life, and publicly beheaded him as a warning. No more was heard from this village in the Old Field, but throughout that part of the country, elderly people still commonly said, *Lock up your doors and bar your windows in the month after Samhaine, for the Old God's children will come, merry for pillage, and mighty Blackhound their consort. Take heed and pray thee to God, for naught the lords and warriors may do shall e'er change this.*

Lucinda sat back with a sigh and rubbed her chin as she sent the appropriate page to the printer installed under the desk. She shook out her hair and felt an abrupt need for tea.

* * *

"There's more than a hint of the 'wild hunt' about it," Desdemona Silver mused as she went over the printout. On a low table between them, Earl Grey steamed in gold-rimmed porcelain. They sat in an upstairs parlour where afternoon light streamed through wide bay windows, and the November day seemed less sombre. "The Blackhound is a straightforward enough reference."

"I've dealt with my share of blackdogs," Lucinda said unconcernedly, recalling Whitby's Barguest Hound and others. "The village is still called Oldfields, halfway between Bath and Bristol. A pattern of death and disappearance surrounds it, going back at least seventy years—always in November, spaced thirteen years apart."

The mistress laid aside the sheets and sipped her tea. "You'll not be referring this to the authorities, I take it?"

Lucinda chuckled. "It's hardly the sort of thing they'd take seriously. And from their perspective, the gaps in the pattern of disappearance—filled by the passing of Oldfields locals—would likely reduce it to the level of mere coincidence."

"So, what will you do?"

The question was blunt, as Lucinda expected. She was more or less alone among her kind in battling for the well-being of mortals when the supernatural raised its head. One thing the Elderling kind had learnt was how to maintain a low profile and not be noticed by the mortals' teeming multitudes. Fighting mortal battles was certainly not on the vampire agenda.

"What I usually do. Get in the way." Lucinda would not elaborate.

"Do you have anything else to go on?"

"Not yet. But there's a feeling in the bones when the 'dark side' stirs, and I've been getting it for a while."

Desdemona smiled thinly over her cup. "It's your forte, dear Lucinda. You know, there are some who resent your crusade. They call you a meddler in the affairs of mortals, always interfering in the natural order of things. It's actually because you make them feel inadequate. The Elderlings have folded their hands for so long that they've become afraid to do battle. They say they're 'saving themselves' for some apocalypse to come, when in fact they're really too lazy to do anything more than enjoy what providence has given them." She sipped again. "Of course, you didn't hear this from me."

"What about you?" The question was pointed.

"Do I look like a warrior, my dear? Never have been, no matter what becoming a vampire changeling has brought me."

"You feel the blood burn now and then," Lucinda said softly over her cup. "We all do, even the mildest of us."

"True. We have little to fear...except the Darklings. And that's where you come in."

"I could use a little backup now and then," Lucinda admitted with a touch more frustration than she had intended.

"What—and incite a fully-fledged war between the two halves of Elderling kind? If the Darklings ever got the impression that we Lightlings had organised any strategy against them, they would awaken *en masse*. We would be slaughtering each other in a very visible way. No, my dear old thing. To them, you are simply an irritation. Admittedly, a formidable one—but they are prepared to deal with you case by case. Since you seem able to cope with that, you may find your greatest success in simply making the more rapacious of the Darkling kind think twice."

"If that's the best I can do, so be it." Lucinda

shrugged. "There's more than vampires in this world." She drained the cup and set it down. "All the indications are that this cult will be on the lookout for its next victim even now. Every recorded incident has fallen between Halloween and Guy Fawkes Night. They might choose one of their own—the proverbial farm accident—but they'd need to be careful. These days, pathologists can smell even a hint of foul play, and the coroner examines almost every corpse. An elderly villager might be chosen, and if the local doctor is in on it, he could certify natural causes. But the potency of such a sacrifice would be meagre. If they're looking for an outsider on this cycle..." She smiled, flint-hard.

"Yes?"

"They'll get more than they bargained for."

* * *

Being of ample means made things simple—and one did not live five centuries without amassing wealth. Lucinda had built subtly and steadily on the fortune she first made in trade in the 1600s. Now, it was diversified across multiple accounts, tax shelters, and investment portfolios. An agent in London—also an Elderling—kept it growing, so she was never without money.

She went shopping on Glastonbury High Street among the New Age and magic shops, bought very different clothing from her intimidating Goth norm, plus a decent digital camera and a new tablet—clean of any identifying files—and spent the night back at the Lodge.

Leaving the Jaguar safe in the capacious garage, Hungerford drove her into Glastonbury in time for the morning coach up to Bristol. Dressed in winter-weight leggings, a colourful sweater and jacket, a tie-dye silk scarf and soft hat, she seemed a different person. Camera around her neck, case between her boots, she waited for the coach at the stop on Magdalene Street, near the gates of the old, ruined Glastonbury Abbey. Henry VIII's soldiers had torn the abbey apart when Lucinda herself was just twenty-one years old.

She kept to herself while the bus passed through the green and sodden countryside, northward to the cold, grey city of Bristol. She caught a cab from the bus terminal to the rental agency where she had hired a three-tonne motorhome—the rates were fair at this time of year, with the summer rush well over, and she paid with a credit card on one of her aliases. Driving licence and smartphone also tallied with the ID, and in an hour, she was on her way east again, this time as 'Sally Robinson,' freelance photographer, exploring Somerset's villages.

Swinging south, she lingered in places with names like Norton Hawkfield, Norton, Pensford, Chelwood, where she wandered with the camera busy, made notes in a flip-back notebook, drank coffee and hot chocolate, and watched the day draw into November's early twilight. This was the time of blowing leaves and an edge in the wind that swept the Levels all the way from the Bristol Channel; of trees growing stark as they laid down a carpet of crackling reds and golds; of grey skies through which the sun fought an unequal battle. Farms stood silent in a landscape declining towards winter, and the villages fell quiet as the grave.

Driving a circle route, south then east, gave every appearance of Sally being exactly what she claimed: a photographer rambling the countryside in search of the perfect image. Within an hour of sundown, Lucinda was perfectly in character when she arrived in Oldfields, a village set amid the irregular patchwork of reaped fields, with Bristol to its west and Bath to the east.

At once, her vampire senses pricked, as they had when she viewed the place from afar. She almost *smelt* something—a taint, an acridity in the air that told her senses, which were razor-sharp after so many years of struggle, that something *wrong* lurked among these seemingly innocent byways. From a low hillock, the Saxon church, with its square tower overgrown by the ivy of ages, presided over picturesque streets of flower-grown cottages, the well-mowed green, a few shops, and a single pub with a thatched roof and leadlight windows.

The people were friendly enough. The publican, a big, bluff fellow named Jonathan Greene, was more than eager to make Sally welcome, and set a fine meal before her while he prepared a room. This far out-of-season, in a backwater farming community, any passing trade was like gold. But as Lucinda ate in the dining annex opposite the bar and the sun set over the rooftops in goldy-greys, she had the unmistakable sense of being *watched*—not necessarily by the patrons in the bar, though many eyes turned her way, but by *something* that peered out from behind those eyes.

Her psychic shields were firmly in place, so nothing of the vampire bled through Sally Robinson's innocent façade. But if the entity that haunted this place were powerful enough, it would break through and *know* her. A blackdog? Lucinda would take it as it came. Smiling, sipping a decent red wine, she watched the flames of an evening fire in the hearth glimmer through the ruby refractions in the glass. She *liked* dogs, and they liked her.

In the evening chill, she shrugged into her coat and took a turn around the village green, sitting and watching the stars until clouds came up before making her way back to the pub. She took a cider in the bar and sat quietly with the tablet, scrolling the news, sure she would be approached. Soon enough, she was chatting with local farm types—a commercial traveller from Bristol, several retirees from Bath.

Something unspoken hung heavily on the air, and more than one person asked if she would be staying long, as if timing were important. "Just till tomorrow," she replied, "but I'm not going far. That's the beauty of a motorhome. I can shoot landscapes till the light fails, pull over anywhere, and get some sleep."

Heads wagged in agreement, and with an almost eerie sense of accomplishment, she climbed the creaking stairs to a room with centuries-old, black-finished roof timbers. She sat on the end of the bed for a while, breathing deeply and concentrating. She *knew* they had taken the bait. If she were mortal, she would be in deadly danger now.

But she was not, and her smile became that of the hunter partway through a successful stalking.

* * *

She chatted with Greene over breakfast in the dining nook, making sure to tell him she would be in the area all day, photographing the charming village. He asked leading questions about family and friends. Was anyone waiting for her? She had crafted Sally's persona to appeal to an abduction scenario: an only child, father deceased, mother with dementia in assisted living. After enjoying a long break away from her home on the other side of the country. Sally would be looking for a new career to fill the void left by a disappointing relationship.

If all this got back to the locals who were ready to perform the snatch, she could be sure Greene was also part of the murder cult. But historically, every public figure in a closed community must be part of such collusion for it to remain ironclad. *No one* in Oldfields could be unaware of it.

She made sure to tell Greene that she would be back for lunch but declined to book the room for a second night. She would use the vehicle, she said, and be ready to shoot the sunrise over the bare fields. Now, she had deliberately cast the bait—and Green had swallowed it, barb and all.

The day became no more than a formality. She cruised a few miles in each direction—found pubs and shops, filled flashcards for the sake of the disguise, and, in the early afternoon, took care to be back in Oldfields for steak and ale pie. Sipping a lazy cider while she read the news, she found herself acutely aware of the locals and their sidelong attention.

There was Joe Costerman, the local farm mechanic—a hard-bitten sort in dark blue overalls, scrappy hair raked back from a troubled brow—who looked in for a quick pint and a ploughman's lunch. Mary from the post office was nervous and furtive, sipping a port and lemon. Then came Deirdre from the village shop, innocent as could be; the distinguished Mr Morgan from the farm machinery sales office over in Bristol; old Donald Crandon from the cottage by the church—the village gossipmonger, whose face, lost in wrinkles, looked like a map of eternity.

They *all* knew. The word had raced around. Sally was

the target.

Everyone was on their best behaviour and would remain so until they grabbed the stranger, though Lucinda had not yet been able to spot the ringleader. There was always an organiser, a facilitator, someone who coordinated the rest. Greene? He was in a position to know what was happening. Costerman had the muscle to perform the abduction, and the village bucks would take on the job with glee. There would be a minister and possibly a solicitor, though Oldfields was too small to have its own bank branch. Whoever was in charge represented the most trusted guardian of an ancient secret. The position might be hereditary; continuity through the ages was one of the best ways to hold any matter sacrosanct.

Part of Lucinda wondered, even now, if she should turn over what she knew to the police. These people were guilty of more than one murder—yet she understood them. They were keeping faith with the traditions of antiquity, venerating a *thing* belonging to these islands that might have been old when Caesar came ashore. She reminded herself that to the tribesmen of the Dark Ages and earlier folk, it was a *god*. Faith had a tendency to endure.

The thought that twitched the corners of her mouth while she concentrated on the scrolling newsfeed was that if these people were asked, no one would believe in vampires. What a towering irony, she decided, that their faith in a long-forgotten god should bring them into collision with powers of which they could not conceive.

Cautiously, she let her shield lower just a little and carefully peered around at wavelengths to which few mortals were ever privy. She felt an inrush of strange, dark emotions—enough to make her nauseous—but they were entirely human in origin. This was the thrill of the chase. The sick expectation of murder. The dark delight was closely related to the hunter's simple, morbid 'kill pleasure,' albeit twisted into a bizarre piety rooted in beliefs from time immemorial. But at that moment, she perceived no psychic 'tang' to suggest that things beyond the ordinary—*her* ordinary—walked here.

Satisfied, she locked the shields back into place and concentrated on the task. She had some vermin to scatter.

* * *

They came for her in the early hours.

She lay awake in her bunk, fighting the impulse to 'do for them' here and now. If she wanted to make a lasting statement, it must be as theatrical as their own ritual, which meant playing along. She lay under several blankets in the chill; the van stood in a siding off one of the narrow farm roads between long, empty fields, situated where she would see the sun rise across the saturated land's ruts and runnels. Rain had gone through earlier in the evening, with a harsh rattle on the roof.

She had slept in sweat pants, top and thick socks, and she wished these people would get on with it. She found herself mildly amused; this was the first time she had tackled a foe with neither sword nor gun. But another part of her was bored. Fond thoughts of a sumptuous guestroom upstairs at the Lodge ran through her mind as the wind rocked the van—and at last she picked up the sensation of impending malice. They were here.

Now, Lucinda smiled, looking forward to the moment when she would turn the tables. She rose in the dark, pushed her feet into sheepskin boots, and wrapped herself in a blanket as if she had merely fallen asleep at the tiny table, working with the tablet and camera. When a crowbar forced the van's locked door and dark figures bundled in to tackle her by torchlight, all she needed to do was cry out as she had heard mortals shout, and let the men do as they would.

Duct tape sealed her mouth and bound her hands. Promptly blindfolded and hoisted over a brawny shoulder, she listened as her keys were snatched from the table, so they could move the vehicle. The psychic flavour of Joe Costerman imprinted on her like a strobing flash before they dumped her into the back of a battered farm truck.

It made its way swiftly through the dark and backed into a yard after just a few minutes' journey, which meant a nearby farm. Costerman lifted her again and carried her into a chilly building that echoed softly and smelt faintly of cows. A hard bed awaited her, and he bound her to the frame by one wrist with duct tape. Then a rough and odorous blanket landed over her, and she heard the door close—bolted from the outside.

As abductions went, this one was workmanlike enough. The fact that she could so easily have escaped made her smile in the darkness, and she settled to sleep, if not comfortably. They would come for her when the time was right—probably tomorrow night. Cults always had rituals to be performed in preparation for a grand sacrifice. All attendees must spend the next day in some form of purification—little details that reinforced that murder constituted a sacred duty.

She slept a while and woke to the lowing of cows in the fields and the thump of gear at milking sheds not far away. A few birds sang, and eventually she sensed that the late dawn had arrived. Eventually, the door opened, admitting a rush of cold air, and she heard two pairs of feet.

A knife slit the tape at her wrist, and a voice grunted one word. "Up."

She sat, and when she raised the blindfold, no one stopped her. A tough, dour-looking man in gumboots, raincoat and knitted hat looked down at her with cold, merciless eyes. At his side, a young woman of sour demeanour held a tray, which she set down on the end of the rough worker's cot—porridge and tea.

"Eat," was the blunt suggestion, and the man nodded at a corner of the grubby, whitewashed stone room, where they had left a privy bucket and roll of paper. "You'll have visitors later. Just behave yourself." They stepped out without another word.

The tape peeled off, and Lucinda took the offered meal. The experience made her heart all the harder as she imagined the stark terror of mortal victims who had suffered this. She was in no danger—no matter what humans did to her, she would heal, repair and return, even from deep coma. She might not enjoy it, but to vampires, pain was an old friend that tended to feed their appetite for a rebalancing of accounts.

But what of the men and women who had seen this shed or others like it around the district—their last place of uncomfortable rest before they were taken out and... what? How would the sacrifice be made? Probably the knife. Bladed weapons were traditional. The fear and depth of prayer into which even an atheist would descend when only hope remained—these were the true pathos here, and the crime to be avenged. If it were not for the blackdog mentioned in the ancient text and the tangible sense of evil that pervaded Oldfields, Lucinda would have assumed she was up against entirely mortal adversaries this time, no matter the supernatural motives. The vampire in her knew better.

The girl returned for the tray an hour later. She said nothing, made no eye contact, and when Lucinda tried to speak to her, begging to know something, she hissed threateningly. From that point, the hours unwound with leaden slowness. In the midafternoon, the big farmer came to fetch her at last. He blindfolded her once more, and, guiding her with a hard hand on her elbow, brought her to the farmhouse.

She let herself be steered to a straight-backed chair and blinked as the blindfold was removed. The farmer faded out of the room. At Lucinda's side was a small table on which stood a cup of steaming tea and a bowl of sugar cubes, yet before her was an incongruous sight. They had strung a bedsheet from the floor on some sort of frame of rods, to create a screen. On the other side of it, the one who controlled this ancient murder cult was anonymous even now—lest the unthinkable happen, she guessed, and she should escape.

"Drink, my child," came an elderly man's deep, soft words, breathy with congestion. "You must be cold."

She took the cup, sniffed, found nothing untoward, and then inspected the sugar. Was there a shadow in the lumps? She added two, stirred, and swallowed half the cup at once. "Who are you?" she ventured in a small voice. "What do you want with me? I have no money; my family isn't wealthy. If you're looking for ransom—"

"Nothing so crude," was the almost paternal reply.

"You have been chosen to serve a greater purpose. One you may take pride in, if you are so disposed."

"Pride?" Chemical relays adjusted in Lucinda's brain; molecules locked into one another. She had just been drugged. Probably a strong tranquiliser, she thought—they were being oddly civilised about this.

"This is an old land. Old ways die hard, as they say. Among the haystacks, ancient memories predate even the Romans' coming. Somerset is one of England's richest farming regions, and it is our modest belief that we have played a role in this. It doesn't matter whether you believe such things, but whether *we* do. And we preserve the ways of our ancestors, who traded something of value...for something of *greater* value."

"My life is not yours!" Lucinda injected anger into the words as well as fear—spirit counted.

"We acknowledge this freely. We have always acted contrary to the laws of God and man, but we recognise a deeper obligation. There were gods before Jehovah, and all the saints' zeal could not remove them from this land. Long, long ago, a bargain was made between a protector spirit and the people over whom it watched. Our ancestors agreed to give up one of their own in exchange for a bountiful harvest. Just as the Maypole and the Morris men have lasted down the centuries, along with the Green Man, the *sheelagh-na-gig,* and all the other country traditions, so have older, darker ways. Ways not spoken of by the light of day. Yet upon them rests our well-being."

Lucinda sipped the tea. "You're the vicar, aren't you?" She fired the observation bluntly, tangentially. His lengthy silence assured her that she was right. "I've heard priests before, and they have the same timbre, the same lilt, when they deliver a sermon." She knew she was speaking out of character; he must sense *something* other than the innocent traveller they thought they had snatched. The time had come to instil doubt.

"That's not your concern. Your only concern is to pass through this ritual with whatever dignity and composure you may. The end is preordained. You see, you are far from the first."

Lucinda let her voice slur a little, though in fact the powerful sedative only made her comfortably mellow. "You hear about all kinds of crazy people in the country. My God, you're going to kill me." In character, *Sally* looked around desperately. She did not see or hear the farmer waiting in the hall to cut off any run she might attempt, but he had to be there.

"Think of it not as death but as a translation to a higher plane where you will be joined with all you believe in. To go in possession of your health and faculties and be spared the depredations of age is an end to be welcomed."

She made noises of disbelief. "I don't want to die!" She said it feebly, as if the drugs were taking hold now.

"Gently, my child," the unseen minister soothed. "If you are a daughter of the Church, be assured that you will receive all the proper ceremony."

She grinned, fought back a chuckle, and spoke again in a slur. "You people are insane! You have no right...no right..." She rose, made plenty of noise as she stumbled a few steps, then let herself go down. "Help me, somebody —" Her last cry was pathetic, with the right mix of desperation and horror as she succumbed to the drugs. Closing her eyes, she heard the priest rise.

His last words came clearly. "Be at peace, child. You merely go ahead of us to that place for which we are all bound."

Heavy footsteps. The smell of muddy gumboots reached her nose. The farmer crouched at her side; she felt his rough touch as he lifted an eyelid and remembered to roll her eyes back in her head. Convinced that she was out, he grunted a confirmation to the priest.

"Prepare her," the holy man said softly. "We will gather in the grove at seven."

*   *   *

Pretending to be unconscious was difficult while they carried her to another room, which was warm and softly illuminated. There, they laid her on a table, and, eventually, women came. She felt their auras, heard their tread, and sensed the reverence of their touch as they stripped and bathed her. They dressed her in a white gown, anointed her with sacred oils, and placed a crown of autumn leaves on her head. They ceremonially bound her wrists before her with a rope made from dry hay stalks. It wound into an ornate corn dolly, forming an infinity loop as it closed.

Scented candles flickered around her when, alone again, she opened an eye to scan her surroundings. The iconography was neither pagan nor Christian, but some strange combination; these people had created and preserved a unique tradition. At the sound of approaching footfalls, she closed her eyes, felt a softer hand on her brow and sensed that it was the priest.

He checked her and spoke softly to others in the next room. "Well done," he whispered. "She'll be out for a while yet. All is ready."

Soon, many other people arrived and whispered in the adjacent room. She heard the hum of many minds before the priest called them to order, and powerful arms scooped her up from the table like a child. All the same, the man who carried her grunted—she was tall and uncommonly heavy for her size.

A procession had begun, Lucinda realised—out into the chill night air, moving without light along a well-worn path. They crossed a field; listening as a gate opened, she heard the soft rustle of night breezes in the fading season's foliage. The crackle of dry leaves beneath many feet sounded like ocean waves. She stretched out with her deeper senses, probing beyond the confines of her shield.

Now she caught her breath, and her closed eyes tightened as she sensed a strange, black space. So, this was where they did it—out here in the woods, under the sky. Perhaps shallow graves in this woodland contained bones dating back decades or centuries. The aura of death clinging to the place was almost nauseating, but she had trodden the line dividing the *here* from the *hereafter* often enough, and she clamped down on the reaction. A thread of bright humour gathered in her heart. In the long history of these devotees, she would be the first to see the looks on their faces when it all went wrong.

A guttural howl broke over the woods, and everyone

paused. Invocations were whispered before they pressed on, and the howl came again. It was more than a dog, more than a wolf. As she had so often before, she felt the etheric brushing of the spirit world.

Blackdog.

They were common throughout Britain—spirits of nature made manifest. People who did not understand the primal energy they embodied often depicted them as figures of horror and terror. Britain's blackdogs were similar to the Scandinavian Fenris, but Lucinda had no fear of them.

The deep rumble of a huge chest issued from the darkness, and the padding of massive paws crunching leaflitter and apprehension flared suddenly as Lucinda acknowledged that, as mortal as this murder cult certainly was, something higher had *always* taken an interest.

At last, she found herself lying on rough stone, and heard quiet movement as the procession formed a circle around her, a good distance away. Most villagers local to Oldfields must be here, and perhaps others from Bristol and Bath. A faint glow filtered through her lids—a taper was lighting candles around the circle. For the illumination not to betray the ritual, they must be deep in the woods. Any passerby might guess precisely what was happening.

At the priest's word, a soft chant began in some language that Lucinda did not recognise. Saxon? She heard his steps as he walked the circle, turning to the left, and opened her eyes narrowly to glimpse him striding with a long, sheathed, ornate knife upheld. Everyone wore dark robes, many with raised hoods—a mockery of the earnest and ancient pagan way. Her eyes followed the priest, a bearded elder whom she imagined delivering sermons on Sunday morning, and she wondered how he struck the balance between his profession and the older tradition he enacted here.

And as the villagers concentrated on their soft chant and the priest worked through his litany of appeal to a grim and forgotten deity, she *saw* it in their midst. Within the circle crouched the blackdog's half-translucent figure

—a mighty and menacing hound, double the size of the largest prehistoric wolf—

But to her sudden surprise, his tail was wagging. To her eyes, he lost the predatory aspect, the shaggy and staring coat, and the manic eyes of the hellhound of old. Little by little, he became just an immense black wolf whose eyes sparkled with entirely canine delight—and recognition.

Lucinda laughed.

The chant died abruptly. The priest turned, eyes wide, as she sat up on the boulder they used as their altar, and the blackdog—by now clearly visible to all—rose and bounded up to her, tail wagging furiously. A huge nose pressed into her middle; she fondled his ears, cuddled the mighty head, and looked up to sweep the villagers with a stare as she shook out her hair.

"You got it so very wrong," she breathed. "For endless centuries, you've been murdering to feed the god of the land, when all you've been feeding is a malicious spirit that thrives on fear and pain—and everything you feel is in your own black hearts. The land takes care of itself because that's what land does." She looked down at the giant wolf in her arms. "He's not here to protect *you*. He never was. He's here as the *psychopomp* who guides the souls of your victims safely across. And he's overjoyed, because this time there's no need."

Easing herself off the stone, she stood beside the wolf in the candlelight—a Celtic spirit, all red mane, white robe, and russet crown. She raised her bound wrists and applied her teeth to the tough stalks. The vampire's canines descended, and she raked their sharp points across the fibres. They parted with a dry snapping sound, and she brushed the remnants off her wrists. "The blackdog walks in eternity...and immortals always recognise *each other*."

Lucinda let the words hang, and wondered if anyone here understood. A moment later, she knew they were not that bright.

The priest drew the gleaming, engraved blade of the heavy sacrificial dagger and, with an expression of fear and outrage, hurled it with all his strength.

An instant later, it stood deep in Lucinda's chest. With a snarl like thunder, the blackdog turned, his hackles rose, and his lips lifted back from teeth that would crunch through bone. His ears flattened as he brought the villagers to bay in sudden terror, but Lucinda's voice cut across the scene like a bullwhip, bereft of any human quality.

"Stand where you are!"

In the soft light, they watched her hunch forward, hands clutching the dagger where the robe had stained scarlet. Blood laved her lips—the blade had buried itself in her right lung. But her eyes blazed with something far from mortal, and the villagers winced in horror as she exerted the vampire's strength to pull the blade free. With a guttural cry, she dropped it onto the altar.

The robe was red to the hem now, but she straightened, face contorted with effort. Her words were like ice water spilling down their spines. "You made of me an angel," she said gravely through a mouth full of blood. "Now, understand the demon."

She took several deep breaths. Blood foamed on her lips as the chest wound sucked, then she threw back her head and *spasmed*. When her head lowered once more, the villagers screamed. They had never imagined any such thing could be possible. The transformation was not merely the extension of her canines; her face had become inhuman, pallid, and distorted; her teeth were the super predator's rending fangs; and her eyes had the pure gloss black of a bird's. Her hair seemed to be flame itself; her hands were the talons of an eagle.

The vampire's battle morph poised as if it would tear these mortals limb from limb. The horrific rictus held for terrible moments before she relaxed and flowed back into human form. Her face returned to normal, and between one blink and the next, her reptile eyes became mammalian.

The blackdog watched and wagged his tail once as if he understood perfectly—but he remained between Lucinda and the priest.

The glade remained utterly silent as, with a smile of dark satisfaction, she glared around the circle. Reaching up, she tore the fabric to examine the wound over her right breast. It had already closed, healed by the transformation. She wiped away the blood with one thumb, sucked it clean, and stared at the ring of faces.

"You made me shapeshift." Her voice was sibilant, a snake's hiss. "That is the first time in fifty years. I don't like it. It reminds me that I have more in common with the Darklings than I find comfortable." Taking their sacred knife, she rammed the blade between two rocks, raised one bare foot, and stamped, snapping it level with the crosspiece. A gasp ran through the crowd. "No more ancient daggers. No more murder." She spread her arms, looked around, and roared, *"Where is your god now?"*

This was sacrilege—the profaning of sacred space, and they must look on it as the most perverse and unnatural reversal imaginable. The victim defied the ancient pattern, failing to succumb to the inevitability of death that ensured life. But the paradox stood before them, tangible yet unkillable, while the blackdog they revered as their spirit protector turned out to be *hers*.

Still, the keeper of this old tradition was not without recourse. Eyes blazing, the priest stepped forward and pointed a blunt, accusing finger. "We have stayed the course for two thousand years at least. The faith we preserve is older than that of the carpenter king. Witch or monster, whatever you are, you shall not prevail!"

With that, he closed his eyes and began another chant, different from the first in subtle ways. The circle joined in, raising power with deliberate intent. Feeling a cold wind swirl the leaves, Lucinda looked around. The blackdog came to her side but crouched low, subdued as he scented the etheric breeze; he might have retreated if not for his automatic loyalty to her. She felt a nexus of force developing as the chill in the air increased and frost glazed the altar—a mere nuisance to any vampire.

Well, I called out their god, she thought bleakly with a sudden sensation of dread in her belly. A moment later—while the wind rose into a swirling torment that sucked up leaves, stripping the trees in its paroxysm—she let herself transform back into the vampire's battle morph. When the wind died away, the hound's tail had tucked between his legs, and Lucinda felt the *evil* enter this place.

A concentrated ball of black energy hung over the grove. The villagers fell to their knees, silent now, terrified even to watch as their faith was reaffirmed a thousandfold. Crouching, the vampire extended razor-tipped paws to meet whatever emerged. When it came, she doubted the mortals saw more than a ghostly outline, but to her, it blazed like the sun.

Her heart fell. Mortals had no monopoly on mistakes, and she might have just made her best, greatest, and last. In the eyes of her psychic senses, it strode out of the night —a giant triple her own height, wreathed in foliage, a holly crown on its shaggy brow. She saw only its silhouette against the burning aura, and made out little but the overwhelming impression.

The Lord of the Seasons, she thought—at a loss, for how could even an Elderling contest one of the very forces of nature itself? A mighty, treelike limb came scything for her. She rolled with all her agility to avoid the stroke, and a rumble issued from the massive chest—frustration and more. Back it came, and she evaded again, claws ripping through autumn's sparse greenery.

She bounded high and struck at its shoulder, all the while wondering what she could possibly achieve. When the giant caught her in gnarled hands, tough as tree roots, and lifted her high, the vampire fury redoubled. But, held immobile and knowing every human eye was by now either tightly closed or transfixed with awe and terror, she stared into the darkness where a face should have been.

The apparition said nothing, as if its mere presence answered every question. She feared it would simply tear her apart—and then, like lightning from a clear sky, that very concept calmed and sobered her. The battle morph faded at once; she hung like a Celtic angel in the grasp of the Holly Lord and, as clear as daybreak, realised this was *wrong*. Her voice carried across the grove, over the giant's rumble and the wind in the trees. Every villager heard.

"The Lords of Oak and Holly demand no sacrifice." She stared into the darkness below the crown of exuberant greens. "They *are* the sacrifice that brings new life. I name thee *pretender*."

With a sudden growl of shock, the entity dropped her, and she crouched in the leaves. It stepped back, one hand raised defensively. The villagers stirred in consternation, still overawed but astonished when their god appeared less than all-powerful.

Lucinda sensed more than mortals ever could. She stepped forward warily, extended a hand, and her wild eyes saw beyond the mundane spaces. The presence was still strong, suffocating under the weight of its malign intent, and its self-righteous power confirmed her impression. Hate had never been in the Green Man's heart; in either phase of the year, he was life and love, not *this*. Never this.

And behind the façade, something very familiar was peering through. The evil that clung to these trees, dripping from the leaves, was the concentrated life essence of the murdered multitudes who had fed this entity—but it was no god.

She had dropped into the crouch of the vampire's bestial fighting pose, flickering between human and battle morph, but at last straightened and reverted resolutely to human form. The hound's ears rose, but he remained belly-to-the-earth as she put both fists on her hips. "Oh," she said softly to the cold air and the vast presence, "it's *you*."

A ripple of outrage raced through the villagers, and the priest blanched, but her attention remained on spaces these mortals only dimly perceived.

"I might have guessed. We've faced each other before, centuries ago. *Groyduur*, thou art a low spirit." At the pronouncement, the woodland shivered. The entity sent up a subliminal cry, which even mortals felt. "Thou art little more than hunger and hate. A master of deception—long have you feasted, posing as the King of the Green, the wheel of nature itself. *Yet thou art an imposter.*" With imperious disdain, she made a banishing gesture.

"Named, art thou, and powerless! I have called thee out, and by it, I bring thy reign to an end." Lucinda reverted to modern speech. "You know this. Take what you came for and go. And never, ever return."

Contemptuous, she turned her back on the half-visible spirit, strode with poise through the crunching leaves, and paused to slap the priest's shoulder with a smile of terrible intent. "The failure is yours. You attempted to serve up an immortal. Who do *you* think will be the demon's final meal?"

Now, the villagers bore witness to the hunger of the ravening entity they had believed was nature itself. They watched their priest scream and contort as a shadow flowed over him. In a seizure, he collapsed, writhing in the leaves. When it was over, the oppressive sensation in the air gradually diminished, and as the villagers' heads cleared, they stood shivering in a chill night.

The circle had broken up into knots and groups, huddling together for support. Many people wept, trembling. The blackdog was mostly transparent now; he began to fade rapidly from the world, since his task was done.

"Listen to me," Lucinda said, her voice carrying to them all. "It is *over*. But I know old ways run deep, so I'll be here again thirteen years from now to make sure of it. And thirteen after that, and thirteen after that. I'll still be coming here when you are all dust." Her voice rose like that of a drill sergeant. *"Do you understand?"*

Heads wagged. They were too shocked not to comply with whatever she demanded.

She walked the arc of terrified villagers, and when she found Jonathan Greene, she threw back his hood. "Your village doctor is in on this?" She gestured at the priest's body. "Better get that death certificate written. Heart failure would seem appropriate." She continued along the line, revealing faces, until she reached Joe Costerman. "You." She smiled like a death's head, and thrust one hard finger into his chest. "Bring my van to the farm."

As he raced to do as he was told, Lucinda turned

back to the circle. With the rush of fury spent, she felt the cold. The bitter night taxed her, making her shiver against the sticky residue of her own blood. "And the rest of you—get this place cleaned up. Get your story straight, and consider yourselves lucky. You should spend the rest of your lives behind bars. If I were the kind of vampire they tell stories about, I'd drain the whole pack of you!"

Her lip curled in disdain as she gestured dismissively before following Costerman's path out of the wood. The blackdog bounded after her, and the last the villagers saw was her pale outline receding into the black of night, with the spirit wolf at her side.

* * *

A handyman on Hungerford's staff repaired the motorhome's door; there would be no questions when she returned it, and Lucinda was quietly pleased. In the past, she had been criticised for being closer to mortal than true Elderling, and fonder of blades and guns than a vampire needed to be. To resolve a challenge without resorting to either was a vindication. True, she had used the battle morph she abhorred, but one must fight with the weapons at hand.

She woke in a broad bed upstairs at the Lodge and was loath to move until the late dawn had past. She looked up at the Georgian floral mouldings, which surrounded light fittings that might have been a hundred years old, and sighed, troubled by the thought that this murder cult could have existed unnoticed throughout all her tenure on Earth, feeding a supernatural parasite with innocent lives. She had learnt—many times over and in a variety of unpleasant ways—that the world is neither a kind nor forgiving place. Her consolation was to eventually put an end to Groyduur's bloody indulgence.

Emerging from her room a little later, she saw Hungerford coming up the stairs. "G'morning, Mistress Crane," he began in his bluff way. "Mistress Silver asks you to take breakfast with her in her study."

"Pleased to," Lucinda murmured, and skipped downstairs with an energy that told her she was quite recovered from the experience.

Desdemona sat at a wide desk, framed by a bay window in which the grey day made a sombre backdrop. She rose to offer her guest a hug. "You're entirely yourself today?"

"And remaining so." Lucinda mimed a shudder. "I hope it's another fifty years before I'm forced to shapeshift."

"I wanted you to see history in the making." Desdemona gestured at the desk's monitor, which displayed a transcript of all Lucinda had told her last night. After a bath and a meal, she had reported the adventure in detail, and had noticed a recorder taking her words down for posterity. Now she saw why.

"*The Vampire Annals,*" she breathed softly. "One always thinks of them as the dusty tomes downstairs, but the tale is never complete."

"Precisely. So long as vampirekind endures, new chapters will be written. Not *every* exploit finds its way into the pages of the chronicles, but enough do to continue the unbroken history of our people."

Across the sumptuous room, a printer slowly delivered a wide sheet of curious stock—a heavy, cream, fabric-finish hemp paper, on which Desdemona's account of the Somerset affair appeared in large type and a mediaeval font. Illuminated capitals embellished it; a digital illustration, in ancient style, of a magickal dagger based on Lucinda's description accompanied the text.

Desdemona flipped the sheet and fed it back to the printer; the job continued with the next page of the account on the reverse side. While it passed through, she ran a hand over the leather-bound volumes on the library shelves. "Not exactly editions of one copy—there will be several. Up here; down below, and copies for the libraries of other vampire Houses. We choose to remember in our own way."

With a knock, Hungerford propelled in a serving trolley bearing a choice of tea or coffee, waffles and syrup, hot rolls, conserves. When he had stepped out, Lucinda arranged a chair opposite Desdemona. "So, which affairs do *not* find their way into the annals?"

"Oh, anything...contentious, shall we say? Far be it from me to advertise your role in the desecration of the tomb of a feared ancestor!" She smiled sweetly. "*Shh.* Those things are for the confidential record. Should the politics ever allow for it, they'll become part of the mainstream register."

"That might take some time," Lucinda said with a wry expression. "I'm still hoping the matter hasn't come to the attention of some very old members of this community."

With a sly look, Desdemona poured coffee. "*They* knew the instant you took the *vincula*. But don't worry. They smiled indulgently, wagged their immortal heads and said *clever girl*. You solved the problem without them needing to get their ancient paws dirty. Nobody else was any the wiser, and the matter is finished." She passed over a cup and unfolded a napkin in her lap. "But not all vampirekind are so tolerant. While your adventures continue to bring rough justice to all manner of occult *things*, our ancient hierarchs are unconcerned. But matters that come closer to home must be assessed for how they disturb the balances between the great Houses. It doesn't do to foster animosity among clans who have found their peace."

"What do you mean?" Lucinda asked cautiously.

"Tread carefully. You chose the solitary life, which is fine. But you know, as well as I do, there is a hidden society dwelling beyond mortal sight. In this modern age, it is more important than ever that we do *nothing* to bring ourselves to the wider world's attention."

"I'm always mindful of this," Lucinda replied, her tone in no way defensive.

"Good. Because for all the good you do, and despite your struggle's fairness and the righteousness of the fights you pick, some of our elders would declare you dangerous. You walk *too* close to the mortals. If you were ever to jeopardise vampirekind as a whole, you would find your battle taking on a dimension you never expected."

Lucinda accepted the advice in the kind spirit in which it was meant, but the warning lay heavily on her.

She had always known she walked a narrow path between the mortal and the immortal, and she had no wish to court disaster.

They finished breakfast, and for now, she focused on the good. *Someone* out there owed their life to her intervention, though they would never know how close they had come to death. At the window, gazing out across the Somerset Levels in the grey autumn morning, she discovered a smile and raised a toast to that unknown soul. "You're welcome," she whispered.

The Last Revenant

York is an old town—old enough for an immortal vampire to feel less out of step with the world than she did in the bosom of the modern era. The city began life in the first century as the Roman Eboracum; it became Viking Yorvik in the ninth, and was ancient long before Lucinda Crane took her first breath. But December's rains and dour skies made a strange backdrop this year as she turned five hundred years old; she could reflect on her wanderings, the crusades, and all the people she had known. True, it was easier for a Lightling to blend into the human world than for the Darklings who haunted the night; this was the chief reason her first and deepest allegiance was to the mortals among whom she was born.

Daniel Tate was a *patron*, one of the network of trusted friends she had built up all over the British Isles. She never asked for more than two or three feedings in a year from any of them; her needs were not onerous to a healthy human being. They gifted the blood that was the staff of her life as an act of devotion, freshly let or chilled in a glass. She never created changelings by drinking directly from the vein. She had learnt that lesson in the seventeenth century and would never repeat it, but she was always there for her patrons when they needed her—she had devoted her life to the service of humankind.

Daniel's email arrived early on this rainy Saturday morning at the house Lucinda leased—a country property in a suitably secluded spot on the Lincoln fens. Intrigued by his approach, she made a booking at the Principal, the elegant hotel by the station, and drove up to York. Now, she sat in the Refectory Kitchen and Terrace Restaurant, looking out over the topiary hedges and green lawns that stretched away to boundary trees, and whiled away the time with Irish coffee.

The Goth look had been her disguise and defence for

many years, but she adapted it depending on the circles in which a particular task compelled her to move. Today, black jeans and high-heeled boots with a russet sweater and long leather coat were all the statement she needed to make. The expensive, branded clothes were appropriate to the venue; her blood-red hair and the strange intensity of her presence completed a picture that fascinated others yet kept them at arm's length.

The restaurant was quiet. She stared out at the clouds lowering over the old city, watching rain mist the outline of York Minster, the cathedral that was once the tallest building in Europe. It had stood for over two hundred years before she was born—as had the nearby city walls, which were repaired and rebuilt in the Middle Ages. Only one remaining tower and the lowest courses of stone in those walls were not Norman but Roman. The ages crowded close, tangibly real to one who felt the currents of time and history, as vampires did. She luxuriated in the sensation of time-depth made resonant by human *doings,* and was almost regretful when her friend's arrival demanded her attention.

Rising, she enfolded him in a brief hug before beckoning a waiter for fresh coffee. Daniel was an academic, a folklorist who knew every legend, every enchanted tree, and stone-of-the-ages from Harrogate to Bridlington, though Southern Yorkshire was his specialty. They had met through an antiquarian society. He was getting on a little now, and his grey hair had begun to retreat, but his delight remained undimmed in knowing a world that was far wider than the five senses revealed most definitely existed.

He stretched a hand across the table to squeeze hers. "Thanks for coming, Lucy, my dear," he said softly, keenly aware that he had become visibly her senior in the twenty years since he had first gifted her with his blood. "Happy *quincentenary*, by the way."

"It's not every year you turn five hundred," she said with a smile. "The actual date is in the New Year, but..."

"You don't look a day over three-fifty, tops," he added with a chuckle.

They were silent as the coffee arrived, along with a couple of menus. They perused the lunch offerings, but after a few moments, Lucinda caught his eye with a stare so direct, it called him right to business.

"Why did I ask you to come up to York?"

She raised a brow.

"Something that might be just the sort of thing you're looking for."

"Are we talking an investment property, an antique—or a *target?*" The last was a whisper.

"Very much the latter."

"Tell me," she invited.

"It's one of the strange ones." His eyes wandered down the menu. "You might tell me I'm either letting my imagination run away with me—or perhaps it's some phenomenon with which you're already familiar."

She smiled enigmatically, looking out at the drizzle over the gardens. "Old lands hide old things," she mused, and shrugged as if it were the most self-evident truth.

The soup of the day arrived for Daniel, and a steak for Lucinda, before he began the tale quietly. His voice almost blended into the rain that wove a silvery curtain outside the long plate-glass windows. Other diners heard nothing. "What do you know about the late-mediaeval belief in the walking dead?"

She looked up, pausing, her knife in mid-cut. "Twelfth to thirteenth centuries," she said slowly. "Widespread in northern Europe. Archaeological evidence has come to light, suggesting it was also far from unusual in Britain. Old tales are borne out when we find graves with occupants who were decapitated or whose limbs were smashed or burnt before burial."

With a wry smile, Daniel raised one grey eyebrow. "Anything to keep the dead from rising once more to the detriment of the living." But his manner became brittle, and he hesitated.

At once, Lucinda sensed something ominous. "What?"

He took his time replying. "Strange things are happening, Lucy. Old legends take hold of people—they live, even now, and not just in folklorists' imagination. Some villagers up in the Wolds are running scared. People lock and bar their doors, close the shutters at night, and farmers keep the shotguns handy. Something makes dogs howl in the night. *Something* scratches gates and barn doors; *something* trips security systems, so floodlights come on, though cameras never catch it."

"An animal?" she wondered, taking a sip of claret.

He shook his head slowly. "Only if it goes on two feet. With all this rain, the ground's often a quagmire. The prints look like a man's—but what man would be barefoot in this weather?"

"Police?" she asked, just as quietly.

"They're looking for someone trying to be funny—somebody who thinks it's a big laugh to reawaken old fears by playing the ghoul. The police are concerned someone will let fly with the old rabbit gun and bag a teenager out on a dare, a university prank or some such thing."

"But you don't think that's likely." It was a statement; she read him plainly enough.

"It's possible. Perhaps." He ate in silence for some moments, then looked up at the planes of her ageless face—the bottomless depth of eyes and character that had captivated him long before he knew why. "The fact remains: cameras *should* have spotted him. The police are no amateurs at debunking nonsense. In the last two weeks, they've got nowhere; now we're finding sheep torn to shreds, gnawed and drained of blood—which is pleasing the UFO nuts no end, of course. A guard dog had his neck broken. No ordinary person can break a rottweiler's neck and yet leave no other sign of violence on the body. It *can't* be done."

"How do the police explain it?"

"They're keeping *schtum.* Whatever the pathologist reported, we're not going to hear it. But people in half a dozen villages from North Grimston to Fridaythorpe are thinking about calling in an exorcist. They're scared, Lucy." He patted his lips. "Now, your experience predates us all. So, how does this strike you?"

She chewed the juicy steak for a long while, thinking, and at last raised one shoulder in an elegant shrug. "You intrigue me," she said simply.

"Just...intrigue?"

"Intrigue is where it usually begins," she added with a sly smile, and rattled the keys in her coat pocket.

* * *

The chequerboard of fields stretching across the Wolds from York to the North Sea coast wore its winter green. In many places, standing water turned mirrors to the sky, and in the days ahead, snow would clothe this land. Global warming had not yet robbed Britain of its white time.

Twenty-four kilometres northeast of York, Lucinda pulled over on a secondary road beside the waterlogged fields, and the 2010 Jaguar XKR's supercharged V8 whispered into silence. The rain had eased. Fingers of yellowish daylight reached between the hurrying clouds, and the vampire relaxed to *feel* the day...the place, the time.

Wharram Percy is a famous heritage site where the foundations of a mediaeval village can clearly be seen alongside roads that have been in use for a thousand years. It is open to the public, though at ground level little remains. Yet this, Lucinda knew, was the spot where, in 2017, archaeologists found a cemetery whose skeletons displayed the kind of mutilations referred to in ancient documents as 'post-mortem measures to ward off the return of the dead'.

In the Middle Ages, it was thought—genuinely *believed*—that cantankerous or ill-spirited people became vampires after death and would claw out of their graves to molest the living.

Lucinda sat in the car for a long while near the old roads' intersection. They were metalled now, but still followed the routes of byways trodden since Norman times. She had been here before; the spot was connected with the vampire tradition—and any place this old was manna to her soul.

She was alone; the weather provided solitude. At last,

she stepped out, zipped her coat against the chill wind, and drew on the broad-brimmed hat.

The car locked with a flash of its lights, and she walked along the road towards the intersection's curve. To her left, a two-storey manor house had once stood—the local squire's grange—while workers' cottages trailed off on the road that crossed this one, all gone now, but for the church and millpond, lower on the slopes. The village had been abandoned a generation before she was born. She shook her head with a sad smile. If Wharram Percy had survived long enough for its existence to coincide with her own, she would have counted her return as a completed circle in time.

Afternoon's low winter sun made a bright halo through a last mist of rain as she stood in the roadway, hooded eyes going from one hummock in the green sod to another. Her mind's eye *saw* this place as it had been when it lived. Centuries before the first spark of electricity was tamed, it was a land of silence and wind, save for the bleat of goats, the ring of a blacksmith's hammer—or the cries of the tormented. They were difficult times when the heavy hand of overlord, soldiery, or church was never far away.

She cast her mind back to her own youth, when she was the proverbial 'slip of a girl' in the 1530s. Her own ill-starred flirtation with marriage—and the age's expectations—ended so badly. She was still unwed in her twenties, and people called her a witch even before she met the vampire who gave her the gift of immortality and, with it, the responsibility to accomplish what mortals could not.

Her name was Henriette of Anjou. In 1541, she gifted Lucinda with eternity and near-indestructibility—powers that continued to serve her in the twenty-first century. Henriette had become the Caroline van Alt who lived on an isolated estate in Norfolk and remained one of Lucinda's most beloved friends.

One of the vampire abilities was the capacity to access the deepest levels of cognition. She had only to extend her psychic senses to perceive the currents of nature around her—and the presence of other vampirekind, light *or* dark.

Her senses were prickling sharply.

Here, in the cold breeze, in the smell of the damp earth where stray sunbeams made the wet road shine, she extended a hand and felt for the world's etheric currents. Her palm tingled with each energetic 'aroma.' Yes, Daniel had been right to call her in. Something was out of place. A current of malice underlaid the shortening days, with their hurrying of life to be ready when the snows came. Its signature was acrid, foul as a burnt corpse, but it reeked of nothing more complex than hunger—unless one counted the bitterness of life betrayed.

Clearly, there was more to this than could be seen at first glance, and she must temper her approach. She had styled herself as a protector of mortals, and whatever had come back into this world in these past weeks faced an opponent such as it had never known.

An angry vampire, driven by hunger, passion, and fury, was terror incarnate. The vampire who was also a consummate warrior, controlled by logic and the calmness of inner peace, took 'lethal' to a whole new level.

* * *

The *thing* walked by night, and night was the vampire's natural environment.

Back in York, Lucinda spent a few hours resting, but when the short day ended—the sun set in flurries of red and angry yellows not much before five in the afternoon—she was alert and already in 'hunter mode.' She spread an ordnance map of the Wolds on the end of the bed and worked with the tablet, studying the landscape in relief—the position of farms, main and minor roads, ponds, bridges. She had hunted things that did not belong in this world often enough to know the deep, dark places where they hid from daylight's scrutiny. Whatever this aberration might be, it feared light as surely as did any Darkling.

She had swapped the designer labels for tough outdoor jeans, boots, and jacket. Any vampire had the resilience to withstand extreme temperatures, but they seldom found the conditions pleasant. Up on the Wolds, the nighttime low would fall close to freezing point, so she took the hat and driving gloves, and from one of her cases unpacked a small thermal imager. It always paid to have the edge; she was one of the few vampires who wholeheartedly embraced modern technology.

The weapons were in the car—she had no intention of testing a modern four-star hotel's security systems by walking in with guns, or the sword in which she placed so much faith. She had long ago learnt to avoid legal entanglements—they complicated matters unnecessarily. It was far more convenient to move from place to place, unencumbered by the facile questions of mortals who *thought* they understood how the universe worked.

She pulled up a screengrab of a Wolds map, marked all the villages Daniel knew to have experienced one or more visitations, and calculated the median point between them all. She marked the spot with an X that fell on open farmland, about a kilometre west of the village of Burdale. Assuming whatever left those footprints was within walking distance of its daytime resting place, the odds were that she would find *something* close to that point.

With a grim smile, she packed tablet and imager, snatched up the keys, and pocketed her room access card. She headed out into the chill early evening, where the lights of York glittered in the sharp air, and, in the rank of parking places in front of the hotel, settled into the Jaguar. While the engine warmed through, she took a deep, even breath before pulling out and threading through the town to join the A166—east across the dark, open countryside.

Now she was hunting. This was the part she was best at.

* * *

She had lost count of the aberrant *things* she had dispatched.

Other vampires chided her for her sense of loyalty to mortals, often holding her at arm's length as a changeling who did not possess the purity of a vampire born. The powerful vampire Houses sat back and watched her war with dispassionate judgement, but they had never interfered in her protection of mortals. Sometimes, she benefited vampirekind too; the world was filled with strange, shadowy entities that cared little for the distinctions between one Elderling and another. She had learnt long ago that her innate strength and vampire speed were no guarantee of survival, let alone victory, and courted the warrior way instead.

Under a starless sky, she parked on a potholed sideroad in the lonely farmlands and stepped out into the knifing wind. Her eyes went to the odd yellow spark at the window of a farmhouse here and there, and the words formed in her mind: *You're welcome.* Few mortals were ever aware of the service she did for them, or of the protector they had. She was content with the anonymity.

Standing in the darkness, pupils wide open to catch the faintest glimmers, she buckled on the double pistol belt that accommodated the 9mm automatics, which she had lifted from the case under the passenger's seat. The razor-honed Katana lay in its own case, in the concealed compartment under the back seat. She secured the harness over her shoulder, locked the car, and walked into the windy blackness.

She never felt more alive than in such moments. Now she was primordial and distanced from mortalkind's petty affairs, the trivialities above which she had been elevated. Much as she loved them, humans could be insufferably naïve and even obstructive of much that was critical to their own welfare. But out here, there was only the night, the prey, the struggle.

Vampire pupils saw a night of greys and deep blues, a range of tones in which Lucinda perceived ripples on water and flurrying clouds as clearly as mortals could see on a deeply overcast afternoon. She found a high point in the landscape—a stile between fields where the night wind ruffled winter's rank grass—and stepped up.

Standing astride the stile, she scanned all around. She was loath to degrade her natural night vision, but used the thermal imager to view the horizon and picked up heat sparks in many places. Chimneys, a vehicle exhaust far away, the sudden flare of lights on a road kilometres off...but no body heat. Perhaps the creature she was after did not produce the heat of a living body at all. She lowered the imager and blinked hard. Her visual neurochemistry reset far more quickly than any human's would have.

With the local map firmly in mind, she marked her orientation from this starting point and jogged back across the open fields. She drove without lights—first north towards old Wharram Percy, then a couple of kilometres beyond, where the living village of Wharram Le Street was merely a hamlet built around an intersection. Pulling over outside the village, she stepped into the silent roadway and *felt* the world. The antennae of her psychic senses were by now hypersensitive to the land's currents.

And then she had it—a spark in the gloom, a stench in the mind, a sensation as if a greater darkness focused and resolved itself into a moving point of hate. She stared northwest across the fallow fields, and recalled the map. Yes, its stalking ground tonight was North Grimston again —a church, a pub, a farm, a horse breeder, half a dozen houses. As villages went, it was not much, but worth terrorising for a creature that was little more than blind and directionless hunger. Just for an instant, Lucinda picked up enough resonance to know instinctively that it was a vampire.

And in the same split second, she realised that it saw her too.

Unseen eyes stared at her across the dark countryside before she snapped off the connection and breathed a shaky sigh. *It knows it's not alone. Element of surprise lost. But there's no comprehension—just hate. No wonder those sheep were drained.*

Chancing the thermal imager again but seeing nothing now, she turned back to the car. The Jaguar followed the secondary farm road three kilometres north to its connection with the B1248, where she accelerated, and approached North Grimston two minutes later. She pulled into a stand of woods, far enough from the village to attract no attention.

With the car secured and the sword across her

shoulder, she ran southwest to close the distance. She fought through the wood's deep gloom, vaulted a wire fence, and crossed the local disused railway. The old track bed ran northwest, where she negotiated the fence on the far side and emerged into open country. Meadows and trees spread out starkly in the gloom.

Somewhere ahead was *something* that did not belong in this world. It might have the characteristic 'tang' of a vampire, but it was like no vampire Lucinda had ever encountered. This creature had no clarity, no purpose, or sense of self—just a hunger that would shame even the most sociopathic Darkling. It might not have taken a human life yet, but murder was inevitable. And if a mortal were accidentally turned by *this* vampire, Lucinda did not dare imagine the resulting, monstrous changeling.

Her task was clear. Moving with the speed of her kind, blurring from tree to thicket, she went to ground among tall, rank grasses before skirting the boggy patches where the land could no longer drain. At last, the quarry's psychic stench became overpowering.

Lucinda paused by trees half a kilometre from an isolated farmhouse, and strained her eyes in the gloom. *It knows I'm here.* Her hackles rose. The guns were silenced, but in a fight like this, she preferred the blade. She rocked the katana over her shoulder; the razor-honed steel gave a soft whisper as she scented the air like a hound, and listened with the vampire's superhuman ability. All her attention focused on this one moment, this single task.

Silence, but for the wind that whispered from the hard, chill dark...

Then she saw it.

It stood fifty metres off, staring fixedly in her direction, as if it were tracking too. She took a moment to force her pupils wider again, and, cat-eyed, made out a hulking, humanoid figure. Her lips compressed in disgust. This was not a troll or goblin. It had once been as unremarkable as herself when it came to passing among human beings. Yet now the beast seemed to have acquired almost gorilla-like proportions—distorted, as if it had tried to put itself back together after the awful mercies of some implement of torment. The head was a low, hunched outline over brutish shoulders; blunt and savage paws tipped the too-long arms. It was not unlike a vampire's battle morph, but this form appeared to be fixed.

After a few seconds, it crouched, emitting a guttural growl. A dog howled at the farm across the way. The tableau held for long moments while a few snowflakes swirled on the breeze—then the creature exploded into a headlong charge, as if it meant to wipe her out of existence.

Her response was automatic. She no longer needed to think when combat was joined. She erupted from cover and came at the apparition with the sword held two-handed. They closed the distance in seconds, and as the creature's battering-ram charge seemed about to overwhelm her, she jinked left, went low, and swung with all her strength. The blade bit between ribs and pelvis, but the juggernaut's terrific momentum carried it on. A baying howl of agony broke out of its throat, and it palmed its side.

They skated to a halt five metres apart, and Lucinda spun with the sword presented in the classic overhead block. Recovering its strength, driven by fury, the creature came at her again. She sidestepped right, twisted and brought the blade around in a scything wheel that matched the first wound with a second on the other side.

Now it howled in pain, stumbled, and came up more slowly, lashing out with huge hook-like paws to bowl her over. She tucked in tight, hit the ground with one shoulder, and rolled back to her feet faster than the eye could follow. The beast towered over her, and the foul stink of its breath reeked in her nostrils. She stroked right and left under the massive arms; the sword wove a tapestry of cuts, and dark blood blossomed on breast and arms.

As she fell back, the fury visibly drained from the creature in one strange and terrible moment. It sank to its knees, mewling horribly, and flinched from her, crawling away. A sudden sensation overcame Lucinda—nothing she had known before. She should have darted in and struck off the head to end the beast's rampage, then incinerated the body with thermite, but something held her back.

Perhaps it was the lost incomprehension in the creature's eyes, the consternation when its strength and hunger were defeated, or the pain as ichor flowed from open wounds that, by vampire standards, were closing only sluggishly. But most of all, it was the withdrawal, the retreat.

Pity was all she felt. She followed, careful to keep her boots out of its trail as it regained its feet and staggered south. Moaning hideously, it cradled its body in oversized arms, and abruptly, all Lucinda saw was a wretched animal looking for a safe place to hide. To die? No, this thing could no more die than she could—but its existence was misery. It stumbled on, at times going to all fours like an ape; she followed, wondering what she could or should do. She must bring an end to its reign of fear, this was a given. But...

She remembered the graves that archaeologists had opened not far from here. If this creature were the victim of postmortem mutilation, and *if* this were not simply a cantankerous mortal but an *Elderling*, then—despite death being temporary—the lack of oxygen in an airtight coffin would have slowed the vampire's healing response. It was just possible that what she had fought tonight was the result of the best repairs the vampire metabolism could achieve in eight hundred years.

How terrible it would have been to wake, buried alive—still physically broken—only to suffocate once more, and perhaps die many times over the centuries while the body laboured to heal. Inevitably, all vestige of sanity would be gone. She could have wept as she considered the creature's plight. This could have been herself or any other Elderling unlucky enough to *appear* to die, whether by accident or violence, in a community that feared vampires and believed mutilation of the dead was the key to exorcising them.

In this case, the people of Wharram Percy were almost correct. Had this Elderling received a gift of vampire blood soon enough and been allowed to heal, all would have been well. But this travesty was the best the body could make of smashed bones, severed tendons, crushed skull, and burns. It was not the individual's fault, but the vicious caprice of fate.

At that thought, Lucinda cleaned and sheathed the blade, still walking a little way behind the beast. *What can I do? Is there any way to reunite body and soul? Should I send it to the grave once and for all, as the only true mercy? No! I would undo this—if I could.*

It lumbered into a wood about two kilometres south, and she followed it through the trees until, at last, in the dimmest illumination her pupils could resolve, she watched the creature halt at a pit scrabbled in the damp earth. Was this it? A revenant's last resting place since the Middle Ages? There was no consecrated ground for monsters from the dark.

Dropping into the grave, it huddled miserably, shuddering and crying softly as its Elderling body strove valiantly to repair the damage. And all Lucinda felt now was regret. Instinctively, the beast hunted by night, suggesting that it had been a Darkling, which did not automatically make it her enemy.

Breathing a shaky sigh, she pulled out a special mobile—an untraceable account reserved for very special occasions. She thumbed a number from the list, one she had never called before.

The vampire House of Gratharn was an isolated country manor in the Pennines mountains, on the moors between Burnley and Bradford, and the closest she was aware of. She had never asked them for anything and had no quarrel with them that she knew of, so approaching them was only a minor risk.

In the sharp, crystal night, phone pressed to her ear, she wondered how to frame the request. At the response— an executive secretary, always available for contact with the outside world—she cleared her throat. "Good evening. You may or may not know me. I am Lucinda Crane, with allegiance to no specific House. I have a *situation* that… might concern you."

After a long pause, the deep, resonant voice said,

"Your name is not unknown to us. As far as we know, we are at peace. Continue."

"What would you do if you came across one of us, quite insane and unable to heal?" A long silence followed, while she shifted her feet in the frost and hugged her jacket closer as she began to feel the cold almost like a mortal.

"We would want to know more," was the reply at last.

She quickly provided details of the horror that had stalked the vales in these past weeks. "I stopped this... creature, but I cannot *help* him or her, except to end the misery that has persisted since ancient days."

"And this concerns House Gratharn—why?"

"You have a reputation for preserving our culture. Among our kind, you are known as champions of peace. This would seem to fall within your purview."

"Wait."

On hold, she stood for what seemed to be an age while fine snowflakes fell, and listened to the creature's faint whimpering as it huddled, alive in its grave. *Come on, come on!*

At last, the voice returned. "You are correct. This is a matter we should consider. Send your location."

She read off her GPS fix.

"Very well. Remain with the lost one."

The call ended without formality or nicety, and she looked at the phone, feeling rather brushed off. But if the Gratharni were as good as their word in their dedication to preserving vampire culture, they would be able to intervene. They would at least bring with them better knowledge of what had happened. Lucinda was seldom out of her depth, but here, she could do no more than kill for pity's sake. Sometimes, she acknowledged as she waited in the drifting whiteness, the way of the warrior did not *quite* cover all of life's bases. But House Gratharn had the resources and know-how, and they were willing to act.

An hour later, an unmarked helicopter appeared in the night sky, and four powerful vampires—silent, taciturn giants in black—alighted with chains and a cargo sling. She watched while they found the miserable, tormented creature; they stood around the grave in the sod and leaves, formed a circle of intense concentration, and gifted peace to soothe the beast's distress.

It had lapsed into the sleep of exhaustion when one of the Gratharni produced a tranquiliser gun. He delivered a heavy dose of sedative that should knock the creature out for some time, so weak was its condition. They chained it, loaded it into the cargo net, and boots crunched in the hard frost as they carried it away.

They had slung it from the helicopter's heavy-lift hook when one of the four offered Lucinda his hand. "We know how to contact you," the square-faced giant said in a whisper, soft as the night breeze, which eddied the fresh snow. "Thank you for your decision, but it is for our elders to decide if anything can be done. If this one's soul is long fled, it may already walk among us once more, and doubtless would not wish this vessel of flesh returned. We will do whatever is fitting."

They climbed aboard, and the turboshaft spun up from the hot-standby position. Locals would have heard the aircraft approach, but no one was willing to investigate on such a night. It flew without running lights, so no one would see it go.

Lucinda stood back and held a hand to her face as the craft generated a savage, freezing gale. Dragging the sling into the air, it receded into the west, on a heading to skirt Bradford on the way home. Soon the night was silent once more, and she was alone, melancholy, and troubled as flakes of virgin snow settled in her hair.

* * *

She kept clean jeans and shoes in the car, and struggled into them before returning to the hotel. Back in York at 3 a.m., she shared a silent smile with the night staff before heading upstairs to draw a hot bath. Vampires were a hedonistic race, and she loved her comforts. Still, she found little to elevate her spirits while the lost one's plight filled her thoughts. What she would tell Daniel Tate when they met again today, she did not know; perhaps merely that she had dealt with the matter and the Wolds villages would no longer be troubled.

Could that have been me? The thought returned over and over, while she lay in the steaming water. *I would have hoped to be shown some mercy—that someone would take pity and help. Centuries to escape a grave I should never have been in, only to find sanity gone and blood hunger all that remained—no, I would sooner not exist.*

She sighed, swirled the water, and shook her head. No matter how long she lived, the vampire life had a way of raising doubt, making her wonder whether its blessings were indeed a curse wrapped up in attractive packaging. If this were one more permutation of being an indestructible immortal, she had to question its value.

There was worse yet. The mutilation of corpses to combat the mortal terror of revenants had been widespread for so long that she must wonder—with a cold knot in her belly—how many vampires, whether Lightling or Darking, had found their way to such ends, ignoble and unknown. How many might still lie half-alive, broken, insane, awaiting their turn to live out a nightmare none deserved?

Vampire House

Lucinda sighed as she stepped out of the Jaguar in the gloom of a damp January night.

She looked down on the glimmering sweep of the River Stour among the bare woods west of Birmingham, and her breath plumed in the chill. She had parked among sodden leaf litter and crackling, fallen twigs off the northern arm of Boundary Lane. A few lights glimmered through the boughs from the Prestwood House apartments to her west and a farm to the east. Here, the woods were thick and stark, with the river a tumbling snake at their heart. Perfect country—for a short, sharp action.

The message had been cryptic and threatening: *Come to these GPS coordinates if you would see Carnelios alive again. Come alone; come by night.*

She called Carnelios immediately, but he was not answering his mobile, and this alone brought her from the solitude of her property in the Lincoln fens—across the country to the sleeping village of Stourton in Staffordshire.

The twin silenced automatics rode the small of her back under her coat. She slid the katana from its hiding place under the back seat and carried the lacquered sheath in her gloved left hand. In the midnight gloom, she stretched out with the vampire's senses, seeking the psychic spoor that would betray her opponent. Who dared lure her to this spot? Every instinct informed her that it could only be a trap—but for Carnelios's sake, she had no option but to spring it.

Nostrils flaring as she scented the night breeze, she sensed as much as smelt a taint that told her something eldritch was abroad tonight. The flavour was familiar—acrid, acid, filled with hate—and she nodded with a cynical smile. In the great rebalancing of life and death, what went around came around.

Once more, the time had come for her to enact final

sanctions. But against whom?

She had parted from the Darkling Anathriel on the best of terms, and to her knowledge, no Elderling stalked her. *I've made no new enemies lately,* she thought. *Maybe an old one?* But no flare of intuition warned her that perhaps Jane Covette had escaped the grave or that creatures even more arcane than vampires had taken an unkind interest in her.

She locked the car with a blip from the lights, pocketed the keys, and breathed a curl of vapour in the faint light. Racing clouds obscured the stars overhead as she unzipped the coat for quick access to the guns, and moved with the tread of a panther. She settled smoothly into the warrior's combat mentality—ready for battle, seeking the foe.

A few confused psychic impressions crowded in from people hundreds of metres away, who were safe behind locked doors. She tried to shut them out. Something carrying a psychic 'tang' like the clenched fist of fury stalked these woods, and in her five hundred years, Lucinda had learnt that the best way to meet such a monster was to be the greater fury.

But hers was the cold fire and refined balance of the warrior. She held her energy on a short leash, conserved for the sudden explosion that would come with *contact*, the moment the foe revealed him- or herself. She never forgot the lessons of a samurai master, long ago, who told her, *Hold rage in your palm as delicately as a flower. Do not crush it by allowing your physical self to react prematurely to the needs of battle. Carry it, perfect and whole, to be turned against the enemy only when the time is ripe.*

The winter forest was frosty under her boots, and she strode with caution, breathing in a slow, deep pattern. She had energy to spare, but husbanded it carefully. The call's urgency meant there had been no chance to visit a patron for the blood that charged the vampire metabolism. She must resolve this matter with what she had.

"Come out, come out, wherever you are," she whispered, sing-song, while her right palm tingled, counselling that she must draw the blade. But the adversary was taking his or her time, playing her like a fish on a line—a thought she found repugnant. She read in it either contempt or studied venom. *Who have I annoyed this much lately?*

She paused, pupils opening wide as a cat's and perceiving the forest in greens and silvers. A damp, mossy boulder lay among the stark trunks. She sat there, the leather tails of her coat masking the sharp cold as she drew the katana. She held it feather-lightly across her knees, waiting. Now, the initiative passed entirely to the foe. She had traded away the advantage of the initiative, and invited them to commit to the attack. But she also forced them to commit to a single course—and if it failed, the situation would suddenly be very different.

And fail it would. The boulder was at least four metres from the nearest trunk; she had space, which translated into time to react. She stretched out with all her psychic ability to search the treetops, catching a distinct impression of something like a huge leopard up there, an apex predator, though it had none of the wholesomeness of a natural creature. This was something else: something that watched with the eyes of focused fury and the poise of a hunter upon an unholy mission. She almost sensed its heavy breathing as it sized up its attack.

It was among the boughs, twenty metres away, invisible in the gloom. If she had brought the thermal imager, she might have seen the gusts of its hot breath, glimpsed the outline of rippling muscles in the infrared energy bleeding through its hide. But she relied on skills she had learnt long before technology came into this world.

Rising slowly, she stared unblinkingly into the maze of bare tree limbs, and raised the sword. She flipped it about her wrist before levelling the outstretched blade and pointing into the psychic spoor.

"Well?" she demanded of the cold, damp air. "Let's not be all night about this."

The moment stretched on. For an instant, Lucinda thought the challenger would withdraw, but the boughs creaked and rattled, and a shower of droplets shook from them as a powerful body moved in a blur. She wheeled the sword in a defensive arc as an impression of something monstrous dropped into her field of vision.

It was a vampire's battle morph—humanoid, muscles grotesquely bloated, with a face out of hell snarling below a hairless skull that displayed fangs to shame a rampant boar. It came at her with all the rage of the wild world. The eyes of madness glittered with the primal urge to destroy, to kill, and the creature moved with a confidence as strong as the world's foundations and near-indestructible. Huge arms flailed, reaching for her with rending claws; jaws clashed with the promise that they would rip out her throat with ease.

But Lucinda had been in this tactical position before. The katana wove a web of razor-honed destruction, leaving red lines across the massive arms as it kept the beast at bay. The creature's feral grunting filled the night; the stink of its maw was in her nostrils, and she fought with deep concentration.

Passing the blade through a vampire body would not end it, but striking off the head certainly would—the only physical injury capable of extinguishing the breed's infernal life. For that, she needed position, angle, speed, and power, but this adversary had the experience to evade every move. *Old! This one is old. It has the feel of the ages about it. It has won more fights than it can remember!*

Adhering to caution, she gave the beast its due. When it came on again after a brief respite, she drove it back with a flurry of parries, seeking a single opening to strike at the head. In a blur of swordsteel, she opened a gash over its right eye. It bellowed, a sound that would surely wake humans—dogs barked at the farm, a distraction she could not afford to acknowledge. The injury gave the creature pause, and she opened a safe space with a great sweep of the blade.

Their eyes met across a few metres. Her pupils dilated to gather the midnight glow of streetlights beyond the wood, and Lucinda strove to block out the urgent psychic pricking that informed her—not far away, humans were waking. She must end this and be away before attracting attention, especially if she were leaving behind a headless corpse that, in death, reverted to human form.

This vampire was ancient and aggrieved. It wanted her dead, but at this moment, *why* was not the most important question. Grasping the initiative, she advanced with a pattern of slashing strokes that drove the thing back, before it leapt like a tiger. It rebounded from a tree and lunged at her flank *almost* fast enough to beat her wheeling defence. She opened wounds across its left shoulder, and it bellowed in anger more than pain. Each wound closed with mesmerising speed. To have so much energy, the beast must have fed immediately before joining battle.

Frustration almost got the better of her. She *almost* overextended her thrust, *almost* became unbalanced, *almost* lost focus, but in the last heartbeat, Lucinda withdrew to recover equilibrium. The flicker of lights, back beyond the woodland, distracted her for a crucial split second.

A flailing paw swept her blade aside. In the next instant, the massive right fist struck home to her heart—not a piledriver blow, but a melding that left her frozen, pinioned helplessly with a dread such as she had never known before.

One bestial hand passed *through* her in de-phased state—occupying the same space as her most vital organ. Rivulets of cold fire raced through her body and, in the stress of battle, she fought to understand what was happening. Her sword arm fell; in another second, the Darkling knocked the katana out of her hand. With an overwhelming dread, she slipped backward from the aetheric impalement and fell to her knees. Both hands slid under the coat, clawing for the automatics, drawing them, flicking off the safeties.

The silencers hissed as both magazines emptied into the beast, point-blank. She watched as the rounds forced it back, step by step, while bloody rosettes opened across the torso and belly. But with the last round spent, the Darkling remained on its feet, the great chest rising and falling in ragged breathing as it exerted the vampire's ability to close the wounds one by one.

Thick fog swirled over Lucinda's mind. She knew she must reload—go for a head shot, anything to slow the beast down until she could cleave its neck—but her hands would not obey. She saw only the spectre of death. Did a five-hundred-year life meet its end in a wood near Birmingham? So much left undone, so many loose ends—she had no wish to die...

As the last wound closed, the battle morph flexed its massive limbs and stroked a hand down its worm-white body to brush away the blood. Its chin rose from its breast; eyes like hot coals burned into hers and a guttural chuckle issued from the massive throat. "Now, you die," it rumbled—and stooped, drawing back its left arm for the blow that would decapitate her.

A flurry of movement in the corner of her right eye—Lucinda caught a confused impression of a human shape, a familiar psychic 'tang,' before starlight flashed faintly on steel. The katana was scooped up from the leaflitter, but, intent on the kill, the Darkling was a split second late to realise they were not alone.

Sword met limb as the blow cut home; the creature's left parted at the elbow, and a monstrous cry bubbled among bloodshot fangs. The beast staggered back. The stump fountained blackly, and before Lucinda's eyes, the creature shimmered into a pall of sulphurous yellow-green flame and faded from existence.

The grotesque arm lay where it fell. She watched the figure at her side pin it with the sword's tip and fling the amputation into the river. Then her saviour turned, and a hand grasped her shoulder.

Focusing with difficulty while consciousness flickered in and out, Lucinda recognised the aura. "Is it Anna—Anna Darkholme?"

"Are you injured?" came the urgent whisper. The hand shook her shoulder. "Lucinda, are you injured? How do I help you?"

A strange feeling, which she identified as mortal terror, uncoiled slowly through Lucinda's mind. Whatever the Darkling had done to her, the effect was not fading. Anna helped her to her feet, and she could only gasp, "John Hales—Shepley Farm, Norfolk—take me to John Hales."

From that moment on, she had only blurred impressions of being fed into a car, not the Jaguar. A rug spread over her; a seatbelt clicked home. Then came rocking movement, as the vehicle left in a rush of blurred streetlights. She knew no more as she fell down a long, dark tunnel to a place from which she feared she would not return.

* * *

The next Lucinda knew, she lay in a bed, a lamp glowing at her side, and John Hales was sitting beside her, holding a glass of his own fresh, warm blood to her lips. His kind, craggy features were drawn with worry, the thrown-on sweater and jeans suggested that he had been woken abruptly. With the iron-salt smell in her nostrils, her fangs extended automatically; she drank greedily, taking every drop and a second glass for good measure.

The window was still dark. A digital clock showed 4.05 am, and she blinked through a haze of confusion. Anna Darkholme hovered behind John, a shadow in the black Goth attire and stark makeup who seemed out of place in the farmhouse's old-world charm. Lucinda coughed, laid a hand on her chest, and felt—not the rhythm of her heart but pricking sensations in her palm, echoes of the eldritch damage done earlier this night. Her T-shirt was gone, replaced with what she vaguely recognised as one of John's.

The fresh blood's rich warmth filled her; she sensed her regenerative capacities moving into high gear, but nothing affected the cold, dead weight in her chest. She blinked, exhausted in a way she had never felt before, and fear swirled around her mind. She found John's hand, squeezed it, and whispered,

"This is beyond me and well past the understanding of human medicine. There's someone you need to call."

He placed her phone in her hand. She pulled up contacts, indicated a number, and passed it back to him before her head dropped onto the pillow and consciousness fled once more.

* * *

The sun was still three hours away when the sound of tyres on gravel brought her around. Footsteps approached the farmhouse, crunching through Marshland Fen's stark quiet. In her mind's eye, she almost saw their owner—one as comforting and familiar as she might ever know in this life. Moments later, the door opened, and she heard the strike of heels on the hall timbers. She forced her eyes open in the lamplight, saw the figures framed in the doorway, and smiled.

Caroline van Alt was old long before Lucinda's birth, and had received the gift of immortality far back in history's mists. The ageless woman paused with an expression of the deepest concern. She wore a long, dark coat and a luxurious Russian fur hat over her blond hair. She tapped frost from the toes of her high-heeled boots. "Whatever has happened, my dear one?"

John and Anna hovered at the door as the ancient vampire swept off hat and coat, revealing a bright sweater and dark pants. She pulled off her gloves as she came to the bedside. Her expression clouded as she took in Lucinda's wan pallor, the fear in her eyes, and with hesitation, she hovered a hand over Lucinda's heart. Her eyes closed tightly; the hand clenched into a fist.

"*Bastard,*" Caroline hissed. "The foul, dishonourable *bastard!*" She mastered her passion quickly and turned back to the mortals' blanched faces. "You did the right thing. I know what has happened, and I can help. You've fed her?"

"A pint, fresh," John said with a ready nod.

"That is all the medicine a vampire should need, but this is—something else." She stroked Lucinda's cheek briefly and frowned at John and Anna. "If you could let me have some hot tea and a blanket...?" They hurried to find both, and Caroline sank into the chair beside the bed. "Trust me," she whispered.

"I always have," Lucinda returned, in a voice almost too weak. "I thought I knew every trick a vampire could play in battle, but not this."

"This is old magic," Caroline sighed. "As old as the Earth. I have not heard of its like in centuries. It will take time. Just sleep, dear girl. Sleep and heal. Leave the rest to me."

As she spoke, John reappeared with a mug of steaming tea, which he set on the bedside table, and a colourful rug.

"Thank you, Mr Hales. There is no more you can do," Caroline assured him. "I suggest you and your young companion take what rest you can. This is not going to be quick. But..."

"Yes?"

"Do you have weapons?"

"Weapons? A shotgun?"

"Load it with *salt*. It is crude, but vampires like it no better than do many other things that are not *quite* of this Earth. Then rest—with one eye open."

With the ominous warning in his ears, John stepped out, closing the door behind him.

"Now, my dear," Caroline said as she draped one knee over the other and wrapped the blanket around herself against the chill, "just relax. Relax completely." She steepled her fingers. Her eyes narrowed in concentration, and her trance deepened little by little as she went to work.

Lucinda nodded silently. Closing her eyes, she opened herself to the mystic touch of the one she trusted before any other.

* * *

Wintry daylight filled the window when Lucinda woke again, and with some surprise, she realised that it was afternoon. She lay in the bed she knew so well, upstairs at Shepley Farm, propped on pillows, with an electric blanket complementing the heavy quilt. The first thing she saw was Caroline, stirring awake in a chair by her side. Smiling, the elder vampire stretched over and enfolded her in a hug. "Welcome back," she whispered into Lucinda's ear.

"How long...?"

"I got here at five this morning. It was not easy, but you will recover." They broke apart and held hands. "Hungry?"

"Thirsty."

"For blood? I am sure the young lass could manage a pint."

"No. Actually, for tea."

"Good sign. Take a while to pull yourself together, then you have visitors who very much want to see you."

Feeling stronger by the moment, Lucinda sat up straighter while Caroline rearranged the pillows. "What *happened* to me?"

"All in good time. I think everyone has a story to tell."

Half an hour later, with tea on the bedside table, Lucinda was ready for guests. Curiosity had overcome her fatigue, and she searched for a scrunchie. Caroline opened the curtains to fill the room with as much daylight as winter might afford, and called the others.

Lucinda had been expecting John Hales and Anna Darkholme, but seeing Carnelios sent her eyebrows up. "You're okay?" she asked at once of the tall, ascetic vampire with the long hair and piercing eyes. "The call that lured me into that trap offered *you* as the bait, and your phone wasn't forwarding to voicemail."

He wore motorcycle leathers and looked as if he had put in a long night of his own. "It was stolen early yesterday," he replied in his pleasant, somewhat mysterious burr. "It took a while to get a fresh account up. I thought I sensed a presence—something on the dark side—but it was there and gone in an instant. Somebody knew just how to set out a bait trail to catch you."

The four pulled chairs up to the bed and balanced cups on the arms. Lucinda's eyes travelled around them— Caroline, her oldest friend and mentor; John Hales, her dearest mortal, looking exhausted with concern but relieved; Carnelios, vampire friend and comrade, hard but reserved; Anna Darkholme, the wildcard in all this, dressed in the subculture's Gothic black and pallid makeup and looking decidedly out of place.

"The last thing I remember is nearly losing a fight,"

Lucinda said softly. "Anna, I think I have you to thank for my life."

"That's where the story begins," John said, glancing at the girl. "We've become acquainted in the last few hours. I learnt all about that business in Shropshire. Miss Darkholme, why don't you tell us how you came to be there?"

Clearly uncomfortable among people, Anna visibly marshalled her thoughts. These were not just *people*; they embodied so much that had come to dominate her life. She set down her cup and spread black-polished hands in leather mittens. "When Lucinda saved me from the thing that'd taken root in my heart, she opened a whole world to me. I'd already gravitated to the dark side. I had the fascination, but since then I've *studied*.

"I had to learn what had happened to me from scratch. It turns out the whole possession—Lucinda drawing that thing out of me—opened the door to a lot more. I can *feel*. I can *sense*, I can *channel*. I recognise Lucinda's presence from miles away, and I know when she's in trouble. So, I came. I haven't seen her since the day I left for Birmingham, but something told me I *had* to be there.

"And it's just as well I did." She smiled, a tough expression in the midst of square-cut, jet-black hair. "Whatever that *thing* was, it won the fight. I didn't think, I just acted—pure instinct. I grabbed the sword and swung it with all the strength I've got. I didn't expect what happened. It disappeared."

Caroline nodded with a sage look. "It teleported, the energy demand for which is huge—and don't forget that it lost its arm. There is *one* vampire who won't be back for some time so, for the moment, we are safe—at least from that one. Go on."

Anna took a sip. "Well, before you passed out you told me to bring you here. That was a bit of an odyssey. I checked your pockets, but your keys weren't on you, so I put you in my car—damn, you're heavy, woman! Iron bones or something. Sorry, I had to abandon the Jag."

Lucinda looked around in sudden concern. "My

weapons? My sword!"

"Safe and sound." John raised both hands, urging calm.

"I hid them in my back seat, under some loose gear," Anna said quickly. "You were a mess, covered in blood—you were in the way when I lopped the arm. I tucked you up in a car rug and just hoped it was enough for appearances when I had to stop for petrol at a servo on the other side of Birmingham. All your supernatural entities aside, that was the scariest thing I ever did. Right in front of CCTV, I've got you in the front, looking dead asleep, with guns and a bloody sword in the back." She shook her head and gulped the tea. "Anyway, I Googled Shepley Farm, figured out the quickest way here—223 kilometres, mostly on the M6. I nailed the speed limit. At that time of night, there wasn't much on the road, so I got here about half past three. I phoned, and Mr Hales picked up. I told him I had a redhead called Lucinda who, uh, needed help."

There, John took over the story. "I know that blood is the best medicine, if you're hurt. I drew a pint at once. You had it at around four o'clock. We got you into the guest room downstairs. Your clothes were too bloody to be saved, but your coat should clean up nicely." He gestured at the wardrobe. "You keep plenty of things here. Anyway, you asked me to call Miss van Alt, and she came right away."

"I have a fair idea of what you did, Caroline," Lucinda said slowly.

With a pensive expression, Caroline deflected the ball of the conversation. "Carnelios first."

He gave a wide shrug. "Mine was the simple part, really. I felt the psychic fallout of the combat, and knew Lucinda's signature, but the other was…dark. In the extreme. I was in Wolverhampton, came as fast as I could but missed the action. I found the Jaguar. As luck would have it, I also found your keys—you lost them in the fight. I dowsed through the area, and there they were.

"So, I used my new phone to trace yours, got a GPS fix on it—heading fast up the M6—and followed. The Jag's in the barn. A friend took my car back, so there's nothing to tie any of us to any disturbance in the Stourton woods. Anyone investigating noises in the night probably found bloodstains, but without bodies, there's nothing to go on."

Lucinda laughed shortly. "Think of it. Vampire blood under a pathologist's microscope. If he only knew!"

"Anyway," Carnelios finished, "I'm here—and you've got me until this is sorted. Whatever *it* is."

"That's my cue," Caroline observed. The others looked at her expectantly. She took time choosing her words, at last speaking with precision and gravitas. "In the old days, what happened to Lucinda was called *Raptor Animarum.*"

"Stealer of souls," Lucinda whispered, her expression grim.

"It is a dishonourable technique. A vampire of exceptional power can de-phase his or her own matter— akin to shapeshifting into battle morph, which we all can do. Even my demure self. In this state, one can pass through living tissue. The trick is to reach in and jumble a foe's chakras, pulling the strings of their very life force. It would prevent Lucinda, from shifting into her battle morph and also prevent her from using metamorphosis to heal severe injury rapidly.

"It can be undone; things can be corrected, but it is a nasty ball of hate to remove. It took hours, then I slept like the dead myself." She smiled guardedly. "All is fixed, and John's gift of blood should have you fit again by the end of the day. But the question remains: *who* singled you out? Why was the attack prosecuted with such vitriol?"

In the silence that followed, Lucinda looked from face to face, deeply grateful for her friends and sorry to burden them. "As it happens, I can answer that. When he phased with me, I caught one glimpse of the mind inside the morph." Her tone was heavy, and she forced out the words. "His name is Vashtanya. He's an old one, a member of an ancient vampire lineage. And he is a brother of Javirand the Face-Changer."

* * *

Dressed warmly against the winter wind, Lucinda and

Anna walked in the wan afternoon sun, taking a circuit of drier ground above fields that lay fallow. Standing water shone in the low areas, and the Fen District ran on, green as far as the eye could see.

"I'm glad for the chance to return the service you did for me," Anna said quietly, hands deep in her pockets. "I look back on those days in Shifnal, and I know how close I came to losing my life. I invited the damn thing in, gave it a place to grow through morbid fascination—I suppose I was angry. Restless."

"You've grown up," Lucinda observed. "I'm glad you had the opportunity."

"I can only imagine the power it took to pull that *thing* out of me." With a remote expression, the young Goth squinted into the grey day. "When I realised what'd happened—and it took a year before I understood—I wanted to find you, beg you to teach me. But you don't want to be found, so I found others. Just shadows of your skill, I'm sure, but they had plenty to say, and I studied hard. Once I realised these things really do exist—not just in imagination, all the stuff we mess about with to blow off time that doesn't have any meaning—but really *exist...*" Anna smiled, an instant of sunshine. "I came alive like I never did before."

"And you want to stay that way." At Lucinda's tone, the girl looked up at her. "I'm grateful for your help, but we're all square. One rescue apiece. There's no call for you to risk your life in this."

Anna blinked scornfully. "Sod that! I learnt that vampires are as real as every other ghoul out there—more than most. I want to know more. I want to know what makes them tick. Hell, knowing immortality and the ability to heal are as close as a nip in the carotid makes me say, *Bite me!*"

The line made Lucinda chuckle. "There's a lot to being a vampire, and I wouldn't wish it on anyone. Living forever sounds great—at first. It can pale, I promise you."

"If that's a problem, it's one I'd like to have."

They laughed, picking their way through the rank grass as a sharp wind hurried across the fields. "This is a dangerous world, Anna. The path I chose is difficult. At times, ignorance really is bliss."

"But the blinkers are off now, for me."

"I know. I also know how fragile humans are. You survived last night by the skin of your teeth, and Vashtanya doesn't forgive or forget. Few vampires do."

"Then give me a fighting chance."

"Enough!" Lucinda spoke more sharply than she had intended. "Now is not the time. We have a mess to clean up, and it won't be easy. If I survive *at all.*" She glanced at her watch. "Time we were heading back."

They wandered towards the tall farmhouse, which nestled among its sheds and grain bins. Clouds flurried in grey-blue banks that blocked the westering sun, plunging the land into shadow. Anna let the point go; she had made her wishes plain, and no more could be said or done at this juncture. As the early January sunset developed into sullen yellows, with a few sunrays slanting through the clouds, they were glad to close the farm gate.

The house's lights welcomed the weary, and in the spacious old kitchen, where the open hearth crackled cheerfully, the long table was set for five. John had ordered half a dozen pizzas and two chocolate Bavarians; several bottles of red and white were open to breathe. When Lucinda and Anna had hung their coats in the hall, he poured all around. Savoury aromas circulated as plates went back and forth.

When each guest had taken a tall glass, the farmer raised his own in toast. "It's a day I thought might never come; the day I welcome Lucinda's friends from the *other* side of life in this world. There are Lightlings at my table and I couldn't be happier than to make their acquaintance." He gave Anna a smile. "And a new friend from similar paths."

The others raised their glasses, and Lucinda was first to speak. "Friends."

They echoed the sentiment, and dug in with good appetite. The sun had set before they were done. Each nursed a second glass and sat back, satisfied, but now was the time for serious discussion.

Caroline cleared her throat. "We have a lot to talk about."

"Like, what's to be done?" Carnelios added with a wry quirk of his brows. "We have an ancient on the loose and wishing you dead, Lucinda, my friend. So, what are we going to *do?*"

John raised a finger. "Pardon my mortal naivete—if that's what it is—but how long do we have to mull this over? Couldn't Vashtanya come back for more at any time? Miss van Alt had me prepare salt loads last night, just in case."

"Caroline," she corrected. "That was before I was sure of the facts. I would now say that we have some leeway. Anna, he left the severed arm behind when he teleported, yes?" At her firm nod, she went on: "Then, he must regenerate it, which means a heavy feeding and a deep sleep while his metabolism works. Two, three days—we are not in danger of attack just yet."

"How did he find you at all?" Anna asked Lucinda.

"Vampire senses," she returned evenly. "The same way you sensed the combat and were drawn to that place, but Vashtanya's ability is a thousand times greater. I *ended* Javirand up in Whitby, some time ago, Vashtanya has obviously emerged from a long sleep to find his kin absent. Perhaps he reasoned that I was responsible, given my long history with his clansman. Or he might have consulted those who know—the Great Houses keep the annals, after all.

"That's the problem, for those who sleep away the ages. They only touch down here and there in years, decades, even centuries, and the world changes so fast. One might wake in some hidden sleeping place to find oneself the last member of a doomed House." She shrugged. "Whatever, Vashtanya is coming for blood the old-fashioned way."

"He belongs to a family, a clan," John mused. "Will he wake his kin for reinforcements? What kind of force are you up against?"

"I doubt it," Carnelios mused. "I had a brush with this one long ago and I came to know something about him. His House is Clan Korsakof, which has member branches from the Balkans to Nepal. Javirand and Vashtanya belong to the Indian branch. Since the Middle Ages, the whole tribe has made merry by night.; some have died along the way, but the clan has managed to stay out of full-scale conflict with other Houses." He sipped his wine. "I remember Vashtanya being proud but egotistical and, above all, *arrogant*. He lived for the next score, the next conquest, the next trophy; he uses human souls like tiger pelts."

"Like Javirand," Lucinda murmured.

"Which probably gives us an edge. The last thing he'll do is wake the family for help. He wants to avenge his brother personally—then claim clan leadership on the strength of it."

"So," Caroline mused, counting points on her fingers, "the odds favour *one* foe, who will not be out of his regeneration for some days, and we are on the alert. There is no way to know when or where he will come, and nowhere in the world to hide. But hiding is not the object."

"No," Lucinda said softly. "The object is to make him fight on my terms, my turf. And I must win." She smiled, knife-thin. "I have to take the fight to him."

"My first thought is to put it on a more formal footing," Caroline murmured, eyes narrowed, sitting back with her glass. "There is a long and honourable tradition of blood feuds fought out under the Great Houses' adjudication. Vashtanya was looking for a quick kill before the matter could come to the old lords' attention. If he had killed you last night, my dear, he would be presenting your head to his kin and embroiling himself in the politics of clan mastery. His attack has as much to do with aggrandisement as revenge. But he failed, and he is on the back foot. He will be the bitterer for it, but House Korsakof *nominally* walks the path of vampire law. We can use this."

John coughed quietly. "Does vampire law apply equally to changelings?"

Caroline made a face, and Carnelios sighed in sympathy. "It depends," she went on. "You would think that after thousands of years there would be some universal understanding among vampirekind, but even now there are ancient ones—the progeny of unbroken vampire lines stretching back into the mists of prehistory—who consider changelings second-class vampires: lackeys and servants, lucky to share the same space with true vampires; definitely lesser, and probably undeserving of legal rights." She nodded at the mortals' surprised expressions. "Oh, yes. No wonder our kind choose the solitary way. Not every House treats changelings shamefully, but prejudice is very real. The trick is invoking the law and getting it to apply—which means appealing to the right ears." She turned to Lucinda. "Who would speak for you?"

"Desie Silver, in a heartbeat."

"But Desdemona is also a changeling. Anyone else?"

"House Gratharn *might* be disposed to give me a fair hearing. I had some dealings with them recently."

Caroline nodded slowly. "I have a clan affiliation via the one who turned me. I have never invoked it—however, there is a first time for all things. Carnelios?"

"Something similar. It'll be a bit of a minefield to explore. What about Anathriel?"

"Anathriel?" Caroline's brows rose towards her flaxen hair. "Where does a Darkling come into this?"

"We had cause to fight in common purpose not too long ago," Lucinda explained. "Carnelios and I found Anathriel to be wise and reasonable."

"All advocates are welcome. The Great Houses maintain an intricate web of allegiances and alliances, with responsibilities and obligations. It is how they have managed to not annihilate each other—which would only benefit mortals. Appealing to them in the right way is respectful. It honours the law and amasses credit for us. We can set the matter before the elders, let them make the ruling. The alternative is to enter into this battle alone: draw Vashtanya to an arena of our choosing, and let the cards fall as they will. The risk is dire."

"Of failure?" Anna guessed.

"Yes," Lucinda said darkly, "but more than my own

life is at stake. As I tried to say earlier—you interfered to the detriment of an old one, Anna, and that's marked you. Vashtanya will take you as sure as day follows night. He'll kill you—if you're lucky."

The girl's brows rose; her pupils were dark orbs in a pale face. "If I'm not?"

"He'll turn you. Use you as the lowest slave, so that your misery is absolute...and eternal."

In the uncomfortable silence, the five shared bleak glances. Lucinda clenched her clasped her hands on the table. "Putting this matter under the purview of vampire law means it should play out according to the most ancient code, which might afford you all some measure of protection." She gave them a brash smile. "All I have to do is kill the bastard."

"The merest formality," Carnelios added with an ironic grin. "How did you take his brother?"

"Silver bullets. No, seriously." Lucinda's face was a granite mask. She raised a hand to claim the floor. "There's another problem we're all ignoring: I see two mortals at this table. They're brave and loyal to a fault, but they have *one* life apiece, and they could lose it so very easily." She squeezed John's hand as she spoke.

"You're not suggesting we let you face this alone?" John asked quietly.

"I'm saying you break too easily—as would my heart, if anything were to happen to you."

"You have mortal allies," Anna added. "Surely that counts for a lot."

"It does, but I've never asked anyone else to fight my battles. Least of all those who don't bounce back so fast. Or at all."

"I'd never forgive myself if I wasn't there for you," John protested. "I don't want to find myself facing one of your darker kind, but I won't let the possibility keep me from helping."

"That goes for me, too," Anna added. "I owe you my life. *And* this wider view of the world. You're important."

Caroline cleared her throat softly. "John, Anna, you know the risk. We can keep it civil and at the level of law, but with one flare of temper in the wrong place, you could be gone. The very old, the very insular, place no value upon mortal lives." She looked from one to the other. "We will protect you as far as we can, but…"

"Correct me if I'm wrong," John said slowly, "but aren't we automatically marked for culling? If this Vashtanya wins, there's nothing to stop him draining us both dry, just to pay us out. Vampirekind would do precious little about it."

"Sadly, quite correct." Caroline sighed.

"Then we're better off in the fight than out," John concluded, folding his arms.

In a long silence, Lucinda's eyes went to each face before she nodded in weary acceptance. "All right. For better or worse, it is how it is. So, what's next?"

With a canny smile, Caroline got to her feet. "Let me start this ball rolling with some phone calls."

* * *

Things moved faster than Lucinda would have imagined possible. Two days went by without word—two days of doubt and concern, when she sought the company of John's bed and hearth almost as if she feared she would not have them much longer. Then Caroline received the news she had been waiting for.

Bringing the five together, she briefed them before making more calls. She paced with the phone in John's study and, at last, sank into an armchair by the hearth with a cautiously satisfied expression. The next day, still with much to do, they moved in convoy for the ten-minute drive southeast to Van Alt Hall, Caroline's Tudor manor.

"It has never happened before," she mused, standing in her stone-flagged hall and looking around at the ancient timbers and plaster. "These walls have seen a lot of guests in their time, some quite important, but never a gathering of vampire lords."

"This just got real," Lucinda breathed, rubbing her arms in a second of chill discomfort.

"You must have known your one-woman crusade against the dark would one day escalate beyond single combat. That day has come. Yes, it will end in single combat, but at this moment, it is political."

"Politics! May the old gods save me from them."

"Too late for cold feet."

"I'm not getting them. But I feel like I've lost the initiative. This is alien to me."

"Incorrect." Caroline put one arm around her shoulders. "You have *taken* the initiative—the only move left open to you."

The others were moving around upstairs in the rooms allotted to them. There was no shortage of space; the manor was three storeys tall, in the old-fashioned style. John and Anna lent a hand while Caroline's domestic staff prepared for the dinner guests. Her valet and assistants, both mortals with an understanding of the eldritch ways, must leave before the august visitors arrived at eight in the evening. In the afternoon, the servants dressed the dining room, spread a rich, vintage cloth on the long table, arranged a dozen place settings, plus candelabra and flowers. A major King's Lynn hotel would deliver a banquet supper by six.

In the back garden, among the season's bare trees, Lucinda met John and Anna under a wan afternoon sky. "I'm sorry to say this, but you two must make yourselves scarce, like Caroline's staff. The Elderlings coming in won't tolerate unannounced mortals under the same roof, and they'll easily sense you. Come six o'clock, I want you to head back to the farm and wait for my call."

"It's an odd feeling," Anna said, not arguing but merely accepting the way things were. "Knowing we're the wrong species to be taken seriously."

"It's more complicated, but essentially—yes. Some of these vampires haven't spoken to a mortal in centuries, and don't want to, if they can help it. You're better out of it. *I* don't really want to meet these types! But if their law is going to oversee the duel, there's no choice."

With that, she walked on, down the garden to an ornamental pool, and lingered under the gloomy sky, thinking deeply and peripherally aware of the mortals as John raised a hand to stop Anna from following. "Leave her be," he advised. "This is vampire business." He checked the time, and they returned to the house to help.

The sun set before half past four, and lamps lit the manor brightly as cars came and went. Caroline's staff were done by five. They were safely away to King's Lynn before a minibus pulled in, and the evening's servants stepped out of it. Caroline did not mention to John or Anna that all were vampires, on loan from Lord Ithrial of House Gratharn.

The caterer's truck arrived shortly after. The newcomers took charge of the banquet before standing back, dourly silent in their incongruous white uniforms. They transferred the hot lockers to the kitchen, and a brief, unnatural calm descended.

Outside the hall's arched front door, Lucinda gave her mortals a farewell hug. John's Range Rover crunched away up the driveway between dark, bare trees, while Caroline and Carnelios took a last, long pause—a deep breath before the night.

"Time to make ourselves presentable," Caroline whispered, and closed the door.

* * *

When she and Caroline came downstairs, Lucinda had to admit that the regal setting was fit for grand dealings. The fire burned in the dining hall, and the decor was all red and white, with an almost Christmas-like feel. Caroline had opted for the boldest possible statement. She wore a blood-red silk gown and heels, and as the manor's mistress, she would command the head of the table. For Lucinda, she had found a figure-hugging, plunge-necked mediaeval gown in leaf-green velvet that counterpointed her flaming hair—and guaranteed no place to conceal a weapon.

Standing by the fire, Caroline said quietly, "There is protocol to observe. It may be difficult, but you must share this table with Vashtanya himself."

"I understand," Lucinda returned evenly. "We're both plaintiffs before vampire law and must appear in amity until the time comes to enter sanctioned combat."

"All will be civil; this is neutral ground. Meaning, no display of hostile emotion is permissible other than confidence—not arrogance—and the tightly-controlled courage of one's convictions."

"I'm on my best behaviour," Lucinda assured her with a faint smile.

"I would be more concerned about Vashtanya. But he is also on display, seeking credibility among his peers. He has a predatory lineage—as do others who will be attending—and he might have been in conflict with other Houses represented here. Carnelios's, certainly. Speaking of whom..."

She gestured at the stairs, where a tall, dark figure was descending. Carnelios joined them, and Lucinda nodded her approval of the old-fashioned suit he had found among the selection in the upstairs wardrobes. A frockcoat counterpointed a cravat and richly-patterned waistcoat; he had washed and brushed out his hair.

"You'll do," Lucinda said appreciatively.

Printed reservation cards lay on the plates. Lucinda's and Carnelios's cards flanked Caroline's at the end closest to the hearth, while other names trailed off down the table. Only a couple were familiar, and at the far end, the twelfth place was set but vacant.

"This is how the elders want it," Caroline said secretively as she walked the length of the table with a slow strike of heels and passed a hand over the tall-backed, intricately carved chair. "We shall see how matters unfold. We may or may not encounter the one for whom this place is prepared."

They gathered by the fire, and Carnelios poured rich port. Glasses chinked, and they shared a look that acknowledged the truth: they had never been in deeper water.

"I couldn't have seen this coming," Lucinda admitted. "I fought Javirand for a hundred and fifty years, tracked him through warzones and massacres, and we duelled a dozen times. You know, his ambition was to make a Darkling of me. He failed. And now..."

"There are always some who'll never let the outcome of a fair fight stand," Carnelios mused. "It's important to keep that firmly in mind." He gestured along the table, indicating guests who were yet to arrive. "Take nothing for granted."

The gold clock's hands moved inexorably towards eight, and Caroline lifted a small video camera from a carved box. She placed it on a shelf, well back from the table, and set it to transmit. "For the one who watches, unseen," she whispered. Then, smiling, she turned, spread her arms to her friends, air-kissed them both, and went to the kitchen door to alert the staff.

Soon, stewards appeared in the hall. One manned the front door, and another waited to relieve guests of their coats. Lucinda's heart thudded painfully. Five hundred years fell away from her like sloughed-off snake skin, and she was again the new changeling, awestruck before the ancient ones whose world she had glimpsed. She knew how so many vampires felt about the humans they turned, and could only accept their arrogance for what it was: the learned behaviour of thousands of years. Having *ended* vampires—and ancient ones—she held them in less awe on the field of combat.

She fell silent as the hour approached. Gravel crunched, headlights swept the forecourt, and the screen displaying 'door cam' showed a line of limousines drawing up. She recognised the silver Rolls-Royce belonging to a certain House in Somerset, and watched Hungerford opening the door for the gowned vision who alighted from the rear. Lucinda took her place beside the hearth as the guests appeared, and a herald called their names as they entered.

"Lady Silver, of House Silver...Anathriel of House Belphegor...Lord Ithrial of House Gratharn..."

They entered in a slow, dignified procession, and Caroline received them with the courtesy of the ages. Lady Silver and Anathriel, dressed respectively in a silver gown and a black suit, swept along the table and embraced Lucinda and Carnelios as old friends. Their places were reserved opposite Lucinda and Carnelios, flanking Caroline at the head.

"Lord Istvan of House Ferringor...Lady Traega of House Sachsillian...Mordecai of House Talos..."

"Now we come to it," Lucinda whispered as the haughty, immaculately-presented Elderlings filled the hall, and Caroline moved among them like a gold and scarlet butterfly.

"Vashtanya of House Korsakof...Lady Kromelech of House Korsakof."

The pair hovered disdainfully at the arch to the hall. Their dark eyes swept the assembly as though they owned it all—or *would* when plans matured—and Lucinda studied them with narrowed eyes.

Vashtanya himself was not unlike his brother: well over two metres in height, with a spare, ascetic kind of build, clad in an Indian suit of the finest grey silk. He wore his hair braided, drawn back from a wide forehead, and his eyes seemed to look into one's very soul. High cheekboned and thin, with a sensual mouth that seemed made for drinking wine—or blood, the whole face expressed mere contempt.

Lady Kromelech was the wildcard. Beautiful in a harsh, discordant way, she was pale as a ghost, as tall as her kinsman. She clothed her reed-like physique in a black silk drape and a corset of mirror-inlaid leather; her expression remained divorced from all around her, as if these proceedings were so far beneath her that she wished only to return to what dark contemplations had occupied her. Luxurious lashes framed eyes that were too bright a violet above an unforgiving mouth outlined in black lipstick, and night-black hair fell to her knees. Few would stand close to Lady Kromelech by choice, though Caroline greeted her cordially and with a deep curtsy—an acknowledgement of status, which Kromelech did not acknowledge with so much as a flicker of expression.

The twelfth chair would remain empty, and Lucinda assumed its occupant would be watching via the transmitting cam. *Hmph—let's see who's playing the cards so close to his or her chest that they won't even show their face till they know which way the wind's blowing!*

The herald rapped his staff three times upon the flagstones and intoned in a booming voice, "My lords and ladies, pray, take your places, and give heed to the

Mistress of the Castle."

With a rustle of rich fabrics, the vampires took their seats—the Korsakofs at the end farthest from the hearth. As the waiters moved rapidly along the table, decanting something rich and red into the pewter goblets alongside each setting, Caroline rose once more.

"My lords and ladies, honoured guests. I am Gwenifre of House Sachsillian. Lady Traega represents the interests of my clan. On my left is Carnelios of House Vendregor, and on my right is Lucinda, who is without House affiliation. Both are part of the affair we have gathered to discuss, and both are my personal friends. For this reason, I have provided my humble residence as the venue for this negotiation." She lifted her goblet. "For those who favour *nectar vitae*, there will be plenty, and I know many of you have provided your own sources of *la nourriture du sang*. So, let us greet in amity. Let us drink to the vampire way and the vampire ethos."

Goblets rose all along the table, and vampire voices echoed her final sentiment. "The way." After moments of silence, each goblet set down, upturned; pewter glimmered in the soft lighting, and when not a drop remained, each vampire paused to savour the glow of digestive thrill.

"Now," Caroline went on, "in keeping with the etiquette laid down in the centuries BC by the Lords Anachrion and Belshazzar, let us first partake of the feasting. Only when all are served in body and in soul shall we turn to business. For those who may enjoy it, we have a sumptuous menu. For those who prefer only wine, I offer a selection from my cellar, which I hope will not offend the palate." She gestured to Lord Ithrial's serving staff, and covered platters made their entry.

Lucinda was quietly surprised. The ancients chatted and made small talk as easily as any society gathering in London or Paris. Most quaffed wine in extraordinary quantities, and more than half of them enjoyed mortal food. A pale chicken broth with hot rolls constituted the first course, followed by fish in white wine sauce, with parsley garnish; then came a baron of beef, which a knife-wielding steward expertly carved. The finest vegetables surrounded each generous portion, flanked by individual Yorkshire puddings in rich sauce.

Time went by to facilitate digestion. An hour later, the guests tackled ice cream cake with flaming brandy sauce. All the while, the wine circulated. Lucinda had not dined in such style in over a hundred years, and she cast her mind back to London's Belladonna Club, an exclusive ladies' establishment she had frequented in the days of Queen Victoria and Sherlock Holmes.

The Darkling Anathriel sat to her right, opposite Desdemona Silver, speaking lightly of recent adventures— the defeat of a false deity in Somerset and the battle with Ignius, the fire elemental in Cumbria. Not every year brought notable events, but vampire lives accrued lengthy records of such noble conflict.

Lucinda heard little from the far end of the table, where the Korsakofs sat opposite each other, refraining from food and consuming vast amounts of wine. They conversed with the lords beside them and maintained tolerant expressions, as if the niceties of vampire protocol were the definition of boredom.

When the last dish had been removed and a final round of wine served, Caroline rose and lifted her glass. "My lords and ladies, honoured guests. The Old Lords' etiquette has been honoured. I suggest we move on to business." Dark heads inclined slowly; ancient faces remained impassive, and she went on smoothly, "I requested this meeting to present an appeal for the adjudication of a grievance between Houses. This uncommon situation *might* have been resolved by entirely orthodox means. However, matters have changed."

She resumed her seat, and her eyes swept the assembly. "I turned Lucinda Crane some some four hundred and seventy-nine years ago. She is my protégé and technically my clan-daughter, but she long ago passed beyond the realm of the student in vampire ways. She chose to wage a campaign on behalf of mortals, among whom she was born—among whom *I* was born—to protect them from the depredations of Elderlings and other occult forces that would harm them.

"This crusade has seen her strike down incubus and elemental, dismiss low spirits, and commune with tree spirits and dragons. Among such battles, in 1865, Lucinda came into conflict with Javirand of the Indian branch of House Korsakof. They battled repeatedly and inconclusively until 2016, when my clan-daughter was victorious."

Waves of hostility from the table's far end swept over Lucinda. She did not flinch, but could taste the hatred. Yet there was more: a distinct *tang* of greed, as if her victory had destabilised the Korsakof lineage and thrown the door open to internal conflict. Ending Javirand's life had presented ambitious Korsakofs with a golden opportunity.

"Recently, Vashtanya, from the same branch of House Korsakof, moved to exact revenge on his brother's behalf. This is honourable." Caroline paused for a beat of five. "What was *not* honourable was for Vashtanya to employ the *Raptor Animarum*."

Brows rose, and several ancients stirred in their seats. One cast a glance along the table at the Korsakofs. Caroline had seized their attention.

"The use of a forbidden technique between Elderlings calls into question honour itself. The fact that Lucinda survived the encounter brings the shame into focus. If this matter is ever to be over, free from the endless, dreary payback that, centuries ago, plagued vampire Houses, I propose that the challenge can only be fought as a formal duel, witnessed by representatives of all Houses concerned. The letter of the law will be upheld, and justice will be *seen* to be done. Regardless of the victor, the matter may then be closed." She spread her hands. "What say you, my lords and ladies?"

A long silence followed, while each ancient glanced at the next. The first to speak was Ithrial of Gratharn. The broad-faced giant—master of the vampire House on the northern moors—cut an imposing figure in a dark suit, his silver mane drawn back in gold clasps.

He cleared his throat. "My friends, I would speak for Mistress Crane. Recently, she hunted a revenant in the

Dales country, and while many would simply have killed the tortured creature and called it the only mercy, she had compassion enough to seek the better solution. She sought out the Gratharni. I am pleased to do what I can for the unfortunate soul. I greatly respect Mistress Crane and hope none from my House should ever find themselves on the wrong end of her sword." He paused, studiously avoiding looking to his left, where the Korsakof delegation sat. "Honour is precious to us. To use the soul-stealer is repugnant."

It was *said*, and Vashtanya bristled visibly, his expression hardening.

"If it is to be a challenge under the Great Houses' eyes," Ithrial finished, "so be it."

Next to speak was Anathriel. The Darkling had mellowed with food and wine, but his stare remained direct, his voice even. "I had the honour to do battle with Mistress Crane—fortunately, on the same side. I found her a worthy warrior of pure intention and consummate skill. Perhaps Master Vashtanya was compelled to use a forbidden technique...if he found himself ever so slightly overmatched."

The Korsakofs sat like statues, strictly controlled but clearly poised to strike like snakes. They were not without support, in the form of Mordecai of House Talos. The wiry, ascetic-looking vampire, dressed in a suit of silver-inlaid fabric and the cravat of centuries gone by, shrugged. He spread his hands in a lavish gesture and spoke in a strong southern European accent.

"The soul-stealer is not nice. Combat is *not* a kind place. Mortals, they say, 'All is fair in love and war'—well, if Mistress Crane would wage war, she must take whatever fortunes come to her." His eyes narrowed. "We have not heard how she came to survive."

Caroline maintained a deliberately bland expression. "She has the good luck to have an ally who intervened at the crucial moment."

Mordecai shrugged again. "Fortunes, as I said."

"You accuse me of using an unfair technique," Vashtanya began, speaking above a whisper for the first time this evening. His voice was bass baritone, his speech careful and measured. "I do not deny it. But the intervention of a third party skews the balances to at least the same degree. Clearly, we both survived well enough."

Lucinda leant forward to look along the table. "The soul-stealer is a curse that cannot be removed by one's own force of will or by any action one might take for oneself. It rots an Elderling away, cuts them down like a wasting sickness. Little wonder it was outlawed. Would you condemn the practitioner who removed your *Raptor Animarum* from my flesh as also interfering?" Vashtanya did not answer, and Lucinda smiled thinly. "How's the arm?"

He balled his left fist but said nothing.

Lady Traega cleared her throat. She was an imposing, bodacious vampire in the prime of strength, with red hair piled high above the neck of a revealing, iridescent purple gown. "I am here to support my clanswoman's veracity and her authority to bring this case," she began in a deep, assured manner. Scandinavian overtones lilted in her accent. "However, in the interests of fairness and not escalating the matter out of proportion, I would point out that Lucinda might legitimately have asked for this meeting to take place in less casual circumstances.

"She had the right to present it to the Council of the Clans. Then, we would not be talking it over after a very fine dinner but arguing before a panel of hierarchs in a cold and forbidding chamber." Lady Traega's gaze swept the others, and a guarded smile came through. "We walk a dangerous path, my friends. This is a dispute—*just* a dispute—and I doubt anyone here would wish it to escalate into a confrontation between Houses. Surely, there is enough wisdom and experience around this table for justice to be served. So, where is the difficulty in acknowledging the claim's rightness and granting the formal conflict, as requested?"

"Perhaps…" The voice was strange, deep, with the quality of a drawing blade. It issued from a throat unused to speaking English—or, indeed, speaking aloud at all.

Lady Kromelech looked up slowly. Her disconcerting stare raked her fellow diners; she did not blink at all. "Perhaps the issue is one with which some of us are uncomfortable, and in this enlightened age, we are reluctant to put our misgivings into words.

"But in times past, none would ever have questioned the actions of a vampire of the ancient blood, especially not when those actions concerned a mere changeling." The room fell silent, and all eyes went to her. "Changelings glimpse eternity only through the debt they owe to us. It is a debt of blood, which ancient tradition deems repayable at *our* whim." Kromelech smiled like a death's head. "A changeling brings a suit before vampire law on behalf of another changeling? This is *risible*. Are we expected to nod politely and accord due process?" She waved a black-clawed hand in dismissal. "We agreed to *behave* for the evening, and we shall. But House Korsakof is more traditional in its outlook. Mistress Crane has made war upon our House. She took our brother Javirand from us, and there will be a reckoning. Of whatever sort."

"It is a reckoning they seek," Ithrial growled. "But before *our* eyes, so that if there are any tricks of the calibre of soul-stealing, it will be *our* blades that end it. This is the nature of the challenge, Lady Kromelech. It concerns us all. If we do this, we accept the blood debt it implies."

An element of challenge underpinned Ithrial's own words. He should not have to spell out the conditions to a panel of Elderlings, and House Korsakof's obstruction on prejudicial grounds seemed shallow. Desdemona Silver was about to speak, but Vashtanya cut her off.

"Before we hear further appeals from *changelings*, let me say that the legal grounds for a formal challenge are weak. As Mistress Gwenifre stated, Mistress Crane claims no House affiliation. In our world of tribe and clan, this is strange. The law deals with conflict between the members of Houses, not rogue individuals—*ronin,* if you will. I am a vampire true, and a clansman, thus bound by this legal code and protected by it. How can a changeling without House affiliation claim this right?"

Caroline pinned Vashtanya with an icy look. "Changelings are not obliged to take House membership. Given the prejudice against us, as defined by you and Lady Kromelech, many of us would not be welcome anyway. Personally, I practice only distant clannish ties. I have spoken only for myself, not on behalf of House Sachsillian. I would refer the matter to Lady Traega."

Lady Traega glanced at each of them in turn. "The formal adoption of Mistress Crane is possible and would grant her the privileges and responsibilities of House affiliation. However, it will also be an escalation. I am obliged to put the question to my people—and abide by their decision. It is they who shall bear the burden of any conflict arising with House Korsakof."

In the following silence, many uncomfortable looks passed around the table. Lady Kromelech's smile was razor thin. "You see that this request is frivolous. The changeling chose her path; let her be victorious if her skills are adequate. Oversight is unnecessary. This is merely a skirmish; it need not grow into war. Vashtanya has the right to avenge his people upon an attacker—and also to enact this justice upon any who aid and abet the malefactor."

Desdemona Silver pinned the dark lady with a glare. "This argument presupposes that the conflict in which Javirand fell was in some sense dishonourable. Have you evidence to that effect?" Seconds passed in difficult silence. "If there is no suggestion of dishonour, the matter should be closed. A fair fight is a fair fight. Seeking revenge does, in fact, constitute inter-clannish warfare. The proposed duel avoids this only because Mistress Crane is without a House. If I were Lady Kromelech, I would be careful about randomly implying dishonour when the only dishonour demonstrated this day is House Korsakof's own."

Kromelech's retort, Lucinda thought, would surely have been, 'Brave words from a changeling.' But a creak from the front door interrupted the dispute, and all present turned towards the hallway.

At once, the herald went to greet the newcomer and

returned moments later, escorting a tall, powerful figure in a robe of red fabric worked with intricate patterns of metallic thread. A hood covered his head, plunging his face into shadow, but the sense of power in this one was unmistakable. He came to rest at the vacant chair at the end of the table.

"His Excellency, Lord Alaric of House Aquila Negra," the herald announced in stentorian fashion, "Lord President of the Council of the Clans."

Realising that their deliberation was not beyond the eye of the body that governed relations between the Houses, the assembled vampires sat up straighter. Even Vashtanya and Kromelech stiffened; a flash of frustration registered around their eyes.

The newcomer raised his gloved hands to lift back his hood, revealing a shaven head adorned with tattoos, the meaning of which was lost to time. His face was broad and strong, with eyes of mysterious depth. His mouth thinned in disapproval.

In the silence, Caroline rose and bobbed a curtsy. "Welcome to my home, Lord President."

Alaric slid elegantly into the seat, and a steward appeared as if by magic, presenting a goblet of blood upon a silver tray. He took it, raised it in toast, and drained it. When the steward had retreated, Alaric's eyes roved around the assemblage. His voice had the quality of an organ, and his accent was unplaceable, lost in antiquity.

"My lords and ladies, honoured Vampires. Though much has been said, it comes down to this. The quarrel between House Korsakof and the *ronin* Lucinda Crane is an old one; it has been a sideshow in our society for a hundred and fifty years, and we have watched it unfold with interest. The *ronin* won. Another scion of House Korsakof would prosecute the quarrel, whether for genuine revenge or to win status is not germane. As far as the law is concerned, their duel could go on forever at this level. But when it threatens to escalate, the spectre of clan war raises its head. This is not tolerable. Too few of us remain in this world for us to expend our blood and lives in a pointless conflict. *This* has been decided by the

Council of the Clans.

"Let us not forget that we have lived into a technological age when mortals remain oblivious to us only by virtue of their endemic disbelief in all things intangible. If we make enough disturbance to be noticed, we can expect to have our unique biology captured, analysed, *weaponised* and then turned against us to expunge us from existence." He smiled, cold and harsh. "Mortals do not tolerate competition on *their* planet. We are far better off remaining in the anonymity of the Darkling's night and the Lightling's discretion."

For a moment, it seemed Alaric invited comment, but no one was willing to break the silence. He went on, "Lady Kromelech stated the ancient conceit: that changelings do not deserve the protection of vampire law—they are beneath legislation. This was part of our cultural heritage for long ages, and is now widely recognised as obsolete, dated thinking that proceeds from assumptions of divine purpose in our own origins, lost as they are to time. Our best scientific minds find *no material difference* between the DNA of ancestral vampires and that of changelings. Our abilities are identical; the variations from the mortal genome we all carry are identical. A difference that makes no difference is mere semantics. As a race, we cannot afford to segregate eighty percent of our numbers on the basis of our origins."

He let the figure hang for a second. "Yes, at the most recent census, vampires tracing their origins back to Neolithic bloodstocks are currently outnumbered by the changelings they have created by four to one." In the long pause, his thin smile reappeared. "I would be most wary of courting division." He addressed the comment to no one in particular, but all knew it was intended for the Korsakofs. "Those who believe in the old way should be thankful that vampire society is not a general democracy. If it were, they would find themselves a minority *within* a minority."

The only one willing to question the president was Lady Kromelech, who turned an imperious eye on the Lord. "Whatever the antiquity of our notions, it is a matter of established fact that three guests at this table desecrated the resting place of Dominius, Lord of Old. Mistress Crane herself, and Masters Anathriel and Carnelios. New brooms sweep clean, as the saying goes; however, to many of us, the reign of Dominius was but yesterday. To strip his bones of their magical binding is an unthinkable act."

Lucinda's eyes met Carnelios's. There was much she was desperate to say, but under the table, Caroline's foot pressed on her own, and she understood the message: *Be quiet!* Perhaps Caroline's other foot also signalled to Carnelios; neither betrayed themselves by so much as a blink.

"Dominius was a tyrant," Alaric replied smoothly. "He was deposed by the massed rebellion of a dozen Great Houses, whose warriors struck him down and bound his remains with the Chains of the Dead, ensuring that they should never reincorporate. He is dust, and his *Vincula* now binds something even more deadly." He smiled in frank recognition of the changelings. "Oh, yes, Mistress Crane, we know all about it. Which brings me to the point I am really here to make.

"The debt in which we stand for services you have done for us." Heads twitched; at least a few dignitaries were taken aback. "In your crusade to place a shield between mortals and the supernatural world in which they steadfastly disbelieve," Alaric continued, "you have also served vampirekind. You have destroyed spirits and entities that are as dangerous to us as to mortals, and it would be churlish to overlook those things. Your motives cannot be faulted, for they are selfless." He bowed before her. "I salute you, Lucinda Crane."

The assembled vampires were doubly speechless and hung on the president's words. Caroline was nominally the hostess, but Alaric had the chair and commanded attention.

"Master Vashtanya raises the point that the law is designed to regulate disputes between Houses. This is correct. To satisfy the letter of the law, I hereby offer Mistress Crane temporary affiliation with House Aquila Negra. If this is acceptable, Mistress van Alt's proposal that the duel with Vashtanya of House Korsakof be ratified and fought under the scrutiny of the Great Houses' becomes a mere formality.

"Under the laws of the challenge, reprisal against the families or associates, of either party, is strictly forbidden." He growled the last words in an overt threat. "Thus, we avoid a cascade of retaliatory events and escalation into open warfare." He glanced between Lucinda and Vashtanya, brisk and businesslike. "What say you?"

Caroline took her foot off Lucinda's. She rose to face the Lord, placed her right hand over her heart, and bowed. "I swear to abide by the code of vampire law, and I accept the Lord President's generous offer."

Vashtanya also rose, stiff and dignified. "This is acceptable to me, and to House Korsakof."

"Very well." Lord Alaric stood, resting his gloved knuckles on the table. "A venue and time will be determined. The official witnesses will assemble, and both combatants will hold themselves ready to prosecute their case...in a battle to the death."

* * *

With midnight utter quiet descended on Van Alt Hall. The dignitaries had departed as the limousines purred back into the dark countryside, and Ithrial's stewards had dismantled the feasting hall's adornments. They placed leftovers in the capacious refrigerators, cleared the table and its decorations, and all but three retired to their coach—the trio Ithrial had assigned to guard the hall during the night against the treachery he and others obviously feared. The rest left with Caroline's gracious thanks, both for their master and their assistance, and the gift of a case of fine wine.

A phone call summoned John and Anna back from the farm, and as the witching hour came around, the five sat in the parlour with a rare vintage, recounting the event before a crackling fire. Both mortals hung anxiously on the news, and Lucinda explained with a calm smile.

"It was very convoluted, but it came down to just one thing. Vampirekind does not want to reawaken the Clan

Wars. Deep-seated bigotry towards changelings notwithstanding, they can't and won't risk it. So, we get our formal duel. Javirand's kin *must* abide by the law, even if they don't like it—which protects *you*." She angled a confident smile at John and Anna.

John sat forward with an earnest look. "Can you take him, Lucy? *Really* take him?"

She reached over to take his hand briefly. "If I had the slightest doubt, I wouldn't be doing this. But for the *Raptor,* I'd have had him in the Stourton woods. Don't worry, my dear. This isn't a suicide match."

Sighing, Anna rolled her glass between her palms. "I never imagined vampires were so *political*. The old stereotypes—monsters sleeping away the centuries—doesn't cover it."

"Not even half," Carnelios agreed. He stretched out in an armchair, long legs spread before him, glass balanced on his middle. He had set aside the frockcoat in the room's warmth. "Some choose to sleep in the age-old way, between bouts of feeding; others hibernate rarely, if at all. It's a matter of choice. I would rather experience the world day by day than sample it in small doses, never staying long enough in any decade to do anything other than mock it."

"To have such a perspective on time must be amazing," Anna whispered.

"It's *different,*" Carnelios allowed, sensing the thrust of her remark and guessing it must be uncomfortable for Lucinda.

Caroline rose, stood by the hearth, and rested one elbow on the mantelshelf, her silk-sheathed figure outlined against the flames. She sipped the rich red, drew the pins from her hair, and shook it out. "We have what we wanted—a formal setting rather than a free-for-all that could overtake any of us at any time. Without the stipulation of the Council, we were all targets, and..." She frowned at the wine. "I do not trust Kromelech at all. I have known vampires who are consumed not by hate but by ambition. It is written all over her. If she can find a loophole, she will use it. So—maximum caution until this is over. We would not want any *accidents*, would we?"

"You're saying we're still at risk?" John breathed softly.

"Not officially."

"But, better safe than sorry."

"You would be best to stick close," Caroline added, and she sighed, moving on to less grim topics. She patted Lucinda's shoulder. "Keep the dress, my dear. It suits you. It belonged to a pagan high priestess twenty years ago." She smiled at the memory. "Wiccans can party as if tomorrow will never come."

Lucinda smiled her thanks, took Caroline's hand, and kissed it, but could not yet move on. "Vashtanya got what he wanted. He has the arrogance to be confident of victory, and by doing it this way, his triumph will be seen by all. It will be acknowledged, written into the annals. Vanquishing me would elevate his position in his own clan, and *that's* what this is all about. All the obstruction was just posturing—playing to tradition for appearances' sake. If he couldn't take me in a trap, a formal duel is the next best thing, and even better in the PR sense."

"You've got him right where he wants you," John murmured with strained humour.

"It's a contest," Lucinda said simply. "It's always been a contest. I'm not afraid, John," she added, to reassure him. In fact, with such a foe, she could not afford complacency.

Caroline drained her glass and set it down. "Well, we have Lord Ithrial's gracious protection, so we can sleep easy. And on that note, I will bid you goodnight. Help yourselves to anything you need; we shall speak again tomorrow."

They each rose with a hug for the lady before she retired to the hall, stairs, and the comfort above. Sensing that the others had much to say, Carnelios made his farewells and followed. With privacy, Lucinda, John and Anna sat by the fire once more, and the vampire said slowly,

"I know what you're going to ask me."

John sighed. "We've known each other quite a few

years, m'love. Those years are catching up with me. I'm silvering now, and the *little* problem that doesn't show is nonetheless making itself felt. I don't want to grow old and die, Lucy. Please don't make me."

She could only squeeze his arm, and turned to the Goth girl. "And what about you, my young friend?"

"I'm coming to understand the scope of all that goes unseen in this world, and I know it'll take many lifetimes to finish that study. I believe I could achieve great things, but I'll need the time—and resilience—to do it. I'm asking you to make it possible."

Lucinda breathed deeply, slowly. "I know you've both given it a lot of thought. John, we've talked about what it means to be a vampire, and you wouldn't make the request without those things firmly in mind. I don't want to disappoint either of you, but you must understand, fully and intimately, that this is at least as much a curse as a gift. It's the proverbial double-edged sword that gives so much, but takes so much in return, not least—if you're not *very* careful—your humanity.

"I know this sounds strange. Vampirekind separated from humanity out of sheer necessity *and* because the ancients consider themselves genuinely different—superior, entitled. You know how it goes. Suggesting to such a mind that they are merely humans with a genetic disease that translates into infinite life and a host of abilities mortals consider magic…*sacrilege*."

She laughed quietly. "Changelings bring human hearts and values to the vampire world. Unlike the storybooks, we don't become cold, distant, monstrous creatures overtaken by cruel imperatives. Except for the need for blood, and the ability to hibernate if we want to, for Lightlings, there's precious little to set us apart. But we do change—how could we not? We live, grow, evolve as people always do, but the changeling becomes a different person, and it's up to the individual what sort of person you become.

"I was lucky enough to be changed by a beautiful soul who carries her own vampire nature with grace. That helped so much. And, yes, before you ask, Lightlings always pass on the Lightling characteristics; Darklings pass on their own attributes. Vampires *never* give rise to opposite mutations, which underscores the fact that this really *is* a transmissible disease."

The others hung intently on her words, unsure where she was taking them but grateful that the subject—never far from their minds—was finally under discussion. Reading them like open books made Lucinda's position all the harder.

"In my five hundred years, I've made only one changeling, and it didn't work out well. Maybe I'm 'gun shy,' but I haven't made changelings the way our people used to in the old days. I've lived on animal blood. It wasn't until this modern age, with the simplicity of giving blood, that I've had human blood as a staple. That's only one of the sea changes this disease brings. Another is the balancing act you find yourself doing between all that is *possible* and all that is reasonably *desirable.*" She raised a brow at them. "What do I mean by this?

"Your ability to heal any injury could take you to some very dark places indeed. Imagine, if you can, what vampire *duress* is like. How do you torment someone who can survive almost anything? If you dwell on it, it's a gateway to madness. Thankfully, such things are rare today, but the ancients remember terrible times."

"You're saying it's our own strength of character that counts," Anna mused. "Keeping control of our base nature, *not* letting the beast out to play."

"Well put. Every human soul has its dark side, and perhaps vampires gained much of their reputation from the fact that Darklings revel in their strength and invulnerability. Some became oppressors, monsters, the scourge of humanity—conceited in their stone towers, looking down upon fragile, short-lived beings from the vantage point of the ages. It was so easy to frighten mortals, hurt them, and thus control them." She shook her head, which was copper-red in the firelight. "This trap awaits every changeling merely by being possible. A vampire must have self-control. a tough mental discipline, a clear understanding of one's place in the universe, and an unwavering moral compass. I'm not questioning whether you have these qualities; I'm asking you to imagine what would become of you if any of them ever failed you."

In the long silence that followed, John stood and stirred the smouldering fire back to life. He resumed his seat with a quiet and loving smile. "The answer is no, isn't it, Lucy?"

"It must be, for now, at least, for you both," Lucinda whispered. "Even after five hundred years, I can't bring myself to overset mortality without better reason than simply *wanting* to. All the responsibility I carry—to live a life that helps, not harms; to deal well with other vampires; to choose only the battles that are winnable and turn away from those that aren't; perhaps even to learn the way of the warrior in the name of survival, and so much more—all this would pass on to you...and I can't do that to you. It is a terrible weight, and you'd carry it forever."

At last, they rose. John enfolded her in a hug and whispered, "It's okay, sweetheart. I promise I'll not ask again."

Lucinda could find no reply. She held onto him with the lost feeling that his ephemeral human nature made him all the more precious. Then she drew Anna into the embrace. Her powers seemed to mock her, for she knew she could not help her friends except by condemning them to share her own purgatory.

If, of course, it really was a purgatory.

*   *   *

The next day dawned windy and clear, and the breeze drove torn clouds over the bare trees amid patches of blue. The house was quiet until late morning, and Lucinda shared a shower with John after some sweet diversions that helped take their minds off the coming battle. They went downstairs late, shared the long table with the others in the stone-flagged kitchen, and nodded their appreciation to the three guards Ithrial had left.

Hot rolls and coffee started the day while they chatted of this and that. The reality of the evening's events was sinking in at last for the mortals; they envied the vampires their senses of fatalism and calm. In an hour, Caroline took coffee and headed into her study to clear some work. Perhaps sensing that Lucinda and John needed a little time, Carnelios coaxed Anna into a game of chess at an elaborate, centuries-old board table.

They went out to walk in the garden, in the chill January breeze. Lucinda pulled her wide-brimmed hat low, and thrust her hands into jacket pockets as they wandered down the long back lawn, past the pond, to the wall of trees that screened the estate. There, she leant against a trunk and pulled John close for a soft kiss.

But serious things must be discussed, and she said with difficulty, "Last night, I spoke about purgatory—the curse of the vampire. This is so difficult to say, and I wouldn't say it to Caroline or the kid, but have you prepared yourself for the possibility that I *won't* win this fight?"

The silence was hard; the wind in the trees made a harsh accompaniment. John looked up at the sky, his features seeming older than the years-old image that had impressed itself into her mind. He could not find words for some time and then began, "Lucy, I *never* know if I'll see you again." Facing realities that he would rather not, he wore a sad expression. "When the next quest takes you away, the chance always exists that some new enemy will be the one that ends your career.

"I faced this many years ago. This duel is no different. I'm as prepared as a man can be to lose the love of his life. I've always known there'd never be everyday normality. I don't expect you to come and live on the farm, drive a tractor, and run the gear. I don't expect to join you on your adventures. We have different worlds, and they converge in the simple fact that I fell for an ageless warrior spirit." He laughed ruefully. "I have no regrets, and I'd change nothing." They hugged for a long time. "If you come home, I'll love you. If you don't, I'll grieve for you. There really are only two choices."

"None of this has been easy for you," Lucinda whispered. "I cultivated a patron many years ago, and you've been the staff of life for me. It became more, but *easy?* It probably never was."

"Only the loving part."

They stepped apart, at a loss for words. The moment seemed to last a lifetime until, to John's eye, it seemed a swirling silver-grey cloud broke over the drab morning, a cloud surrounding a vaguely anthropoid form that enveloped Lucinda in its arms and dissolved from existence as if it had never been—taking her with it. He froze in shock, watching her hat tumble into the grass where she had stood. With trembling hands, he clawed out his phone, punched a number from his contacts, and gasped one word.

"*Caroline!*"

* * *

A roaring nothingness surrounded Lucinda for long, terrible seconds before she plunged back into the world she knew—a tipping, swirling world of sky and land. She fell through thin air, aware that the creature's powerful arms still enfolded her. She had time to glimpse forests and villages below before the rushing void consumed her once more.

There was no pain, merely disorientation, and she rapidly conquered both reactions. When the world sprang back into view, she saw farmland, sodden with the season, and felt the sting of the icy wind before they raced on through a blustering gloom in which there was neither up nor down.

The next time the world solidified, she recognised the long grey waves of The Wash in winter and realised what was happening. *He's navigating visually. Heading north? A teleporter who needs to see where he's going...okay, you can do nothing till he gets there...*

She relaxed, counted the jumps, and guessed he was bolting twenty kilometres at each transit. On the eighth, they rematerialized at a much lower altitude, and she saw a sprawling city in the middle distance. After the ninth, they appeared on *terra firma,* in the grounds of a dilapidated manor house, but she had too little time to gather her bearings before a final jump took them through solid matter.

They reappeared somewhere dark and echoing, and Lucinda had no chance to register any more before she found herself shoved bodily into an unyielding wall. Her temple cracked against stone, and she went out cold.

Time passed, but not so long. Her vampire metabolism, fuelled by the surfeit of blood the previous evening, repaired her hurts, rebalanced her body and mind, and she opened her eyes to the dim radiance of a light source somewhere far overhead. She growled a sigh as she discovered her shackled wrists.

She hung in the manacles. Getting her feet under her to ease her hands, she looked around and a thrill of foreboding rushed through her. "Well, this is new."

In fact, it was extremely old—so old that she had never actually seen one before. Her flesh crept at its grimness. She stood with her back against a stone pillar set on a featureless disc of smoothed rock, perhaps four metres wide. Darkness gathered beyond its rim; only the daylight from far above cast wan illumination over the worked-stone walls, ten metres away, that rose out of even darker depths and soared towards the spot of light.

Twisting her neck to look upward, she made out a circular patch of sky, like a divine eye looking down on her. She heard only the faint drone of wind across the opening. Opposite, the iron-bound timber door and the stone ledge in the wall were as solid and stout as a castle's main gate.

It's an oubliette, she thought bleakly. *A place of forgetting.*

A place where prisoners could be locked away, out of sight, out of mind, to reflect upon their situation for as long as it took for utter privation to change their minds. Shushing her misgiving, she laughed derisively. Vampires were made of different stuff.

She rattled the shackles and craned her neck to see them. They were heavy-gauge iron forgings welded to a thick chain—designed to defeat vampire strength.

Okay, but what's wrong with this picture? If the teleporter wanted me dead, he could've dropped me from a mile up. Not even a vampire can heal that kind of damage. Ergo, he wants me right where I am. So, why?

The vault echoed thinly with a taunting hint of sounds from the world above, and she sighed. She might have a while in which to reflect, since the energy penalty of the teleporter's main trick was so great that he was likely exhausted. He would need both nourishment and rest. She already knew how to get out of the shackles—a somewhat messy but effective process. The problem was the door. She could jump the ten metres, but the ledge was so narrow that the odds were she would rebound from the timbers and go into the pit, however deep it might be, doubtless joining the mouldering bones of victims who had lain there since Norman times.

There's a better way. Given her healing abilities, she had been unconscious for only ten minutes; the wound would be fully healed, the blood dry. But the vampire who brought her here had to make up a gigantic energy debt, and it would take hours. *No time like the present*, she decided, and with bleak humour, brought her hands together.

The shackles made her clumsy; she fought for alignment and grip but at last found what she needed. She breathed deeply for some time, and with the survivor's terrible resolve, committed to what must be done.

With all the force of her left thumb, she broke the right.

A sheet of pain flashed through her, making perspiration break on her brow. Her knees trembled for several seconds before she gritted her teeth and pulled her hand through the manacle. She could not rest yet. Grimly, she took hold of the thumb with her left hand and straightened the bone—another knifing wash of pain—and only then relaxed. She rested the shaking hand against her left shoulder, in the crux of her upswept arm.

Now, she needed only patience. She concentrated on good memories, thinking of the light in which she walked, which was eternally denied to the Darklings, and the good food she enjoyed, which they often could not. Soon the pain faded from her hand, and when the thumb responded to conscious control, she knew it had healed.

With the grimmest fatalism, she reached up and repeated the process for the other hand.

* * *

Caroline paced on the patio behind the hall, mobile against her ear, gesturing with her free hand, while John, Anna and Carnelios sat in the kitchen and watched her outline rove beyond the ancient diamond-pane windows. The humans were tense with apprehension and pale with fear. When Caroline came in, they saw her disquiet and anger.

Tossing the phone onto the long table, she thumped onto a stool. "Lord Ithrial has referred the issue to Lord Alaric. Both agree that it's a blatant transgression of the laws of ritual combat. Their best adepts are already dowsing for Lucinda's aura, and all known teleporters are being questioned. Vashtanya can teleport, but on the honour of her clan, Kromelech asserts that he has not left his room this day."

John made a disgusted noise. "And we believe that?"

"Not for an instant." Caroline paused before inviting speculation with open-handed gestures. "What is their play? Where is the *point*? They already have what they want."

"If Lucinda fails to appear at the appointed time, she forfeits," Carnelios said bitterly. "If Vashtanya isn't sure he can take her, this would be a way to avoid the fight."

"The officers overseeing the challenge know it is an abduction; they will not force the letter of the old code. I brought the challenge on Lucinda's behalf; why would she run out on it? Any suggestion of cowardice—that she has run while we report an abduction—is outrageous enough to undo the amity we built between all concerned just last night." Caroline took a difficult breath and, after a long moment, whispered, "Lucinda may be dead."

"Do you feel that?" John asked gruffly. "Because I don't."

"I feel *nothing*, as if a conscious shield is blocking me." She squinted, thinking back. "There was a trick the ancients could do. They would infuse a place with an 'aura of intent'—in today's parlance, a 'jamming' field—that damped vampire abilities; not our physical skills or strength, obviously, but certainly our psychic abilities. Something like that might block our senses, Carnelios." She stalked to the coffee pot and set it up with quick, angry motions, merely for something to do. "I seldom *lose my rag*, as the mortals might say, but if anything has happened to her..." She flicked the switch and, for some time, would not turn back to the others.

"Let's assume she's *not* dead," Carnelios suggested. "Nothing else is acceptable. She's been taken somewhere, where communication can be prevented." He grinned brashly. "I wouldn't like to be the one trying to hold her. It's a thousand to one against this abduction being connected with anything outside of this challenge, so—who benefits from stopping the duel?"

"Vashtanya needs a victory to avenge Javirand," Caroline turned and folded her arms. "All along, we have assumed that victory is his strategy to gain status. Could we be wrong?"

Anna shook her jet-black head. "No. That's the way the world works. If I've learnt anything, it's to put *nothing* past ambition and greed. Since the minute he set the trap in Stourton, he's been playing the revenge card. He accepted a formal challenge, and he can only work with the hand he's managed to deal himself."

"So, who else might want Lucinda out of the picture?" John murmured.

"Over the years, she has amassed a scrapbook of enemies," Caroline admitted, "but most are dead. She has fought vampires comparatively rarely—a few duels in a decade. The clans have long memories, but..." She counted off on her fingers. "Jane Covette still sleeps in her grave, and the revenant was in no position to instigate this sort of problem. In the last decade, Javirand is the only Darkling with whom Lucinda has fought. I recall no battles that remain unsettled; all are finished, done with." She shook her head. "No, only Clan Korsakof is in this picture. So, *what* is their angle?"

"To weaken her before the challenge," John

speculated. "Is there some harm they could inflict that her healing abilities won't put right?"

"Essentially, no," Caroline mused. "But as Jane Covette demonstrates, body and mind are different things. The worst fate I can imagine would be to reduce her—Lucinda Crane, Paladin of the Mortals—to insanity, so she will never again be a thorn in the flesh of those she opposed. Just a sad, mad creature who spends eternity in the misery of a broken mind and is so dangerous that friends must keep her caged. Or else be punished themselves by granting the final mercy."

"There is no honour in this," John growled. His face had grown pale.

"None." Caroline smiled cynically. "How is immortality looking now?"

* * *

As noon came, a disc of light from the opening overhead moved down the wall in a shallow arc, then started back up. In the summer, it would strike deeply into the pit, but January's low sun made little inroad into the hole's damp misery.

Lucinda sat with her back to the pillar. Her mind had cleared, all pain was gone, and she spent some time preparing herself for the coming struggle. She would hear the door unlocking and have time to get to her feet. Until then, she pitted her psychic abilities against the fortress around her and, to her consternation, found her thoughts not merely blocked dead but reflected back at her.

She dimly felt the outside world through that tantalising skylight. It was probably intended to drive prisoners mad with a glimpse of freedom that was forever denied. But she was far less concerned than many a previous 'guest' would have been. Her senses had not failed; this was a deliberate measure to render her as blind on the psychic plane as a mortal.

The object is to hold me for a time, she thought. *Not to kill, but to keep—why? This game is kill or be killed. If they don't press the advantage, they're fools.*

The situation reeked of Javirand's kin. He had invoked them with his dying breath, and it seemed his vow had come true. The ancient Clan Wars festered through the law's inability to control Elderling passions; Darklings too often recognised no hierarchy except clannish obligation. Even now, only the Houses' participation in the Council system—their *agreement* to be bound by rules—made any difference. If that agreement failed, vampire society would plunge into chaos.

Nobody wants war. The reaction was automatic, but Lucinda's eyes narrowed as a new thought occurred. *Unless...somebody does.* Vistas of possibility opened up, none of them attractive. *If someone were to sabotage the Entente Cordiale between the clans, we would have no means to prevent open bloodshed. It would become a question of strength. That's how you fall from a union under our elected Council into an empire under the rule of whoever is the strongest, meanest, and has the fewest scruples.*

She breathed deeply, shaking her wild, tangled hair. This abduction was a move on the chessboard, but whether it was pivotal to grander events or merely incidental, she could not yet tell.

Time passed as she brooded and the pit became chilly. She concentrated on the door, listening with inhuman senses, and when at last she heard a key slide into the clumsy old lock, she bounded to her feet. She grasped the shackles, with the chains dangling just right. From a dozen metres away and in poor light, it would appear that she remained bound.

The lock turned, a bar moved, and hinges creaked as the door swung back into the tunnel beyond. Lucinda's eyes narrowed on the harsh LED torchlight that outlined a svelte figure in thoroughly modern clothing. He wore a fine, silver-blue suit; the features were tanned and lean, and the hair severely cropped.

The newcomer stood at the brink of the drop and clasped his hands behind his back, staring at her for a long and insolent moment. "You have been a great trouble to my kinsmen, Mistress Crane." The deep voice boomed in this hollow space; his accent sounded—somewhere *east?*—the Balkans or Carpathians? Classic vampire country. This one might have lived in the age of Vlad the Impaler himself. "You perplex us, first with your simpering concern for the mortal scum—I swear, if you were human, you would be freeing cattle from fields and monkeys from laboratories."

He regarded her scornfully, as though her convictions had made her demented, and raised a finger. "But, more so, with your unwillingness to embrace the power that could have been yours. Javirand, my distant cousin, made it his life's work to cultivate you and, at last, bring you into your rightful place as a powerful warrior for our race. Changeling though you are, your skills are phenomenal, and a resource that should not be wasted."

He was rambling out of complacent self-indulgence, Lucinda thought. She let him talk. Accosting him with verbal abuse served no purpose, and she could not jump the gap to the tunnel before he could teleport. No, she must move with less warning, which meant awaiting the opportunity.

"The project was Javirand's undoing, and he vanished from the face of this world. We are satisfied that no other hand was involved. Only his eternal foe could be responsible. You *are*, of course?"

"Oh, I killed him," she replied quietly. "Sometimes I miss the endless conflict, pursuit, the duels all over the world. But only for a moment. Then sense returns." She stared at him with the directness of a locomotive. "And you are?"

"Pardon my manners; I have had the advantage. I am Josephus Caspar, of the Carpathian branch of House Korsakof." He gave her a mocking bow. "My kinsmen talk politics and kowtow to laws." He scowled and spat into the pit. "These are twisted times, when strength has taken a back seat to civility. I say, to hell with it."

"What do you want from me?" Lucinda fired the question bluntly.

"Want? Other than your head, or to drain the blood from your living body...why, your life, woman. But not *quite* yet. All things in their time." He smiled, speaking with his hands as he expounded his point. "You see, while you were a masterless samurai, you were but a nuisance to be ignored or dealt with as such. But with this official challenge—" He clicked his tongue. "Now, you recruit the attention of the Great Houses, and the oversight of the law. This allies you with vampire society, something you have always repudiated. It makes you stronger through your association with them, and this will never do."

"A Great House, threatened by a single individual?" She made a face. "Join in honourable combat with me, and end it—if you can."

"As Vashtanya wishes to do. But the possibility exists, however remote, that your skills might outmatch his. We cannot have you whittling back the flowers of our Korsakof warriors. Not when there are simpler methods." Josephus Caspar smiled, apparently enchanted with his own cleverness. "You will never reach that duel. It will not be difficult to plant a seed of suspicion that will quickly grow into the conviction that your request for the match was sheer bravado, just a time-winning tactic, while you wasted your superiors' time and goodwill.

"Once disgraced, you will never recover it. We shall destroy your reputation for honesty and forthrightness; take your honour; make you a pariah among those who have so recently gifted you their support—the President of the Council of the Clans! And when you have become a stale joke to those whose attention is fixed not upon trivial matters but upon eternity...when you are without even the protection of the law...then we shall exact such revenge as the world has not seen in centuries. The Great Houses will not even care. But it will teach them to *fear* us."

"That's your play?" Lucinda shook her head sadly. "Sophistry. The last resort of cowards."

Caspar laughed richly. "Semantics. I call it husbanding resources against more important battles. We do not squander our best blood in swatting aside troublesome flies."

"Look me in the eye and say that," she hissed, injecting all her loathing into the challenge to his vanity—

Caspar took it up without thought. In a *thud* and *shush* of displaced air and matter, he dissolved on the ledge and reappeared before her. Red-rimmed eyes bored into hers, and as he inhaled to deliver some damning retort, she released the chains. She dove headlong into him with a rugby tackle, carrying them both off the rock tower into the nothingness of midair.

Adrenalin spiked, and Lucinda sensed Caspar clearly enough to feel the instant of panic as he realised he was in freefall in his own pit. He had only one recourse, and no time to plan the move. He navigated by sight, and as she had planned, the only thing he saw while he plunged backward was the disc of sky.

In a split second of dislocation, she registered the transition; then they were out in the afternoon light, which her distended pupils found suddenly brilliant. As a Darkling, the Korsakof scion began to blister immediately. Lesions opened on any skin that was bare to the daylight. The wounds inspired a roar of pain; they would heal with every teleportation jump, but he would burn afresh, and his agony was very real.

They were just six metres over an unkempt green lawn by a rockery, in which yawned a mediaeval well. She flung her arms wide to release Caspar, and pivoted in midair as he transitioned. She rode the landing on ankles like steel springs, rolled, and rebounded.

To a vampire, the leap was nothing, and she came up with every fighter's instinct in high gear. When he materialised behind her—skin unblemished before the daylight began to burn him again—she swung low under his grasping arms. She dropped and swept his feet out from under him with a scything boot. He landed hard on his back, and a snarl of rage twisted his features, but before she could land a blow, he jumped away in a burst of vapour.

Moments later, she picked up his signature disturbance as he dropped in again, intending to enfold her. This time, she back-kicked to his groin and used the instant's shock and pain to turn and place a kick to the head. Still falling, Caspar teleported once more, and this time materialised some distance away.

Lucinda crouched, turning this way and that, every

sense wide open, and *sniffing* for his trace. If he came close, she could strike before he could snare her. His fury communicated as clearly as spoken words, and she realised that the psychic plane was open now, humming softly. They were beyond whatever isolation field Caspar had conjured.

He bounced in again, appeared before her as a distraction, vanished in the same instant, and a second later, his arms encircled her from behind. With a convulsive jerk of the neck, she snapped her head back, hit him in the face—and felt his nose break. This time, she had time to spin, drop into a crouch, and land a blow to his middle. It knocked him off his feet, but he snapped away once more.

She heard him materialise forty metres away, beyond the shaggy arbours, and snarled in frustration. "Fight me, you coward! You miserable one-trick pony!"

* * *

Caroline and Carnelios felt it simultaneously. Their heads rose, their eyes met, and she snatched her phone from the bench. In seconds, she was speaking with Lord Ithrial himself. "We have her—she just appeared like throwing a switch. But the trace is very faint, so she must be well north of us."

All four in the kitchen heard Ithrial's reply. "Our people also registered her. The JetRanger is on standby—I shall run down her bearing and call you the minute I learn anything."

"We shall be waiting." Caroline stared at the phone as if hardly believing it, then turned to group-hug the others. Lucinda was alive. Nothing else mattered.

* * *

In the brief time while Caspar hesitated—healing the burns and allowing his metabolism to recover from the jumps—Lucinda took in the old crenelated manor house's dilapidated upper floor, which reared over the untended gardens. Bare woods framed the building; the chill afternoon breeze rippled the dark water of a stagnant pond. Centuries ago, this had been a grand residence, but it looked as if it had not been occupied for fifty years. That made sense. If the oubliette had been discovered under the ornamental well, vampires—old enough to recall such horrors and cruel enough to have a use for them—would take a keen interest, and move the mortals out at the first opportunity.

Renewing his attack, Josephus Caspar teleported in once more, but this time he had also shapeshifted. His battle morph was a loathsome worm-white *thing* with slavering jaws and rending talons. He had taken time to set aside the elegant suit before the metamorphosis destroyed it, and the beast he had become could tolerate daylight for some time.

Deprived of a weapon, Lucinda had few choices. Throwing off her jacket, she shapeshifted with a feeling of revulsion—felt her limbs grow and change while her features distorted into the vampire's animalistic battle morph. Her jeans and T-shirt split as she reached the morph's full expression.

They clashed in a burst of energy, all flailing claws and ravening jaws. As they scrabbled on the damp lawn, guttural cries startled birds from the trees. Clods of earth flew as they struck and parried. Bloody gashes opened on them both, but while Caspar was reduced to pure animal savagery, Lucinda maintained an awareness of *self*, and the importance of tactics. She still fought with her head.

Her gnarled, rock-hard fist crashed home on Caspar's jaw and sent a fang whirling. When he threw himself forward to pin her down, she rolled under his lunge, came up fast, and snap-kicked to his forehead before he could rise. He pitched backward and jumped out, which allowed the rematerialisation to instantly repair his injuries.

With his special ability, he began a fresh series of sniping passes, and Lucinda knew she had him on the ropes. Caspar was a talker, not a doer; he had invited a fight that was well beyond him. She had called him *a one-trick pony*, and now she was sure of it. She dodged and rolled with inhuman agility to stay out of his grasp—anything to keep him from teleporting her back into the pit.

Near the tumbledown bowers, she snatched up a fallen branch, a long, thin, jagged staff, and instinct guided her hand. She whirled, stepped in close to the half-materialised creature, and thrust. Caspar took shape around the branch—naked, impaled, trapped in a fugue of conflicting forces as two objects tried to exist in the same space.

He shuddered helplessly; a bubbling cry burst from lips that suddenly slackened, and he dropped to his knees as he lost control. As he began to die, he shifted back to human form. His eyes met Lucinda's in a confusion of rage, hate and fear, and he had grasped the branch, trying futilely to draw it out of his flesh, when consciousness fled.

Morphing smoothly back into human form, Lucinda stepped around behind him, took Caspar's skull in the crook of her arms, and gave a convulsive wrench. His neck broke with a dry *snap*, and he collapsed to the grass, hands still knotted to the branch, blood drooling in slow, scarlet strings. Daylight was rapidly burning the body, and Lucinda had only minutes to act.

With the proper care, Caspar would recover soon enough, but like any Darkling, he would shrivel away in daylight. This day was thickly overcast and approaching evening; no hot, yellow sunlight caressed the Korsakof's naked, Darkling skin, but even so, she must be quick. Kromelech would hold her accountable if Caspar were utterly destroyed, while Lucinda's efforts to save him might earn some small credit with the lady's house. And Caspar must be tried before the law and punished by the Council of the Clans.

The body had blackened when she tore out the jagged wood, but Caspar had fallen into the strange state where the vampire was not dead yet not alive. He knew nothing while she dragged him into the nearby bower, into shadows that were as thick as twilight. For good measure, she buried him roughly in a mass of leaflitter and loose earth. "You'll keep," she told the body. "In fact, you'll survive, damn you."

Panting, she stepped back, arranged her ruined

clothes with a hard, cynical smile, and pulled on the jacket for warmth. Repairing the injuries Caspar had suffered would take many hours, depending on his energy levels; she could keep him in check simply by watching for the first hint of animation.

She was still standing beside the bower, listening for signs of life, when House Gratharn's black helicopter beat down out of the overcast. It settled on the lawn, and she raised a hand in a tired greeting to Lord Ithrial.

* * *

No further risks would be entertained. The party regathered at Gratharn Hall, on the high moors a few kilometres from Haworth. The helicopter made a number of flights, one to Van Alt Hall to bring Caroline's group and their guards, and another to fetch House Korsakof's representatives.

From an upstairs parlour, Lucinda—dressed in the fresh clothes she had asked Caroline to bring—stared down on the wide front lawn within its ornamental hedges and watched the Korsakofs arrive. Alighting from the helicopter, they strode with arrogant confidence towards the front steps—Vashtanya and Lady Kromelech, in black from neck to toe.

Caroline had also brought Lucinda's weapons, and she gratefully took possession of blade and automatics. Given the treachery of her foes, she had received permission to be armed—even within Gratharn Hall itself.

She regarded her companions with a raised brow. "Now we shall see," she murmured, and turned towards the door as a quartet of vampire guards in Gratharni livery arrived to escort them. She surrendered the weapons only reluctantly as the group was ushered into the Master's presence.

Gratharn's council chamber was buried deep within the house and windowless for the comfort of Darklings. Lord Ithrial wasted no time in bringing the group together. Lord Alaric attended via encrypted video link; his face appeared on a multi-directional screen on the long table, with a reciprocal cam feed.

Those with a vested interest assembled around the

table. Anathriel and Desdemona Silver had returned to their respective lodgings, but Lady Traega of Sachsillian remained close to oversee her clan's interests. She sat beside Carnelios, on Ithrial's left, where he commanded the head of the table. Lucinda and Caroline were on Ithrial's right. Isolated at the far end, the Korsakofs sat several empty chairs away, and their expressions could not have been less convivial as they watched the four guards take station, flanking the chamber's closed doors.

"With Lord Alaric's permission, we'll begin," Ithrial grunted. The tattooed head on the screen inclined silently, and Ithrial continued without preamble. "Lady Kromelech, we have in custody one Josephus Caspar, scion of the East European branch of your clan. He is the teleporter who abducted Mistress Crane from Van Alt Hall this morning. He was unable to hold her, and she had defeated him when we reached the scene."

The unnatural lashes blinked once in Kromelech's pallid face. "Pray, continue."

"Caspar was using the old Aldringham estate, in the woods near Parlington, a little way east of Leeds. It has been disused since the 1950s. We discovered a previously unidentified mediaeval ruin on the property. An *oubliette.*"

"How interesting," was her cool reply.

Ithrial's eyes narrowed; he held his temper with the skill of a diplomat. "Master Caspar imprisoned Mistress Crane in this structure and must have been planning his actions for some time. An aura of interference still lingers in the estate's stones. As we both know, this takes considerable effort."

The strange Darkling eyes passed unblinkingly over the room as if the news were a mild curiosity. "I am more interested in the release of my kinsman from your *custody.*" Kromelech pronounced the word as if it vastly amused her.

"We hold him under Article 27 of the *Vampira Codex* for interference in a sanctioned trial by combat between clans. He has been placed into an enforced sleep, and will not be teleporting anywhere." Ithrial smiled grimly. "In the interest of amity between the Great Houses, judgement and punishment remain the province of the Council of the Clans. You must petition *them* for Caspar's release—if his actions can be justified in any way. But we have not addressed his purpose."

"Was this purpose extracted under duress?"

Ithrial laughed, inspiring a flare of anger in both Korsakofs. "Not at all. Caspar was so certain of his position that he was willing to divulge his intentions. It appears that he acted very much on behalf of his clan."

Lady Kromelech spread her pallid paws and smiled her death's head smile. "You will excuse us if the word of a changeling is not enough. Mistress Crane intimates that House Korsakof treats with its fellows without honour. I deem this a desperate attempt to sow disunity and destabilise vampire society, made by a rogue individual hellbent on overturning our ancient traditions."

The accusation hung in the air for some time before Lord Alaric's voice spoke from the screens. "There is no prior suggestion of such motives. I will not waste this Council's time by asking you to present evidence of your claim—and there is no need. If it were true, it would merely constitute one more thing for which the only solution is the duel upon which we have already agreed. Do the combatants stand ready?"

Vashtanya nodded. His mysterious and not unhandsome features settled into a studied, confident smile. "I am ready, Lord President."

"I am ready," Lucinda echoed, a deep burr in her throat as she inclined her head to the cam.

"Very well. Mistress Crane was recently in combat; it is appropriate that she be allowed to feed and rest. The Witnesses to the Dispute will gather at Gratharn Hall by eight, so let us set the duel for...midnight."

"The arena will be ready," Lord Ithrial promised, and the screens darkened. "Council closed." Rising, he beckoned the guards. "Escort our guests to their quarters, where they will remain until the appointed time." The Korsakofs made a regal departure with forced, brittle dignity, and, given privacy, Lord Ithrial said quietly, "We must speak when this is over. *Whatever* the outcome."

With those ominous words, he touched Lucinda's shoulder in passing and left in a swirl of robes.

* * *

In the chambers assigned to them, Lucinda, Caroline, Carnelios, John, and Anna gathered for coffee—a fine brew in a tall silver pot. For Lucinda, something extra arrived from the Gratharn stocks: a pint of premium-quality chilled blood. She drank it in one draught, sank into an armchair, and sighed as the restorative energy radiated through her tissues. Eyes closed, she rested, utterly relaxed.

With the hour set for the duel, this confounded the mortals, but Caroline cautioned them with a tiny shake of her head as she poured the coffee, and they said nothing. Lucinda opened her eyes to take a cup, sat forward, and raised it in salute.

"To friends. John, Anna, you might be the first mortals to set foot in this house in a hundred years. Consider yourselves favoured."

"You've told me so much about vampire society," John mused, spooning sugar into his cup. "I knew it was ancient, ordered, and complex, but I never imagined it could exist so close under the surface humans know. Tourists pass right by this house; they come to walk these hills in the footsteps of the Bronte family. No one would ever guess what it contains—other than rich, eccentric recluses."

"Humans need never be aware of anything more," Caroline said wryly. "Same with my home, Desi Silver's place in Somerset, and many others. This land has countless sprawling estates, left over from the days of royal favour and the birth of international trade and industry. Some have been…repurposed."

Carnelios cleared his throat. "What do you suppose Lord Ithrial meant by that last comment?"

"Ithrial sees the bigger picture," Lucinda replied simply. "The implications of all this for the future." For the moment, she would say no more. "Now, my friends. Without meaning to be morbid or pessimistic, there are matters we must discuss. If the duel should go against me, I want you to know that I've made a will under mortal law, covering the disposition of my assets. I own a lot of property that's under lease through various agencies. I have antiques, cars, and a fair amount of liquid cash—all perfectly legal and contracted under one or other of my aliases. I've named Caroline as my executor. John is the main beneficiary, but *all* my patrons, all my friends, receive something."

"Trust me to do what is necessary," Caroline whispered. "To satisfy the law, we shall need to, um, produce a body."

"Make it a car crash," Lucinda suggested. "Roll and burn, something like that, leaving the remains beyond identification. Not the Jag, though; John gets that." The others laughed, but the sound was forced and difficult. "Then finish the job properly in a crematorium; scatter my ashes in the fens. And remember me fondly."

No one could speak. Anna and John were pale with the realisation that an indestructible immortal had made provisions for death. But the painful awkwardness passed, and as she finished the coffee, Lucinda hunted for a smile, more for the mortals' courage than her own.

"I'll need to meditate for a while to centre myself. When we're done here, I'll use this suite's bedroom, and I'd appreciate absolute quiet. The only one I want to help me is Caroline." She reached over to take John's hand. "Don't take it personally, dear one."

"I won't," he sighed.

She knew he was wondering if he would ever see her again. He and Anna spoke in quiet, desultory snatches, acknowledging this transitional moment. Before Lucinda left them, she hugged each in turn, but she could say nothing that had not already been said many times.

Withdrawing to the bedroom, for some time she sat on the lavish bed, deeply aware of the lives closest to her, human and changeling. In the past, she had valued and even *used* solitude; far from isolation being her bane, it kept her loved ones far from harm, so that her only worry was for herself.

She sank onto the room's rich carpet, assumed the

lotus position, and cleared her mind. She must find the right headspace for the duel, and nothing was more grounding than inner contemplation. She relaxed, reduced her breathing and heart rate, let her thoughts move with glacial slowness, and was unsurprised when a glance at a clock showed an hour had flown by.

The chilled blood had recharged her metabolism; the energy she had spent earlier was fully replaced. All that remained was to *consummate* her relationship with House Korsakof—in the most final way.

* * *

At ten, Lord Ithrial's retainers escorted Carnelios, John, and Anna from their room and took them to a small annex. A light meal had been set out, but no one spoke to them, as if they were merely tolerated. A strange changeling and two mortals were an unwelcome graft upon even a forward-thinking vampire House.

In the suite, Lucinda and Caroline listened to the coming and going of staff as the witnesses arrived, and a mutter of voices in the main hall as Ithrial welcomed the dignitaries. Caroline offered an embrace. "Have faith," Lucinda whispered, her manner mild, her control absolute.

"I have faith *in you*," Caroline returned with a sad smile. "I am sorry it has come to this, but your chosen way has guided you towards this time and place since the moment you first took a stand for mortals. It is the life you made, and I would not change you."

All Lucinda needed had been delivered. The sword and automatics had been cleaned, serviced, and laid out on the bed. Beside them lay a folded garment—ritual combat attire, as approved by the Great Houses. The tough, black spandex jumpsuit would tolerate morphing, if either combatant opted to shapeshift. Boots made of similar material stood at the bedside.

Lucinda belted on the guns over the form-hugging suit. Caroline gathered her clan-daughter's hair into a thick braid and pinned it behind her head, leaving nothing for Vashtanya to grasp. Lucinda buckled on the baldric; the polished blade, in its lacquered wood scabbard, snugged into the rig. Last of all, she swirled on the cloak in the Aquila Nigra colours. The Black Eagle clan.

Gold and red shimmered among the black, and the eagle's head motif on her back made her feel almost like a prize fighter as they walked out. A taciturn guard escorted them to an elevator, and they travelled down three floors, where Caroline left her with a last swift embrace.

Now, Lucinda stood alone and silent in a gloomy chamber. The guard observed the proprieties with an inspection of her weapons and quickly passed a metal detector over her to ensure that she carried no undeclared tricks. To her elevated senses, it seemed she waited an age, but in reality, only minutes went by before a soft chime preceded Lord Ithrial's deep voice.

"Combatants, stand ready."

Her heart thudded with a steady rhythm, and adrenaline edged her movements, making her flex her muscles, bounce a little on the balls of her feet, and ache for the door to the arena to go back. She had seen ritual combat more than once in centuries gone by—as Caroline's guest, on the occasions when she visited House Sachsillian, back in the days of the Clan Wars. She knew what to expect and did not have long to wait.

The door purred aside, and she stepped out into the hall's undercroft, a chamber some ten metres wide and fifteen long. Its walls were ribbed with stone buttresses that flowed together into weight-bearing Gothic arches. The floor was laid with tan, and floodlights bathed the scene in the reddish frequencies Darklings preferred.

Four metres above floor level, an open gallery held a long, double row of seats. There, Lucinda saw them all. Desdemona Silver, Carnelios, Anathriel, Caroline, and Lady Traega sat to the right of Lord Ithrial, while Ithrial had positioned himself in the centre of the front row. John and Anna sat beside their friends—quarantined as far as possible from the opposition and present only by dispensation of the Master of House Gratharn. Lady Kromelech had taken a seat on Ithrial's left, and other dignitaries filled out the line of witnesses, along with senior members of House Gratharn. Lord Alaric sat in the rear row's centre, as if providing an oversight for the oversight, and his brooding face set the tone for the conflict.

Vashtanya strode into the arena from the opposite end. He wore the same combat uniform, the cloak emblazoned with his clan motifs: the steppe falcon and crouching tiger. His face was impassive, a mask of confidence. The grips of twin weapons extended from the cloak—a sword on the left hip, and something rare and unusual on the right. It had the hilt of a sword, but a metal strip encircled Vashtanya's waist. If he carried a firearm, it could only be at the small of his back.

The duellists paused five paces apart, the guards still flanking them. A Gratharni herald entered the arena with the traditional scroll of pronouncement, which the audio system's pickup he wore in his right ear rendered anachronistic. He bowed to Lord Ithrial and, receiving a discreet signal, began,

"Let all present know that the dispute brought by the designates of House Sachsillian on behalf of the scioness of House Aquila Nigra and answered by House Korsakof shall be determined on this night by Rite of Combat. Lucinda Crane of House Aquila Nigra and Vashtanya of House Korsakof will do battle to the death. The matter will be mutually agreed by the Houses concerned to be concluded with the fair and honourable discharge of this burden. This specification protects all members and associates thereof from reprisal or retribution outside the specific terms of the agreement, and any such action will be considered an act of war between the named Houses." The herald took a dramatic pause. "Let all present bear witness to the honour of this combat and to the verity of its settlement under the precepts of the *Vampira Codex.*"

He rerolled the scroll and motioned to the guards, who took the cloak from each fighter. The three noncombatants withdrew from the arena, and the doors rolled closed. The silence was absolute—a perfect moment, as if it were suspended in time. Lucinda stared into Vashtanya's features, into his soul, sizing him up as Lord Ithrial stood.

The Master of House Gratharn raised one hand for several seconds before bringing it down. "Begin!"

In a heartbeat, she rocked the sword forward over her shoulder and poised with the katana outstretched in a samurai guard position, but Vashtanya made no move. His stare was snakelike, his fixed, faint smile a calculated slur. Several seconds passed before his gloved hand moved to the grip at his right hip. He released a retaining thong there, and something bright and deadly sprang from its sheathed position—it had been coiled about him like a glittering cobra. An urumi whip-sword. The blade was two metres long, and it swayed and flexed like a serpent.

Lucinda smiled now, a thin, lethal expression. She came forward on nimble feet that barely touched the tan and paused just outside the urumi's deadly reach. Stillness lasted a scant few seconds before Vashtanya erupted into action. He flailed the strange weapon in a pattern of strokes that filled the air with the crisscrossing flicker of razor-honed steel. Lucinda retreated, parrying with a scratch and slither of contact. Her sword moved in lightning responses, and the air *whirred* over its edge as it kept the urumi away.

At this instant, Vashtanya had the advantage. His weapon was lighter and covered a larger area, while Lucinda expended more energy in defence than he did in attack. He kept the strange blade circulating, creating a shield before him and sending it sniping high and low. The urumi slithered through her defence, leaving a red wound on her left shoulder, another on her right shin. Her concentration did not waver; she offered no reaction—the wounds were irrelevant—and circled warily, changing the angle to put the lights in Vashtanya's eyes.

The urumi shone brightly in her vision now, and she tracked its motion better. Her breathing was quick but light; energy pulsed in her veins and nerves. The katana moved like lightning to repeatedly sweep aside the whip-sword. With a snickering of steel, Vashtanya cut through her defence just once more—

Her right arm bled copiously for a few moments, but in the next rain of blows, Lucinda moved to her right, inviting the urumi to follow. Vashtanya swung low, going for her shin again, and overextended himself. Her foot lashed out in a blur, trapping the glittering strip of metal against the tan. The katana whistled down in a wheeling stroke, and the Indian blade parted with a piercing chime.

Vashtanya stepped back convulsively, staring at the stub of his weapon. Less than a metre of it remained, and Lucinda raised her own blade for his inspection. "This is a seventeenth-century master's weapon. The steel was folded one thousand times. There are few things in this world it can't cut." She palmed her left arm, working the shoulder around—the wound had already almost healed. Satisfied, she resumed her stance.

No sound came from the gallery, and the combatants did not spare a glance for the witnesses. The entire universe contracted to this space and time.

Throwing aside the useless hilt, Vashtanya drew his second weapon with a rasp of fine steel. This time, his choice was a hengdang sword from India's eastern provinces. The Chinese influence was obvious; it had gentle curves, like the katana, but somewhat less reach—but it was also lighter and easier to manoeuvre. The Darkling cast aside the elaborate, red-tassled metal sheath and presented the blade two-handed, his gloved fists lightly clasping the lengthy grip.

When they clashed now, the style became a fascinating blend of *ken-jutsu* and *thang-ta*, each with its flowing and graceful motions, its focus, and intent. The arena filled with the sweet, bell-like contact of the blades.

Concentrate—feint—parry—thrust. Lucinda moved in the purest state of coordination, as she had learnt so long ago. In recent times, she rarely fought blade-to-blade, but this was the real thing—a duel such as she had fought before firearms became compact and convenient. The thought of drawing the automatics never crossed her mind; she carried them because they were part of her, but this challenge was like the disputes that vampirekind had fought since time immemorial. In this much, changeling though she may be, she honoured vampire tradition, and the witnesses must approve.

In two minutes, both black suits were lined with red. The wounds would have incapacitated any human, but vampires shrugged them aside. Lucinda was never in jeopardy until Vashtanya dove in under her thrust and sank the hengdang's tip into her abdomen.

She dropped to one knee as a sheet of pain washed through her, and felt the hot run of blood. Her sword swung in a blocking stroke as she forced her way to her feet, far more slowly than she should have. The first tiny kernel of doubt kindled—she needed time to heal this wound.

At once, Vashtanya knew he had the advantage, and he pressed it. A flurry of blows rained on the katana with the lighter weapon's greater speed, and Lucinda drew on every shred of experience she possessed to weave around the attack, contain it, deflect it.

At last, the katana enveloped the hengdang. She plucked it out of his grasp, sent it whirling in a glitter of steel, and it impacted solidly in the polished timber *above* the viewing gallery—almost exactly over Lady Kromelech's head.

For seconds that seemed elastic, the katana's point hovered in line with Vashtanya's heart, until he teleported across the arena in a rush of vapours, opening space between them. Slyly, he looked up at the blade, which still quivered in the wood—stretched up a hand as if to teleport and snatch it free, but Lord Ithrial's stentorian voice cut across the chamber.

"*No!* The weapon has left the arena. It may not be retrieved, as specified in Article 6 of the Rules of Combat. Without weapons, you will fight open-handed." No need for a reminder that this was a fight to the death.

Vashtanya glanced up at the witnesses just once. Lucinda watched Kromelech's features set into a glare of hatred. It was mostly directed at Lucinda herself, but at least some of the fury appeared to be for the kinsman who had squandered his advantage.

Now Vashtanya turned back into the arena, gathered his strengths, and shapeshifted into the hideous battle morph Lucinda had last seen in the forest. Releasing a bellow of rage, he teleported around the enclosure in several swift jumps—showing off. *Wasting energy* was the more practical assessment, Lucinda thought, but the flurry of transitions brought him closer, and the abdominal wound had not yet healed.

Constantly turning to present the katana pulled at the gash, making blood flow. Vashtanya kept her turning, jerking one way or another to prevent the injury from mending. At last, he came close enough to rake his talons across her hip and side, and she grunted in pain. Her return swing cut only air and, a split second later, she twisted to counter his next sniping pass.

I'm losing, she thought bleakly. *Change the game, girl, or you'll die.*

The next time he teleported, she bolted to the arena's exact centre, below the central seats, and bent over the wound panting. Vashtanya reappeared some distance away, and they stared at each other. His confidence had returned; the red-rimmed eyes in his white, animalistic face bored into her, seeking any weakness. She freely acknowledged that he was equally as formidable as Javirand had been—but also reminded herself that she had killed Javirand. She was not done yet.

He seemed to take perverse pleasure in allowing her a brief respite, but as she raised the blade to a samurai guard stance, feather-light on the balls of her feet, and closed her eyes, she sensed his puzzlement. Vashtanya teleported again and again; the thudding displacement of air made his movements simple to track around the chamber, but each time Lucinda declined his invitation to spin and cover that quarter.

She neither flinched nor turned, but maintained a neutral expression that looked profoundly peaceful, face a little upturned, weapon balanced gently in both gloves. Vashtanya reappeared well outside her reach and hesitated. He could not entice her to open her eyes, and she felt his consternation grow. He jumped several times in quick succession, getting a little closer with each, but nothing would make Lucinda react. Blood no longer seeped through her suit; the wound had closed. Her breathing remained even and deep, and she poised like an ebony statue.

She knew Vashtanya was fully aware of the fighting arts' spiritual aspects. He could think through a situation, and recognise a trap when it was laid for him. But this was not a trap; like this whole match, it was a test. Each warrior gambled their life on speed, strength, and skill. She had just offered Vashtanya one last hand—the turn of a single card.

The katana outreached him, but he must come in point-blank, to strike a disabling blow. Who was faster? She gifted him with the enticing, deceiving advantage of fighting blind, but she was *not* using her vision to track him. All he had to do was come close enough.

Eyes closed, she sensed him a few metres away, and they faced off like gunfighters in a dusty street. No more cleverness; no more tactics. Now it was all down to reactions. He jumped twice more, thudding into different parts of the arena, now in front, now behind, studying her. Only one angle of attack gave the katana its greatest distance to travel in any countermove, winning Vashtanya an extra split second. He must strike from directly behind Lucinda.

"Well played," he rumbled through his fangs, though she sensed the raw emotion behind the words. She had chosen this game, and he was compelled play. He was the one without any option, so he gathered his strength again, poised, tense as a runner on the starting blocks, and committed.

He thudded into being one metre behind her, and his massive right paw lashed out to impale her with his claws, clean through her back, beside the sword rig. But in the same instant—before even properly feeling the wound—Lucinda whirled with the katana outstretched.

The twisting movement tore the claws free with a blinding wrench of white-hot pain, and air whistled over the blade as it took off Vashtanya's head. He reverted to human form just as his slumping body hit the tan, and the head that bounced under the arena lights looked up with human eyes, its expression midway between profound surprise and simple regret.

Lucinda coughed a spray of blood. Her chest bubbled—the right lung was pierced. She fell to her knees, sword point-down in the tan, and blinked up at the witnesses. She saw the faces of the friends who had remained staunchly silent throughout, as custom demanded, and the last thing she knew was Lord Ithrial, rising to his feet to make a sweeping gesture, declaring the contest—the feud—over by law.

* * *

Rain was pelting the tall windows when Lucinda woke, comfortable, warm and, at first, not quite sure where she was. She lay in a sumptuous four-poster bed; a fire burned cheerfully in the hearth behind a brass guard. When her eyes focused properly, she saw John and Caroline, both asleep in armchairs beside the hearth, rugs over their laps, as if they had not left her in—how long? Long enough for her to heal. As she remembered the sword thrust, then the impalement, she ran a hand down her body and palmed her abdomen. To her interest, she found herself dressed in a true vampire gown of revealing, blood-red silk, and someone had brushed out her hair.

An antique timepiece at the bedside showed 9 a.m. After sleeping the clock around, she felt better, stronger. But most of what she felt was relief. She stirred, trying to sit up, and the movement woke Caroline.

The elder vampire touched John's knee, and they came quickly to the bed. John enthusiastically fluffed the pillows; Caroline gave Lucinda an arm to pull herself up. Neither could speak, and Lucinda broke the tension with a weary grin. "These days, I always seem to be in bed, surrounded by relatives."

They laughed as emotion released, and shared a hug. "How are you?" Caroline whispered.

"Tired, but good. Need to cough. I'll be coughing clots out of this lung for days." She relaxed back. "Hungry. Have I had blood?"

"Anna and I each stumped up a pint," John said, holding her hand. "Lord Ithrial's people assure us you're fine."

"I'm pretty much healed already. A quart of fresh blood and a good night's sleep is all it takes." She coughed again and stretched. "You can let them know I'm through it."

John sat beside her as Caroline took the message, and soon enough, Carnelios and Anna appeared to take her hands and speak quietly. They were allowed only a little while before Caroline and Lord Ithrial stepped in.

"Mistress Crane," the latter rumbled quietly, "I am overjoyed that you prevailed. It would have been a black day, had you fallen. If you are up to it, you have a visitor who needs to make formal vows regarding this affair."

Lucinda wore a sombre expression. "As is the custom." She offered John her arm. "Help me up; I'll do this on my feet."

He steadied her to the hearth, where she put an elbow on the mantel, creating a deliberately striking image of red hair, red silk, and firelight. The mortals left, as protocol insisted, and Lady Kromelech appeared.

She stood tall and prideful, her face rigid as a marble statue, clad in the blacks and purples of her position as a clan hierarch. She inclined her raven head in a half-bow. "I acknowledge your victory, Mistress Crane, and assert that the contest was fought fairly, with honour, under the rules of the *Vampira Codex*. I assert on the honour of the Korsakofs that this matter is at an end, and no further action will be taken in reprisal."

The words had clearly been rehearsed. Something in her manner made Lucinda doubt her sincerity, but protocol demanded she accept the bald statement. Kromelech composed herself, haughty and stiff once more. "As for cousin Josephus, his actions have had their way with him. House Korsakof relinquishes him to the Council's jurisdiction, and we shall take him to task for his treachery when his sentence has expired."

Again, something in her cold, dead eyes made Lucinda doubt. She had the sudden intuition that Josephus Caspar had acted on Kromelech's instructions in a bid to control the situation—prevent it from going to ritual combat and risking ancestral vampire blood.

Instead, two of their ancient lineage had fallen in one day, one to a judicial verdict and the other to the reaper.

"It is my fervent hope that the feud between House Korsakof and the changeling presently awarded status among the Black Eagles will at last be over. Too much proud blood has been spilt in its name, and the time has come for us to concern ourselves with less destructive affairs." Lady Kromelech managed another ghost of a bow to punctuate her speech.

Lucinda could have added a great deal, but merely nodded with a faint smile. "Thank you, Lady Kromelech. I also am glad the matter is behind us."

There was no more to be said, and the lady strode out with a measured striking of heels on timber. Caroline opened the curtains while Lucinda sank into a fireside chair and looked up at her companions. "She must be smarting. I defeated a vampire of ancestral blood with a mortal weapon, mortal fighting style, mortal technique. I didn't even have to shapeshift."

"So, the closed eyes...?" Caroline asked.

"Zen," Lucinda said simply. Then she frowned at their host. "Lord Ithrial, you mentioned needing to speak when it was over."

"Yes." He hooked his thumbs into his belt, and his gaze swept the others. "I say this with the knowledge of Lord Alaric and special bodies under the Council. Lady Kromelech's words are very sincere and satisfy all protocols, but we have reason to believe that the Korsakofs might be intending to withdraw from the Union of the Clans." He paused, frowning into their grave faces. "It has never happened before, but any clan no longer bound by the *Codex* becomes rogue. It is the responsibility of the rest to subdue that House. Secession invites civil war. Should the seceding clan have struck deals behind the scenes to divide the world among allies in such a conflict, we would return to the Clan Wars overnight. It would be madness, because there is no possibility that another war among vampires could fail to come to mortal attention."

Lucinda shook her head with a grimace. "They

obviously think they have the leverage and strength to make a bid for supremacy—replace the Union with an imperial or even feudal structure, with themselves at the top. If humans finally realise the Elderlings actually exist...the mortals are too many, and we are too few. We couldn't expect to prevail, no matter our abilities. Oh, we'd give good account of ourselves, but—" She sighed. "I've fought for mortals all these years, but if it comes to war, understand this: humans make no distinction between Lightlings and Darklings. We would *all* be eliminated." The thought was bitter, especially for one who had given so much for the human race.

"Well," the master of Gratharn added quietly, "you needed to be apprised of our suspicions. Your feud served to expose at least some of their dealings. Once more, we owe you a debt of gratitude. Perhaps there is yet time to avert catastrophe." He accorded Lucinda a small bow. "Stay as long as you wish. When you are ready, one of our cars can have you back in Norfolk in a few hours."

As he withdrew, John and Anna returned, and Lucinda brought them up to date in a few terse sentences. "Among the World Unseen, there's a lack of stability. We have a truce for now, but it feels to me as if Korsakof's feud is already simmering. When I took up arms for mortals, I never imagined I'd be inviting the division of vampirekind—or that my longest battle would be against a clan with ambitions of domination. I don't want my compassion for humans to be used as an excuse to precipitate war! But I also can't tolerate being forced to choose. Fight for mortals and foster catastrophe? Or ward off doomsday but leave mortals to their fate." She shook her head. "It's too much, too soon. But I'll tell you this: finding a path through this mess will be the fight of our lives."

Later, when afternoon cloud shrouded the high moors, Lucinda stepped out into the forecourt of Gratharn House. Back in jeans and leather, hat brim pulled down low, she took a last look around the vampire House before joining the others in the back of a long, black limousine. Anna had seen more of vampire reality than she could have imagined just days before, while John was overwhelmed by the enormity of the world he had wanted to join. Both were uncharacteristically silent; both had so much to think about.

The car purred onto the road that ran down through Hebden Bridge and on southward. The five looked ahead with guarded optimism. Difficult times lay before them, but they had seen what could be accomplished with a sword, a true heart, and faith in what was right.

That belief must be their guiding star.

www.ingramcontent.com/pod-product-compliance
Lightning Source LLC
LaVergne TN
LVHW011946060526
838201LV00061B/4228